HUNTER'S FALL

SHILOH WALKER

BERKLEY SENSATION, NEW YORK

THE BERKLEY PUBLISHING GROUP
Published by the Penguin Group
Penguin Group (USA) Inc.
375 Hudson Street, New York, New York 10014, USA
Penguin Group (Canada), 90 Eglinton Avenue East, Suite 700, Toronto, Ontario M4P 2Y3, Canada
(a division of Pearson Penguin Canada Inc.)
Penguin Books Ltd., 80 Strand, London WC2R 0RL, England
Penguin Group Ireland, 25 St. Stephen's Green, Dublin 2, Ireland (a division of Penguin Books Ltd.)
Penguin Group (Australia), 250 Camberwell Road, Camberwell, Victoria 3124, Australia
(a division of Pearson Australia Group Pty. Ltd.)
Penguin Books India Pvt. Ltd., 11 Community Centre, Panchsheel Park, New Delhi—110 017, India
Penguin Group (NZ), 67 Apollo Drive, Rosedale, Auckland 0632, New Zealand
(a division of Pearson New Zealand Ltd.)
Penguin Books (South Africa) (Pty.) Ltd., 24 Sturdee Avenue, Rosebank, Johannesburg 2196,
South Africa

Penguin Books Ltd., Registered Offices: 80 Strand, London WC2R 0RL, England

HUNTER'S FALL

A Berkley Sensation Book / published by arrangement with the author

PRINTING HISTORY
Berkley Sensation mass-market edition / June 2011

Copyright © 2011 by Shiloh Walker, Inc.
Excerpt from *Departed* by Shiloh Walker copyright © by Shiloh Walker, Inc.
Cover art by Danny O'Leary.
Cover design by Richard Hasselberger.
Interior text design by Kristin del Rosario.

ISBN: 978-0-425-24180-6

BERKLEY® SENSATION
Berkley Sensation Books are published by The Berkley Publishing Group,
a division of Penguin Group (USA) Inc.,
375 Hudson Street, New York, New York 10014.
BERKLEY® SENSATION and the "B" design are trademarks of Penguin Group (USA) Inc.

PRINTED IN THE UNITED STATES OF AMERICA

10 9 8 7 6 5 4 3 2 1

*My thanks to Maili and Natalie,
for all your help.*

*Thanks to my wonderful editor,
Cindy Hwang,
who listened for hours one night while I tried
to hammer out some issues with this book.
And Sylvia Day . . . who did the same thing.*

*For all of those who asked when
Nessa would get a story.
Originally, I didn't have one planned for her.
But she had other plans.*

*To my family . . .
always to my family . . .
I love you more than life itself,
and I thank God for you, every day of my life.*

*A special dedication . . .
this book was finished shortly before
the terrible earthquake that struck Haiti
in January 2010.
I'd like to dedicate this book
to Fatin and Joy B,
as well as the other readers
who donated money to help the relief efforts.*

*And a special thank you to the charities
like Doctors Without Borders, World Vision
and so many others.
You went where many of us couldn't go,
where many of us wouldn't go.
Thank you.*

PROLOGUE

H<small>E</small> was watching her again, the old bugger. She could feel his eyes on her and they made her feel dirty. She quickened her steps and slipped out of the village, melting into the shadows of the forest.

William—why in the hell had he been out this late? It was past midnight. No reason for any sane soul to be awake.

Of course, she was awake. But there were things she needed to do. Out in the forest—the sort of things the good people of the village were better off not knowing about. The sort of things that would likely have her branded a witch, if they knew what she was doing.

And of course, she *was* a witch. She took no shame in it, either. It was a God-given gift—a gift that saved lives, a gift that helped people.

The skin on the back of her neck crawled. She could still *feel* the weight of his stare. Casting a look over her shoulder, Agnes stared through the trees, but she could not see him.

He was not there now.

But he had been.

He always seemed to be watching her. There was something about it that made her feel tainted, foul. Almost as bad as that one time he'd touched her.

Damn that bastard. She should have taught him a lesson then. Nessa moved deeper into the forest, trying to shrug off the nervy, twitchy feeling between her shoulder blades.

She was uneasy.

Not afraid, she insisted, squaring her shoulders as she continued to move through the night. Agnes was a Hunter of the Council. She did not fear the dark. She did not fear the monsters lurking there.

The darkness feared *her*. And she was quite certain if she told herself that enough, she would even believe it.

But something was not quite right tonight. She could feel it. Smell it. All but taste it. She wanted to go back to her home, cuddle in bed beside her man, Elias, and hold him tight. But she could not.

Something evil was afoot, and it called her.

Called her from the safety of her bed into the darkness of night.

Part of her still feared, no matter how much she might insist otherwise.

She did not rightly know if she would ever get over that fear. After all, she knew what monsters hid in the darkness— she knew them truly and well—she knew their names, their faces, their blood and their magic. She was right to fear them.

But fear or not, she had responsibilities. Uneasy or not, she had a sworn duty.

Agnes was more than just a witch.

She was a Hunter, called to protect others. She had been sent to this small village to deal with the rogue werewolves roaming in the forest, preying on the villagers. It had been the first task assigned to her and she knew she had done well.

The werewolves were gone.

They were not responsible for this uneasiness inside her.

Perhaps it was just William, she thought. He always made her feel twitchy and jumpy. Dirty.

Not for much longer, though. Soon she would be away from him and she would never have to see that nasty man again.

Soon she and Elias would be leaving Oneoak. First they would go to Brendain, the home of the Hunters. It had been home to her for nearly six years, since she was twelve. She was almost eighteen now. Although she had lived in Oneoak for the past year, it was not home. Not for her. No, Brendain was home and soon she would return there, and this time, she would take her man with her.

The two of them would take a bit of a rest. Nessa would see if there was some place she was needed.

Needed . . . it warmed her heart to think of it.

Nessa was needed.

Absently, she fingered the tip of her braid, lost in thought. It was not just by the Hunters, either. She helped people. She saved people. A grin lit her face as she thought of one person in particular—she had saved his arse, even if Elias tried to argue.

She knew the truth.

Elias could tease her and call her a foolish girl all he wanted.

He knew the truth. She had saved his life. It had been almost a year since she had met him, just one week after she'd come to Oneoak. The wolves would have torn him apart that night. There had just been too many of them— his silver dagger could kill them, but not if there were ten of them and only one of him.

They would have killed him if she had not come and burned them to nothing but dust and ashes.

The entire pack was gone now, the bloodthirsty monsters sent straight to hell where they belonged. A new pack would come here, a healthy pack, one that would roam this land and care for it the way it deserved to be cared for.

The taint in the land would be cleansed. And it was in part because of one little witch, a Hunter called Agnes.

Nessa. Elias called her that, said that *Agnes* just did not suit her. It was his mother's name also, and she knew that was partly why he did not think it suited her. Thinking of him made that uneasiness return, stronger, more powerful.

"Stop it," she muttered to herself. With a sigh, Nessa started to head south. One last trip through, just to be certain. They would leave in the morning.

But she froze. Icy fear wrapped a fist around her heart.

Pain plunged a fist into her stomach.

Fire danced before her eyes.

A cacophony of voices assaulted her mind.

Witches—we have to kill them.

Do not kill him yet. We need him to get her back here. To make her confess before she dies.

She is just a girl—be sensible. A nice girl. We cannot do this. We will take them before the priests. If there is something wrong, they will know what to do.

Be silent, woman!

She is a witch . . . oh, aye. I have seen her, using fire, casting spells—she has tried to bewitch me. Tried to seduce me, that witch.

Rage wrapped its fiery grip around her. She knew that voice. It belonged to Sir William. Oh, she would tear his eyes out. Slamming a hand against the trunk of a tree, she braced herself to keep from stumbling as everything struck her at once.

Adrenaline surged through her and she spun around, running through the trees. The very night had fallen silent—too silent. The forest was never this still.

A voice rasped through her head and she heard him speak even though he was far away.

Run, Nessa. Do not come back here, Elias said in her mind. Elias had no magic, no power, nothing save the bond their love gave him. But he knew that if he spoke out to her, she would hear him.

And likely, he knew she would not listen.

The anger and fear in his voice added to her own fear, but it spurred the part inside her that made her warrior as well as witch. She only ran faster. If he thought she would run away when he was in danger, then Elias did not know his wife very well at all.

She tore into Oneoak looking exactly like what she was. One very angry witch.

William *had* been watching her—watching to make sure she left before he sprung this nasty trap.

Nessa knew she was losing control of her magic but she did not care. And then she saw that they had tied Elias to a pole, hay and branches at his feet.

Sir William, the sodding sheriff, stood at her husband's side, ready to burn him. Nessa's grasp on her control fractured even more.

Elias lifted his head, glaring at her. It was dark, but her eyesight had always been keen. Even in the dim light of the torches, she could see him well. They had beaten him. One eye was black, and both his nose and mouth had been busted, blood painting gory streaks on his handsome face.

"Nessa . . ."

She met his eyes and shook her head.

"Let him go," she said quietly, clenching her hands into fists. There was nothing she wanted more than to release the power flooding her right now. Release it all, into the smug face of Sir William.

Oh, he would pay for this, Nessa swore, her body trembling with anger and fear. He'd pay for this.

William folded his face into pious lines. "Agnes, you and Elias have fallen into a dark path, practicing magic, worshipping dark, foul monsters."

"We worship no monsters." She arched a brow. "Elias practices no magic."

But she'd be damned if she would lie about herself.

They leaped on the one simple thing that she left out. "So you admit it! Witch!"

They moved closer, and Nessa narrowed her eyes. "Stay back, you blind fools," she said softly. "Let him go."

William dared to take one step forward. "You say he is no witch—we cannot take the word of a woman who openly admits she uses the dark powers. If we let him go, will you let us bind you? Will you go through our tests? Cleanse yourself?"

She'd openly admitted nothing. She just had not denied it. Looking at William, she suppressed the urge to snort as she stared at him. *Cleanse myself?* "I do not fear your tests, William. Let Elias go. He has done nothing wrong."

William smirked. "If he has done nothing wrong, then by all means . . ." He glanced at one of the men and nodded. "But first you must agree. You will be bound. You will submit to the tests. You will be cleansed."

"Your men will untie him as I come to you. If you dare be foolish, Sir William, you will know pain like nothing you have ever felt," she warned.

"Nessa!"

She lifted her head and stared across the distance separating them. *They use ropes, Elias. You think I cannot get rid of a few paltry ropes? Run into the forest—to our cave. I will meet you there. And these simpletons can rot. We wasted months protecting them.*

His dark brown eyes stared into hers with fury and desperation. *Do not let him touch you, Nessa. I do not trust him.*

She just shook her head. She would not risk Elias. She would not. She walked arrogantly toward William, holding her wrists out in front of her. He just smiled benevolently and gestured to one of his men.

"I shall deal with your husband," William said, his voice quiet and dignified. His eyes gleamed though, with something she did not like, not one bit. *He* would deal with her husband? Lower himself to free him? Instead of ordering his men . . . ?

Her ears pricked at those words. Her instincts screamed.

Rough rope bit into her wrists but she barely even noticed as she watched William walk over the uneven ground to where his men were cutting Elias free.

Elias shrugged away from them and started toward Nessa. She shook her head at him and she could see the argument in his eyes. *Run*, she said into his mind. *Now.*

She heard the argument in his head. Felt his refusal.

And then there was nothing but icy, sharp pain. She felt the brutal echo of it in her own heart.

They were soul mates—meant for each other even before birth. It would have been better if that blade had killed her as well as Elias.

"No!" she screamed out. She shoved at the sheriff's man, pushing away from him as though he was naught more than a child.

"Grab her—cover her eyes," one of the men bellowed.

All around her people shouted—although some screamed in horror as they realized what one of William's men had done.

She barely even heard them. She was aware of nothing.

Nothing but the screams . . . and the blood.

It was Elias's blood, dripping from the dagger of a treacherous snake.

Without even looking at her wrists, she gave in to the rage and used her magic to set fire to the ropes, and they fell to the ground still flaming. Nessa didn't remember closing the distance between her and Elias, just catching him as he sagged to the ground.

William stood behind him, his thin mouth curved up in a smile. In his hand, he held a jeweled dagger and the blade dripped with dark, dark red blood.

"You will be mine now, Agnes."

"Not even in hell," she whispered hotly, lifting her eyes from Elias's face for one second. "And hell awaits you."

William fell back a step as he looked at her. Behind her, she heard people moving up. Power exploded through her and then heat surrounded her. Fire now wrapped a deadly ring around the three of them, Elias, William and Agnes. He paled, his eyes widening as the fire seemed to reach out and grab him.

"Help me!"

Elias laughed, the sound choked and full of pain. "Listen to him scream for help, love. You came and answered their cries. And this is what they have done."

Nessa looked down at Elias, pressing her fingers to his lips. "Hush," she whispered, forcing the words past the tears that were threatening to choke her.

Then she looked back at William. "Filthy swine—there is no help for you. Murderer, filthy, evil murderer. Rot in hell."

William shrieked, the stench of his burning flesh heavy in the air. All around people screamed, and then they scattered. Their fear was ripe—she should have been choking on it, but she didn't care.

Nothing mattered.

Nothing but the sight of Elias lying so still in her arms, his face growing more and more pale as his blood flowed so hotly from his body.

She reached under Elias, pressing her hand to the wound. It was too close to his heart, though. "Elias . . . God, please," she sobbed, hugging him to her. His breath rattled in and out of his chest. "Do not leave me!"

"Hush."

"Do not tell me to hush, you fool!" she shrieked. Magic sparked out of her and she tried to focus it. Witches could heal. Damn it, she could heal him. She had not yet learned that magic, but she had to try.

She couldn't focus it, though, not to save her life.

Or his, it seemed. More and more blood drained from him as she tried to use her wild magic to heal that nasty, jagged wound. "You cannot leave me, Elias," she whispered. "You cannot leave me. You are my life."

He reached up, touching his hand to her face. Nessa gave up trying to hold the jagged edges of the wound together and caught his hand, pressing it to her cheek. "Ah, Nessa . . . my beautiful, foolish, wonderful girl. I love you so much. I will come back . . . I will find you again."

He coughed and a sob wracked her body as she saw the blood trickle from his lips. "Promise me!" she choked. "You promise me! Promise me you'll come back."

"Only God Himself could keep me from you, love," Elias whispered. He sighed and his entire body trembled. She could feel the pain tearing through him and she forced herself in between, using her power to separate him from the pain as she filtered it away. She could not heal him, could not save him—but she could damn well stop him from hurting.

The tension eased from his body and he breathed a little easier.

"Elias . . ." she moaned, wrapping her arms around him.

"Just hold me, Nessa," he murmured. His voice was weaker. Lifting her head, she stared down at him, brushing his hair back from his battered face. "I do wish I had listened to you, my beautiful witch."

Closing her eyes, she whispered, "Just come back, Elias."

"My Nessa."

CHAPTER I

PRESENT DAY

THERE was smoke.

And there was blood.

The air was thick, and he was going to choke on all the blood. Even if he didn't have it pooling in his throat, he wouldn't have been able to take a breath.

The pain wouldn't let him.

It stole through him, turning everything to ice.

She was crying. He could hear her. She cried and wept and pleaded with him not to leave her. But he had no choice. Death was coming, coming to rip him away from the one person who mattered.

Even though he slept, he felt the sting of tears. Felt them well up under his eyes, felt them burn their way down his cheeks. He wanted to wipe them away. Wanted to wake from this awful dream.

But he was helpless, locked in his slumber.

Ah, Nessa . . . my beautiful, foolish, wonderful girl. I love you so much. I will come back . . . I will find you again . . .

BROWNING, IDAHO

"You're too pretty."

"Am I?" he asked, a grin tugging at his lips. It was a mouth made for kissing.

"Yes."

She was dreaming. Nessa knew she was dreaming. If she had any sense, she would lie back and just enjoy it.

Well, I already did that. And she had—three, no, four times over.

There was no way any red-blooded, straight woman could lie in bed with this man, dream or no dream, and not enjoy it. Not enjoy *him.*

His eyes were dark, rich as melted chocolate, framed by thick, curly eyelashes. His skin gleamed a soft, mellow gold. In the sun, she imagined that smooth, sleek skin would deepen to a darker gold. His hair was black, blacker than onyx, and thick. It had just the slightest curl to it and when she ran her hands through it, the jet strands twined her fingers.

She knew that from experience—she'd spent half the night with her hands buried in his hair.

They hadn't spent much time standing up, but she guessed he was about five ten. He had a long, lean build, and she sensed strength inside him. Massive strength, but when he touched her, he did it with gentleness. Reverence.

As well a dream lover should, she supposed.

He reached up and traced the line of her mouth with his fingertip. She shivered under that light touch and felt heat flicker through her. Catching his finger in her mouth, she bit lightly.

Hunger blazed in his eyes.

She felt a response and leaned forward, pressing her lips to his. "Well, if I had to dream you, I must say, it turned out rather well," she mused.

He laughed against her mouth and asked, "How do you know I'm not the one who dreamed you up?"

"Oh, believe me, I'm the one who is dreaming. There is no man out there pining for me."

No man waiting. No man longing. No man searching. No matter what was promised.

I will come back . . . I will find you again . . .

"You're so sad," he whispered. "Why are you so sad?"

Nessa forced a smile. "Of course I'm not . . . well, I won't be for long. That's why you're here, isn't it?"

"*I* WILL *find you. No matter where you go. No matter how far.*"

With a snort, Nessa looked away from the TV and focused on Mei-Lin's hair. The teenager grinned up at her. "It's romantic, Nessa. You can't snort like that when Daniel Day-Lewis is on the screen saying a line like *that*." With a sigh, the girl rested a hand on her heart and gazed at the TV with rapt eyes.

The Last of the Mohicans was the girl's favorite movie. They usually watched it once a month.

Unless Nessa could see a way out. Today was Mei-Lin's seventeenth birthday, though, and she'd wanted to watch the silly film before she went out with some friends.

Weaving the girl's silky hair into a tight braid, Nessa glanced at the screen. Spectacular scenery. Strong, sexy men with big guns, innocent-looking girls with simpering eyes. Romantic bits like, *I will find you.*

It stuck a knife in her heart.

Although it had been five hundred years, she could still hear Elias's voice.

I will come back . . . I will find you again . . .

Only God Himself could keep me from you, love.

And God Himself had spent the last five centuries doing just that. Nessa couldn't watch this damn film without reliving her memories. A time when she was torn away from her husband.

Not by pissed off Natives, but by death.

By God.

He had taken her lover from her, and had kept her from joining him.

She was alone, and empty. So empty inside. Not even her dream lover could ease that ache. At least not for long.

She blew out a sigh and used an elastic band to keep Mei-Lin's braid from unraveling. Rising from the couch, she gathered up the ice-cream cartons from the floor and carted them into the kitchen to dump them in the trash.

From the corner of her eye, she saw Mei-Lin and despite herself, she had to smile.

This girl had pulled Nessa back from the edge of madness, despair.

Even as she tried to draw her mind away from the memories, she found herself caught in them again. It had been a few years since her life had been turned upside down.

One last battle . . . she'd been so sure when she went to face the young witch that it would be her *last*.

And after more than five hundred years, she was so very, very tired. So empty inside, but she'd become accustomed to that. The exhaustion, though, weighed on her more and more, with each and every year.

The thought of just being *done* had been such a . . . sweet relief. She'd yearned for it, ached for it. Longed for it. She'd gone to battle with a young woman who used her magic to steal life and power from others—Morgan Wakefield. She had practiced blood magic, and it was addictive. Once a witch gave in to that lure, it became a hunger, a need. Fighting it was almost impossible, and Morgan hadn't wanted to.

The only way to keep her from killing was to end her life—a sad, sorry fact, but one Nessa had been prepared to handle. She'd been prepared for all likely outcomes—including her own death.

She hadn't been prepared to live. She certainly hadn't been prepared to live like this.

Absently, she glanced at the ornamental mirror hanging over the sofa and studied her face.

Morgan's face.

No. She hadn't been prepared for this. She'd fought the young, deceptive, blood-thirsty witch, and as she'd expected, her body hadn't survived the battle. But somehow, her spirit had. She hadn't planned for it—hadn't done a damn thing to make this happen—at least not consciously. Nessa had wanted death, craved it. Craved it the way Morgan had craved blood. The way a drug addict craved their next fix. She'd needed it.

But instead of the sweet relief of death, she lived. In Morgan's body.

For so long after it had happened, Nessa had been lost—trapped in a muddle of depression, despair, memories and madness. Even as she began to emerge from that fog, she'd hated it—she'd yearned for the sweet, oblivious cloud where she'd lived.

Until Mei-Lin.

They had met just a few months ago, but already, this girl had settled inside Nessa's heart, forged a place there. Given Nessa a reason to believe again. A reason to hope. A reason to live.

She looked at Mei-Lin and saw the echo of her own youth. Kindred spirits, she supposed. That was why she'd felt so drawn to the girl, why she'd taken Mei-Lin under her wing instead of shipping her off to Excelsior.

Almost a year earlier, Mei-Lin's mother had died and the girl had ended up in foster care, only to run away after one of the other foster kids had tried to molest her.

The night they met, Nessa had been walking through the dark streets, looking for a fight, a drink, both . . . anything to occupy her mind.

What she found was Mei-Lin. Or rather, Mei-Lin found her. The girl had quick hands—she might not have even noticed the theft if the girl hadn't unconsciously used her magic as well.

Untrained witches—they were a danger to themselves. Nessa had planned to dump the girl back at Excelsior. She needed training, that was for certain, and she also needed to finish high school. She could do both at Excelsior. Kelsey and the other Hunters would see to it that Mei-Lin was trained and care for.

But in the end, it was Nessa who took the girl in. It hadn't taken but a few hours to realize she needed the girl as much as the girl needed her. Perhaps more.

The two of them, they were both lost, lonely souls.

Meeting the girl had pulled Nessa back from the brink—she'd reminded Nessa of who she was.

She'd reminded Nessa of *what* she was.

She might be a lonely witch still pining over her lost lover, but she was also a fighter.

Nessa was a Hunter—a warrior, a witch. She'd devoted her life to protecting the innocent from the monsters in the world. She'd never given up in her whole damned life.

Mei-Lin helped her remember that about herself.

She owed the girl.

More, she loved her.

Leaning against the counter that separated the kitchen and the living room, she tucked her hair behind one ear and watched as the teen finished watching the movie. As the credits started to roll, Mei-Lin patted her heart and said, "If you're still wanting to find me another birthday present, I want *that*. Gimme a man like *that*."

"I looked but they'd already sold out at the mall." Nessa rolled her eyes. "Darling, you are seventeen. You have plenty of time to find a man."

"They do still make them like that, right?" She wrinkled her nose and said, "I want a *real* man, not one who spends more time messing with his hair than I do. I don't want some dumb boy, either. Real men still exist, right?"

Nessa grinned and thought of some of the men she knew. Chortling, she tried to picture Malachi messing with his hair. The vampire had seen millennia come and go, and while he was a vain bastard, he wasn't one to primp.

Images of other men, other friends—Hunters she'd worked with over the years—flashed through her mind. Would they stand in front of a mirror and primp? Tobias, Declan, Vax . . . no. Not a one of them.

Eli, perhaps, but he had always been a peacock.

She had a quick flash of her dream lover. That thick, silken hair, tousled by her hands. He wouldn't spend his time studying his reflection, either, she knew.

Of course he wouldn't . . . he isn't real. He was just her dream lover, a man her imagination created to help with the emptiness inside her, to help wile away the long, lonely nights.

A dream lover . . . and he belongs in those dreams, only those dreams, so for the love of all things holy, stop thinking about him during the day.

She shoved off the counter and went to turn off the television. "Yes, Mei-Lin. I promise, there are plenty of men who are less than enamored with their pretty reflections."

Outside, Nessa heard footsteps and she tugged on one of Mei-Lin's braids. "Your friends are here."

"*How* can you hear them?" she asked, cocking her head. She squinted her eyes as though it might help her hear better.

"Practice." Nessa shrugged a shoulder. "You'll get there."

The doorbell rang and Mei-Lin moved to answer it. As a gaggle of giggling girls entered the small house, Nessa tidied up the living room. Living with a teenage girl, she was constantly picking up, straightening up, doing laundry.

She didn't mind, oddly enough.

Other than Mei-Lin's training, this was the closest to *normal* Nessa had ever known.

Mei-Lin reappeared in the door, surrounded by her friends.

"Hi, Ms. Chandler!"

Nessa managed not to make a face. *Ms. Chandler* was only one of the many names she'd used during her life—she'd much rather be called Agnes or Nessa than anything *Ms.* Made her feel as old as she truly was. Ancient.

Giving them a smile, she said, "How are you this evening, Kim?"

"Oh, you know." She rolled eyes heavily made up with black liner and said, "I'm sort of on probation. Brought home a C on my final and Mom said if it happened again, I'd lose the car until I brought home something better."

"You could have a better grade if you wanted." Nessa knew the line she should use and she did. Mei-Lin's friends, the teachers, all the people they knew thought Nessa was Mei-Lin's stepsister. They even had legal papers to document it. "Your mother just wants you to do your best."

"I know." Kim sighed and shrugged. "Chemistry is just so *boring*. I can't wait until I'm done with school and don't have to worry about that sh . . . uh, crap anymore."

Dryly, Nessa said, "Paying bills is quite boring as well. You'll have to do things you don't enjoy the rest of your life. The good comes with the bad." She gave Mei-Lin a bright smile and said, "Speaking of which . . ."

She dumped the armful of shoes, books, an iPod and socks into Mei-Lin's arms. "Before you go out, please put these away."

Mei-Lin rolled her eyes and obediently trucked up the stairs.

One of the newer girls asked Nessa about her accent, and another started rambling on about how *sssexxxy* accents were. Kim enviously told the others how Nessa had taken Mei-Lin to France for spring break.

The new girl—Ashlyn—rolled her eyes and said, "Man, Mei. You've got the coolest mom. Mine would never let me go that far away without her."

Mei-Lin appeared on the stairs and pain flashed across her face. Nessa gave her a gentle smile and whispered mind-to-mind, *Are you okay?*

Mei-Lin gave her a tight smile.

An awkward silence fell, and one of the girls leaned in and in a loud whisper said, "Way to go, Ashlyn. Mei's mom died last year. Ms. Chandler is Mei's stepsister—her guardian."

Ashlyn went white. Nessa patted the girl on the shoulder. "It's okay, Ashlyn. You didn't know, now did you?" Then she gave her a smile and said, "I imagine your mum is quite the protective one. I'm sure you find it quite irritating, but she loves you. Enjoy it . . . enjoy her, because you never know how long you'll have her."

Ashlyn gave Mei-Lin a slightly sick smile. "I'm sorry, Mei. I didn't . . ."

"It's cool," Mei-Lin said, shaking her head.

Changing the subject, Nessa looked at Kim and said, "So, what plans do you girls have tonight?"

Mei-Lin gave Nessa an exasperated look while Kim smiled. In a singsong voice, she replied, "We're going to get some dinner at Applebee's, then we're going to a movie. The movie is at the Multiplex and it starts at nine fifteen. It should be over by eleven thirty. I have to drop the other girls off first, but we'll be here by midnight and I'm spending the night. And yes, Ms. Chandler, my mother will be calling at midnight so I hope you're awake."

"Cheeky girl," Nessa murmured. She looked at Mei-Lin. "You have your phone?"

A few minutes later, Nessa shut the door behind them. Alone in the house, she rested her head back against the door and sighed. Alone . . . and it was too quiet.

When silence came, the voice was louder.

The voice . . . Morgan's voice. Yes, she had Morgan's body, and she also had Morgan's . . . ghost, for lack of a better word.

"This is just too cute for words, you old hag. Look at you, playing house."

It was a taunting, angry jibe, but Nessa pretended to ignore it. Once she had noise, once she had something to occupy her hands, the voice of the dead woman would fade.

For a time.

How much longer, she wondered. How much longer would Morgan linger?

Even now, months, years later, the girl haunted her.

Damn her. Even in death, she'd managed to ruin things. If the woman's body had just *died*, then Nessa could have died as well.

"Is this the reason you stole my body, so you could play Holly Homemaker?"

Nessa shoved away from the door and reached out. With

the slightest flex of her magic, she turned on some music. *Loud.* But Morgan wasn't going to go quiet *that* easily.

"This is a fucking waste. Why did you take my body if this is all you're going to do? Shit, can't you even go out, find a guy, get drunk, get fucked? Something—anything—would be better than watching you play mama witch to that little idiot."

Nessa smirked. "Not while I've got a dead witch whining in the back of my head."

"I don't see why not. It's my body."

"Actually, no, it's not. If it was *your* body, you'd be able to take it back. But you can't." She knew what the girl was about—Morgan wanted to make Nessa feel guilty, wanted to exploit any and every little weakness.

"It damn well is my body," Morgan snarled, her mental voice an angry, ugly growl. *"Your body died. That old bag of bones is gone. Hypocritical bitch. How in the hell can you condemn me for taking blood when you took my damn body?"*

Narrowing her eyes, Nessa turned to the mirror and stared at her reflection. She saw her face—the face that had once belonged to Morgan. "You didn't just take *blood*, child. You took *lives*. You ended *lives*. When I came upon you, you stank of death. How many have you killed? Can you even remember?"

"The strong kill the weak. It's the way of the world."

"We could write your death off that way if you like." Malicious cow—she knew just what words to use, when to use them. Guilt tried to settle inside Nessa but she cast it off. "And here's another way of the world. You can call it karma. I prefer 'you shall reap what you sow.' You killed. Blindly, indiscriminately, and you enjoyed it. You would have sucked my body dry of magic, sucked me dry of life, and then moved on to your next victim and your next. But you couldn't beat me. And I didn't *take* your body. Trust me, precious, I didn't *want* your body. I didn't want this *life*. You don't like it, and I understand that. I don't like it, either. But we're both stuck with it."

"I'll find a way to get my body back."

"No." Nessa shook her head. "You won't. You're just a ghost, Morgan, clinging to life. You need to let go and move on. It's not like there's much of anything keeping you here now, is there?"

"There's plenty keeping me here. My body, for one."

Nessa stared at her reflection, knowing the ghost in the back of her mind would see the insolent smile on her face. That was where Morgan existed now—that was the *only* place Morgan existed.

"It's not *your* body. You went and got greedy, precious. Tried to take things that don't belong to you. This is rather karmic, don't you think? You took power, you took blood . . . and your body was taken from you. It's mine now."

"Because you stole it."

Nessa sighed. "No, I didn't."

After all, *stealing* another's body would imply that Nessa wanted to live. She'd wanted anything but. She'd gone into that battle with her eyes wide open, *knowing* that after more than five hundred years, she could finally rest. She would die, and on the other side, she'd find Elias. Finally.

But fate hadn't worked out that way.

Nobody else knew. Nessa had told no one about Morgan. Morgan was her burden, her problem. And she'd learned how to deal with the problem relatively well.

Smiling at her reflection, she leaned in and kissed the mirror. "I must get to work now. Toddle off now, precious. We living witches have things to do."

In the back of her mind, she heard Morgan shriek . . . just before she blocked her off.

Her workroom was tucked away down in the basement, and she might as well spend some time working on Mei-Lin's next lesson—the poor girl was still having trouble with basic grounding and shielding. Until they had that down, they couldn't start even the more rudimentary magics.

Focusing on the work, she lost track of time. It wasn't until she felt a brush against her senses that she looked up with a glance at the clock. Nearly ten. Time enough.

"You might as well come in, Mal. I'm alone for now."

The vampire appeared in front of her, materializing out of thin air. He cast a look around the small, dimly lit room and grimaced. "Fuck me, love. You could do far better than this, you know."

"*This* will do me fine, thank you." She made a few more notes in the margin of the paper and tossed her pencil down. Rising from the chair, she moved around the desk and rose on her toes to kiss Malachi's cool cheek.

The vampire was her oldest friend—in more ways than one. He was so old, he'd forgotten just how old he was. Nessa knew he'd been a Roman slave at some point during his human life.

She had met him shortly after she'd returned to Excelsior after Elias had died. Five hundred years of friendship.

She knew his moods. Though that pale, poetically handsome face showed no expression, something was bothering him.

He was worried.

"Where is Kelsey?"

"At the school." He brushed an absent hand down her hair and turned away. Restless, he roamed around the small room for a few moments before coming to a stop in front of the shelf of books.

Many of the books were old. Not a few decades or even a couple of hundred years. They'd belonged to Nessa for several centuries. He studied them and then turned around, looking at Nessa with an unreadable expression.

Nessa sighed. "What it is, Mal?"

"I don't know." Dark, deep red hair fell to hide his face as he lowered his gaze to the floor. He stood in silence for long, long moments.

Her skin started to buzz and adrenaline started to course through her. She didn't feel anything. But something had Malachi on edge. The bastard had walked this earth for even longer than Nessa—whatever bothered him, it wasn't going to be some mild little annoyance.

Finally, he lifted his head and pinned her with midnight

blue eyes. "Kelsey wanted me here, pet. I don't know why. She doesn't know why. But she wanted me here."

"That doesn't sound quite good." Nessa rubbed her eyes and then lowered her head, mentally extending her senses. She felt nothing.

Absolutely nothing.

No nasty, hideous supernatural monster creeping close— *that* she would feel, just as she'd sensed Malachi's presence. The small town of Browning, Idaho, had a nearly nonexistent paranormal population. It was why Nessa had chosen to live here after she'd made the decision to take care of Mei-Lin. She didn't need to worry about any vampires or werewolves. The nearest wolf pack was close to a hundred miles away, and the nearest vamp was even farther. There were one or two lesser witches, a family of cat shifters and the odd random psychic.

If anything *new* had moved in, Nessa would have felt it.

"I don't feel anything," she pointed out, although she knew it was unnecessary. Malachi might be a vampire and she a witch, but they were both Hunters, which meant they were tuned into the monsters—the non-mortals that hunted and preyed on the innocent.

"Neither do I." A muscle twitched in his jaw.

Nessa felt the bottom of her stomach drop out. The look in his eyes, it nearly froze her to the bone. She closed her eyes and reached out, extending her mind until it brushed up against Mei-Lin's. She sensed the younger witch, sensed her surprise as Mei-Lin felt Nessa's presence.

She gave the nonverbal equivalent of *Shhh . . . it's okay. Just wanted to check on you.* And that she did—the girl was most definitely in the theater, as were her friends.

Feeling a bit reassured, she opened her eyes and focused on Malachi's face. "Mei-Lin will be here shortly. It's her birthday and she's gone to the pictures." She paused and took a deep breath. "She was to have a friend spend the night, but I guess I should reschedule that."

Malachi just watched her.

"She'll be cross with me," Nessa said, forcing a smile.

"She's a good lass. She'll understand."

"Hmmm. Perhaps. Although if I knew whatever the trouble was, it might make it easier to explain, wouldn't you agree?"

THEY left Nessa's small house to drive to the theater. Malachi wouldn't go for remaining at the house. Truthfully, Nessa was glad he came along, and not just because it was amusing to watch as the big vampire forced his large body into the front seat of her Ford Fusion.

"I'd have more room in a tin can, love."

"Oh, nonsense. Besides, you can't drive a tin can." She started the car and backed up, zipping along the roads with careless speed.

"You can't crash a tin can, either," Malachi muttered, maintaining a white-knuckled grip on the doorframe.

Plastic cracked and she shot him a disapproving glance. "If you make a mess of my car, vampire, I'll have your arse."

She could almost *see* how much it took for him to ease up. "How did you get any sort of license, driving like this?" He gave her a sour look. "You didn't magic some fool into it, did you?"

"Of course not." Nessa smiled serenely. "I don't have a license."

She checked the opposite lane of the narrow two-lane highway and darted around a semi, grinning as the driver laid on the horn when she squeezed in front of him.

"Fuck me," Malachi mumbled. He closed his eyes and rested his head against the back of the passenger seat. "Damn good thing I'm not mortal—you'd give me a heart attack."

As they neared the interstate, she reached over and patted the white-knuckled fist he had resting on his knee. "You worry too much, my friend. Turning into a boring old fusspot."

He shot her a narrow glance. "Very few people would dare call me a fusspot."

She opened her mouth but the words locked in her throat.

Blood roared in her ears. She barely had the presence of mind to pull the car onto the narrow shoulder before she wrecked it. Her hands shook, cold and clammy on the steering wheel.

"Mal . . ."

It came as a cold wind.

Death. Uncaring, unstoppable.

Malachi felt it as well—she could tell by the tight expression on his face, the blue light glowing in his eyes.

She shot him a dazed look. For a few short moments, she could hardly breathe.

The sound of her mobile phone buzzing hit like a fist, stealing the breath from her lungs. She grabbed it, recognizing Mei-Lin's picture on the display.

"Nessa, hey, you didn't answer the home phone."

"Mei-Lin, what's wrong?"

"Oh, nothing." Then she paused.

In the background, Nessa could hear the girls talking and their voices lacked the excited, happy tone from earlier. Then Mei-Lin sighed and said, "Kim ran into this guy she was dating at the theater. He started being a real jerk and I told him to back off. He started yelling at me and some guy in the row in front of us told him to back off and then . . ." Her voice trailed off. She was quiet for a minute and then said, "Kim just wanted to leave. So we left. I wanted to let you know we'd be there soon and—"

There was a scream.

A crash.

And Nessa felt it as death came in and claimed yet more lives.

S HE cried.

His pretty little witch was crying.

Standing in a field of stone, surrounded by people, yet utterly alone.

Day bled into night and the people drifted from her side and still she cried. She was alone now, save for one woman and one man.

Anger bit into him as the man—the *vampire*—dared

to lift a hand to touch the witch. Dared to wrap a big arm around her slender shoulders and draw her close.

Tears choked him.

Her pain racked him.

He wanted to reach out to her. *He* wanted to be the one to comfort her, to hold her against him as she wept.

But when he whispered her name, she didn't hear him.

D OMINIC came awake with her name on his lips and a tearing pain in his heart.

Snarling, he fought free of the covers and dashed a hand over his damp face. Crying. Damn it. Again. Dreams of some woman he'd never met and he wakes up crying. He stared at the pink smears on his fingertips and stormed into the bathroom to wash away the blood-tinged tears.

With water dripping from his face, he looked at the mirror. A muscle worked in his jaw and he gripped the edge of the marble counter.

"This is fucking ridiculous," he muttered.

He was obsessed. Obsessed, dreaming about the same woman, night after night, year after year. And now he was even crying like some fucking pansy in his dreams.

"What in the hell is this?" Shoving away from the counter, he strode to the enclosed shower and turned on the water with an angry flick of his wrist. He needed a damn hot shower, he needed a good hard run, maybe even a down and dirty fight—if he could get all three of those, it might lighten his dark mood.

But somehow he doubted it.

The dreams were getting worse, and he had a bad feeling he knew why.

Dominic Ralston was going crazy.

F IVE minutes later, he climbed out of the shower and stood naked in front of the mirror as he towel-dried off. Although legend might say otherwise, vampires did have reflections, and Dominic's looked the same now as it had the night his human life had ended. Five ten, 170 pounds of lean, ropy muscle stretched over a frame that probably needed another twenty pounds on it. He'd been in medical school when the Change had been pushed onto him.

Now he'd forever look like that medical student, running on caffeine, nerves and not enough food or sleep. It was a fact he'd come to accept, and he was grateful he'd been on the skinnier side since this was the body he'd live with until somebody put a silver knife through his heart or relieved him of the burden of his head.

There was no telling how long that could be, though. It could be tonight or it could be in a couple hundred years. Hunters lived erratic, somewhat dangerous lives. And very often, they were lonely lives.

Damned lonely. Damned empty.

Oh, he could have found a lover. He could maybe even have found one who understood his life, who would share those nights and days with him.

But unless it was the *right* someone, he wasn't interested. And lately, it seemed the right someone only existed in his dreams.

Dreams about a sad, blue-eyed witch, dreams that left him crying in his sleep.

Yeah. He was pretty sure he was going crazy.

CHAPTER 2

*So high up. What were people thinking, making some-
thing reach so high into the sky?*

Nessa peered down at the earth far below, so far that the
people down there didn't really look like people. More like
little bugs scurrying back and forth.

"Why don't you just jump?"

It was only the third time Morgan had said it. If Nessa
didn't know better, she'd think the ghost was getting bored.

"I won't jump because that would be too easy for you,"
she said, her voice flat and cold. "Too easy for us both."

*"Easy . . . what in the fuck do you care if it's easy for you?
You want it over, so just end it already. Be done with it."*

Nessa swayed forward. Tempted. So very tempted. But she
wouldn't do it. It *was* too easy. Just too easy. Which meant
something would go wrong. If she jumped, she wouldn't
die. She might well break every bone in this body and end
up a fucking vegetable, but she suspected deep down that
she wouldn't die.

God hated her too much to let her die.

"You know one thing I finally figured out, Morgan? I

can't die. Not the easy way at least." She smiled humorlessly and murmured, "It would seem you're stuck with me."

Even as she swore, Morgan faded away. She wasn't strong enough to come to Nessa's mind for too long anymore. Definite plus, there. Nessa might not care for her body as she should, but the weaker *she* felt, the weaker Morgan was.

"Have you lost your mind?"

She glanced behind her and the wind whipped her hair into her eyes, blinding her. She caught it in her hand, holding it back from her face as she stared at Malachi.

Lifting a brow, she said, "Where the bloody hell did you come from?"

"What in the bloody hell are you doing?" he fired back. "Damn it, you have gone insane."

Malachi didn't look too impressed with the view from the top of the skyscraper. "I thought we had already decided on that particular subject, Mal."

Although he didn't age, Nessa decided he looked older now than he had a year before. Something akin to guilt tried to stir within her, but she simply didn't care enough.

She'd tried. Well and truly, she'd tried to settle back into this life that had been thrust upon her, tried to view it as the *gift* everybody else made it out to be. But then the one thing she had viewed as a gift—Mei-Lin—had been torn from her. That girl . . . Nessa had loved that girl like a daughter. More than.

She'd loved her, and just like Elias, Mei-Lin had been taken away from her.

It was just too much. That precious girl, all of her friends, all dead.

If this was the sort of gift *life* offered, Nessa wanted none of it.

Malachi, the poor fool, he worried. All of her friends did. Nessa wished she could care.

But she just didn't.

Looking from Malachi, she cocked her head and stared down at the street. "They are all in such a hurry," she murmured. She slid Malachi a glance and asked, "Why do you think mortals always rush to and fro, Mal? Don't they know that all that rushing accomplishes nothing? They'll still get sick. They'll still suffer. They'll still die."

"Lovely, morbid thoughts there, love." He blew out a disgusted sigh and edged a little closer. Stretching out his hand, Malachi quietly said, "Come down, Nessa."

"Hmmm . . ." A gust of wind picked up and as she held out her arms, it slapped against her with an intensity that made her clothes flap around her and had her swaying near the edge of one of the tallest buildings in the world.

In the middle of the fucking day. Malachi stared at her and then made the fool mistake of glancing down. While he tried to pretend he wasn't dizzy, Nessa giggled like a loon and murmured, "It almost makes me feel as though I could fly, Malachi. Truly fly, like a bird."

"You're not a bird, pet. What you'll do is fall—like a stone." Without feeling the least bit of shame, he backed away from the edge.

After walking the world for a good two thousand years, there was little that bothered him, but he had to admit standing on top of the Sears Tower was on the list. Wouldn't be so bad if she'd decided to do her sightseeing from *inside* the tower.

No, she was outside, on the roof, a place that wasn't exactly open to the public. He doubted she cared about that little detail, however. It was possible they wouldn't have too long before somebody came to investigate.

Mortals, they had their cameras everywhere. He scanned the area, looking for one of the infernal things, and found a number of them. "You know, there are cameras. Where there are cameras, there are often security types watching for suspicious activity. I hope you kept them in mind when you decided to visit this particular spot."

Nessa glanced at the cameras and rolled her eyes. "Bunch of silly electronics. They're all scrambled, and if I know security types, they'll be too busy trying to find the reason inside with their computers, gizmos and gadgets." She laughed. "Not a one of them will think to come looking out here and see if maybe a witch was in the area. We're bad on devices of an electrical nature at times."

Witches and technology didn't always mix well. She could short-circuit a camera from ten paces away . . . if she chose.

"Yes. I'm married to a witch, and I've been around them long enough to know they can fry those computers, gizmos and gadgets practically on purpose if they've a need."

Nessa slid him a sidelong look. "Then I imagine I had a need. I want peace, Mal. Some privacy."

"And you had to choose this spot to find it?" Nothing here worth seeing, at least not worth seeing from the outside. The huge antennas spiraling up into the sky weren't anything worth looking at in his opinion. "If God meant any of us to be this high up in the sky, He would have given us wings," Malachi muttered. From the corner of his eye, he saw Nessa standing as close to the edge as she could without actually going over it. "Bloody hell, would you move a little farther back?"

Grinning at him over her shoulder, she asked, "Why do you look so worried?"

As if he couldn't believe his ears, he repeated, "Worried? You're standing on the very edge of the *fucking Sears Tower*, all but dancing there."

"It's not called the Sears Tower anymore, darling." She slid him a glance from the corner of her eye, smirking. "It's the *Willis* Tower."

"Willis Tower. Sears Tower. I don't care if they renamed it the fucking Eiffel Tower. You do know that if you fall, it could kill you."

"Do you think?" Nessa cast a hopeful glance over the edge and hummed under her breath. A mournful sigh escaped her and she murmured, "If only."

"Nessa, damn it."

"You can be such a bore sometimes, Mal." She blew out a breath. "How does your wife even tolerate it?"

Malachi's face twisted in a snarl. "She's too busy trying to keep you alive to worry about me being boring." Hell, he and his beloved spent so much time worrying about Nessa that they didn't have time to wonder if they were boring these days.

"Becoming a bit harder to handle me than you'd expected, eh?" She arched her brows and smiled at him.

Malachi wanted to shake her. She didn't seem to bloody care about anything anymore, and it was getting more and more disturbing.

For a time, she'd done well. She'd seemed stronger . . . almost like she'd once been.

But then Malachi failed her.

He'd never forgive himself for that.

The loss of the girl she'd loved like a daughter had damned near destroyed her. Malachi hadn't been able to do a damn thing to stop it. He hadn't been able to stop a drunk driver from plowing into the car Mei-Lin had been riding in. He hadn't been able to save the four girls, and he hadn't been able to do anything but stand at Nessa's side and hold her hand while she wept at Mei-Lin's funeral.

Useless bastard. All these years he'd walked this earth and the few times one of his dearest friends had needed help, he hadn't been able to do anything.

Just as he couldn't help her now. She was slipping into madness, he feared. Kelsey, his love, his heart, his soul, seemed to fear the same thing.

They were losing her, bit by bit.

Remember why you came here, old man, he told himself.

Not that he thought he'd have any impact on her. But he couldn't give up. And if *he* didn't come, he feared Kelsey would. As mindless as Nessa was these days, Malachi feared his wife even being near her.

If Nessa wanted to court death, Malachi would do his damnedest to stop her and he'd do his damnedest to hold Kelsey at bay, too.

"You found a nest of feral vamps," he said.

Nessa grinned. She looked like a damn schoolgirl standing there, a pleased grin on her face, her blond hair whipping around her face. Flinging her arms to the sky, she said, "Yes . . . Yes, I did. And it was quite a lot of fun."

She stood there like that for a moment, poised as if getting ready for the dive to end all dives. Then she lowered her arms, rubbed at her neck with one hand.

Malachi walked over to her, tugging the neckline of her sweatshirt aside so he could see the ugly bite mark on her neck. "Got bit, too, I see," he murmured, keeping his voice neutral. He'd known that before he'd come. That was why Kelsey had sent him.

Nessa had been courting death with a vengeance ever since Mei-Lin had died. Each time, she moved a little closer. But he wasn't sure what would claim her first—death or her own demons.

He'd been so grateful to have her back that he hadn't noticed how broken she was. Hadn't realized what returning had done to her.

Then Mei-Lin came into her life, and Nessa seemed to find herself again. She'd been whole . . . or closer to it than she'd been in a good long time.

She was worse now.

All these years, Nessa had been strong. He'd counted on that strength, he supposed. Counted on it to see her through this.

But even the very strong break.

Malachi suspected the girl's death had proven to be too much.

Nessa wasn't broken—*yet*—but neither was she whole.

He had been so pathetically grateful to have her back. Nessa was one of the few constants in his life. He'd known her when she was little more than a girl and he'd watched her grow into the powerful witch she'd become, a witch whose power was so great, it had kept her soul alive even after her body had shut down.

But they'd all been fools thinking that she would eventually adjust. And Malachi was the biggest fool of all for thinking it, because of all of them, Malachi knew her best. He'd known how tired she was, how lonely, and it had nothing to do with a frail, weakened body.

Whatever miracle God had wrought upon Nessa, it

wasn't one that she would thank Him for. She hated every moment of her new existence. Right up until Mei-Lin. But that peace had been too short-lived and now, things were even worse than they had been before.

It was no longer simple loneliness and heartache tormenting the powerful witch. It was more.

Something dark had settled inside of her, something broken. She was fractured inside, a fact that all of them had overlooked until it couldn't be any longer.

Now, he had to face every day and wonder if this would be the day he was forced to hunt down his oldest friend and kill her. As yet, she was no threat to any but the ferals and herself, but he wondered how long that would last. She chased death with a passion, and she moved closer and closer to a line that no Hunter could cross.

It was as though she'd forgotten who she was. What she was. He looked into her eyes and saw madness. He saw a decided lack of control, and she cared little. No, she wasn't a danger to them yet, but he feared she would be. And when that happened, he would have to kill her. It was a knowledge that festered inside him. All this time, as long as he had walked this earth, nothing had broken him. It had been close when he had thought Agnes had died, but Kelsey had pulled him through.

He worried though that his wife wouldn't be able to pull him through what he feared was coming. Not because she couldn't. But because she *wouldn't*.

Kelsey . . . he loved that woman more than life itself. For her, he could survive centuries in hell if he knew she would be waiting for him at the end. But if he had to kill Nessa, Kelsey might never forgive him.

In her heart, she still hoped that Nessa would survive this. But Malachi was a pragmatic man. He had admitted what Kelsey's soft heart had yet to accept.

Nessa didn't want to live and she was getting desperate enough to do the unthinkable, just to see that she got what she wanted.

Death.

This time, she'd almost found it. And at the hands of a mangy, miserable feral vamp that she could have killed with her hands tied behind her back, if she chose.

Nessa shifted and smoothed her shirt so that it mostly hid the bite on her neck.

Inside his mind, he could still see those ugly, gaping holes in her pale skin.

"He took too much blood," Malachi said softly, his voice tight and controlled. Controlled, because if he wasn't careful, he would start shouting and he'd learned quite some time ago how shouting affected Nessa—she either laughed, or did something that would make him want to shout louder. "You're running a pint or two low there." He could see it in the pallor of her skin, and more, he scented it in her blood. Another few minutes and she would have been completely drained.

Nessa shrugged. "Nothing I haven't dealt with before." Then she grimaced, glancing down at her rail-thin body. "Granted, not in this particular body."

"That particular body is the only one you have. Perhaps you should care for it better. You need food, red meat. Rest. Hell, even a pint of Guinness would do you a world of good."

"Hmmm." She turned around and peered over the edge, staring down. The naked yearning in her eyes turned Malachi's gut into a cold, empty pit.

She wanted to jump. If he hadn't come when he did, would she have tried it? Would she try now . . . with him watching?

"Come back to Excelsior with me," he said quietly. He held out a hand and watched as she turned around. "Come home."

Come home, he thought. If he could just get her back to Excelsior, back to the school, they could help. There, perhaps she could find herself again. Perhaps she could heal.

He hoped. He prayed.

"Home." A faint smile curled her mouth upward, but it didn't reach her eyes. She never really smiled anymore. "Home is where the heart is, isn't it, Malachi?" She slid her gaze east, east over land and ocean, to a village that hadn't existed for centuries. "My heart's been buried for so long, there's not even dust left of him. I have no home."

An impish grin appeared on her face and she added, "Besides, there are still some nasties out there that I missed the other day. A good Hunter never leaves the job undone and all that rot."

"You don't need to be Hunting right now, Nessa," Malachi snapped. "You're weak, you're low on blood." *You're insane.* He kept that part to himself. He reached out, grabbed her wrist and jerked her back from the edge. She went flying and if he hadn't still held her wrist, she would have flown halfway across the roof before she landed. "It's a bloody miracle you can even stand."

Tugging her wrist, she said, "Oh, nonsense. You don't really believe a couple of pesky, bloodthirsty vampires are that big a threat to me, do you?"

His eyes raked over her from head to toe, lingering on the barely concealed bite mark at her neck. "Right now? Yes. You're vulnerable, damn it. A toddler having a temper tantrum could well prove to be a threat to you in your state."

"Vulnerable?" Blond brows arched over wide blue eyes. "I haven't been vulnerable since—well, since I don't remember when. At least not to vampires. And obviously, you haven't spent much time around toddlers—toddlers in a tantrum are a threat to damn near everything."

She tipped her head back and murmured softly, "They're out there now, waiting for the sun to set. I feel them . . ."

Recognizing the look on her face, Malachi started toward her. "Fine, then," he growled. "We'll go after them together. Just like old times, eh?"

There was no way he was going to let this demented woman out of his sight, not until he knew she was stronger. If he were the hopeful sort, he would even wish that perhaps the two of them working side by side as they had so many times before might remind Nessa of who she was.

"Let's go then." He held out a hand to her.

But instead of putting her hand in his, she smirked. "I'm used to doing things on my own, Mal."

A mischievous smile flirted with the corners of her lips.

Not this time, old friend, he thought, ready to grab her once more.

"Oh, no, you don't." Malachi lunged for her, but she disappeared, right in front of him, and his hands closed around thin air.

Tʜᴀᴛ big bully of a vampire worried too much, Nessa mused.

"You should have just jumped," Morgan whispered, her voice faint, but malicious. *"Then you wouldn't have to worry about him anymore."*

"Shut up, bitch," Nessa muttered, swallowing the knot in her throat.

She might despise this life, might despise the God who'd trapped her here yet again, but she wouldn't do that to Malachi. The poor vampire, he worried so, and he felt guilty, although none of this was his fault.

She might hate her life. She might not care if she lived or died. She might not care so much that they worried about her. But she wouldn't do that to him—wouldn't jump while he watched.

Her stomach rumbled demandingly and she followed her nose to a street vendor. A hot dog, loaded with chili, onions and cheese, wasn't going to do much more than ease the emptiness of her stomach, but she wasn't going to take the downtime she knew she needed. She needed a decent meal, a lot of calories, a lot of water and a lot of rest before she'd feel even close to strong.

And she might . . . later.

Just not right now.

A glance up at the leaden sky didn't tell her much about the time of day, but experience had her placing it at roughly noon. Gave her about five hours before the sun set. Five hours to make sure those vampires were dead. At least the old one. The two younger ones she could deal with even after sunset. The old one though—

A cold ache spread out from the slow-healing vampire bite in her neck. He'd sought to bleed her out and he'd been low enough on his own blood that his vampiric gifts hadn't been particularly strong. When vampires wanted, they could leave bites that were almost surgically neat and their saliva had a rather miraculous healing effect. At least they did when the vampire wasn't hovering just this side of death.

She finished up her hot dog and then turned the corner, heading for the subway. The red line would take her close enough to where she needed to go and it would save her much-needed energy.

She moved slowly down the steps, hating the weakness in her body, hating how heavy her legs felt, how gritty her eyes felt. She plugged some money into a machine and got her ticket before joining the other bodies waiting on the platform.

The train came to a halt in front of her and she moved on, surrounded by commuters, college students and construction workers. She breathed in the scents of life and felt a curl of envy whisper through her. These people were rushing home, rushing to work, living lives that revolved around work, family, dates.

Everything Nessa wished she could have.

Everything she never would.

The envy flowered into full bloom. Nessa glanced around at the faces of the mortals and wished she could be anywhere but here.

"Then go. No reason you can't be anywhere but here."

That insidious cow. She couldn't linger for long, but she could sure as hell speak up often enough to drive Nessa completely insane. Or try to tempt her into something foolish.

On a good day, Nessa could ignore the bitch.

But today wasn't a good day. On the bad days, it wasn't just lucidity that took a vacation. It was her common sense and self-preservation. On a good day, she'd never even dream of using her magic where mortals could witness it.

Today, though, was obviously a bad day and if she was just a little stronger, she might have even done what Morgan wanted and let the magic carry her away.

Weak and tired as she was, flying wasn't just unwise, it was dangerous. The ability to move herself from one place to another, miles away, was almost as easy as breathing when she was at full strength.

Nessa hadn't been at full strength in months. Logically, she knew she needed to take better care of herself. On her lucid days, she did try. But there were other days when it seemed insanity had the stronger hold. Days when she couldn't tell reality from the nightmares inside her head, days when she couldn't separate the future from the past.

When she was stronger, the lucid days came more often. Those days, however, came with painfully clear memories. Memories she would do nearly anything to avoid having. Keeping her mind occupied helped—which meant Hunting like a demon. Or letting herself become weak enough, tired enough, that she slipped out of lucidity. Usually a combination of both worked best.

Except doing both tended to make people fuss over her like she was some kind of daft old bat or a reckless young child.

With a curl of her lip, she muttered, "I tried the daft old bat route—it wouldn't stick." So now she was stuck inside the body of a reckless youth.

Morgan had been young when they had stopped her murderous rampage.

If Morgan had lived, she would have been in her twenties, Nessa thought. She wasn't sure. The years had all run together on her, but she knew this body was still in the bloom of youth. She wondered how many more years she was going to be trapped inside it. How many more years of emptiness and loneliness she must endure.

It was enough to infuriate her. A sharp hiss escaped her and she shoved to her feet. Danger be damned. Common sense be damned. She forced her way through the bodies, heading to the back of the train, looking for just a little bit of privacy. The closest she was going to get was the second to last car. One drunkard, a bored-looking woman who Nessa suspected was a prostitute, and a dozing commuter who would probably end his trip minus his wallet and briefcase if he didn't wake up.

She met the insolent gaze of the woman and held it. Standing up, Nessa imagined the other woman would probably have a good six inches on her, and easily forty pounds. But physical presence didn't always add up to everything.

Attitude counted for a great deal. Attitude and arrogance. Those two things Nessa had in spades.

Their gazes connected and Nessa smirked at the other woman, watched as the gaze fell away. In that second, when nobody was looking at her, Nessa let the magic take her.

In the back of her mind, she felt Morgan's delight.

It left Nessa feeling more than a little sick, and downright furious.

She alit on the front stoop of the worn, run-down house on the lower east side of Chicago. "Honey, I'm home."

CHAPTER 3

Dominic hated heights.

He hated heights, and he couldn't stand outside during the midday, not even on a cloudy one. Unless he wanted to burn to a crisp. At least not yet. In a few more decades, he might be able to handle it.

But right now, he couldn't. And even if he could, he wouldn't be outside *here*. Nausea hit him and he knew where he was. Chicago. He'd been to Chicago before and he'd even been in the Sears Tower—no, the Willis Tower. They'd renamed it. But he'd been inside before. *In* the tower, not on *top* of it.

"I'm not really here now, either," he muttered, shooting a look at the sky.

He was dreaming.

He didn't even have to see her, didn't hear her voice to know he was dreaming. He just knew.

He heard voices. Two of them—both women. Although they sounded the same, they weren't. One was accented, with the crisp, lyrical sound of England, and the other was good old American with the slow, lazy drawl of the South.

"Why don't you just jump?"

"I won't jump because that would be too easy for you. Too easy for us both."

"Easy . . . what in the fuck do you care if it's easy for you? You want it over, so just end it already. Be done with it."

Dominic felt his fangs throb in their sheaths, ready to emerge. His body tensed, ready to attack as he searched the rooftop for the other woman. He'd kill the bitch—whoever she was, taunting this woman to jump, he'd kill her.

But there was no other woman.

Just the witch.

Just *his* witch.

Looking at her made him ache.

It had been months since he'd held her . . . even in his dreams. You'd think a man's libido would kick in and he could at least have her in his dreams, but not lately.

Not since the dream where she'd stood crying in a field of stone.

Since then, his dreams had taken a drastic turn, and not a good one. Either he was reliving that dream where she held him as he died, or he was in one where he was nothing more than an observer, watching as she drifted through life like a heartbroken ghost. Dreams where he couldn't touch her, couldn't hold her, couldn't talk to her.

Because she wouldn't let him.

She had isolated herself, even in her dreams.

No . . . not *her* dreams. They were *his* dreams.

Whatever . . . none of it made sense, and he couldn't try to make any of it now, either, not when she was there.

He wanted to go to her. Hold her.

He wanted to tell her to come away from the ledge, that she wasn't alone up there on the roof. That she wasn't alone, period. He was there . . . he was with her.

And then she wasn't alone, but Dominic wasn't the one standing just behind her.

It was another vampire.

Dominic couldn't reach out to the witch. Couldn't touch

her, couldn't make her hear him if she spoke. Couldn't save her if she tried to jump.

But the vampire could.

Don't you let her jump, you big bastard, he thought darkly.

And still, in some part of his mind, he wondered why he was so worried about a dream-woman jumping off the Willis Tower. It wasn't like she was real. It wasn't like it would hurt her. The next time he slept, she'd be there . . . waiting for him.

Not if she jumps, he thought.

If she jumps, I've lost her.

He knew it. If she jumped, she was lost to him. Somehow.

N ESSA swayed as a wave of dizziness washed over her. Had been a bad idea, flying here. It was too late to walk away now, though. Besides, if she knew Malachi well enough, he'd show up. He'd be here to back her up. As she checked her reserves, she flexed a hand, an absent gesture. She frowned as she realized just how very low her energy was. She didn't even know if she had fumes to operate on.

But she couldn't walk away. She felt the pulse and ebb of the vampires inside and despite her lack of interest in life itself, she still had a keen interest in fighting the good fight.

"A good Hunter never leaves the job undone and all that rot," she mumbled to herself.

They were resting now—or rather, two of them were. The older one had enough years behind him that he didn't immediately collapse when the sun breached the horizon. He had been the one to bite her.

For a few moments, she'd almost let him win. Blood loss would kill her. That was a certain fact—all animals needed their lifeblood, and witch or no, she was just another animal.

But then she'd heard the wail of sirens. Somebody had called the police, some kind soul probably thinking they were doing something good. Or maybe it had just been somebody annoyed by the noise.

It didn't matter, though. The police had been coming and they weren't equipped to deal with vampires. If she died, then the police would stumble blindly into something they couldn't handle.

So, once more, with death just a wish away, she'd fought back. Hating every last second of it.

She reached for the doorknob but a wave of weakness washed over her. In the back of her mind, Morgan laughed. Even in death, the bitch continued to taunt Nessa. *Go on inside, old woman. He could use a tasty treat.*

"Hmmm, perhaps. The silver I pumped inside him will be munching away at his insides by now, though."

It had been sheer luck on the vampire's part that he'd managed to bite her at all. They'd both been weakened by the battle, but the vampire had been running perilously low on blood. He had a gaping wound in his gut that wasn't healing as it should and there'd been internal organs trying to slide out as he fought to pin her to the ground. She'd stopped fighting long enough to shove the vial of silver nitrate inside him, and that was when he'd bit her.

Her blood had given his body the strength to start healing, but he had a slow, insidious poison inside his body. If the vampire hadn't been as old as he was, if he hadn't had her blood rushing through his veins, it would have already killed him.

Now, she imagined he just wished it would. Silver nitrate would eat at him like he'd been injected with battery acid. He'd have to feed heavily to recover his strength and sunlight had kept him trapped all day. If she knew vampires, he'd send the two younger ones out as soon as dusk fell and whoever was brought to him wouldn't live through it.

There was little that Nessa cared about in life anymore, but she wasn't going to let that monster kill another innocent soul.

Somehow, Morgan was aware of Nessa's thoughts and as Nessa stood there staring at the door, the bitch laughed.

It was a ghostly echo that none save Nessa could hear and it chilled her, infuriated her. *Let him just kill you, precious. That would make both of us happy.*

"Precious," Nessa crooned aloud. "Please don't be so ridiculous. What on earth made you think I'd even consider making you happy?"

She reached out and closed her hand around the door. She concentrated a bit, using her magic to manipulate the elements on the other side of it. The air formed itself into a "hand" of sorts and turned the lock. It opened with a quiet snick and she pushed the door open.

Darkness greeted her and when she took in a deep breath, she could smell him. Smell the silver that was poisoning him, smell the stink of burning flesh as it ate away at his body.

As she stepped over the threshold, she felt a rush of wind behind her and she glanced back, smiling as Malachi materialized. She might as well have a homing beacon on her, she decided. He was just that good at tracking her.

But Hunters always seemed damned good at sensing each other.

"Crashing the party?" she asked. Some part of her, the part that had tried to chide her into resting, recovering, was glad to see him. That part of her, the part that wouldn't give up, was glad to see him, glad that she wasn't going to walk into a fight she couldn't survive alone.

"Bloody fool witch," he growled. He stormed past her, sending her an icy look. "You might not give a damn if you live or die, but I do."

Nessa sighed. "I know."

CHAPTER 4

Tucked inside a warm, soft bed, Nessa rolled onto her side and clutched a pillow to her chest.

She was back at Excelsior.

She'd been at the school for three days—something she hadn't had much choice in. During the fight in Chicago, she'd collapsed. If it wasn't for Malachi, she would have died there. Part of her couldn't quite manage to be glad for that fact.

Not just yet. Maybe not ever.

Outside her rooms, she could hear the low murmur of voices, sense the rush of life. Her shields were shot, and everything just felt too intense. She couldn't block a soul out to save her life.

She was far too weak, far too vulnerable just yet.

Closing her eyes, she reached up and touched the smooth skin where she'd been bitten. Kelsey had healed her, good and fast, but Nessa didn't remember. According to the other witch, she'd spent the first forty-eight hours unconscious.

She'd woken in this room to find herself healed, bathed

and dressed in a long, cotton nightshirt. It resembled the chemises she'd worn for much of her life, gathered at the neck and hanging to her ankles. The first thing she'd done when she woke up was tear the damn thing off.

She'd made the mistake of looking at the mirror and it had been like being flung back into time.

It was an ugly, awful irony that Morgan's former body bore a striking resemblance to Nessa's. The shape of the eyes were a bit different, and her hair was blond now rather than brown, but the differences were so slight they could have been sisters—nearly twins.

Seeing herself in that chemise and wearing a face that looked far too much like the one from her youth had been too much.

Now she had echoes of Elias's voice in her mind, the low, rough sound of his laughter, the heated whispers in her ear as he made love to her. The tormented, awful rasp of his voice as he lay dying in her arms.

My Nessa . . .

Only God Himself could keep me from you.

Pain wrapped around her heart and squeezed. It poisoned her, darkened everything and stole the breath from her lungs.

Closing her eyes, she buried her face against the pillow and whispered, "Please, just let me rest. Please . . ."

K ELSEY stood outside the door, her hand frozen just inches from the door. She'd been about to knock, but then a wave of pain had threatened to send her to her knees.

Helplessly, she turned toward Malachi and rested her head against his chest.

"What's wrong, sweet?" he whispered, stroking his hand up her spine.

She shook her head, unable to explain the maelstrom of pain coming from Nessa's room.

"Kelsey," Malachi said, his voice low, rough.

Lifting her head, she looked at him. In his midnight

blue eyes, she saw the warning. If she didn't explain, he'd go look for himself. Sighing, she rested a hand on his chest and lowered her shields, projected some of the pain she felt from Nessa.

It hit him like a sledgehammer. She watched as he stumbled back a step before righting himself. She cut the flow off and took his hand, guiding him away from Nessa's room.

They had their own quarters, tucked in the east wing— or rather, *under* the east wing of Excelsior—and that was where her footsteps led her. Once inside their bedroom, she curled up in a chair and hugged herself, watching while Malachi started to pace.

"What in the hell are we supposed to do?" he finally bit off, turning to stare at her. Fury and worry warred in his eyes.

Kelsey understood completely. "I don't know." She sighed and rested her head against the padded back of the chair. Closing her eyes, she muttered, "I just don't know. But she can't survive with that kind of pain inside her, Mal. It's going to drive her mad."

"I think it already has." He laughed, but there was no humor in the sound. "You didn't see how weak she was, sweet. If I hadn't seen her, I never would have believed it, and yet she plunged feetfirst into a fight with a couple of ferals. She passed out—right in the bloody middle."

She'd heard this already. Several times. But she said nothing. If she was shocked just to hear it, she couldn't imagine the shock it had given him to watch.

Nessa was courting death too closely these days.

"How can we help her?"

Kelsey opened her eyes and stared at her husband. It broke her heart, in so many ways. Just to see him look so confused, just to feel how helpless he felt—this was *Malachi.* The oldest of them all. He went where angels feared to tread and did it with a laugh. There was nothing he couldn't handle . . . or so it would seem.

He couldn't handle this, though. And she didn't have

any idea what to say to him, how to help him. She didn't know how to help Nessa, one of her dearest friends.

Quietly, she said, "I don't think we can." Rising, she crossed the floor to stand in front him. Wrapping her arms around his waist, she rested her head against his chest. She sighed as his cool body began to warm from the contact. He ran his lips down her neck. Cupping the back of his head, she tipped her head to the side and pressed him close.

They both hurt. They both worried. After so many years alone, it seemed as natural as breathing to press herself closer and take comfort in his nearness.

She wasn't alone any longer.

Neither of them was.

He nuzzled her neck then sank his fangs into her. Kelsey shivered as heat danced through her veins. She could feel his mouth drawing against her flesh, feel his cool body warm. The tension in the air grew thick, hot, wrapping around them.

When he pulled away, she groaned, instinctively trying to draw him back to her, but it was too late. He licked the small wounds at her neck and she felt the faint tingle as her body healed it. Lifting her head, she stared up at him and trailed her fingers across his mouth. She needed him. She needed the strength of him, the warmth of their love. The comfort they could offer each other.

"Take me to bed," she murmured softly.

Malachi's dark, midnight eyes glowed. He lifted a long-fingered hand and cupped her cheek. "You have students and teachers awaiting you, pet."

She reached between them, stroking him through his jeans. "I don't care."

"Well, then." A smile curled his lips and he lifted her into his arms.

BECAUSE she knew she'd come too close to death, Nessa didn't leave the school the minute she had the strength to climb out of her bed.

She should have felt at home here. After all, she'd taught in this school for many, many years . . . back in that other life. *That other life.* She smiled without humor. She could break her life into two parts now . . . no, three.

Life with Elias. Life after Elias. And now . . . life after death.

Nessa didn't want to be here. She didn't want to be around another soul—not a friend, not a student. Nobody. She couldn't risk it. Another loss would destroy her.

Where's your strength now, you stupid old bitch?

The sly, insulting whisper of Morgan's voice stirred something inside her, the first embers of anger, self-disgust. Something. But she couldn't very well get angry, now could she?

After all, the girl wasn't wrong.

Nessa's strength was gone. She couldn't find that strength again, and she didn't want to.

She just wanted oblivion and if she couldn't have that, then she wanted peace and solitude.

If she was alone, then she wouldn't come to care about anybody again and if she didn't come to care, she wouldn't be shattered by another loss.

"Too many losses," she murmured to herself. Far too many.

As her strength slowly returned, so did lucidity. Clear thoughts weren't particularly welcome, but she had to face the facts. She couldn't keep doing this to herself. Even if she didn't particularly want to live, she didn't want her friends to pay the price, and sooner or later, that would happen if she kept to this road.

Kelsey visited often, using books, movies and bribes of French chocolate and plum wine to draw Nessa out of her shell. As fond as Nessa was of her shell, though, she let her friend coax her outside.

As little as she cared for her own neck, for her own life, she did still care for her friends and she was tired of making them worry.

Within a week, her energy was back.

Thanks to the food they'd been pushing on her, she'd put on a few pounds.

And her mind was all too clear. That was the bothersome part about taking care of herself. It was harder to avoid thinking about things.

Memories taunted her, and the ever-present Morgan renewed her assault with glee.

She was tempted—for the first time since she'd realized that the bitch had taken to haunting her—to tell somebody else about her hitchhiker, see if anybody might have a clue how to get rid of the annoying ghost.

But she didn't. If she seriously put her mind to it, she could probably think of a way to rid herself of Morgan.

It's a sad thing in life when one hesitates to rid oneself of an enemy. But if nothing else, Morgan was a constant in Nessa's life.

"How low I've sunk," she whispered, staring off into nothingness. She tolerated the presence of a murdering ghost, just because it meant she wasn't alone inside her head.

The irony wasn't lost on her.

S HE came awake to hear the high-pitched chatter of laughter and she groaned, rolling onto her stomach. She tugged the pillow over her head and tried to block out the sound of the students, but to no avail. She'd left the blasted window open the night before, forgetting that the students resumed their studies today.

For the past week, it had been relatively quiet. The students had been on spring break, but now the time for quiet was over. School was back in session.

Kicking her legs over the edge of the bed, she rose and stormed to the window, half tempted to mutter a spell that would darken the room again. She could pretend it was still nightfall.

Staring out the window, she watched them. They were laughing amongst themselves. A few were griping about an assignment they'd failed to do over the break. Others were loitering here and there, with that feigned air of apathy teenagers had long since perfected.

Across the broad expanse of green grass, Nessa could see the front steps of the school. Kelsey was there, along with some of the other instructors. They spoke to the children, answered questions and waved the students on when they lingered too long.

On the surface, it looked like most any other school. That was exactly what the mortal world saw—a school for the gifted and troubled. *Gifted* meaning *highly capable*, though, since naturally the mortal world didn't tend to think in terms of witches, shapeshifters or vampires.

And Excelsior was a damn fine school—it provided a top-notch education, one of the finest private educations money could buy. It provided that . . . and a lot more. Many, though not all, of the students had no family to guide them through the training needed to attain control of their gifts.

Once the sun set, a new set of students would emerge from the secured, safe rooms under the school—the newly Changed vampires—there to learn control over their bloodthirst.

Excelsior was small. No fewer than two hundred minor students and maybe half as many adult students. A little world, isolated from the rest of mankind.

Nessa closed the window and jerked the heavy curtains into place. Turning, she stared at her room. She dismissed the bed without even looking at it. There was no way she could rest now. A headache pounded behind her eyes.

There was a neat stack of books on the little table near the window. Yet another offering from Kelsey. Depressed and tired, Nessa moved to the chair and sank down. She blew out a breath and glanced at the paperback on top. A pretty girl, dressed all in black. She flipped it open and saw another image just inside. The same girl, this time with a man. They stood close, not quite embracing.

Blood roared in Nessa's ears as she stared at the man. Black coat, worn open over a bare chest, the long ends of it flapping about his legs.

Nessa's hands trembled. Her heart began to slam against her ribs.

Dark hair . . . a strong jaw. She couldn't see his face well, but her imagination was quite content to fill in the void. In her mind's eye, she could see him.

Her dream lover . . .

The book fell from her slack hands, but she didn't notice.

His face. There was something about his face . . . then the image faded away—or perhaps *she* faded . . . into the image, for the girl was no longer there. It was him. He lifted his head, staring at her. His face—almost too pretty for a man.

You're too pretty, she'd told him.

Dark, velvety brown eyes.

Long-fingered hands . . . almost elegant.

Her heart skipped a beat as her imagination kicked into overdrive. He was touching her and she was helpless as he lifted a hand to cup her cheek, angling her head back.

Tears burned her eyes.

Just before he would have kissed her, she flung herself out of the chair, landing in a heap on the floor.

"No," she whispered, shaking her head. She couldn't do this. She'd refused to let herself dream of him in the past year, refused to let herself take comfort in his presence. In those dreams, she'd felt almost happy . . . and she couldn't be happy. Would never truly be happy and having it in her dreams, only in her dreams was just too much.

Too painful.

"No," she whispered again, shuddering.

The spell was shattered and Nessa found herself on her hands and knees, staring at the book. It lay just inches from her hands.

Swearing, she shoved upright and kicked it away. It ended up under the bed, but she didn't bother retrieving it.

Nessa cast a look around the room.

Enough. She'd had enough.

"Damn it." She shoved a hand through her hair, fisted it in the blond strands. She jerked at it, hoping the light tug would help clear her mind, but it did nothing.

Her head ached, her heart ached.

Confusion and chaos reigned inside her.

All from a bloody picture on a damned book.

And she was so fucking *tired* of it. So tired.

"I'm stronger than this," she muttered. Slowly, she turned and stared into the mirror hanging over the fireplace.

She *was* stronger than this.

"By God, it's time I started acting like it then, isn't it?"

Lifting her face upward, she gathered her magic, and in moments, she was gone, letting it carry her away.

CHAPTER 5

"I'M not doing very well, darling."

Nessa was talking to a stone angel.

The marble headstone held Mei-Lin's name, her date of birth and the day she died. Such a short time she'd walked this earth. Seventeen years, to the day.

Below the dates there was an angel, etched into the marble with amazing delicacy. Brushing her fingers over the wings, Nessa said, "I'd ashamed if you could see me now, what I've become."

There was no answer, but she hadn't expected one.

The past week had passed with startling, unpleasant clarity. Ever since she'd left Excelsior, she'd been all too sane, all too aware. She hated it, and some part of her yearned for the oblivion of the past year. She hardly remembered much of it. It was a vague, hazy blur, one she longed to find again.

But it wouldn't be so easy this time.

Grimacing, she touched her neck. The skin beneath her fingers was smooth, unscarred, no sign of the nasty bite that could have killed her—it likely would have, if she were human.

Or if God had any intention of letting her die.

Damn Malachi for saving her. Damn her own hide for collapsing and giving him the opportunity to get her to Excelsior.

Just being at the school had reminded her. She knew who she was. She knew what she was meant to do with her life. Finding her own death wasn't in the plan, no matter how much she longed for it.

Pushing her hair back from her face, she stared off into the night. It was past midnight. The cemetery was closed and she wasn't supposed to be here right now.

Not that she cared. Nessa didn't listen to or follow rules that kept her from doing what she wanted. If she wanted to visit a loved one's grave, why couldn't she do it at whatever hour she chose?

The mild spring breeze teased her hair, carrying with it the scent of rain and blooming flowers. It smelled of life, and of new death. Why did people always feel the need to offer flowers to their dead?

"I can't keep going like this, can I, darling?" Nessa stroked the marble headstone and then pushed herself to her feet.

Tucking her hands in her pockets, she said, "I think it's time I say good-bye."

Since Mei-Lin's death, Nessa had made it habit to come visit her grave as often as possible. She'd done it in part because she wasn't ready to let the girl go, but also because she wanted to remind herself—punish herself. Using the pain, deliberately inflicting it upon herself, like jabbing a needle into an open wound.

Logically, Nessa knew there was nothing she could have done to save Mei-Lin. It had been an accident—a horrible, terrible accident in which four young women lost their lives.

She needed to let the girl go, and she needed to let go of her grief. She rested a hand on the headstone. "I'm sorry, Mei-Lin, so sorry. You should have grown up, found a man who looks like Daniel Day-Lewis and lived happily ever after. I'll miss you, darling. But I need to let you go."

Tears rolled down her cheeks and she wiped them away.

"Good-bye." She turned on her heel and strode away from the stone, refusing to look back, no matter how much she wanted to.

There was one more good-bye she needed to make.

One more dream to kill.

Once she was out of the cemetery and away from any prying electronic eyes, she lifted her face to the sky and called her magic.

It carried her away, sweeping her across miles and miles, over land and ocean. It was nearing dawn when her feet alit on the ground.

She breathed the air in, filled her lungs with the scent of the forest—trees, moss, the morning dew. She stared around her, amazed to realize she barely recognized the place. Centuries had passed since she'd seen this bit of land. No sign of Oneoak remained and logically, she hadn't expected to see anything of the long-gone village.

Even the trees were different. The land. Peering up at the sky, she searched for something that she recognized. But there was nothing.

Swallowing the knot in her throat, she started to walk.

Although the land no longer seemed familiar, she knew where he rested. She could have found his grave had she been forced to stumble blindfolded through a snowstorm.

There was nothing to identify it. No marker, no stone. But she knew. Deep inside, she knew. Settling on the ground next to his grave, she rested a hand on the earth and said, "Hello, lover."

*H*ELLO, *lover* . . .
It was a bad time to get distracted. Dominic barely managed to evade the werewolf's clawed hand, aimed straight for his throat.

The woman's voice echoed in his ears and he scowled, blocking it out of his head.

Not now. Can't lose my mind right now.

No way could he afford to get distracted right then. He

wasn't fighting alone—Sheila, one of his fellow Hunters and his best friend's wife, was with him. If she got hurt because he couldn't pull his head out of his ass, he'd never forgive himself for as long as he lived. And that wouldn't be very long.

Rafe would kill him.

Gripping his knife, he waited until the werewolf came at him and ducked under the strike, using the wolf's speed to his advantage and driving them both to the ground. He plunged his knife deep, and the stink of burning meat filled the air.

The heart—had to destroy the heart. He twisted the knife, making sure the wolf was completely and utterly dead before he shoved himself upright. The dead body was changing back to his natural state, revealing a middle-aged, slightly plump man, his body nude.

Dominic lunged for the other wolf just as the creature went to belt Sheila. Judging by the bruises on her face, she'd already taken quite a beating. Oh, yeah. Rafe was going to have his hide. He wrapped his arm around the wolf's neck and pressed—unlike vampires, werewolves did still need to breathe, and Dom used his strength to choke the wolf into submission.

"Don't kill him," Sheila warned. "Rafe wants to know where the rest are holed up."

Dom grunted as the were tried to smash his head backward. "Maybe he could save us the trouble and just tell me now."

"Go fuck . . . your . . ." The were gasped, struggling to breathe. ". . . self."

Dom grinned. "Be nice. There's a lady present. Tell us where the rest of them are and you can die nice and fast."

"Fuck off." He tried to drive an elbow backward.

"Fine. Have it your way—the Master will get it out of you if he has to bleed you one drop at a time." He squeezed tighter, tighter, until he felt the wolf go slack. He held another minute or so and then he let the unconscious sorry bastard fall to the ground. Reaching for the reinforced silver cuffs at his belt, he gave Sheila a narrow look.

"Well, that was fun," Sheila said, her face pink and her eyes gleaming at him despite the bruising around her left eye.

Normally, Dominic would have stared at her and laughed. She was black-and-blue, and that was her idea of fun? But just then, he heard another whisper. *It's long past time that I do this.*

What . . . ? He staggered, all but swamped by a wave of misery—*her* misery. His woman . . . his witch. Pressing the heel of his hand to his temple, he braced the other against the brick wall nearby, barely aware of Sheila's odd, worried gaze. "Hey . . . you okay?"

No. No, he wasn't.

He was hearing *her* voice again. He could hear her. Clear as day. Clear as a bell. Like she was standing right next to him, murmuring in his ear.

Past time she do what? he thought, half panicked. He was so focused on her, on her voice, he wasn't aware of anything, of *anybody* else.

I have to let you go. All these years, I waited for death . . . knowing I'd finally be with you, and now, death has denied me. I'm not meant to find you.

The hell she wasn't—he wanted to scream. To snarl in sheer frustration. Over a *dream*. Over a woman who didn't even exist.

The blood roared in his ears. Dimly, he heard Sheila shouting his name. Heard the scrabble of claws on concrete. There was a howl. *Danger—danger—*His body tried to scream the warning at him, but he was lost, caught in the spell of his woman's voice as she continued to whisper inside his head.

I don't know why. But I'm not. So I need to let you go. Good-bye, my love . . .

His heart no longer beat that much, but it still functioned and as her voice echoed in his mind, Dominic felt a tearing pain, unlike anything he'd ever known.

Unlike anything he had ever imagined. It was worse than the pain he'd gone through when he Changed. It was worse than the sickening, terrifying nightmares that still haunted him—the nights he'd spent helpless as a feral Master toyed with him.

It was the worst pain he'd ever felt in his life and he went to his knees, unaware of Sheila, unaware of anything but *her*.

It was the pain of a heart shattering into a thousand pieces.

And then there was a very *real* pain—the pain of his own blade, cutting deep, deep into him. The pain of it was enough of a shock to force him out of whatever spell held him captive, and he stumbled backward and saw Sheila struggling with the wolf he'd neglected to restrain. Blood splattered across her face and her eyes glowed. As his blood gushed out of him, too much, too fast, he heard another whisper.

Good-bye, my love . . .

"So what did her voice sound like?"

It was a full twenty-four hours later, and Dominic was still trying to get past the ache in his heart. It was worse than the pain from the slowly healing wound in his gut, worse than *anything. Good-bye, my love . . .*

He'd collapsed into a healing sleep not long after the other Hunters had arrived on the scene, but even that had provided no respite from the haunting echo of her voice. Hell, even now, facing a very disgruntled Master, all he could think about was *her*.

"Dom?"

Dominic surged out of the chair with such speed it toppled back behind him, falling to the floor with a clatter. Shooting a dark look at Rafe, he ground out, "I don't know—a woman's voice. Sounded English. I've never heard it in my life."

At least not awake, he thought bitterly. Her voice was eerily, haunting familiar, but he knew, as sure as he knew his own name, he'd never spoken with this woman, never heard her whisper his name in the night, never held her in his arms while they slept.

"Can you be more specific? Is she young? Old?" Rafe

asked, his black brow rising. There was a certain amount of skepticism on his face.

Dominic couldn't blame him. Fuck, he'd all but ended up getting disemboweled because he zoned out right in front of a feral. He hadn't bothered getting the bastard restrained, and the wolf had come to, seen Sheila staring at Dom, seen his chance. The werewolf had screwed up by trying to do a little more damage, by assuming Sheila's preoccupation with Dom meant she was as fucked in the head as Dom had been.

Sheila had killed the feral but not before the feral had all but laid Dom open like a gutted fish.

He could still feel the cold ache of the silver, could still feel the itch and burn of healing flesh.

And he felt like he losing his damned mind. The dreams . . . the dreams were bad enough, but *this* hadn't been a dream. He'd been wide awake and on the tail end a fight, not exactly a safe zone. He could have gotten killed, Sheila could have gotten killed—innocents could have died if the feral wolves had managed to evade capture. They *still* didn't know where the rest of the small feral pack was holed up, either.

Rafe was skeptical? Hell, why *wouldn't* he be?

Shoving a hand through his hair, Dominic turned away and stared out the window. He'd only been awake for four hours, but he still felt weak. Despite feeding, he was already hungry. Exhaustion pulled at him, and he knew he'd have to rest again soon. Injuries caused by silver— shit, he'd heard they were bad, but this was the first time he'd taken more than a nick.

"Look, Rafe, I don't *know* what happened. I don't know if she's real, if I'm going crazy, or what."

Rafe leaned back in his chair and watched him with dark, intense eyes. "I don't think you're going crazy. But we need to figure out what's going on. This could have been bad, Dom. Hell, it *was* bad. You almost got yourself killed. If Sheila hadn't been there, you could be dead."

"I *know* that." His voice sounded more than a little

frustrated, more than a little pissed off, but he couldn't help it. "You think I'm a fucking idiot as well as a nutcase?"

Rafe sighed and said, "You're not a nutcase." Then, forcing a smile, he said, "And you've always been an idiot. That's beside the point. Look . . . I want you to get some rest. You need another solid eighteen hours of rest and another good feeding before you'll feel a little less like hell."

"A little less like hell?" Dominic passed a hand over the fading pink scar that bisected his middle. It was nothing short of miraculous that he was moving around at all, but this lingering weakness, the exhaustion, it pissed him off. Still, although he was tired, he was reluctant to believe Rafe was going to let it go as easy as that. "So that's it? You want me to rest, feed? You're not going to smack my hand or anything?"

Rafe shifted his gaze away, a muscle jerking in his jaw. "I'm not going to smack your hand after you all but had your guts spill out at my wife's feet, no. I'm tempted to beat you senseless for it, but I won't." Then he lifted his gaze and focused on Dominic's face. "Go rest. And when you get up . . . pack."

That caught Dominic by surprise.

He stilled and turned to face the Master. Rafe was more than just his Master—he'd been the one who brought Dominic through the Change, the one who'd helped him find a purpose after he'd found himself in a strange and fucking terrifying world where monsters really did exist.

Rafe was also Dominic's best friend . . . and he was sending Dominic away.

Swallowing, he managed to force something out of his tight throat. "Pack . . . Master?"

Rafe curled his lip. "Don't call me that, and don't look at me like that. I'm sending you to Excelsior—I want you to talk with Kelsey, or one of the healers. Somebody. See if they can figure out what in the hell is going on, so we can fix it."

He kicked his feet off the desk and rose, stalking around to stop just a few feet from Dominic. "I'm *not* dismissing you," Rafe said, his voice edgy.

Dominic looked away, staring out the window behind Rafe's desk. The bastard knew him too well, read him too easily. "Sure as hell feels that way," he muttered.

"Don't be any more of an idiot than you have to be, Dom." Rafe rubbed a hand over his face. "You're half out of your head right now. I don't know what the hell the problem is, but as long as you are like this, I can't have you out there, risking *your* life, innocent lives, the lives of my Hunters . . . you know that." He blew out a breath and then added, "I came too close to losing one of my best friends last night—I'm not doing it again. We're fixing this, you got me?"

"Yeah." The ache in his throat eased enough for him to force a smile. "Ever heard of one of us going crazy like this?"

"Hell, no. But you were always a hard case." With a cynical smirk, Rafe moved back to sit behind his desk. "You're not going crazy. But something's going on and we need to figure out what it is."

ST. AUGUSTINE, FLORIDA

The water was so blue, it hurt to look at it. Didn't help that the sun was reflecting off it and causing it to sparkle as though millions of diamonds were scattered on the surface.

Nessa lowered her shades over her face and leaned back in the hard plastic seat, ignoring the spiel of the tour guide.

They stopped at the Old Gate and the guide went on, harping about how old the bloody structure was and what purpose it had served. *It's a bleeding gate, children—it does what a gate is supposed to do—it keeps people out.*

The trip went on and on, with stops here and there so tourists could take pictures of a church, an old tree, the oldest building left in the city.

"Do those bloody Americans even know what *old* is?" she muttered.

The woman next to her caught her eye. "I'm sorry?"

Nessa forced herself to smile. "Pardon me. I'm just rambling to myself."

When the bus stopped at the Spanish Quarter, the tour guide gave her a brilliant smile. "Stretching your legs? Or are you going to check things out, miss?"

"I'm going to walk a bit," she said, drawing some bills out from her pocket to drop in the little coffee can he kept near the front. She gave him a decent tip—it was the least she could do since she'd been riding around listening to his tour talk for the past two hours.

Moving away from the small throng of tourists, she made her way to the Spanish Quarter.

She liked this quaint little town, she decided.

She liked the Irish pub, wandering along the beach, walking through the old fort, combing through the shops in the Spanish Quarter.

And she adored the winery. That was her current destination.

Right now, she was working her way through the wine list.

She was trying a different kind every day.

She already knew which kind she was going to try today and had plans that involved the bottle of wine, a new book and a bubble bath. She'd get her wine and head back to the little house on the beach. She was renting a room from a sweet couple there.

Nessa would walk it, too, so as to spare the poor tour guides. After two days of riding around on various trams and trolleys, she had probably freaked out half the locals.

She was walking down Orange Street when she sensed something. Stopping in the middle of the road, she closed her eyes, uncaring of the people bumping into her, unaware of the disgruntled looks.

She felt . . . *something*.

Cloaked. Whoever she was, the witch had cloaked herself. Clever little witch, Nessa thought. And a very talented one, at that. If Nessa hadn't been close, very close, she never would have sensed this, she suspected.

Avarice. Malice. Nasty, cloying hatred and pure, unadulterated evil.

And joy. The kind of joy truly decent people couldn't comprehend. After all, decent people couldn't understand *this* sort of pleasure. It was the pleasure that evil found in causing pain. A unique, singular sort of pleasure.

Nessa stood there a moment longer, soaking it up, breathing it in. Then, once she had the scent of the magic, she shouldered through the crowd fighting to get past the crush of bodies.

Low in her gut, she felt something hot unfurl through her.

One thing hadn't changed—she still loved a good Hunt.

S HE found the victim first.
A young man—probably here on his spring break. He barely looked old enough to shave. Nineteen, perhaps twenty. He was stripped naked and sleeping the sleep of the exhausted, dumped in the narrow alley like so much garbage. Somebody had dragged some cardboard over him, hiding him from sight.

But Nessa hadn't needed to see him—she could feel him, sense him—the fading sense of magic led her right to him.

Curling her fingers around his wrist, she lowered her shields and looked him over with a healer's eye. She discovered a couple of things—he'd been drugged . . . and he'd been fucked so many times in the past few days he'd need a doctor to look him over. The witch, whoever she was, had gone and torn him a bit.

"Puts a new spin on the idea of being fucked raw," Nessa mused.

The one thing that disturbed her the most though was his energy.

While somebody had done him some physical damage, it wasn't enough for him to be so very weak, so very close to death.

His energy was all but gone. Siphoned away.

Somebody had fed on his life force, the same way a vampire fed on blood.

Her skin crawled.

She'd had her share of run-ins with those who could tap into a life force like that.

One of them was her hitchhiker. But witches with that ability were rare. Other than Morgan, Nessa had only encountered perhaps five of them in all her years.

"I don't like this. Not one bit," she muttered.

The fact that one had almost killed her would be enough to explain why Nessa suddenly felt so uneasy.

But what really bothered her was the way she could feel Morgan unfurling inside her body. The *eagerness* she sensed coming from her hitchhiker.

"*Thank you, you old bitch,*" Morgan whispered inside Nessa's mind. "*You finally did one thing right. You brought me home.*"

The words were like an icy cold blast and as Nessa forced Morgan's presence back, she cursed.

NESSA didn't want to leave the young man there alone in that alley.

But she didn't have much choice.

If she lingered, when the police arrived, she'd have to answer questions.

She couldn't spare the time. She'd already wasted most of the day playing disgruntled, unfriendly tourist. In just a few more hours, it would be dark.

Plus, Nessa figured it would be best if she avoided mortal law enforcement. In life, Morgan Wakefield had lived to do as much wrong as possible. Before some enterprising souls had intervened, Nessa had been the inheritor of Morgan's very long rap sheet.

That rap sheet was gone now, along with any and all records that could have connected Morgan to Nessa. There were no fingerprints on file, no criminal records, no rap sheets, no mug shots.

But they couldn't do anything about the people who'd known Morgan, and if this *was* Morgan's home . . . well, it just wouldn't do to have somebody from Morgan's life recognize her, now would it?

"Don't borrow trouble," she told herself, leaving the man alone in the alley. He needed medical attention, but he certainly wasn't going to die from his injuries. Once she was a few streets away, she called 9-1-1 from a pay phone, leaving the information anonymously.

Then she continued to focus on that faint, almost hidden trail.

Iт was a Hunt that took her most of a day. It was closing in on midnight by the time she'd followed the trail to its end . . . a house. Hardly more than a shack, really.

The cool night wind blew her hair back from her face as she studied her surroundings. The little house was back from the road, surrounded by grass that desperately needed the attention of a lawn mower and by stunted trees.

Off to the left, there was another house, barely visible through the trees. It was nothing but a burned hull—a fire, the best Nessa could tell. The only other house was across the street and it was abandoned. Nessa could feel the utter desolation wrapping around the area like a smothering, cold blanket.

Inconspicuous, quiet and rundown on the outside, it didn't look like much.

But staring at it made her gut roil. Breathing in the air that smelled of stale cigarette smoke, marijuana and booze made her heart clench. She didn't understand why tears burned her eyes as she started toward the door.

She was only on the middle step when the door opened.

It revealed a girl—fourteen, maybe fifteen.

She stared at Nessa and her eyes rounded. Then a brilliant smile split her face. Nessa sensed what was coming before it happened, and by the time the girl had her arms wrapped around Nessa, she'd tensed up, prepared to defend herself.

But not against a hug.

As the girl clung to Nessa, she whispered under her breath, "I knew it. I knew Mama lied. I knew you weren't dead, Morgan."

Morgan.

The young girl's face was familiar—disturbingly so. A younger, more innocent version of the face Nessa saw in the mirror every morning. Softer, perhaps a bit less jaded.

A sister, then.

So Morgan had had a sister.

"Well, well, well." From the porch came a low, throaty murmur.

The bottom of Nessa's stomach dropped out at the sound of it. She made herself look up at the older woman.

If the girl was a younger, more innocent version of Morgan, then this was an older, harsher version. Crueler, too, although Nessa wouldn't have thought that possible. *Well, precious, at least I know where you got it from.*

The woman smelled like the man Nessa had left back in the alley. Smelled of his skin, smelled of sex . . . and life. The boy's energy all but crackled around this woman.

There was little doubt what had happened to him.

This malicious cow had stopped just short of killing him.

And she'd killed others. Nessa could feel it—the stain of death clinging to the woman like an oily cloak.

"Precious," Morgan said, *"I'd like you to meet my mother. You can call her Mommy, if you like. Or Isis. If you have time, before she kicks your ass screaming into hell."*

Isis? Nessa smirked.

A cold smile twisted the older woman's lips and she said, "Jazzy, get the hell away from her. That isn't Morgan."

"But . . ." The girl stared at Nessa's face, confused.

"I told you. Morgan is dead." Isis grinned, a sharp-edged smile that revealed perfect white teeth. "And that would mean this bitch is your sister's killer."

Staring into the girl's face, Nessa watched the bloom of anger, the darkness of grief dance across her face. *I'm so sorry, child. I'm so sorry.*

In the back of Nessa's mind, she heard a cold, hard voice. *"How do you like my mother, you old bitch?"*

"If you thought to surprise me, precious, then you're in for a disappointment. I'd already figured that much out," Nessa said to Morgan, but her heart wasn't in it. She couldn't give two damns about sparring with Morgan.

"No," the girl mumbled under her breath. "No. No. No . . . she's lying. Morgan, she's lying, isn't she?"

Unsure of what to say, Nessa peeled herself out of the girl's arms. Pain and rejection turned the girl's face pink, and Nessa felt a twinge in her heart.

As she turned her head, Nessa could make out the healing shadow of a bruise on the girl's cheek. Anger settled inside, hot and potent. She could handle anger.

She caught the girl's eyes once more, saw the plea in them. Saw the loneliness. The girl was walking down a troublesome road. Nessa could already see the darkness on her, but she wasn't too far gone. Yet. She had only a fraction of her mother's gift, of Morgan's.

She wasn't that strong—ironically her weaker gift was probably what made it possible for her to hover just shy of going too far. The darkness craved power. The child didn't have enough inside to appeal to it.

There were tears welling in the girl's eyes, and as Nessa stared at her young face, one broke free and rolled down her cheek. In the back of her mind, Nessa felt Morgan's reaction to the sight of the girl's tears.

Oh, honey . . .

Nessa stilled at the sound of Morgan's voice. It was unwelcome, but more . . . it was surprising. There was a note of . . . well, Nessa couldn't quite put her finger on it. It almost sounded like she cared.

"I did care, you old bitch," Morgan snarled, her voice an angry roar in Nessa's head. *"She was my sister."*

"What's her name?"

"What in the hell do you care?"

From the corner of her eye, she saw the mother on the

porch, watched as she took a step down. Aggravated, Nessa spoke silently to Morgan. *"Look, you insolent, arrogant, foolish little bitch, I asked you a damn question, and unless you just want me to kill them both, you're going to give me an answer."*

There was a hesitation. Then, angrily, Morgan said, *"Her name is Jasmine. I used to call her Jazzy."*

Finally.

The mother was still moving closer. Nessa ignored her, focusing on the girl. Judging by the look in the girl's eyes, she wanted to believe that Nessa was her long-lost sister—no matter what her mom said.

Fine enough. If it would keep the girl safe for a bit, Nessa would act like her sister, then.

"Is it true?" Jazzy asked, her voice breaking. "Is my sister really dead?"

When Nessa spoke, it was with no trace of an accent. "Come on, Jazzy. Do I look dead to you? She's just messing with your head." Slanting a look at the woman on the porch, she added, "That bitch's favorite pastime is to mess with people's heads, after all."

"Oh, for fuck's sake." The older woman threw down her cigarette and snarled at Jazzy. "She's a fucking liar. You think she'd honestly tell you if she'd killed your sister? Why would she do that? Hell, if that really was Morgan, do you really think she'd come back here? Why in the hell would she?"

Confused, Jazzy looked from one face to the other. Can't lay it on too thick, Nessa suspected. It seemed Morgan had cared for her sister some, but if Nessa laid on the protective sibling bit too much . . . well, it probably wouldn't ring true.

She didn't know the woman, but somehow, Morgan's mother struck her as the greedy sort—she might not love her daughters, but she wouldn't want to share them, either.

Focusing her thoughts, she projected them toward Morgan. *"Did you ever tell her you'd come back for her?"*

For a few seconds, it seemed as though Morgan wouldn't answer, and then finally, there was a reluctant assent.

"I'm here for you, Jazzy. I told you I'd come back, didn't I? She didn't want me coming back for you, did she?" Nessa said.

"Lying cunt," the woman snarled. Her voice was thick with hate, with anger.

Jazzy's eyes were wide . . . almost glowing . . . hopeful. "Morgan?"

"Come on now, Jazzy. You go on inside and let me talk to Mommy Dearest, okay?" Nessa gave the kid a reassuring smile.

"Don't even think about it, Jasmine." The mother's blue eyes narrowed as she spoke.

Heavens, she stank. Reeked with the same foul magics Morgan had practiced.

"Jazzy, go inside."

"You don't get to order my kid around," she drawled, lifting a cigarette to her lips and taking a deep, hard drag. It was hand-rolled and judging by the pungent scent in the air, there was more than just tobacco in it.

Nessa gave the woman a hard smile. "Jazzy, go to your room. Now."

The mother glanced at Jazzy and said in an offhand voice, "If you move one inch, Jasmine, I'm going to beat the shit out of you when I'm done here."

"No, she won't." She had, though. Nessa could see the fear bloom in the girl's eyes and she knew, as surely as she knew her own name, this woman had beaten the girl. One of many sins, she supposed. "She's not going to touch you, Jazzy. Not again. I told you I'd come back, told you I'd take care of you. That's what I'm going to do."

Jazzy darted into the house.

Dimly, she heard Morgan's voice. Heard it jeering her on. She tucked her hands in her pockets as the other woman shot an ugly, hate-filled gaze at her.

"Well, then." She smiled at the older woman as the door slammed shut behind Jazzy. Not bothering to hide her accent, Nessa cocked her head and said, "Let's get this started, shall we?"

Nessa was covered in blood and half of it was hers.

She ached from head to toe and her head . . . oh, her head.

Staggering, she shoved upright and glared at Isis. "You know how this ends," she snarled.

"Yeah, with me killing you. I'll get a good charge from your blood," Isis said, but her voice shook as she said it.

"You'd choke on me." Nessa swiped a bloodied hand over her eyes. From the corner of her eye, she saw a blond head. Swore hotly.

The girl.

Isis took advantage of her distracted state and attacked. The energy bolt sent Nessa flying. Even as she crashed to the busted-up pavement, Nessa sent an energy bolt of her own hurtling back.

Isis screamed, but Nessa barely registered the sound as her head smacked against the ground with enough force to set her brain rattling.

It took a few minutes for her head to clear, and a few more to realize that Isis had taken off.

Ran away, the malicious cow.

Now I'll have to run her down again.

Damn it.

Exhaustion, heavy and cold, hit her, square in the chest.

Gray dots swarmed in on her vision and Nessa lay there, staring up at the night sky.

"I don't want to do this anymore," she whispered. "I don't want to fight. I don't want this life."

Tears burned their way out of her eyes to trickle down her cheeks, mingling with the blood.

"I don't want to remember this life."

The gray dots merged together, forming a huge, enveloping gray cloud that came up and swallowed her whole.

CHAPTER 6

I T was too fucking early for him to be up and moving. Rafe had literally forced Dominic out of the bed, using the bond between them and giving Dominic a command he'd been physically forced to obey. The sun was hours away from setting—*fucking* hours. The sun wasn't even kissing the horizon. In a foul mood, he trudged around his room, trying to clear the cobwebs from his brain. Rafe's Master strength might be enough to have Dominic out of bed, but it wasn't enough to wake his mind up. Everything was foggy and surreal. Even the scalding hot shower didn't help.

As he shuffled out of the bathroom, there was a knock at his bedroom door. He sniffed and scowled as he recognized the scent. It was Lindsey Sue Whittaker, a relatively new addition to the Memphis enclave.

If he knew Rafe, he had no doubts about why she was here.

Snagging a towel, he wrapped it around his waist and headed to the door.

It took a minute or two. He felt like he was walking,

wading, through a room stuffed with cotton. He was pretty sure his head *was* stuffed with cotton.

Opening the door, he stared at Lindsey. She was one of Rafe's newer recruits and had a habit of flirting with anybody with a dick. Dominic didn't read much into it. It was just her way.

Right now, she had a semiserious look on her face and she gave him a quick smile. "Rafe sent me down—he wants you to feed."

Dom grunted and turned away from the door. He'd figured that much out. "I can get my own food."

"You won't have time tonight, and he said you weren't eating bagged blood right now. You need something to help you wake up and you're still healing. Bagged won't cut it and I'll do a better job than mortal, too."

Grabbing a pair of jeans, he disappeared back into the bathroom and dropped the towel. Once he'd pulled the jeans on, he threw the towel over the rod and went back into the bedroom. "So basically, you're my wake-up call."

"Yeah." She grinned at him. "I grabbed me a double mocha with extra espresso before I headed home. You might even get a caffeine jolt."

He didn't need the caffeine, not if he was going to feed from a werewolf. Their blood had more than enough kick in it. And considering how much trouble it was just to think, he needed that buzz. Sighing, he sat on the edge of the bed and waited for her to come to him.

Her voice was slightly husky as she asked, "Where do you want me?"

There had to be something seriously fucked-up with him. Lindsey was adorable, slender and cute, with big breasts, a tiny waist and a voice that just screamed sex. She had short, spiked black hair and big green eyes and she dressed like a gothic version of Tinkerbelle. If the look in her eyes was any indicator, she'd be more than happy to give him something besides blood.

All he could think about was a blonde with big blue

eyes and a sad smile. The words *Good-bye, lover* were still haunting him.

He patted the bed beside him, watched as her brow arched, as her smile widened. But when he took her wrist, she sighed.

Dom didn't look at her. As he sank his teeth into her, he focused on just that—the hot, potent rush of shifter blood and the energy it sent hurtling through him. He drew at her flesh, shuddering as a second hunger roused.

Blood and sex—for a vamp, they often went hand in hand. When he fed, his body wanted sex. When he fucked, he craved blood.

Lindsey seemed quite happy to give him both, curling close. She rubbed her cheek against his shoulder, her warm body a welcome invitation. Her scent, wild and rich, grew heavier.

He kept it businesslike, even though his cock was pushing for more. He withdrew his fangs and flicked his tongue over the pierced flesh. Between his saliva and her own hyped-up healing, the small wounds were closed in seconds.

"Thank you."

Lindsey chuckled. "Oh, no problem, honey. If you're ever in the mood for . . . well, much of anything, you come find me. Rafe said to haul ass once you fed. He'll be waiting in the garage—you're being taken to the airport in one of the vans."

He didn't look at her as she left.

Now that he'd fed, his head was clearer. It wasn't an improvement though, because now he couldn't stop thinking about just what it was that had him out of bed before sunset.

Shit. He'd much rather walk around in a fog for a while.

Too late now.

J UST as Lindsey had promised, Rafe was waiting in the garage. He wasn't alone, either.

Toronto was with him. Toronto, one of Rafe's lieutenants, was a werewolf and a general pain in the ass. He had

pale, pale hair—almost too white to be called blond—and
it fell in a straight line more than halfway down his back.
His eyes were also pale, a faint silvery blue. He looked
almost too pretty for a man, a fact that Dominic loved to
razz him about, under normal circumstances.

Today's circumstances weren't normal and Toronto's
smart-ass ways weren't welcome.

As he stormed into the garage and caught sight of the
werewolf, he stopped dead in his tracks and met Rafe's
gaze. "Fuck. Shit. Damn it. Rafe, find somebody else."

A faint grin tugged at Rafe's mouth.

Toronto popped a piece of gum into his mouth. The
scent of Hubba Bubba filled the air.

"Sorry, Dom. There isn't anybody else. You need a pilot.
Tor flies. Nobody else here does."

"Fuck. Shit. Damn it." Dominic whirled around and
drove his foot into the base of the concrete wall.

"Lighten up," Toronto said, grinning at him. "You act
like I'm flying you to your own staking."

Dominic climbed into the back of the plain white van.
"You need to do something about your van, Lassie. Don't
you know serial killers just love this make and model?"

Toronto flashed his sharp white teeth. "Don't worry,
Dom. You might be pretty, but you're not my type."

Memories—ugly and hated—flooded Dominic's mind.
Slowly, he turned and gave the werewolf a look.

"Ease up, Dominic."

It was a quiet order.

Sliding his gaze past Toronto's shoulder, he glanced at
the Master. Rafe stood just a few feet away, his face dark,
his mouth unsmiling. To a stranger, it might have looked as
though the vampire was in a shitty mood.

But Rafe looked the same on good days, which made it
harder to tell when he was really pissed.

He might not be really pissed now, but he was heading
that way as he gave Toronto a dark look. "You're playing
chauffeur today—so be a good little chauffeur. As in get
your ass in the driver's seat and drive—leave Dom alone."

Toronto obviously wasn't as skilled at gauging Rafe's moods as the others were. "We touchy today?" He cocked a brow. "Gotta suck, losing your punching bag. Don't worry. While Dom here is gone, I'll let you pound on me in the gym. I might even let you win a time or two."

"Just shut the fuck up and get in the van," Rafe snarled.

That clued Toronto in and his brows drew together, something swirling in his eyes. Tension mounted in the air, heavy, thick, like a summer rainstorm about to open up over them.

Toronto might be happy to play at serving a Master, but he was powerful enough to *be* a Master if he chose.

Werewolves were notoriously hot-natured, too, and Rafe's pissed off mood looked like it was now feeding into Toronto's. A growl rumbled out of his chest.

Rafe narrowed his eyes and said quietly, "You gave a vow when you settled here, Toronto."

"I'm aware of that." Toronto's eyes began to pinwheel, swirling with shades of gray, black and blue.

"Then why don't you—"

"Rafe." Dominic settled on the floor of the van and closed his eyes. "Just drop it, okay?"

Rafe grunted under his breath and backed off. Toronto opened his mouth, but then he glanced at Dominic. The shadowed interior of the van didn't do a damn thing to conceal him, and Dom didn't need a mirror to know there were dark, ugly secrets written all over him. He knew it, and even though he blanked his expression, he didn't do it quickly enough.

The anger faded from Toronto's face, quickly replaced by self-directed disgust. A red flush crept up his neck and he rubbed it. "Dom—"

Without saying anything, Dominic slammed the door shut behind him.

He wished he could have waited for full night. Then he could have just taken one of the bikes and driven himself to Excelsior. Would have taken two nights to make the trip, though, and that was the problem. Rafe wanted him there quicker than that, which meant flying.

Outside, he heard Rafe snapping at Toronto. If he focused, he could have heard the words. But he didn't want to. He didn't want to think, didn't want to remember.

I T was just after midnight when they landed at the private airstrip a half hour from the school. The entire flight had passed in tense, uneasy silence. Toronto, sensing Dominic's uneasiness, hadn't attempted to break it, not even once—proving he actually *did* possess two brain cells in that pretty blond head of his.

As the plane touched down, Dominic took a deep breath and braced himself.

All the *what-ifs* in his mind were screaming. What if he was going crazy? What if there was something wrong with him? What if . . . what if . . . what if . . .

Kelsey would be here waiting for him. No matter what Rafe said, Dominic had the worst feeling she was going to look at him and tell him he was going insane.

As he climbed out of the little plane, he glanced around. It was still and quiet, the air cool and damp, smelling of spring flowers and grass. The air smelled different here. Different kinds of trees. Different people. He grabbed his duffle without waiting for Toronto. Up ahead, he could see Kelsey at the hangar.

"Let's get this shit over with," he muttered. Behind him, he heard Toronto trotting to catch up.

As the blond wolf fell in step beside him, Dominic shot him a dark look. "I don't need a babysitter."

"Wanted to say I'm sorry."

Well, shit. Maybe the bastard didn't have those two brain cells.

Thanks to his preflight meal—courtesy of Lindsey—Dominic had plenty of blood circulating in his body. Right now, it circulated right up his neck, settling in his cheeks as humiliation and shame curled through him.

He worked to bury it—it had been years. *Years.* He wasn't

helpless anymore. He'd been in medical school before the attack and since then, he'd worked with so many victims—he knew all the logistics. The feral vampire that had Changed him had done a hell of a lot more than that, showing Dominic just what it felt like to be brutalized.

Dominic had done his time in hell. He knew it wasn't his fault, he wasn't to blame.

But even now, the memories still had the power to sneak up on him and sucker punch him like this.

"Leave it alone, Lassie," he said, hearing the edge in his voice and not caring.

Toronto sighed but said nothing else, ambling along at Dominic's side, hands tucked in his pockets.

Kelsey met them halfway between the hangar and the plane, smiling at Toronto. The werewolf caught her hand and brought it to his mouth, kissing the back of it. "Kelsey, you look gorgeous. Leave that fucking vamp of yours. You need a warm-blooded man."

A smile curled Kelsey's lips and she leaned forward, kissed Toronto on the cheek. "I'll be sure to give him your regards, Toronto."

Toronto grinned at her. "You do that."

As Kelsey focused on him, her smile faded. Dominic's gut clenched. She arched a brow at him, her green gold eyes curious. "Well, you don't look happy to be here."

Dominic didn't say a word.

He'd rather be sunning himself on a beach somewhere. Even though it would leave him with a murderous sunburn—literally.

Charred vamp sounded a hell of a lot better than having some witch play armchair shrink for him, and he had a feeling that was what lay ahead for him.

T HE drive to Excelsior took place in silence. Dominic appreciated that. He'd much rather the interrogation start once he was wherever he was supposed to crash for

the duration. Preferably some place loaded with tequila. If
he got enough of it in him, maybe it would dull the effects.
Might take a tank of Patrón, but he could do it. He thought.

Toronto wasn't hanging around—one small favor, at least.
Dominic's mood was pushing toxic and if he had to listen
to the werewolf's wisecracks for too long, he'd lose his own
damn temper.

That wouldn't help things at all. Physically, he was
strong and could hold his own against non-masters.

But if he went after a Master werewolf, he'd be doing
the same thing he did when he sparred with Rafe—wiping
his own blood off the floor.

Nope. Wouldn't help. Although a good, vicious fight . . .

"You know, I don't bite."

Dominic slanted a look at the witch. She looked like a
schoolteacher, he decided. He'd met her once or twice, but
hadn't ever seen her for more than a few minutes. She had
strawberry blond hair, big hazel eyes and freckles sprin-
kled across her nose. She'd be the kind of teacher half the
boys had a crush on, and the girls would love her, too. She
just had that way about her.

Right now, she was smiling a little, glancing at him from
the corner of her eye as she drove the sleek little Mustang
down the road. Her brow arched and he remembered—she'd
said something.

Oh, yeah. He remembered now.

But he didn't how to respond to her comment, so he just
shrugged.

Kelsey sighed. "Will it make you feel better if I tell you
that you aren't going crazy?"

"It might." Cautiously, he shifted in the bucket seat, studying her profile. "You think you'll be able to tell me that?"

"Oh, I can already tell you that." Kelsey shot him
another smile and then hit her blinker. As she slowed the
car down for the turn, she shrugged. "I don't know what's
going on and Rafe wasn't able to tell me much . . . probably because you weren't telling *him* much. But it seems
his main concern is you—because *you* think you might be

losing your mind. He says you aren't. I agree with him. So does that make you feel better?"

Dominic scowled. "You don't even know the kind of shit going on inside my head. There's no way you can know."

"You haven't been around witches much." She sighed. "That's fine. But yes, Dom, I *can* tell. All I had to do was look at you when you got off the plane. I'm a witch and I've got healer tendencies. I know madness, I know insanity. Whether it's organic, or induced by magic or trauma, I know it. You're not losing your mind. Which is good, because I really don't need another tetched Hunter running around."

"Another?"

She scowled and arrowed the car into a parking space, slamming on the brakes just in time to avoid hitting the curb. The serene smile on her face was gone, replaced by a tight, cold mask. "We're here."

"You've got another crazy Hunter running around?"

With a withering look, she said, "No, I don't have *another* crazy Hunter. You're not crazy. Anything other than that isn't your concern."

He might have pointed out that she had been the one to toss it out there, but he saw the sharp glint in her eyes. He might have some smart-ass tendencies of his own, but he wasn't about to give this woman grief. Whatever else was going on, it was hurting her. He saw it in her eyes before she managed to hide it.

Silently, he climbed out of the car and grabbed his bag from the miniscule trunk. Then he moved to join her on the sidewalk, glancing around.

Excelsior looked the same. It had been a couple of years since he'd been here—the last time had been at Rafe's insistence as well. Dominic was apparently showing Master traits but he seemed too young for it. He had been sent to the school for a second opinion. Which added up to a waste of time in his opinion.

Yes, he was showing Master traits. Yes, he was young. Then he was shipped back to Memphis after spending just a few days at the school. He wasn't ready to go off on his own, there weren't any problems developing, so right now there wasn't any need for concern, big fucking deal.

The school was quieter at night, although he could hear the sounds of training coming from the gym. Nightwalkers like himself getting their training in like good little Hunters, well before the sunrise.

Rubbing the back of his neck, he glanced around and sighed. "Where do you want me?"

"You can take a dorm room or one of the empty houses. Up to you." She smiled at him and said, "I'm not locking you up in a holding cell."

His eyes closed, he managed, just barely, not to blow out a sigh of relief.

She really, honestly believed he wasn't losing it. And she should know, right?

"You really don't think I'm going crazy."

Kelsey chuckled. "Honey, I *know* you're not. Relax, okay?"

"Relax." Dominic snorted. "Hell, that's so much easier said than done."

He hadn't been able to relax, really relax in forever. He closed his eyes and took one slow, deep breath. Held it as his senses processed the stimuli. Lavender . . .

Something familiar . . .

Her.

He caught the echo of it on the breeze that drifted by in the next second.

Every muscle in his body went rigid.

Kelsey said something, but he didn't hear her. Didn't notice he was moving, didn't even notice she was trailing along behind him.

That scent. He sniffed the air again, flooded his senses with it. Would have wrapped his body in it, if he could have. It was stronger now, but still so faint.

He found himself standing on the small stoop of one of the cabins. They were reserved for the teachers who preferred not to live in the dorms, or guests. Resting a hand on the door, he breathed the scent in again. Blood filled his mouth for just a second as his fangs dropped from their sheaths, cutting through his gums, throbbing and ready.

Hunger tore through him.

Her . . . it was her.

Gripping the doorknob, he turned it, but it was locked. Focused on nothing but getting inside the cabin, he turned again, harder. He was a fucking vampire—he could crush the damn locking mechanism, force the door open . . .

Except it didn't open. Stepping back, he studied the door.

That was when he realized where he was—he was being watched by a very curious witch. She had a look on her face like she was trying to decide if she wanted to chuckle or not. "The door is locked, Dom. We reinforce them here, remember?"

"Then unlock it."

"I had a different cabin in mind." She propped her hands on her hips, and now she didn't look so inclined to chuckle. She looked pissed off.

Dominic didn't give a damn.

"I want this one."

Kelsey's brows arched. "It wasn't designed for vamps, Dom. The only place in there where you'll find safety from the sun is the closet. Maybe under the damn bed."

"Fine." He turned back to the door, resting a hand on it, breathing in more of that elusive scent. Fading, bit by bit. He wasn't waiting for a damn key. He stepped back and before Kelsey could try to stop him, he kicked the door in.

"What in the hell . . . ?"

But he didn't hear her.

Feeling half-drunk, he staggered into the room. *Here.*

She had been *here.*

Voices danced through his head.

You're a foolish girl.

Foolish, am I? Not so silly that I couldn't save your arse—those wolves would have had you for dinner.

Can't have that, now can we? And she laughed as he pulled her close, held her tight.

Then pain. Hot and burning bright, tearing through him. Blood bubbling up in his throat to choke him.

And Nessa . . . crying.

Promise me! Damn it, you promise me! Promise me you'll come back.

Only God Himself could keep me from you, love. The pain was hideous and darkness tried to close in. Death. It was death. He was dying . . . leaving her. But he'd come back. He'd find her again.

I do wish I had listened to you, my beautiful witch.

The tears in her eyes, the pain on her face, it tore him apart—even worse than the feel of the dagger in his chest. *Just come back, Elias.*

My Nessa.

His.

She was his.

As he was hers.

Distantly, he heard a voice. A male voice. But it made no sense to him. The words made no sense. His knees buckled and he sagged to the floor, bracing his hands on it, flexing his fingers, as though that might somehow ground him.

Something peeked out from under the bed and he leaned forward, grabbed it. The second he touched it, his skin buzzed. Her scent grew stronger. She'd touched the book.

She *had* been here. He could all but feel her. Where was she? His skin vibrated and he ached, deep inside his chest. His heart began to beat quicker, pounding, hard and insistent.

With each beat, his mind seemed to scream at him.

Find her.

Find her.

Lifting his head, he searched for Kelsey and found her standing at the door, staring at him with a bemused expression on her face. And she wasn't alone.

There was a man with her.

A vampire.

The vampire barely glanced at Dominic, rested a hand on Kelsey's shoulder. "I need to speak with you."

The voice was familiar. So was the face.

The dream—that fucking dream.

With startling clarity, he could remember the dream.

His witch, standing at the edge of a skyscraper, staring down like she longed for nothing more than to step off the edge into oblivion. And the vampire.

This vampire.

He didn't realize he was growling.

He didn't realize he had lunged for the vampire.

Not until a pale hand closed around his throat and he was suspended in the air. Dominic didn't give a flying fuck—he couldn't choke to death.

"You fucking moron, do you have a death wish?" the vampire snarled.

Lashing out with a foot, Dominic demanded, "Where in the fuck is she?"

"Who are you talking about?" Dark blue eyes stared at him. They glowed with banked power. Dominic could *feel* that power, battering at him, slamming into him and threatening to send him back to his knees. Except he was still dangling several feet in the air.

Half-crazed, Dominic felt the bloodlust rise in him and he tore at the other vampire's hand, instinctively trying to break that grasp. Pain shot through him as the vamp's hand tightened, crushing his throat.

"Where in the fuck is she?" he demanded again.

Or at least that was what he *tried* to say. It came out "Waaaa . . ." His throat was crushed and he could taste his own blood.

Yield.

The vampire hadn't spoken.

His blue eyes bored into Dominic, glowing. *Yield.*

But Dominic could still smell her. Could still feel her presence, though it was fading.

The fingers on his throat tightened. But instead of scrabbling at the hand that held him effortlessly in the air, Dominic took his fist and used it to smash at the vampire's elbow. Distantly, he heard bone crack.

He hit the floor, but he had only about two seconds to enjoy it before he was sent flying across the room. He crashed into the wall, oblivious to anything and everything.

CHAPTER 7

A SAVAGE growl rumbled in Malachi's throat.
There were times when hearing that sort of sound made Kelsey's knees all wobbly and weak, but this wasn't one of them. Adrenaline shot through her as she got in front of her husband and rested her hands on his chest.

"Don't."

He glanced at her, his dark blue eyes narrowed. "Don't?" he echoed, his voice silky and menacing.

"Yes. Don't."

But he wasn't hearing her all that well.

Desperate times . . . she rose up on her toes and fisted her hands in his dark red hair, slanting her mouth over his. She nipped at his lower lip and rocked her hips against him. He hesitated for just a few seconds, and then he groaned, wrapping an arm around her waist and hauling her close. He kissed her roughly, his fangs slicing her lower lip, and the taste of blood filled their kiss.

He eased back, pausing to lick her lip slowly, tracing the edge of the wound. As she settled back on her feet, the injured flesh was already knitting itself together. Malachi dipped his head and pressed his brow to hers. "Damn it, Kelsey."

She cupped his face in her hands and smiled. "Hey, a girl's gotta do what a girl's gotta do."

"And keeping me from beating that little shit into nothingness was something you had to do?"

"Yep."

His eyes narrowed. "Perhaps you saw a different set of events than I did. He attacked me. For no reason."

"Yes, he did." Then she eased back, eyeing Malachi's right arm. It hung weirdly, and she grimaced. "He also broke your arm."

Malachi lowered his gaze, staring at his injured arm, disgust written all over his face. "Damn right, he did. Nasty break, too."

Kelsey rested her hands on it and looked at him. After giving her a pained look, he let her take his arm.

It must have hurt. Vampires healed miraculously quick, but they still felt pain and a bad break was still a bad break. She couldn't even be nice about it, because with every second, his bones were knitting together and if she waited too long, they'd have to break it again just to set it right.

By the time she was done, she was in a cold sweat.

A muscle jerked in Malachi's jaw, but that was the only outward sign he gave of his discomfort. He'd had far worse than a broken arm in his life. Far, far worse.

She kissed his chin and then stroked his jaw.

Behind her, she heard Dominic grunting as he started to come back to consciousness. Placing her hands on Malachi's shoulders, she squeezed lightly. "Promise me something."

"No."

Kelsey pouted and looked at him from under her lashes. "Pretty please?"

"No. Because I've got this peculiar feeling you're going to ask me not to teach that little fool a lesson." His eyes gleamed. "He broke my arm. I owe him something."

He brushed around Kelsey and went to kneel by Dominic. The younger vampire was moaning under his breath, but he was still out of it. Kelsey suspected she knew why—the little cabin was made of brick and Malachi had thrown him so hard, it was a miracle the back wall was still standing. He'd hit his head on the brick—she could see the blood seeping out from under his head and when she rested a hand on his brow, she could sense the injuries.

"You're even, big guy," she said, slanting a look at her husband. "His skull is busted—he's going to be a few more minutes waking up."

"We're not even. He broke my arm. I broke his skull. But he attacked me first." Malachi studied his face. "Isn't this the boy Rafe was sending us? The one worried he was losing his mind?"

"Yes."

"Tell Rafe he was dead-on. This one is fucking insane."

"No." Kelsey sighed and stood up, surveying the damage to the back wall. Between the front door Dom had busted and the back wall, this cabin wasn't going to be useable for a few days. It needed renovations in a major way. "He's not crazy. I already looked."

"Attacking me wasn't exactly the mark of a *sane* man," Malachi pointed out.

"I don't think he was trying to attack you." She licked her lips and turned, staring at the room.

Even before Malachi had shown up, Dom had been acting weird. It hadn't started though until they'd arrived at the school. Actually, a few minutes after. They'd been walking up the path.

She narrowed her eyes thoughtfully, thinking back.

She could remember seeing the change come over him—a look had entered his eyes—she'd been speaking to him, but he hadn't heard her. He'd been focused on something else. Someone else.

Where the fuck is she?

That was what he'd yelled at Malachi as he lunged at the older vampire.

Kelsey looked back at Dom and murmured, "He's looking for somebody. He thinks you know her."

CHAPTER 8

HE didn't know where he was when he woke up.

It was bright, that much he knew.

Bright . . . and he could smell Nessa.

Lavender. She always smelled of it.

The scent was fading though, fading more and more.

Squinting his eyes against the harsh, bright light—too bright, it seemed—

He looked around, searching for her.

He wasn't alone, though.

There was a woman with reddish blond hair. A man with dark red hair. But he didn't see his wife.

He licked his lips, his mouth painfully dry. Bugger, his head *hurt*. Squinting at the woman, he asked, "Where is my wife?"

The woman's brows drew together, a confused expression on her face. She looked as though she didn't understand him. The man with her moved toward him and the woman reached out, laid a hand on his arm.

"Your wife?" the man asked, his voice low. The look in those dark blue eyes could have turned blood to ice.

Fear, worry, sank into him, cold and vicious.

"Yes. My *wife*."

The woman continued to stare at him, the puzzled frown on her face giving way to a reassuring smile.

He didn't want reassurance. He wanted his *wife*.

"Who are you looking for?" the man prodded.

"Are you daft?" he snarled. "My *wife*. Agnes."

The woman went pale.

The man looked at him as though he'd lost his mind.

Pain throbbed behind his eyes. Darkness swirled.

"Your wife, you say? What's your name, then?"

He had no time for this. He didn't understand how he knew that, but he did. He had no time for questions or games. There had been trouble. She had been in danger—both of them had been.

He needed to find her—he'd already been away from her for far too long. How long . . . but even thinking about it had pain ripping through him.

Glaring at them, he swore under his breath and then went to push past them. His steps were unsteady and the ache in his head intensified. He reached up and touched the back of his head where the pain was the worst, touched something wet. His head felt strange, too soft, giving under his questing fingers.

A wave of dizziness washed over him as he lowered his hand and stared at the smear of blood.

Behind him, the man spoke.

"Elias . . . ?"

The pain in his head exploded, and like a stone, he dropped to the ground.

CHAPTER 9

MALACHI moved in a blur of motion, too quickly for her eyes to track him. After working with vampires for decades, one would think she'd get used to it. But their speed still caught her by surprise.

Kelsey saw Dominic stagger, then fall, but Malachi caught him before he could hit the ground.

He lifted his head and stared at Kelsey, his dark blue eyes unreadable, his face tight, hard as stone.

"*Elias*?" she repeated.

"He was Nessa's husband." Malachi's voice was cold, flat, devoid of any accent, any emotion.

"I know who he was." Kelsey swallowed past the tight knot in her throat. Confused, and more than a little freaked out, she looked at the unconscious vampire.

His voice had been different. *Seriously* different. She hadn't understood him at first; the accent had been too thick. It had sounded vaguely British, but not quite. Older. Archaic, almost.

Rattled, Kelsey remembered the way Dominic had looked at them, like he'd never seen them before. Now *that* she could attribute to his head injury. Even vamps got their brains scrambled every now and then.

But there was also how he'd been acting earlier—the way he'd come at Malachi . . . *Where the fuck is she?*

Blood pounded in her ears, and she rubbed her hand over the back of her neck as tension mounted there.

Who had he been looking for?

But deep inside, she knew.

Nessa.

Even though it had been more than a week since she'd been in the cabin, her scent would still linger, especially for those with sensitive noses, like vamps. He'd scented her . . . and somehow recognized her.

He was looking for Nessa.

Elias . . .

Even thinking about it made her head ache and pound. Something light and euphoric tried to dance its way into her heart, but she didn't want to examine it too closely. Shattered hopes were often painful.

So instead of trying to think it through that very moment, Kelsey took the easy way—she focused on her job.

"Be careful with him," she told her husband as he shifted the vampire in his arms. She drew on the cool cloak of serenity that kept her sane when she healed. "I need him on the bed, on his stomach so I can see his head."

Without saying a word, Malachi did as she asked.

Kelsey grimaced as she gently probed the back of his head. The bone was still knitting together—he was healing, she could feel the energy as his body dealt with the damage. There was a lot of damage, too. If he'd been human, he'd be dead. As it was, it was taking quite a while, and he was going to be utterly drained once his body was done.

"I didn't do . . ." Malachi's voice faded off and then he took a deep breath, as though to brace himself. "Is he healing well?"

"Yeah." She shot him a strained smile and said, "He just took a really bad blow. You bashed his head in. Although you didn't seem too worried about that a moment ago." She cocked a brow in his direction, wondering if he was thinking along the same lines as she was.

A muscle jerked in Malachi's jaw. He stared at her, an impassive mask on his face. That careful lack of expression never boded well. Malachi hid his emotions when he was very, very pissed off, when he was hurt or when he was worried.

A few moments ago, he'd been angry, so angry it had stung her skin like hot little needles. But he wasn't angry now and she knew he wasn't hurt, either.

So he was worried.

Personally, Kelsey was scared shitless. Her mouth was dry and her heart raced away, pounding in her chest like she'd gone and popped some speed. Feigning casualness, she tried for a smile and asked, "So, do you believe in reincarnation?"

"Fuck me." His face twisted in a scowl and he went to shove a hand through his hair and then stopped. He studied his bloodied hands and then went to the sink in the small kitchenette, scrubbing them clean. "I don't know that I'm ready to have this conversation just yet, pet."

"You better get ready," she advised him. "I don't think it's one we'll be able to put off."

As he turned around, he took a towel from the counter and dried his hands, taking a lot more time with it than necessary. But Kelsey recognized the look on his face. That canny mind was turning everything over, looking at it from every possible angle.

Finally, he tossed the towel on the counter and then folded his arms over his chest. He stared at Dominic as he said, "I never met Elias. Nessa was young then, just a girl. It wasn't until after Elias died and she came back to Brendain that I even met her. She was . . . broken." A haunted look settled on his face and he closed his eyes, remembering the girl who had arrived at Brendain—the home of the Hunters. "So broken," he murmured. "You wouldn't recognize her, you know. She's not the woman that you'd remember. Lost and uncertain. Terrified."

Malachi opened his eyes, gazing off into the distance. He wasn't seeing her. He was too lost in his memories.

"I have forgotten more of my life than I've remembered." His voice was rough and low, thick with the sounds of Scotland. So often, Malachi could speak without any trace of an accent, but at certain times, it slipped out . . . like when he was grieving, as he obviously was now. "But I canna forget the first time I met her. So sad, she was. Poor little lass, so broken and so angry. They killed Elias, right in front of her. There was a man in her village—he wanted Nessa for his own, you see."

He sighed and opened his eyes, staring once more at Dominic's still body. "For years after he died, she waited. Bloody hell, all her *life* she waited. He'd promised her—told her he would come back. Come back for her. So she waited. And waited."

Abruptly, he spun around and slammed a fist into the marble countertop. It cracked under the blow and Kelsey saw his blood splatter. His head bowed, he rasped, "She waited for five hundred fucking years."

She checked Dominic one more time and then moved to join her husband. Slipping her arms around his waist, she rested her brow against his back. As she did, she lowered her shields.

Malachi sensed it, tensing. The tension slowly melted away as she let her magic work . . . the pain, she couldn't help with, but she could ease some of his confusion. His big body shuddered in her embrace and then he turned in her arms, cuddling her close. Resting his forehead against hers, he whispered, "Five hundred years, Kelsey."

"I know." She rubbed her mouth against his, a gentle, soothing kiss. Then she pulled back, snuggling close and resting her cheek against the hard, muscled wall of his chest. "Do you think it's possible?"

"I don't know." He lowered his mouth, kissing the top of her head. She couldn't see his face, but she knew he was looking at Dominic. Looking and wondering. "I haven't the slightest fucking clue."

Knowing Malachi, that probably had him as bewildered as the puzzle of Dominic. Malachi, it seemed, *always* knew what to do.

He sighed and stroked his hands down her arms. "We have problems, pet."

Easing back, Kelsey looked at him, a rueful smirk on her lips. "Such an understatement. We'll handle it, though. We just need to let him wake up and then we'll see if we can figure out what's going on. *Before* he finds Nessa."

"No." Malachi shook his head. "He's not the problem I was talking about. It's Nessa."

Wincing, Kelsey said, "Please tell me she isn't in trouble again . . . not already. She hasn't even been gone two weeks."

"I don't know if she's in trouble or not," Malachi said, scowling. He rubbed the back of his neck, his eyes on the floor. "I can't tell where she is . . . how she is doing. Kelsey, she's missing."

"Missing?" Kelsey frowned. "What exactly do you mean by *missing*?"

Once more, he had that remote, expressionless mask in place. "Just that, pet. She's missing, and I can't sense her. I'd wager you can't, either."

There had been a time not too long ago when Nessa had served on the Council. Over time, the Council members forged a bond, a way of tracing each other. It was a handy thing, especially for vampires who could dematerialize—like Malachi—or witches with the ability to fly—not through the air, but just disappear from one place and arrive in another in the blink of an eye.

Lowering her gaze, Kelsey reached inward and focused.

A lump settled in her throat as she looked up at her husband. She swallowed and tried to speak around it, although it felt like it was choking her. "You're right. I can't feel her."

T HE lumpy mattress was uncomfortable as hell. Rolling onto her side, she pounded her pillow with her fist and then snuggled up, drifting back into sleep.

Back into her dreams.

He was there. They were together, lying on a bed, and he stroked his hand up and down her arm. Midnight black hair framed a lean, golden face . . . an angel's face, she thought. He was as pretty as an angel. His dark brown eyes stared into hers and he smiled.

"I miss you when you're not here," he murmured.

Pushing up onto her elbows, she smiled and kissed him. "Then I should just stay here all the time."

"You're never here. I'm never here." Then he sighed and rested a hand on her stomach. "Why is it taking so long?"

"What?"

He opened his mouth but instead of speaking, he bellowed, a deep, gut-wrenching sound of sheer agony. Startled, she jerked back and then she screamed, too.

He was bleeding. It was just a few spots at first, staining the tunic he wore. But it grew, and grew, a vicious rose of death. "No."

Tears spilled out of her eyes and she rested a hand on the wound, summoned the power. She could heal him. She knew how—she could do it.

But the magic wasn't there.

"You haven't learned how to heal yet," he said, his voice quiet and level, as though his heart wasn't pumping his life's blood out of him.

"I know how to heal," she whispered. She knew how—

But it was too late.

He was already dead, and even as she bent over him, sobbing, his body began to shrivel until it was nothing but dust. She sobbed and pounded her fists against the bed where he had lain. "Damn it, come back! You swore to me, you bloody bastard. You swore you would come back to me!"

It was the sound of her own screams that woke her.

Jerking up in bed, she sucked in a desperate breath and wiped her hands over her tearstained cheeks.

"Bad dream?"

Looking up, she saw Jazzy standing in the doorway. She forced a smile. "Yeah, I guess so."

"Must have been a doozy. You've been crying for the last ten minutes." Jazzy gave her a pained grimace and said, "You woke me up *again*. Geez, I don't know what in the hell you've been up to since you disappeared, but it must have been hella bad, right? You've had nothing but nightmares all night."

She tried to smile, but she couldn't. "I'm sorry I woke you up."

"It's okay." Jazzy came up, gave her a smile. She settled down on the bed and curled up next to her. "Maybe . . . Maybe it will help if I stay with you a while? I really missed you when you were gone. You remember the dream?"

Shaking her head, she whispered, "No. Just that it was awful."

"What about all the time you were gone? Have you remembered any of the time you were gone or is it all still like a blank slate?"

Morgan closed her eyes and rested her chin on Jazzy's crown. "Just a blank slate." There was nothing in her mind, save for the past day or so. The first clear memory she had was coming to the grass with this girl leaning over her and begging her to wake up. It was like her life before that simply did not exist. She patted Jazzy's arm and said, "But don't worry. It will be okay."

CHAPTER 10

By necessity, they decided to move Dominic to the quarters Kelsey and Malachi had in the lower floor of the school. Sunrise was only a few hours off and she wasn't going to have one of her patients resting on the floor. Nor was she going to just protect the room from the sun. That would work, but his instincts would keep him from resting as well as he should.

Dominic was still out, although his head wound had healed. Dawn edged ever nearer, and Kelsey was more than a little worried that he hadn't woken back up. As Malachi logged onto the computer and set things up for a videoconference, she rested a hand on Dominic's brow and closed her eyes.

"How is he?"

Opening her eyes, she looked at Malachi to find him watching her, arms crossed over his chest. Over his shoulder, she could see the familiar faces of Tobias, Niko and Andreas, fellow Council members on the screen. She might hate technology but it had made convening with the Council easier in recent years.

"How is he?" she echoed with a sigh. "Healed. Tired, though. He's been injured recently—I feel the echo of it. And he's weak. He's going to be as hungry as a bear when he wakes up."

Malachi jerked a shoulder in a shrug. "Not overly concerned about his appetite, pet. I'm more concerned about who we'll be talking with when he wakes." Then he spun around in his chair to face the monitor, tapping a button. Kelsey moved up to stand behind him as he said, "We've got problems, mates. Nessa has up and disappeared."

Kelsey hoped against hope one of the other Council members would be able to sense Nessa, but she knew it was unlikely. If Malachi couldn't, if Kelsey couldn't, there was no reason the others could.

Tobias ran a hand over his face and muttered something under his breath. It was too low for Kelsey to hear, but Malachi said, "Yup. One massive fucking problem."

Niko glanced from Kelsey's face to Malachi's.

The relationship between Kelsey and Niko was somewhat strained. Truth be told, the relationship between Niko and the rest of the Council had gone past strained and well into the area of dislike.

The vampire hadn't been particularly helpful in the days after Nessa was . . . reborn. Part of Kelsey understood that—she still couldn't understand exactly *what* had happened with Nessa. The woman had been frail, old and physically very weak when she faced off with a young, feral witch.

Morgan had been something of an anomaly. She could steal power through blood, using it to bolster her own magic—doing so was addictive and it was a bad, bad path for a witch to take. But Morgan's thirst for power hadn't just stopped at taking power through blood—she could also take it through dreams. She had been able to steal her way into dreams and siphon energy that way. Kelsey suspected she'd drained more than one person's life away in just that fashion.

She'd been young, brash and arrogant—a happy little

psychopath, one the world was well rid of. But the cost had been very, very high.

Focus on the here and now, girl, Kelsey told herself. *Not the there and then.*

"How long has Nessa been missing?" Niko asked quietly.

"Missing, as in gone from Excelsior? A couple of weeks. Avoiding me for a few days," Malachi said, shrugging restlessly. "I was trying to give her some privacy." He slumped lower in the seat and closed his eyes. "She seemed . . . better the last time I tried to reach out to her. The grief that choked her had lessened."

"You spoke with her?" Tobias asked, cocking a black brow, his shrewd eyes watchful.

"No." Malachi shook his head. "I was just checking on her." A humorless smile tugged his lips and he said, "I know her moods almost as well as I know my own and all I have to do is reach for her. The pain was there—just less."

"What else did you sense?" Niko asked.

"Resolve." Malachi shoved back from the chair and started to pace. "She was almost as she was when she first joined the Council." He paused and looked at the monitor. "You remember that time, Tobias?"

"Yes." He was the only Council member old enough to remember. Niko and Andreas, twins, had been born in 1701 and they'd been vampires since 1742. Nessa had first joined the Council in the 1600s. By that time, she had no longer been the broken girl who'd arrived at Brendain a century earlier. Though the sadness had still been there, it no longer crippled her.

On the screen, Kelsey could see Tobias's face, could see his reflection as his thoughts turned inward. She suspected he was remembering the earlier years with Nessa, much as Malachi had. The bond between the three of them was a deep one. There were times when Kelsey had envied them for that, even though she shared one with Nessa, as well.

"And how long has it been since you were able to sense her?" Andreas asked. He was the quieter twin and in the months since Nessa's change, he'd finally stopped blindly following his brother's lead so much.

Malachi grimaced. "A day, perhaps. But . . ." His voice trailed off and he murmured, "It's not right. There's something wrong. I sense a darkness. One of us, at least, should be able to feel her."

Kelsey tensed as several gazes shifted to her. Although she was the youngest, her abilities were the most closest to Nessa's. "I can't feel her," she said flatly. "I've already tried."

"Are you concerned about this?" Tobias asked softly.

Concerned? Hell. *Concerned* didn't touch it. None of them, save for Malachi, had any idea of the pain Nessa was living with. None of them. If they did, perhaps they'd understand *why* she was concerned.

"Yes." She gave him a tight smile. "I'm concerned."

"So what do we do?" Andreas asked.

Andreas, more than his twin, had acknowledged what they had almost allowed to happen years earlier, when the change between Morgan and Nessa had transpired. Niko shied away from it, but Andreas faced reality. They had almost killed one of their own. If that didn't change a man, what would?

Kelsey looked away from the monitor, watching Malachi as he prowled the room. He didn't speak. Settling in the seat, but careful not to touch the computer setup, she looked at the other Council members. "I really don't know what to do."

"Could she be dead?"

Kelsey stared at Niko. Sometimes, she really disliked that vampire. Giving him an icy smile, she said, "No, she couldn't be dead. *That* we would have felt."

"Not if she chose to hide it," he countered. "And we all know how depressed she has been. Borderline suicidal, even."

"*Borderline* suicidal isn't the same thing as suicidal."

"All it would take is a nudge in that direction." Niko

shook his head, returning Kelsey's stare with a dark one of his own.

To give him credit, she could tell he wasn't happy with the news of Nessa's disappearance. Although Niko had fought tooth and nail to resist the truth of things, once he acknowledged Nessa still lived, he had shown her the same respect he'd given her in the past. Even when Nessa was acting more batshit crazy than normal.

"She's not as strong as she used to be," Niko said quietly. He looked away, his mouth unsmiling, his face grim. "We all know that."

"She's stronger than you think," Malachi bit off, stalking up to the monitor and giving Niko a scathing glare. "She lives with pain the likes of which you cannot imagine. A weak soul couldn't do that."

"She's strong. But she's not who she once was. She doesn't welcome this second chance she's been given." Niko didn't back down, although Kelsey could sense his wariness, even though hundreds of miles separated them. He feared Malachi.

But then again, just about every vampire on earth feared Malachi.

"She doesn't view it as a second chance," Andreas murmured. "To her, it's a curse. A punishment. Would it be so unlikely to see her ending it?"

Kelsey's heart clenched. Tears stung her eyes, but she didn't let them fall. Her voice was husky as she replied, "I know she suffers. I've felt it—and I'm sorry, but you cannot understand that grief unless you *have* felt it. But Nessa's not a quitter. She never has been. If nothing else, that alone will keep her from ending it."

Nibbling on her lower lip, she shot the sleeping vampire a look. She truly didn't think Nessa had gone and killed herself—she was alive. In her heart, Kelsey believed that. But there was a small doubt, one that whispered *what if they are right . . . ?*

What if they were right . . . and what if that truly was Elias there, reborn centuries later and now a vampire?

He'd live a long life this time.

If she *had* killed herself . . .

If that *was* Elias, and he'd come back for Nessa . . .

So many ifs. So many questions.

Most of them, she couldn't even voice yet. She wasn't going to say a damn thing about Dominic to *anybody*, not until they knew what was going on. They couldn't risk Nessa hearing anything about it—it would be too cruel.

Of course, first they had to *find* her.

"Nessa isn't a quitter," Tobias said, echoing Kelsey's words. "She's a fighter, a born fighter. In both lives." A faint smile curled his lips and he met Kelsey's eyes, gave her a sad smile. Shared pain, shared miseries. They both loved Nessa.

"Could she just be hiding herself from us?"

Toying with one of her braids, Kelsey shrugged. "I really don't know. I'm a good witch." It was simple fact. She was good. She knew her power and she knew that as she aged it would grow. The longer she lived, the more powerful she'd become. In time, she might even outreach Nessa—especially since Kelsey was mated to a vamp. Malachi and Kelsey shared a bond between their souls and through the bond, she'd inherited his near immortality.

For as long as he lived, Kelsey would—unless she was killed. Old age, sickness, they couldn't kill her. She wouldn't fade and wither away as Nessa had done.

"I'm a good witch," she murmured again, staring down at the floor. Then she looked up and met Tobias's gaze. "But Nessa's better. If I lived a thousand years, I might eventually be her equal—assuming she never grew any stronger. Which isn't likely. I would say that *I* couldn't hide my presence from my fellow Council members—I could cloak myself, and I could hide. But you would still feel me. Nessa, though, I just don't know. If any Hunter alive can do it, it would be her."

After a few strained minutes of silence, Tobias glanced at the two vampires with him and then he said, "Right now, I fear there is nothing we can do but think on the matter. Perhaps we should convene again in the evening. Could you come to Brendain?"

Kelsey winced and shot a look at the vampire lying on the

bed. Tobias tried to follow her gaze, but the bed wouldn't be visible to the little camera. Giving him a weak smile, she said, "Now really isn't a good time for me to be leaving. I've got a battered vamp on my hands—he took a bad blow to the head, crushed his skull. Until he wakes up, I'm not leaving him."

Niko opened his mouth to say something, but Malachi cut him off. "We needn't come to Brendain, Tobias. We need to figure out what to do about Nessa, but we have a bit of problem here as well."

"Could we be of any help?" Andreas offered.

Kelsey hoped the panic she felt inside didn't show on her face. Since the others weren't in the room, they wouldn't hear the jump in her heartbeat or scent her nervousness. As long as nothing showed on her face, they were good. With what she hoped was a convincing smile, she said, "No. It's just the vampire. He was in a bad way even before he got hurt."

They agreed upon a time to speak again later in the day and then Malachi shut the computer down, smiling as Kelsey continued to keep well away from the monitor. "You know, pet, just touching it isn't going to harm the bloody machine."

She made a face at him. "Don't bet on it. Computers hate magic. More, they hate *me*."

"Likely because you hate them." Then he folded his arms over his chest and studied Dominic.

In that moment, the younger vampire stirred. Tension spiked in the air—a sure sign the vamp was coming back to awareness.

Three seconds later, his eyes opened. A heartbeat later, he was on his feet and staring around in confusion.

His gaze lit on Malachi and his eyes narrowed. His body tensed like he was going to pounce.

"You."

DOMINIC didn't know what the hell was going on, but he recognized the vampire right away. Kelsey pushed between them right before he would have lunged for the bastard.

"Let's not do that again, okay?" Kelsey put a hand on his chest and shoved. He went to go around and she just sidestepped with him, neatly keeping her slender body between the two vampires.

"I just want to know where in the hell she is."

Kelsey rolled her eyes. Her voice was placid as she said, "Then perhaps you should ask nicely instead of attacking *Malachi*."

Extra emphasis on the *Malachi*.

Dominic stilled, staring at the big, red-haired bastard. *Shit. Malachi.* Yeah, he'd felt the bastard's power earlier but he hadn't realized who it was. He'd seen the ancient vampire a few times, on other occasions when he had visited Excelsior in the past, but nobody had ever mentioned who in the hell he was.

Every Hunter alive knew that name, though. It was the name handed out in case one of them screwed up. If the screwup was bad enough, his name was mentioned—you didn't want *Malachi* coming to clean up your mess, because he'd also come kick your ass while he was at it, if he decided the screwup was in part your fault. Or worse—all your fault.

Yeah, every Hunter knew that name.

Even now, even banked, the vamp's power slammed against Dominic. He had an instinctive urge to go to his knees, lower his head and a bunch of submissive shit that didn't sit at all well with him. Rafe had once told him it was the strength of a budding Master that let a vampire resist any submissive urges. Dominic couldn't care less about being a Master, but if it kept him from kneeling before this guy, he was more than fine with it.

Jutting his chin up, he spat out, "If you expect me to kiss your old ass, you're out of your mind."

"And you are out of your nut," Malachi shot back, his blue eyes swirling, spiking with power. Then abruptly, his face relaxed. His eyes gave nothing away as he asked, "So, Elias, if you want to ask me something, be on with it."

Dominic scowled. "My name is Dominic."

The vampire shot Kelsey a look. Then once more, he

focused those unreadable blue eyes on Dominic's face. "Well, then. Dominic it is. What did you want to ask me, Dominic?"

Where is she? The question danced on the tip of his tongue. Rubbing the heel of his hand over his chest, he glanced all around and then looked back at Kelsey. "The cabin we were in earlier . . . who had been staying there?"

"A fellow Hunter," Kelsey said, her voice cautious. Her eyes were as unreadable as Malachi's. "A witch."

"What's her name?"

Neither of them spoke.

Silence stretched out between them.

Taking a step toward Malachi, he snarled, "What in the fuck is her name? I need to find her."

"Why?" If he was at all irritated by Dominic's spiking temper, it didn't show. "You don't even know her name . . . why it is so important to you? Who is she to you?"

Dominic closed his eyes. Years of dreams slammed into him, the weight of all the longing piling on his shoulders, damn near driving him to his knees. The ancient vampire couldn't do it, but his need for this woman *could.*

Nessa . . . my Nessa. Pretty little witch.

Her voice a husky murmur in his ear. *I love you, Elias . . . Elias.*

His eyes flew open and he stared at Malachi. "Elias . . . you called me Elias."

Malachi inclined his head. "Indeed, I did. But that isn't your name, right, mate? It's Dominic. Answer me, then . . . who is she to you? This woman whose name you don't even know?"

Dominic fisted his hands, pressed them to his head, fighting the onslaught of memories, trying not to get lost in them. "I know her . . ." he muttered. Lowering his hands, he stared at Malachi. "A few weeks ago, I had a dream. You were standing with her, on the roof of the Willis Tower. The fucking *roof.* They don't let people go up there, but then again, dreams don't always make sense. In my dream, you were there with her . . . and she acted like she was going to jump."

A muscle jerked in the ancient vampire's jaw. Off to the side, Dominic heard Kelsey's breath hitch in her chest.

"How did you know about that?" Malachi asked, his voice low and hard, demanding.

Dominic shook his head. "I just told you . . . I fucking dreamed it. A year ago, there was another dream, and both of you were it. The two of you . . . and her. The woman. You were all in a cemetery, and she was crying."

Malachi closed his eyes.

"Why did you call me Elias?" Blood roared in his ears, and his heart began to beat slowly at first but then faster and faster. Damn thing hadn't beat like this since his Change. It was enough to make him light-headed. What was going on? "What in the hell is her name?"

Malachi opened his eyes. Through his lashes, they glowed, sparked and swirled. That banked power began to pulse. "If you're who I think you might be, you should already know her name . . . Elias."

I love you, Elias.

Nessa . . . my Nessa.

Remembered pain tore his chest.

Dear God, that pain.

He could feel it, feel that knife tearing through him, fiery hot, then icy cold. The blood as it pumped out of him, in a hot, unending river of red. And her tears as they fell on his face.

He could feel it . . . like it was yesterday.

Staggering, he clapped a hand over his chest, but there was no wound. The pain had been in a dream—a dream he'd dreamed hundreds, maybe even thousands of times. A dream . . . or a memory.

Where he lay dying in the arms of the woman he loved . . . leaving her alone. Alone, with nothing more than a promise to find her again.

From the time he'd been just a kid, he'd dreamed of her.

Dreams that made no sense to a child, dreams where he'd been making love to a woman even though he had no idea what sex was. They'd come sporadically for most of his life, but the past few years, he could hardly sleep without dreaming of her. Since he'd become a Hunter, they'd gotten stronger. More real.

Somewhere inside his head, some semblance of sanity, some semblance of logic, tried to stir. None of this made sense. None of this was possible.

He couldn't possibly have dreamed of a woman he had never met.

Yet he had. He did.

Dominic clenched his hands into fists, then forced them to relax. Slanting a look at Kelsey, he asked hoarsely, "Do you have any pictures of her? I need to see her. I need to see what she looks like."

"Don't you already know what she looks like?" Malachi asked quietly. "After all, you saw her up there with me, dancing around like she might fly if she fell. If you dreamed of her, you know what she looks like."

Dominic shook his head. "Right now, I don't know whether I know anything. Nothing makes sense."

"Describe her for me," Kelsey suggested. "If it sounds like her, maybe we can find a picture."

Impatience tangled inside his gut. He didn't have time for this. He'd wasted so much time already. Crossing his arms over his chest, he stared at Kelsey.

The red-haired witch returned his gaze levelly.

"You have any idea what's going on?"

Kelsey shook her head. "I have no clue. But if you work with me, I'll do my damnedest to help you figure it out."

Dominic pinched the bridge of his nose. Lowering his hand, he sighed and stared off into the distance. "This won't make any sense. In my dreams, she doesn't always look the same. Hell, I don't think I look the same. Sometimes it's like a different time, I don't know when. History isn't my thing. But it seemed like a long time ago. The

clothes . . ." His voice trailed off, and he glanced at Kelsey.
"Back before I was Changed, I had a girlfriend who used
to like those ren-fairs. You ever been to one?"

Kelsey cocked a brow at him. "I think I've been to one
or two." She had a bland look on her face.

Off to the side, Malachi snorted. "One or two, pet?"

"A year. One or two a year," she amended.

"In some of the dreams, everybody was dressed like that.
The simpler clothes, though. Does that make sense?"

Her voice cautious, Kelsey replied, "Yes . . . I think it
does."

"I'm glad it makes sense to *somebody*," Dominic muttered. He rubbed the back of his neck. Closing his eyes,
he brought her face to mind. "She had long hair, golden
brown, and she wore it in a braid. At night, she would sit by
the fire and I'd watch her brush it. Sometimes, when I woke
up, I could still smell wood smoke."

He glanced up, found both of them watching him with a
heavy intense gaze. Spinning away from them, he stared at
the wall. "You have no idea how long I've been wondering
if I've lost my mind. I've dreamed of her for years."

"Well, mate"—Malachi sighed—"if you've lost your
mind, then I'm right there with you. Because I believe you.
Tell me more about these dreams. In your dreams, who
was she to you?"

"Everything." In those dreams, for whatever time he
was with her, he felt whole. He felt complete. And when he
woke, and realized he was alone, he felt that much emptier
for it. "In my dreams, she's everything."

"Soft bastard, aren't you?" Malachi grinned at him.

In that moment, Dominic was glad he hadn't fed yet.
If he had the blood to spare, he knew he would've been
blushing.

Malachi's grin faded as quickly as it had come. His face
solemn, his voice somber, he said, "Tell me more, then. Put
aside your romantic inclinations, and tell me *who* she was.
A friend? A lover?"

"My wife." Dominic closed his eyes. "In the dreams, she's my wife."

"Is it the same in all the dreams?" Kelsey asked. "Is she the same?"

"No." Dominic shook his head. "Only in the ones that seem like they happen a long time ago."

"Tell me more." Malachi's face showed no expression.

Dominic narrowed his eyes. "You're awfully interested in my dream life, old man."

Malachi gave him a toothy smile. "If you want my help, you'll indulge me."

"Shit." Dominic started to pace the small cabin, feeling restless and edgy. Trapped. He needed to find her. He needed to go to her. He *needed* her. That restless energy built inside him, brewing, boiling, threatening to burn out of control. The taste of blood filled his mouth. Dismayed, he lifted a hand and felt the bulge of fangs behind his upper lip.

Control. He needed to get control. But it was hard, so fucking hard. It had been years since he had this much trouble finding self-control.

Stalking to the corner, he braced his hands on the wall. Although he didn't need to breathe, he still did on occasion. There was something soothing about it, something calming in the passage of air traveling down his throat and into his lungs. He forced himself to take a long, slow breath, then a second, and a third. That restless boiling energy began to ease. After a minute, he was able to sheathe his fangs.

Keeping his voice low, and his hands on the wall, Dominic quietly whispered, "I need to find her. Are you going to help me or not?"

Behind him, he heard Malachi sigh. "Look, lad. Whether you believe it or not, I do want to help. I need to know what's going on first. So you have to help me before I can help you."

"If I *knew* what was going on, I'd tell you," Dominic snarled. Low in his gut, something began to burn. *Leave.* He needed to leave.

The urge started as a whisper, slowly and steadily spiraling up to a wail. His fingers dug into the brick wall, as though some part of him wanted to claw his way out of the cabin.

Behind him, he heard a whisper of sound. It was Kelsey; he recognized her scent, and her warmth—vampires didn't have that warmth. Setting his jaw, he turned to face her.

Her golden hazel eyes watched him with sympathy. She lifted a hand.

Uncertain what she wanted, Dominic eyed her warily.

"It's okay," she drawled, grinning at him. "I told you earlier, I don't bite."

"So, what? You want to shake my hand, is that it?" Dominic gave her a dubious stare.

Kelsey sighed. She continued to stand there, holding her hand out patiently. "You took one hell of an injury. Malachi bashed your brain in, you know. Wouldn't have surprised me if it had come leaking out your ears. It takes a lot of energy to heal, you know that. That's part of why you're so edgy, so restless right now. I can help."

Dominic stared at her as though she had lost her mind. "I'm not going to feed from you. Do you want him to kill me?"

"Oh, for Pete's sake." Kelsey reached out and snagged his hand.

The second her hand touched his, the turmoil inside him eased. It didn't disappear. Dominic suspected only two things would rid him of it completely—finding *her* or dying. But it no longer dominated his mind. He could think. Somewhat.

She let their hands remain linked for a few seconds and then she pulled back. But that sense of peace lingered.

"The dreams," Malachi prodded.

Dominic scowled at him. Then he leaned back against the wall and shoved his hands in his pockets. Once more able to think, he studied the older vampire and then turned to examine the witch. Malachi's face gave nothing away, but the same couldn't be said of Kelsey's.

She stared at him, her pretty, pale face unsmiling. Her expression was somber, but there was a light in her eyes and he could hear the rapid beat of her heart. She was excited, anxious or worried . . . maybe all three.

Tell them. That was what his gut insisted, that was what his heart screamed. Blowing out a breath, Dominic rested his head against the wall and said softly, "The dream started changing on me a few years ago—sometime after I Changed. I really don't remember when. She still looks close to the same. There is just something different, subtle things. Her hair is blond—up until a few years ago, she had always had brown hair. Still got blue eyes, but her eyes are sadder. The shape is just a little different, too. Face shape is similar, almost the same, but not quite. The physical differences aren't big, but they are there. They don't mean jack. Not to me. She's the same woman, but she isn't the same."

"What else is different?"

Turning his head, Dominic looked to Kelsey. "In the dreams when I see her, it's like I haven't seen her in a hundred years. Two hundred. It doesn't make sense, I know, and I can't explain it. But it's like I lost her in one dream and I found her in another."

"It makes more sense than you realize," Kelsey muttered under her breath. She toyed with the end of her braid and started to pace.

"And you've always had dreams about her?" Malachi stared at him, that gaze focused, intense.

Dominic closed his eyes. "Always."

"But the dreams didn't really change until the past few years?"

"No." Absently, Dominic rubbed the heel of his hand over his chest. He ached, deep inside.

Malachi asked, "These older dreams of yours, do they change much?"

"Hardly at all." That phantom ache began to throb, starting in his back, radiating forward. He flexed his shoulders, trying to ease the pain.

Cold. Cold pain, followed by the heated rush of blood

as it pumped out of him. Then the cold was gone, and there was just the pain in his blood . . . and in her. Nessa. Holding him while she cried. While she pleaded with him not to leave her.

"What happens in these dreams? These older ones that never change?"

Lifting his eyes, he stared at Kelsey's face. "I die. I die, and I leave her alone."

Lowering his lashes, he pressed his hand to that phantom ache in his chest. He could feel the blade. He could feel the blood. He could smell the blood.

And her tears, he could feel them falling on his face.

He could remember the pain, as clearly as though it had truly happened—just days ago. He could remember the shock of it, then the burning, followed by the icy maw of death as he bled out.

He could remember clinging to life, so desperate not to leave her. Making a promise. A promise he had no way of keeping, but damned if he wouldn't find a way.

"Dreams." That rational voice in his mind tried to fight its way to the front. "None of this makes sense. No way could this have happened."

Quietly, Kelsey said, "You know, some people would insist that there's no way vampires could exist. That there's no way a man can turn from a man to a wolf and then back. The mortal world would insist that true witches aren't real." She gave him an understanding smile. Warmth and compassion glinted in her eyes. "A few years ago, you would've been one of them, wouldn't you? Would that bright, clever medical student really believe in vampires, shapeshifters or witches? Or would he have been too logical for that?"

"Good point," he said, his voice tight and rusty. "But how can I know? How can I know if these dreams mean anything at all? How do I know they're not just a sign that I'm going crazy?"

"You're not crazy, lad," Malachi said. The ancient vampire slanted a glance at his wife, and he looked back at Dominic with a rueful shrug. "Trust me, if you are crazy, she would know. And I would've already dealt with you."

"How reassuring," Dominic said dryly. Oddly enough, it *was* reassuring.

The ancient vampire might be capable of compassion, but he understood necessity. He wouldn't let emotion interfere with duty. Once more, Dominic rubbed the heel of his palm over his chest. Then he studied his hands.

In the dreams, the older ones, his hands were a little different. Bigger, broader, his palms calloused and scarred. His body had been shorter, more solidly built.

Dominic couldn't even believe he was considering this. He stared at Malachi through his lashes. Once more, his heart raced inside his chest. He calmed it, fought to control that restless energy before it spiraled too high.

"Will you tell me her name now?"

A queer smile curled Malachi's lips. A strange light glinted in his eyes. "Lad, you and I both know this: *you* already know her name. You already know who she is."

Quietly, he whispered, "Agnes. Her name is Agnes . . . Nessa. *My* Nessa."

"Indeed she is," Malachi murmured.

While Dominic stood there, reeling, trying to force his mind to accept what his heart already knew, the big bastard just watched . . . and *smiled*.

D OMINIC snarled at Malachi, ignoring the shapeshifter standing behind him. "I don't have time for this. I need to find her."

"I know that." Malachi waited patiently at the door, one brow lifted. "You've told me—a good fifty times. And as I told you—she's not here. You've only a few minutes of night left and you can't find her before sunrise, so you might as well feed and get some rest. It's almost time for sunrise—or hadn't you noticed?"

Oh, Dominic had noticed. He could feel the burn of it. It

mingled with the restlessness and anger, adding to it. The anger was enough to help stave off the exhaustion, but not for much longer. He knew he'd have to sleep.

But he sure as hell didn't feel like feeding.

"So you just plan on going hungry until you find her?" The ancient vampire watched him with an inscrutable expression on his face. "Not a wise idea and you know that."

"I'm fine." He wasn't though. Hunger was an ugly song in his head and he knew he wouldn't be able to wait too long before he fed. Frustrated, he glanced at the shifter standing patiently behind Malachi and then he turned on his heel. "Fine. Let's just get this over with."

Malachi stepped aside to let the shifter enter but he followed closely behind. Dominic shot the vampire a dirty look.

"What . . . you're here to make sure I clean my plate?"

Malachi didn't answer.

The shifter gave Dominic an easy smile. "I don't mind being an evening snack. But if it's all the same to you, I'd rather you take it from my wrist."

Not a problem for Dominic.

A few minutes later, it was done and the shifter left. But Malachi didn't.

Dominic licked the last few drops of blood from his lips and took a deep breath, forcing his fangs to retract. A heady rush hit his system hard, and for a few minutes, it was hard to think past that euphoria.

The exhaustion clouding his mind cleared.

But it wouldn't last. Sunrise was only minutes away. Dropping down on the bed, he slid Malachi a glance and asked, "What are you still doing here, old man?"

Malachi gave him a tight smile. "I'm not entirely sure."

"*I'm not entirely sure,*" Dominic mimicked. "That could be my new motto. I'm not entirely sure of jackshit."

His body felt heavy, like lead lined his very bones. Heaving out a sigh, he kicked off his shoes and tugged off his T-shirt. His lashes drooped low. He rubbed his tired, gritty eyes and then looked at Malachi. He had about ten million questions he could've asked but he didn't know where to start.

There was one that nagged and tore at him, and he knew he had to have the answer. Staring at the older vampire, he said quietly, "How long have you known her?"

"Nearly as long as you have, I would say." He watched Dominic with shrewd eyes. "She came back to the school after that day. How much of it do you remember?"

"Remember of what . . . me dying?"

A sympathetic smile tugged at Malachi's mouth. "For a lack of a better way to put it, yes."

Dominic sighed and dragged his hands over his face. "I don't know if *remember* is the right word. I guess some part of me remembers, but all I know is what I've seen in my dreams." Restless, he rolled his shoulders—that phantom ache was back.

"And what have you seen?"

"Me . . . dying." Dominic flexed his hands and stared at them. "Those dreams aren't very clear. I can remember not wanting her to come back. I remember this man—I can't remember his name, but I knew I hated him. I remember him, I remember her, and I remember dying while she held me and cried."

He shook his head and murmured, "But that's about it."

Feeling the exhaustion creep closer, he shoved himself upright and started to pace. He needed to sleep, but right then, he needed answers more. Needed to understand.

He paced the cabin, toward the door and then down the length of the floor, pausing by the far wall. A fireplace took up much of the wall and what was left was lined with bookshelves. Or at least, it *had* been lined with bookshelves. Most of them were busted now, books, dust and wood littering the floor.

Dominic was pretty sure it hadn't looked like that when he first came into the cabin. Scowling, he asked, "Did it look like that earlier?"

"No." A reluctant smile curled Malachi's lips as he

studied the damage. Then he glanced at Dominic and murmured, "You poor bugger. End up with a blade in your gullet in one life and here you are trying to straighten this life out, and I damn near put you through a wall."

"Huh. Okay. Some of that's coming back to me now." Part of him felt like he needed to apologize for attacking earlier, but since Malachi had all but handed him his ass, Dominic didn't see the point. He turned away from the wall and started back down the floor, but with every step, it became harder and harder to move.

Too tired. Too damn tired. When he passed the bed, he sat down. It was either sit down or just collapse. He'd done enough damage to his pride today—collapsing wasn't going to happen.

Settling on the edge of the bed, he leaned forward. With his elbows braced on his knees, he watched Malachi through his lashes. "So you've known her a long time."

"A very long time." Malachi leaned forward, elbows on his knees, mimicking Dominic's pose. He gave Dominic a tired smile. "She's a friend—one of my dearest friends, certainly one of the oldest. I know her well, just as she knows me well. But she's just a friend, lad. Never anything else."

The knot in Dominic's chest eased.

He had enough crazy shit in his head—he didn't need to sit there thinking about *what-ifs* and other crap that wouldn't really do much but cause trouble.

But he couldn't help it.

She was *his*—deep in his gut, deep in his bones, he knew that. She was his.

"You'll drive yourself bloody insane if you keep letting your mind wander down those paths."

Looking up, he found Malachi watching him. A bitter smile twisted the older vampire's lips and he said, "Bloody insane, trust me. I know."

"Stay out of my head," Dominic said tiredly. Fuck, he was exhausted—it pulled at him, a gaping abyss of darkness, determined to suck him under. But he fought it. He still had so many questions. Despite the fact that he knew he couldn't leave Excelsior until sundown, everything inside him screamed—*Find her!*

It was a good thing his body would take the choice out of his hands soon. Otherwise Dominic would spend the day trapped in the little house, driving himself crazy and pacing the room as he waited for sunset.

"I'm not peeking inside your thick skull, Dominic." Malachi jerked a shoulder and stared off into the distance. "We get bit—it does something to our bodies, brings all these crazy hungers. But it doesn't change the fact that in our hearts, we're still human. In the end, we're still men and we have the same foibles and fallacies as every other man who's ever walked the face of the earth. You're wondering the same things I'd wonder, if I took a walk in your shoes."

Dominic cocked a brow at Malachi. "You have foibles?"

Malachi didn't bother responding. Coming off the chair, he prowled the cabin, studying the windows and then turning to look at the door. "Not the place for a vampire to bed down, you know. It's safe enough, Kelsey saw to that, but your instincts won't like it. You won't rest well."

"I'll be good. Going to crash under the bed. It'll be dark enough, and it's not like I move around much when I'm out." Absently, he reached for a pillow and brought it around, holding it in his lap. He could smell her on it. He'd just missed her . . . by a few days. Bringing it to his face, he breathed her scent in. "I've slept in worse places."

A wave of exhaustion rose up, slammed into him. Outside, the sun began to breach the horizon. Dominic fought against the siren's call of sleep. His tongue felt thick in his mouth as he glanced at Malachi. "You'll tell me where she is? When I wake up?"

He swayed forward and if Malachi hadn't been there, he would have fallen flat on his face. "Sleep, lad. We'll speak more when you've rested. Come on now . . ."

Sleep pulled. Beckoned.

Vaguely, Dominic was aware that he was no longer on

the bed, but under it. Dim light surrounded him, and he caught the scent of something dusty. Blindly, he flailed around, not even aware of what he was searching for.

Then something soft was pressed into his hands.

Lavender and vanilla . . . it smelled of her.

Peace surrounded him, and then he was lost to the darkness.

CHAPTER 11

M ORGAN knew one thing.
    She seriously hated mornings. With a passion. It might be a new development, but somehow, she doubted it. She suspected she had always hated mornings.

She woke up with a skull-splitting headache. Weakness plagued her, and the dream she couldn't remember haunted her.

If she had her way about it, she would just stay in bed. But she couldn't do that. So she sighed and rolled out, her body aching, her head pounding.

Stumbling in the small, shabby kitchen, she dropped into the chair and glanced at Jazzy. Her sister stood at the stove, singing along with her iPod as she fried up some bacon.

Jazzy caught her eyes and then tugged out her earbuds. "Wow, Morgan, you fucking look like shit." Her voice was heavy with the drawl of the Deep South.

Morgan wasn't sure, but she thought Jazzy had lived in Georgia or Alabama for a while. She didn't remember which—big surprise there.

She didn't remember *anything* important.

Oh, she remembered the simple things—like how to tell time, how to tie her shoes, how to turn the TV off and on.

She'd started to remember more complicated things as well. Like the fact that she was a witch. She wasn't even surprised by that fact. She wasn't disturbed by the fact that witches existed. She remembered how to cast illusions, how to make fire, although both left her weak. She also remembered how to bolster that weakness by drawing strength from others using her magic.

And she also knew that doing so made her feel . . . dirty. Dirty in a way she couldn't explain, so she didn't do it, even though Jazzy insisted that was how Morgan had taught her to use her power. Why drain yourself dry if you didn't have to, right?

All Morgan knew was that it felt *wrong*. Off, in some way she couldn't explain. She knew she should know *why* it felt wrong . . . but it was another one of those things she couldn't remember.

There were too many of those things. Her life was nothing but one gaping black hole. Anything, everything personal, it was all gone. Her life. Her sister. Her mother.

The lost memories of her mother weren't any tragedy, though. She didn't need those memories to know the woman was bad news. All she had to do was look into Jazzy's haunted blue eyes when the girl even mentioned their mother and she knew. More, she *felt* it. In her bones. Bad news? No, the woman wasn't just bad news.

She was a catastrophe.

Morgan wasn't going to forgive herself anytime soon for leaving Jazzy alone to deal with their crazy, mean bitch of a mother. That crazy, mean bitch of a mother wasn't in the picture now, though. For all Morgan knew, she was hell's problem now.

But sensing Jazzy's concerned stare, Morgan looked at her sister and forced a smile, reminded herself—Jazzy had said something. What had she said . . . ? *Oh, yeah.*

"I didn't sleep well. I fucking feel like shit." She sighed

and pushed her hair out of her face and then glanced at the coffeepot. The smell of it was rich and she could use the caffeine, but she didn't care for the taste of it.

Jazzy picked up the pot and wiggled it. "Decided you still have a taste for it after all?"

"No." Morgan wrinkled her nose. "I'll make some tea."

Jazzy made a face as Morgan went about doing just that. While Morgan made her tea, Jazzy started getting out stuff for breakfast and talked about their plans for the day.

"He's a good mark. Seriously. I'm talking *money*. And he's a wuss—I'm talking major chicken. All you need to do is throw a few illusions at him, maybe a couple bursts of fire, and he'll do whatever we want. Trust me—he is *not* getting that money in nice legal ways . . . so we don't really need to worry about him running to the cops."

Morgan's lips twitched in a smile and she shrugged. "Well, it's not like he could really file a report about how somebody had stolen his money using magic, right?"

Somewhere in the back of her mind, a quiet voice argued, *This isn't who you are—a con artist, a grifter.*

Morgan ignored it. After all, it wasn't like she had a whole lot of opportunities at her feet. She couldn't even produce a high school diploma so she could pick up a minimum wage job.

She had responsibilities. Her sister depended on her.

Taking care of Jazzy was more important than the morality of how she was able to do it. It wasn't like she was bilking honest people out of hard-earned money.

But you know this isn't your way.

Damn that voice, anyway. Little wonder she was always so tired.

She poured herself a cup of tea. With a massive headache pounding at the base of her skull, she turned to watch as Jazzy started whipping up some scrambled eggs. Jazzy caught sight of the mug of tea and grimaced. "I don't know how in the hell you can drink *tea* like that."

"You Americans went and ruined a fine drink," she said, her voice cool, crisp . . . unfamiliar, but not.

The cup fell to the floor and shattered. Shaken, Morgan spun around and rested her hands on the counter. *Shit.*

The kitchen was silent, save for the hiss and crackle of the bacon as it cooked. Then a soft step, Jazzy coming toward her. Glancing over her shoulder, Morgan scowled, "Stupid bitch, you want to cut up your feet?"

Jazzy went pale.

Appalled, Morgan clapped a hand over her mouth. "Shit. Shit. Damn it, Jazzy, I'm sorry." She looked away as blood crept up her neck to stain her cheeks red. She grabbed a broom and dustpan. From the corner of her eye, she watched Jazzy.

"I . . . I'm sorry. Honey, I'm so sorry."

Jazzy sniffed and wiped the back of her hand over her eyes. But her voice was hard and cold as she said, "Yeah, sure you are. You know, here I was actually thinking maybe you did love me after all. But you sound just like the mean bitch who left me alone with Mom."

A nasty, biting, cruel voice whispered inside Morgan's head, grating and harsh. *"And you sound just like the annoying, whiny brat I was desperate to get away from."*

But under that cold, uncaring voice there was pain, and regret. Swallowing the knot in her throat, she cleaned up the mess. Jazzy remained where she was, motionless by the stove.

On her way out of the kitchen, she paused. Looking back at the kid, she said quietly, "I am sorry, Jazzy. Really."

Then she retreated back to her small, dank room and huddled on the bed. Hours passed, Jazzy left, and sometime later returned. And still Morgan hid.

She didn't know what the hell was wrong with her.

Her head. It had something to do with her head . . . that vicious, pounding pain. And her mother. Jazzy's mother. Their mother.

There'd been a fight. Morgan didn't know what happened. She couldn't remember that night—hell, try as she might, she couldn't remember *anything.* Not even Jazzy. Somehow she knew she was responsible for the girl, but she didn't *remember* her.

She just knew she had to take care of the girl.

"Lousy job you're doing," she whispered to herself.

Yelling at the kid, looking at her and feeling so angry.

So lost.

So unlike herself.

At least, that's the way she felt. But since she could barely remember who she was, how did she even know?

D UST and dim light.

That was what Dominic awoke to—there was a musty scent in the air, something flat and dark over him and off to the side, he could see light filtering in.

For a second, confusion crowded his mind.

Scooting out from under the bed, he glanced around, trying to place where he was. He came to his feet as he studied the golden light creeping in through the narrow slit in the curtains.

Even without the sun's light, his internal clock told him it wasn't quite full night yet. The sun wasn't quite yet ready to set—it was damn early for him to be up. He shouldn't be awake at all. But here he was, and he wasn't even that groggy.

Just confused as hell.

Rubbing a hand down his grizzled jaw, he studied the cabin, from the windows that would let in enough sunlight to fry his ass, to the busted bookshelves along one wall.

A familiar, elusive scent tickled his nose and he looked down, realized he was holding a pillow.

The scent came from that. Lifting it to his face, he breathed it in and then shuddered as her scent hit him.

Memory followed two seconds later.

His hand fell slack to his side. He stood there, staring stupidly at nothing as those crazy, rushed minutes from the past night and morning started to spin through his mind.

He was at Excelsior.

According to Kelsey, he wasn't crazy.

And according to his gut, the woman he'd been dreaming about was real.

She was alive.

Not a figment of his imagination.

Swearing, he dropped down, sitting on the edge of the bed. He covered his face with his hands and held still, stiff as logic tried to creep up.

You don't know this woman.

You've never met her.

She's not who you think she is.

But logic wasn't getting a very good foothold. Lowering his hands, he stared all around the little cabin, replaying every last second from the previous night. Arriving here. Following Kelsey across the grounds to one of the rooms designed for the vampires.

But he'd caught a familiar scent in the air, and he'd followed it.

Followed it to this cabin, and the moment he'd stepped through the door, he'd been overcome by a sense of possessiveness, a determination unlike anything he'd ever met.

And longing.

Then seeing Malachi—telling him about his dreams.

There was a quiet knock at the door, and Dominic looked up with a scowl. He was still scowling when he answered the door. Automatically, he flinched against the vivid light of the setting sun but it brought him no harm, no discomfort. It caused a faint sting—the way it might after one had been in the sun a little too long, but that was it.

Kelsey stopped in her tracks and then glanced back over her shoulder at the sun. When she looked at him, she asked, "Doesn't it hurt?"

"No."

Her brows arched. "Wow. That's pretty damn good . . . how long have you been a vamp?"

"Ten years."

She whistled under her breath. "Real damn good. I thought I sensed you moving around, but I didn't expect to really find you awake until the sun was gone."

Dominic just stared at her.

"A man of many words, aren't you?" she asked, tongue

in cheek. Then she shoved the door shut behind her and shrugged. "That's okay. The sexy brooder thing works for you."

"Sexy brooder." He snorted and shook his head. "You sound like Sheila." He stood aside to let her enter the cabin.

Glancing around, he found his bag sitting by one of the chairs, as well as his shoes. The shirt he'd worn the previous night was tossed over the arm of the chair, but he didn't remember putting it there. Come to think of it, he didn't remember settling down under the bed, either, although that had been the plan.

The last few minutes before the sleep hit him were always blurred, but not this bad. Pushed it too long, he figured. He had probably been operating on some level just barely above autopilot.

Snagging his bag, he tossed it onto the bed and unzipped it.

"So . . . you in here questioning your sanity?"

With a humorless smirk, Dominic muttered, "How did you guess?"

"Because that's what I would be doing." Kelsey shrugged and settled into the chair near the fireplace.

A memory flashed through his mind—Malachi. Before he'd fallen under, Malachi had been in the cabin, and he'd sat in that same chair.

More . . . he'd told Dominic they'd talk. He would tell Dominic where to find Nessa.

"So does this mean you've changed your mind?"

Her voice was carefully devoid of any emotion and her face was a smooth, expressionless mask. But there was a scent in the air, one he recognized. Humans learned to read facial expressions. Vamps and shifters took it a bit deeper than that. They could even read the faintest shift in body chemistry—fear, worry, excitement.

Kelsey was worried.

Looking at her, he said softly, "No. I want to see her. Hell, if nothing else, maybe I'll look at her and realize this is nothing but bullsh . . . bull. That I'll look at her and not know her."

"You don't really think that's going to happen, though, do you?"

Those eyes of hers saw too much, Dominic thought sourly. Shooting her another glance, he shook his head. "No. I think I'm going to look at her and realize I've spent my whole life waiting to find her."

Something hot and painful crept through his gut as he added in a rough whisper, "My whole life—thirty-four fucking years. It seems like forever. But if this is real, if all this is really happening, then it's been a hell of a lot longer."

His gut in a tight, hot knot, he looked at the silent witch. "How many years, Kelsey? Do you know?"

"Yes." She sighed, watching him with sad, sympathetic eyes. "I know."

"How long?"

For one long, strained moment, she didn't speak. Then finally, she looked away and murmured, "Five hundred years."

Blood began to roar in his ears. His legs went numb and he sagged against the bed. He curled one hand around a carved wooden post. If the bed hadn't been close, he damn well might have ended up on his ass.

"Five hundred years," he repeated, his tongue thick in his throat. "I left her alone for *five hundred years*?"

"You didn't *leave* her." Kelsey drew a knee to her chest and rested her chin on it, watching Dominic with a compassionate gaze. "You were taken from her—you didn't have a choice. Not in how you were pulled away, and not in how you ended up back here. How . . . why . . . when. You had no say in the matter."

Dominic closed his eyes. "The past few years, something has changed in my dreams. *She* changed. I don't know why, don't know what caused it, but she's different. I feel it. The pain . . . the pain I feel inside her, it's worse. I feel her more. I feel her pain more, and that pain . . . God, I don't know how she lives with it."

Lifting his lashes, he stared at Kelsey. "How long has

she been like that? Has she spent every day feeling *that* empty?"

Kelsey looked at him, her pretty face unhappy. But she gave him no answer.

Dominic shoved a hand through his hair and looked away. Grabbing his duffel bag, he headed for the bathroom. "I need a shower."

When he came out of the bathroom ten minutes later, Kelsey was gone. But the room wasn't empty—Malachi was there.

He rubbed his damp hair with a towel as he met the older vampire's gaze. "Where is she?"

"And good morning to you, too." A faint smile curled Malachi's lips.

Dominic bared his teeth. That restless energy was back, and he'd be damned if he waited around here—not even for another ten minutes, another twenty. Hell, he'd be out the door this second if he knew where to go. "You told me you would tell me where she was. Tell me."

"Now that isn't exactly what I told you now was it, lad?" Malachi arched a dark red brow.

Dominic snarled at him. "You damn well did. This morning—right before I passed out."

"No. What I said was that we would discuss it when you awoke. Now you're awake—we'll discuss it."

Dominic clenched his fist, and just barely managed to keep from jumping the older vampire. It didn't matter that the guy would pound his head in. What mattered was that he was keeping him away from *her*. His voice was a low growl as he bit off, "What's there to talk about? I just want to know where to find her."

"Well, that's the thing." Malachi settled on the edge of the chair and leaned forward, bracing his elbows on his knees. Dark red hair fell forward, shielding his face as he stared at the ground. One big pale hand curled into a fist.

Dominic wasn't as good at reading emotions as others. He couldn't rely on his nose, not with non-mortals. Some of his fellow Hunters could have read a vamp's emotions the same way others read a book.

Malachi was a very closed book, but that one clenched fist gave him away.

The bottom of Dominic's stomach fell out. His legs turned to water. For a minute he thought he just might go to his knees. In a low raspy voice, he demanded, "Tell me. Enough with the bullshit. Tell me what's going on."

Malachi sighed. Slowly he looked up. Through a curtain of hair, his dark blue eyes gleamed. "She's missing, lad. She left here nearly a week ago and I wasn't worried about that. But a few days ago she . . . well, it's like she's gone off our radar, so to speak, and none of us have any clue where to find her."

"What do you mean she's missing?"

"Just that." Malachi leaned back in the chair, big body slumped. "She's missing, and not a one of us know where she is."

"You mean you can't fucking find her? Don't tell me none of you have any way of tracking her down. Damn it, she's one of us. Somebody *has* to be able to find her."

His eyes troubled, Malachi replied, "Under normal circumstances, yes, one of us should be able to sense her. I can sense Tobias almost as easily as I can sense Kelsey—I've worked with that old wolf for a long time. Almost as long as I had worked with Nessa. But she's not the same woman she was—you don't know Nessa. She's the strongest witch we have—the oldest witch we have. She's one of the oldest among us. And trust me—age will grant you a few tricks. Nessa knows how to use them. If she doesn't want to be found, she will not be found. At least not by us. Going to take some tricks I just don't know." Now Malachi leaned back in his chair and eyed Dominic, a sly smile curling his lips. "We can't find her. But I suspect you can."

I suspect you can . . .

Those words circled around in Dominic's head. Could he? Could he really?

But he didn't even have to think it through. Yeah, he could find her. That's why he was so fucking anxious to get out of here—something was pulling at him, drawing him toward her. Damn straight he could find her.

So what in the holy hell was he waiting for?

With that thought in mind, he turned away from Malachi and started to pack.

"I need wheels."

"Wheels?"

Glancing over his shoulder, he said, "Yeah. Wheels. As in something to drive. I wasn't planning on sightseeing when I left Memphis and I didn't bring my bike with me. I don't have a vehicle with me. I need wheels."

Malachi lifted a brow. "Well, I imagine we can find something that will work. So . . . does that mean you're going to try to find her?"

"I'm not going to try. I *will* find her."

"You sound sure of it."

Humorlessly, Dominic smiled. "What other choice do I have? This is why I'm here, don't you think? Why I'm here, why I'm here *now*." He shook his head. He hadn't ever been much of one to spend a lot of time thinking about fate, or things meant to be, but he also wasn't one to ignore something after it had been all but thrown in his face.

Fate couldn't have been much clearer on this if it had wrapped it up in a shiny red bow.

"Before you go, perhaps we should talk a bit. There is some . . . information you should know."

Dominic shook his head. "Whatever is it, I don't care. I'm going after her, and I'm going after her now." There was an urgency in his gut, one that was just now making itself known, and rather loudly.

Slanting a look at Malachi, he said, "I have to go. I have to go *now*."

"Do you even know where you're going?"

"No." He had no clue. But he wasn't going to let that stop him. He could feel *her*. Feel her pulling at him. He'd just follow.

* * *

"WELL, that was a good night's work."

Morgan swallowed, her throat dry. Nausea roiled in her stomach. She wanted nothing more than to find someplace dark and quiet so she could hide. From the rest of the world, from her sister and herself. The pain at the base of her skull was back, dancing and twisting around and around. Jagged, ugly streaks of nauseating red flashed through her line of sight, obscuring her vision.

She couldn't believe what she had just done.

"Would you just stop your bellyaching? You did good. Bastard is out of business, you can't say that's a bad thing."

Desperately, she slammed up a mental wall. She couldn't listen to her own self-doubts, her own self-recriminations right now. She was having a hard enough time staying on her feet.

Pain throbbed inside her head. Bile began to churn its way up her throat and she swallowed reflexively, determined not to throw up.

Not here. If she started, it would be a good long time before she could stop. No. They had to get far away from here. Back to the safety of their home.

Jazzy slung an arm around her shoulders. "Why do you look so nervous? Why are you so upset?"

"Probably because I just killed somebody."

Oh, dear God, please forgive me. What have I done?

Jazzy stared at her. "Morgan, he was a fucking pimp. He beat his girls on a regular basis. He cheated them out of their money. He ran a fucking whorehouse. Hell, a couple of the girls he had working for him aren't any older than me. The world doesn't need another man like him around. We did the world a favor."

Morgan looked down. Although the blood had been washed away she could still see it. She could still feel it, the hot, wet slickness of it. She'd killed him.

She could live with that.

But she was having a hard time accepting *why* she'd killed him.

For all the wrong reasons, she knew.

The right thing . . . for the wrong reason. It was entirely possible, she knew.

Quietly, she murmured, "But we didn't do it to do the world a favor. We did it for the blood. For the blood, and for his money."

"You're probably just all rattled from the high. Getting the energy fix always leaves you rattled." Jazzy shrugged. "You'll settle down and you'll feel all better."

No. She wouldn't. Stopping in her tracks, she waited until Jazzy slowed and looked back at her. Once her sister's eyes locked with hers, Morgan folded her arms over her chest. It did nothing to ease the chill inside of her.

"I didn't take his energy."

Jazzy gaped at her. *"What?"*

"I didn't take it. I don't need his energy and I . . ." *I can't live with that evil inside me.* She clamped her mouth shut and shook her head. "I didn't take it."

Then she started to walk. When Jazzy reached out to grab her arm, Morgan shrugged her away. She needed a shower. No, she needed a bath, scalding hot and laced with Clorox. Maybe then she could feel clean again.

But somehow she doubted it.

Morgan didn't think she'd ever feel clean again.

She stumbled, and almost fell. Weakness flooded her and it took everything she had just to keep walking.

"You should've taken the energy. You need it. You're still weak. How can you take care of her when you're still weak?"

"No."

Morgan still didn't understand who she was. She still felt utterly lost inside. But she knew if she tapped into the energy she'd get from spilling blood, she'd remain lost—she'd never find herself again and she would fall into madness.

I can't fall. I can't.

But somewhere deep inside, she feared she'd already done just that.

CHAPTER 12

H^E dreamed of blood.
     Of pain.
Of madness, confusion and loss.
He dreamed of *her*.

Dominic came awake with the bitter taste of blood lying in the back of his throat. His hand ached as though he'd held something too tight, and for too long.

The dream came to him in a rush.

She had been holding a knife, and there had been somebody dying at her feet. A man. He had tried to hurt her, but he hadn't realized what a mistake it would be. Nessa had killed him. She'd taken his life, but she almost hadn't stopped with just that.

There had been a hunger inside of her—Dominic had felt it, and it terrified him. He understood hunger—he craved blood, dreamed of it—needed it to survive.

But this was something different. This was something dark.

He didn't need to *kill* when he took blood. He only took enough to sate the hunger. This hunger he felt from her . . .

only death would slake that hunger. He had felt her magic, curling from someplace inside of her and reaching for that blood, reaching for some power within it . . . reaching for the death.

It was getting worse.

It had been two weeks since he left Excelsior, and every day when he lay down to sleep, he dreamed of her.

The dreams were awful . . . the sort that made nightmares look pleasant.

Dark, ugly dreams where she walked the streets like a predator.

Sad, heartbreaking dreams where he shared her pain and awoke to find bloody tears on his face.

He no longer questioned whether they were real or not—whether she was real.

She was . . . and she was slipping. Falling into a darkness so deep, so complete she'd never be able to find her way back.

It almost happened this time.

Dominic didn't understand much about magic or witches, but in his gut, he knew that if she had reached for that blood power, it would have been too late.

He sat up, shifting in the bed until he could prop his back against the headboard. Although his hotel room had no windows, he knew the sun was still up. It was probably a good hour before sunset. Every day, it seemed he woke a little bit earlier.

Heaving out a sigh, he reached for the phone. He might as well order room service. He placed an order for a steak, medium-well, salad and a baked potato. The smells would torment him. He missed eating food. He just hoped whoever delivered the room service had decent hygiene.

After placing the order for food he wouldn't eat, he climbed out of bed and headed for the shower. He was checking out tonight. Heading farther south. Maybe Georgia. Maybe Florida.

Room service arrived about ten minutes after he finished in the shower. He paused long enough to check the air—a man. *Figures*. When he had the choice, Dominic

preferred to feed from a woman—to him, they tasted better—
but he didn't plan on lingering around town, so he couldn't
be picky.

Without even opening the door, Dominic knew the guy
was clean enough, even though he had gone a little heavy
on the AXE. That garbage ought to be illegal, he thought.
It stank to high heaven, and being a vampire only made it
worse.

He opened the door, caught the man's eyes and smiled.
All it took was one look, and his flimsy mental shields collapsed, allowing Dominic to lead him.

"Why don't you come in and set it down for me?"

Ten minutes later, Dominic sent the man away, with a
fat tip and minus half a pint of blood, but none the wiser.
After he had fed, Dominic had planted a suggestion about
taking a break and getting some food. After all, he didn't
want the man collapsing later. He hadn't taken enough to
do any harm, but it might make him a little dizzy if he
skipped a meal.

It took another ten minutes before Dominic had all his
stuff packed up. By the time he checked out the sun had
set and he had most of the night left ahead of him. If he
drove straight through, he could probably make it across
the Florida state line before dawn.

Florida. He needed to be there. Could feel it pulling at
him. He wanted to think it was *her* pulling at him, but he
was afraid to hope.

God, please. Let her be there.

R OADKILL would've looked more appetizing.
Morgan eyed the tray in front of her, and then forced
a smile for Jazzy. "Thanks, honey. It looks delicious."

Jazzy cocked a brow. "If it looks so yummy, then prove
it. Eat all of it."

All of it? Morgan eyed the sandwich and a steam-
ing bowl of soup. She would start with the soup. It was
more likely to stay down. Giving Jazzy a game smile, she

grabbed the spoon. Her hand shook so badly, some of it spilled as she took the first bite.

Next to her, Jazzy watched with a concerned look on her face. "You're getting weaker."

"Nonsense."

"Don't give me that. I might be a kid, but I can tell when somebody's losing weight. You hardly eat. You don't sleep much. And if you do sleep, you have nightmares. You're getting weaker, and every time you use your magic, it gets worse. The one thing that could help you, you won't do. What's going on? Why aren't you using the blood?"

Because I can't. But she almost had. She hadn't been able to sleep last night. Something had drawn her out of the house—some unseen summons. She had followed it and ended up stumbling onto a drug deal.

She should've walked away. She wanted to believe she *could* walk away. Generally, the only time drug deals interested her was when they could benefit her.

That one could have proven beneficial, she supposed. After all, the drug dealer had a big fat wad of bills shoved in his pocket.

But she hadn't taken it. Even though the dead man would've had no use for it, she had left it. Just as she left his blood alone. Dirty bastard—he'd been out to double-cross the kid working for him, too. Manda. The kid's name was Manda. She was all of fifteen.

Why had she gotten involved? She didn't understand . . . didn't understand.

But she did. Because when she'd touched the dealer, she'd felt what he'd been planning. He'd owed money to one of his "business" partners, and that "partner" had his eye on this particular employee, Manda.

That was why Morgan had cared. The dealer's partner had been lurking, lying in wait. The partner got Manda, and the dealer didn't get his legs broken.

That was why Morgan had gotten involved. But she didn't understand *why* she cared, why she *had* to care. Thinking about it, *trying* to understand was a fucking mistake, too, because when she thought about it, she remembered the call of his blood.

Remembered how much she'd wanted it—how much she'd craved the power she could siphon away from him as he lay dying.

Because she wanted it so badly, she'd made herself walk away. She'd spared only a few minutes to seek out the partner's hiding spot and conceal herself under illusion as she whispered, "Run away. And do not speak of this, unless you want me to come after you as well."

He'd run screaming into the night . . . and she'd stumbled off into it, trying not to sob.

She'd slept the day away, and now, she was even weaker than she'd been before. Weak, too weak. Too tired. No amount of rest, no amount of food was helping. Her power supply was dangerously low. At this rate, she would burn herself out in another week or two at the most.

She needed her magic, because without it she couldn't protect Jazzy. Couldn't take care of her sister. Jazzy needed her. The kid was still so young.

It was more than that, though. She couldn't explain it but somewhere inside, she knew Jazzy was vulnerable. *Too* vulnerable, and it was her weak gift for magic that made her so.

Had to protect her . . .

That knowledge circled inside her head, even as part of her asked, *Protect her from who?*

Her hand continued to shake as she ate more of the soup. When she got half of it inside her belly, she laid the spoon down and focused on the sandwich. "As delicious as this looks, I might not be able to eat all of it, sister."

"That's a shocker." Jazzy rolled her eyes. "Considering how little you eat anymore, your stomach is probably shrunk down to the size of a hummingbird's." She settled on the foot of Morgan's bed and brought her knees to her chest. "So where did you go last night?"

Morgan paused. She gave her sister a puzzled smile and asked, "What do you mean?"

Jazzy made a face at her. "Come on, Morgan. I'm not stupid. And maybe I'm not as strong with the magic as you are, but I can tell when you're not there—I feel it."

"I just needed some air. I thought maybe a little bit of exercise might help me sleep better." The lie rolled off her tongue without hesitation. She wasn't about to explain to her sister that it felt as though she had been drawn away— that she'd felt compelled to leave.

"Did you run into anybody?"

Flicking a glance at her sister, Morgan pretended to think. "No, nobody I know . . . at least, I don't think I knew any of them. I saw a few people, but I'm still not remembering names."

"Did you talk to anybody?"

Morgan shrugged. She didn't think she had said anything to the drug dealer. But she had spoken to the girl. Morgan was pretty sure that her exact words had been *Get the hell out of here. And get your act together.*

She had laughed at her first. But then she'd seen what Morgan did with the dealer—she'd gone white as a ghost, and Morgan wasn't sure, but she thought the girl might have pissed her pants.

"You notice anything weird?"

Hearing the persistent note in her sister's voice, Morgan sat her sandwich down. Focusing on Jazzy's face, she folded her arms across her chest and asked, "So what's with the Spanish Inquisition? Is there something going on?"

"Well . . . yeah." Jazzy shifted on the bed. Even though they were alone in the house, the younger woman looked around, as though expecting to see somebody pop out from behind a door. "Do you remember Lamar Hedges?"

Morgan stared at her sister balefully. Then she tapped her brow. "Amnesia, remember? I don't remember much of anything."

Jazzy wrinkled her nose. "Sorry. I guess I keep hoping something will stir your memory. Anyway, Hedges was a small-time punk—liked to talk big, about how he had all these contacts and how you didn't want to cross him."

"So, is this going to be a new mark?" Jazzy was always looking for new marks.

"Hell, no." She caught her lower lip between her teeth and then shot Morgan a nervous look. "I didn't like him. He always freaked me out. Mama used him some—for drugs, for sex, or if there was somebody she wanted roughed up. Hedges liked to hurt people. I always stayed away from him."

"Smart girl." Even though the name wasn't at all familiar, a cold chill danced down Morgan's spine. The man she'd killed last night—he'd liked to hurt people. She had seen it in his eyes. "So what's this about, if he's not a new mark? Although, he sounds rather ideal to me."

"He's dead." Jazzy came off the bed and started to pace the room. She shot Morgan a look over her shoulder. "I saw it on the news not that long ago. So far nobody is saying what happened, but I got a funny feeling about it."

"Did they mention how he died?"

Jazzy shook her head. "They're not saying anything." Nervous, she toyed with her hair, twisting one thick lock around and around her finger. "They haven't even given his name. I guess they're waiting for next of kin."

"If they haven't released his name, then how do you know it's him?"

Jazzy stopped pacing. She turned to look at her sister. With a jerky shrug, she said, "I just know. They flashed something about a murder victim across the screen during the morning news and I just knew."

Jazzy looked incredibly young as she stared at her sister. Her blue green eyes were turbulent with worry and her face was pale. "Did you have anything to do with it?"

"Why would you think that?" Morgan folded her arms across her chest. "And sweetie, don't take this wrong, but why are you so upset that he's dead? Aren't you the one telling me how we're doing the world a favor by getting rid of some of these marks?"

A stubborn look settled on Jazzy's face. "The world ain't gonna cry over the likes of Lamar Hedges. He's dead, and whoever killed him, let's give him a round of applause. But I've got a bad feeling about this—a really bad feeling. Now can you answer me? Did you have anything to do with this?"

Before Morgan could answer, Jazzy's phone rang.

A NOTHER day. Another hotel.
This one didn't have any interior rooms, so instead of sleeping on a bed, he was sleeping on the couch inside the "sitting" area. There weren't any windows and that was good enough for him. Although the couch opened into a queen-size bed, he'd bypassed that torture device. His feet hung over the edge, but, in and of itself, it was fairly comfortable.

Once he'd stretched out, he was out to the world.

He'd had a few hours of solid, blank sleep before tumbling into a deep, troublesome dream. One of those that he really didn't want to dream.

Dominic was trapped on the sidelines, forced to watch and listen while she fell further and further away from him.

Nessa faced a man who watched her with greed and avarice.

"I saw you. I saw what you did to the boy."

Fear made her voice shake as she replied, "I don't know what you're talking about."

But she did. She knew. It was there in her eyes, on her face.

Dominic could taste the lie on her. But he wasn't the one she had to worry about. Locked in his dream, forced into a spectator's seat, he could do nothing but watch as she faced a man who reeked with evil. Just as he could taste the lie, Dominic could taste the evil. The greed.

"Now don't lie to me. I'm not going to tell anybody. I just thought . . . that perhaps you and I should get to know each other better. We could both benefit from such a relationship."

Dominic muttered under his breath, "Walk away. Just walk away."

As though she'd heard him, she turned on her heel and walked. But before she reached the door the man spoke again.

"It's so nice to know that little Jazzy has somebody

around who cares for her, to protect her, is willing to do anything to make sure she stays safe. You want that, don't you—for your sister to be safe?"

The dream faded—reformed.

Dominic was no longer stuck in his spectator seat. He sat on the beach, staring out at the water as the sun beat down overhead. It was high noon, but in his dream the heat of the sun was no threat to him.

She could be, though. She could be an awful threat.

For the first time in more than a year, he could touch her. She lay next to him on a towel, wearing nothing but a brightly colored triangle that barely covered her butt.

"You're getting into too much trouble," he murmured. He held a bottle of sunscreen in his hand. As he spoke, he opened it and squeezed some of it into his hand. He slicked it over her back and she arched into his touch, making a soft sound, almost like a kitten purring. "You have to stop before it's too late."

One eye opened lazily and she peered up at him. "I can handle it. I'll be fine."

"No." His lotion-slicked hands went lower, trailing over her hips, over the curve of her butt, then down to her thighs. He kneaded the muscles in her legs. "I don't think you can handle this. You don't know what you're getting into."

She squirmed around until she could turn onto her back. When his gaze dipped lower, she gave him a cheeky grin. "Don't you know who I am? Trust me, I can handle this."

Dominic shook his head. *Focus*, he told himself. *Focus on something other than the fact that she's lying here with those beautiful breasts bare. On something other than the fact that she's all but naked.*

It wasn't easy. His cock swelled—ached. His fingers itched, longing to reach out and touch her. And his mouth watered—longing to taste. He realized he was lowering his head to do just that, and he swore, stiffening as he pulled away.

"You only think you can handle this. You don't know what you're getting into—because if you did, you never would've started down this road."

Nessa smiled at him and reached for his hand. "Must we talk now? I can think of so many things that would be far more fun than *talking*." As she spoke, she brought his hand to her breast. Then she reached out and curled a hand around his neck, drawing him closer. "Come to me . . . kiss me. It's been too long since we were together like this . . . I feel so empty without you."

"This isn't a good idea." Even to his ears, the muttered words sounded halfhearted at best. He let her pull him lower.

His fangs throbbed in their sheaths, but he didn't let them emerge. Carefully, he used the straighter, blunter human teeth, raking them across her soft, sun-warmed flesh. She tasted like coconut lotion and woman—sweet, so sweet. Groaning against her, he sucked one pink, swollen nipple into his mouth.

Beneath him, she whimpered and arched up, pressing herself closer. "Don't be silly. I think it's a fine idea." She pulled him over her, her hands strong and certain.

As she pushed his swimming trunks down over his ass, he caught the strings of her bikini bottom and tore them. She laughed against his mouth, breathless. "Yes . . . now you see, this is much better than talking."

Dominic growled and slanted his mouth over hers. He ached to press his mouth to her neck, pierce her flesh and feed from her as he sank his cock into her body. But he didn't.

She reached between them and caught his rigid flesh, stroking him with a teasing, light touch. He crowded against her, trapping her hand between them as he nudged the head of his cock against her slick, wet heat.

"A lovely thing about dream sex," she murmured. "We won't get sand everywhere."

"Quit talking now." He nipped her lower lip and caught her hands, guiding them over her head. "Open for me, Nessa . . . open . . ."

She brought her knees up, hugging them to his hips. As he pushed inside, she whimpered in her throat. "Faster. Harder. More."

"No." He brushed his mouth against hers and began

to retreat, pulling back bit by bit, and then surging inside her. She was tight, so tight around him, her silken tissues caressing and squeezing him even as she resisted him. She whimpered in her throat.

"Shhh . . ."

He trailed his lips over her neck, biting her gently, just above her pulse. She shuddered, pressed closer. The taste of his own blood filled his mouth—a warning. His fangs slid lower but before he could pierce her flesh, he tore his mouth away.

Her legs twined around his hips, and she arched, rubbing herself against him. "Please don't leave me . . ." she begged. "Promise you won't leave. Let's just stay here . . . always."

Her desperate plea tore through him, like a poison blade, leaving pain and death in its wake. What he wouldn't give to be able to make that promise, to know he could keep it. "Dreams don't last forever," he whispered against her lips. "But one day, I will find you. Once I find you, I won't lose you again."

He ran a hand down her side, cupped her breast. Gently, he pinched her nipple, rubbed it back and forth between his finger and thumb. Kissing a path from her mouth down to her swollen flesh, he worked his arm beneath her, locking her lower body in place.

He sucked on her nipple, drawing it deep, pressing it against the roof of his mouth with his tongue. Under the fragile shield of her skin, he could scent her blood, feel it coursing through her veins. He shuddered, trembled, as he fought the urge to mark her, to bite her, to bind her to him.

Her nails tore across his back. The sharp, quick sting brought a harsh groan to his lips.

Nessa caught his face between her hands. She rubbed her thumb over his lower lip. From under her lashes, she watched him. "You're holding back. Please don't hold back . . . not here, not with me. I want everything, everything you are, everything within you."

She didn't know what she was asking. But then it was

just a dream . . . right? Swearing, he fisted a hand in her hair and pulled, angling her chin up and to the side, baring her neck. He scraped her skin lightly with his fangs. Reaching down with his free hand, he cupped her ass, canting her hips up. He drove into her hard, fast.

She screamed.

Dominic twisted his hips, rubbing his body against her right . . . there. Her scream died abruptly. She bucked in his arms, thrashed and whimpered.

This time, when he tasted his own blood, he didn't pull back. His fangs dropped and he pierced her flesh, just as she started to come. As her blood flooded into him, he emptied himself into her.

I T was nearing sunset. Dominic dreaded it—once the sun set, he'd waken and the dream would end.

Already his body tried to wake him, but he didn't want to leave the dream. Pulling her closer, he nuzzled her neck. "Tell me you'll be careful."

"I'm always careful." She tipped her head back and smiled at him.

"No, you're not. If you were careful, you wouldn't be in the trouble you're in right now."

Golden brows drew low over her eyes and she scowled at him. "You keep telling me about this trouble, but I'm telling you, I'm fine."

Feeling cold, Dominic pushed away from her arms and sat up. He stared out at the ocean, watching as the setting sun painted it a thousand shades of gold. "You're not fine. You killed somebody the other day—you *wanted* the blood."

But she acted as though she didn't hear him. She trailed a hand over his back, and Dominic couldn't help but remember the phantom pain of the knife piercing his flesh—right where she touched. "You seem so real."

"I am real," he said quietly, cupping her face. "I am real. And stop changing the subject. You need to be careful."

She rolled her eyes and asked, "What are you so afraid

of? I'm more than capable of taking care of myself. What has you so worried?"

He shook his head and whispered, "*You* have me so worried. I'm terrified . . . scared I'm going to lose you before I even find you."

"So real," she murmured again, stroking his face. "If you're real, then where are you? How I can find you?"

He reached around and caught her arm, pulling her into his lap. Nuzzling her neck, he murmured vaguely, "Tell me where *you* are."

"I asked you first." With a devilish grin on her lips, she straddled him and linked her arms around his neck. "Tell me your name."

"Tell me you'll be careful," he countered.

She opened her mouth, but even as she started to speak, she faded away.

Dominic awoke in the next second, jerking upright on the couch in the empty hotel room.

Alone.

"So . . . do we have a deal, Ms. Wakefield?"

Morgan wanted to tell the man to shove it. She wanted to turn on her heel and walk, keep walking. She'd find Jazzy and the two of them could disappear.

Peter Sanders smiled, as though he knew every thought running through her head. "I wonder what Social Services would think, you taking care of your baby sister, and no idea where your mother is. She's only fifteen. You're not her legal guardian."

"It's so good of you to be concerned for her welfare," Morgan said scathingly.

Peter shrugged. "Tell me, did your mother say anything before she disappeared? Did she run off with one of her johns?"

A sharp pain twisted through Morgan's head—for one second, she could see her mother, superimposed over her vision. She was laughing, and in one hand, she held a bloody knife.

Then it was over.

With a lazy shrug, Morgan replied, "I have no idea where she is. And I don't really care. I can take better care of Jazzy, anyway."

Peter tapped a finger on the arm of his chair. "You'll have a hard time doing that once the state gets a look at you. You never graduated from high school. You don't have a job." He smirked and added, "Although I suppose you can put robbery down as your sole source of income. That will impress them."

Then he leaned forward. The smile on his face was cruel, cold. "She'd be taken away from you. And that's just the best case scenario. Things I could do . . . things much, much worse. Your sister is a pretty girl. She still has that look of innocence—so young, so fresh. She might even be a virgin."

Fear wrapped a cold fist around her heart. She crossed her arms over her chest, fisting her hands so tight her nails bit into her palms and drew blood. "Don't even think about it," Morgan murmured. "Don't."

Satisfied that he'd made his point, Peter pointed to the chair across from his. "Have a seat, Morgan. We'll talk business."

CHAPTER 13

"Y OU can't be serious."
Morgan stood in front of the bathroom mirror as she finished weaving her hair into a tight braid. She'd taken a nap, but she still felt groggy, half-sick, completely exhausted.

She definitely didn't feel up to facing Peter Sanders again.

In the back of her mind, she heard a voice murmur, *Walk away. Just walk away.*

Disoriented, she shoved it aside and looked at the mirror, meeting her sister's gaze in the reflection. Jazzy stood behind her, a worried, angry look on her face.

"Look, I know you don't remember a lot of things. Or *anything*," she mumbled under her breath. "So you're going to have to trust me on this. Peter Sanders is bad news. Very. Bad. News."

Jazzy took a deep, unsteady breath. "We have to leave. *Now.* The bastard has people all over the place who feed him information, but if we get out now, we might have half a chance."

"We're not leaving," Morgan said.

"Damn it, Morgan. You can't work for him."

Ignoring the cold slippery ball of fear in her belly, Morgan said, "I'm not working for him. I'm working *with* him. We have similar goals. This is more a partnership than anything else."

Jazzy shook her head. "Yeah, I can just guess what sort of similar goals you have. Sanders wants to get rid of all the dealers who don't work for him. And he thinks you can do it."

That cold, slippery ball expanded.

"What the hell happened today?" Jazzy demanded. "You need to tell me."

Morgan reached up, stroked a hand down Jazzy's hair. "Honey, please don't worry about this. I'm going to take care of you."

Jazzy knocked Morgan's hand away. Fury glinted in her eyes and her voice all but shook as she said, "I'm not the one who needs to be taken care of right now. I've been taking care of myself ever since you left. You just disappeared, remember? Disappeared and left me alone. You don't actually think our mother gave a damn, do you? I wanted to eat, then I had to find food, had to buy it or steal it. I needed clothes? It was up to me to get them. I don't *need* to be taken care of. Hell, I'm not the one getting ready to go work *with* Sanders." She said it so scathingly, it almost hurt to hear the words. "You're the one who needs a damn caretaker."

Morgan closed her eyes. The pain in her head exploded, lancing throughout her body, spiraling through her chest.

Remnants of a forgotten dream whispered to her from her subconscious.

You don't know what you're getting into.

You have to stop now before it's too late.

A low, warm voice, masculine and rough, familiar but not. Hands stroking over her body. Dark velvet eyes, full of concern and worry.

Forcing her eyes to open, she stared at her sister. Haltingly, she said, "Jazzy, I'm sorry, but I don't have a choice." She licked her lips and shifted restlessly on her feet.

Finally, she took a deep breath and made herself look her sister square in the eyes. "You were right to have a bad feeling about Hedges. I did kill him. And I don't know how, but Sanders saw me. He didn't say outright just what he saw, but he saw too much. Now he knows what I can do. I have to work with him. He's not giving me a choice."

Jazzy blinked. The warm flush of anger faded from her face, leaving her pale. Under her breath, she muttered, "I knew it." She backed out of the bathroom, but she didn't leave. Instead, she paced the narrow hallway, her hands jammed in her back pockets. "Damn it. I knew it."

A minute passed, and then she stopped. Her face was still ashen, and there was fear in her eyes, but her face was set in stubborn lines. "We'll leave. That's all there is to it— we will just leave. Yeah, he'll be looking for that, but it's not like we can't give him the slip. He doesn't know what all we can do. We can get away."

"If I try to leave, he's going to hurt you. I'm not risking you." She caught her sister's arm, tugged her close. Slinging an arm over her sister's narrow shoulders, she touched her brow to Jazzy's. "We'll be okay. I'll figure a way out of this. But you have to trust me."

Jazzy backed away. She stared at Morgan with cold, distrusting eyes. "I already knew a way out of this—we don't get into trouble to begin with. If you had listened to me, if you had trusted me, we wouldn't be in this mess."

The bitch of it all? Jazzy was completely right.

I T was late. After one. The streets of St. Augustine, Florida, were mostly empty.

Dominic was exhausted—bone-deep exhaustion, the kind brought on by stress, heartache and worry.

Where was she?

In another few hours, he'd have to call it a night. There was a Hunter safe house in St. Augustine and he'd be bunking there for however long he was here. No more hotels, thank God. At least not for a few days.

The good news about the safe house—he'd been able to arrange to have his bike brought in, too. It had been waiting for him when he got into town late last night—or rather, early this morning. He'd traded the car Malachi had loaned him for his bike. Lindsey had taken the car off his hands. He had his bike and he'd fed.

He should have been good to go, but he was drained and dragging and so damned frustrated.

As tired as he was, though, he wasn't turning in yet. Not yet. Had to keep his mind busy, had to keep from thinking. Worrying. Wanting.

He kept to the shadows as he prowled the streets. Some of the bars were still open, the smells of tobacco smoke and alcohol mingling with the night air. He blocked those out, relying on his ears and instincts for now.

Those instincts were screaming at him right now, clawing. He felt as though he was being jerked in a dozen directions all at once. He just couldn't figure out which was the right way to go. So he walked. Gradually the sounds of the night life faded, the pulsing rhythm of music slowly replaced by the sounds of the night.

He could hear breathing. The occasional snore. The soft buzz of music coming from a radio. And infomercials—the cure for insomniacs everywhere.

The air cleared as well, the stink of cigarette smoke replaced by the salty tang of the ocean.

He breathed it in, checking.

He scented no blood, no fear, no violence.

Nothing.

And still, he felt something calling him. Pulling at him.

He was so focused on that, at first he didn't recognize the familiar roar of the motorcycle cruising down the street. *His* motorcycle—son of a bitch. His bike—that bike he'd put together himself, over a period of three damn years, and somebody was trying to steal it?

He took off at a quick run, swearing under his breath. He caught sight of black paint, silver chrome—and a petite form perched upon his bike, waiting nonchalantly at a stop-light, like she hadn't a care in the world.

You're about to have a fucking care, he thought. The signal turned green and he put on an extra burst of speed, closing his hand around the leather collar of her jacket just before she could take off. She whipped around—fast.

But she wasn't vampire fast. He caught her fist in his hand and focused the weight of his gaze on her face.

She wore his helmet—a safety-conscious little thief. It was too damned big for her. Behind the visor he glimpsed blue green eyes, now wide with terror.

Young eyes. Young kid, he realized. *Just a scared kid.*

A scared kid who stole my bike.

Then he caught a familiar scent on her skin.

Very familiar.

His instincts, already kicked into overdrive, went on red alert, screaming.

It took less than a second for him to make a decision.

"You're going to scoot back," he ordered, flatly.

Those blue green eyes took on a glazed, glassy appearance. Docile as a lamb, she scooted back.

Dominic mounted the bike in front of her and took off.

Low in his gut, anticipation began to bloom.

Anticipation that bled away into apprehension.

He smelled something in the air now . . . blood. Death. And power.

THE blood.

Thick and slick.

The power of it sang in her veins and Morgan almost went to her knees, sick with the knowledge of what she'd done. It hadn't been intentional . . . but it didn't matter.

His energy, his life force now buzzed inside her. No remnant of her lingering weakness remained. Physically, she felt strong—invincible.

She also felt like a murderer.

The door opened. She didn't have to look up to know who it was.

Morgan stared at the blood staining her hands and then looked up at Sanders. "I thought I was supposed to be helping you take care of 'business' competitors."

The man who lay dead at her feet wasn't a competitor. He'd worked for Sanders, too.

And his blood was on her hands, her soul. Literally. Figuratively as well.

Standing in the doorway, Peter tried to look surprised. Tried, but failed. There was satisfaction in his eyes. "That was our agreement, yes." He eyed the broken, bloodied body and then shifted his gaze to her. "What happened?"

As if you don't know, she thought bitterly. Shouldering past him, she walked down the narrow, dimly lit hallway until she came to the bathroom. She'd taken the time to walk around earlier, after she'd "reported" for her first day on the job.

She knew every exit in the building, although at the time, she hadn't been sure she'd be able to make it out of this dirty hell, even if she had to.

She could do it now. Hell, with all the energy churning inside her, she could *make* her own exit. If it came to it, that was exactly what she'd do, once she knew Sanders didn't have any sort of contingency plan that involved Jazzy.

Jazzy . . . the girl was the only thing keeping her here now. Were there men watching the girl even know? Possibly. Hell. *Likely*, knowing that bastard Sanders. Jazzy—she had to think about Jazzy, make sure she was safe. Whatever that took, and then they'd get the hell out of this place, away from here.

She wished she'd listened to her. Man, she really, really wished she'd listened.

She scrubbed the blood from her hands, and even when it was gone, she kept scrubbing. She might have scrubbed her hands raw if Sanders hadn't come into the little bathroom behind her. Turning off the water, she whirled around and narrowed her eyes at him. "So did you get your rocks off, watching that?"

His thin-lipped mouth curled into a smile.

If a snake could smile, it would look like that, she decided. Sanders was a snake from head to toe.

A snake . . . idly, she wondered if snakes could smell fear, taste it. Looking into his flat, lifeless gaze, she decided *this* snake could. Throttling down the nausea, Morgan returned his stare without flinching. Deep inside, she felt sick at what she'd done. She was terrified of the line she had crossed. Horrified.

But she didn't let it show. She couldn't. Sanders already knew her biggest weakness—Jazzy. She wasn't going to give him any more ammunition to use against her.

Giving him a cold smile, she asked, "So. Are you going to tell me what that was about?"

"I was about to ask you the very same question. You killed one of my men."

"If you didn't want him dead, you wouldn't have sent him after me. Or maybe I should say, if you cared whether he lived or died, you wouldn't have sent him after me."

"What makes you think I sent him after you? What purpose would that serve?"

"You did it. I know," she told him, her voice flat, emotionless. She studied his face, the cunning, measuring look in his eyes. "You were testing me."

Sanders inclined his head. "A wise man knows his tools, his weapons."

Tools. Weapons—

She'd been fucking *used* . . . And even though she'd suspected it, it pissed her off. As she stared at Sanders, the rage inside her began to pulse, growing and throbbing, burning away the lingering cobwebs left by weeks of exhaustion and weakness.

Blood roared in her ears. Her head began to pound. But she didn't let it show.

The bastard—using, conniving, *murdering* bastard. He

thought to use her, did he . . . the fool didn't know who he was dealing with—

Vaguely, she realized she was smiling at him.

She was talking to him.

"That doesn't quite answer my question, does it? I suppose that means wisdom isn't your forte because if it was, you would know precisely what you're dealing with, dear."

She *sounded* nothing like herself. Her voice was cool, confident, taunting.

And not exactly . . . American.

She felt nothing like herself—she felt strong, certain and clear-headed. It wasn't from the blood, though. In fact, she felt *too* strong. The power of blood couldn't do this. She couldn't siphon this much energy even if she slaughtered two hundred people. This kind of power didn't come from blood.

It flooded her with more than just strength. It flooded her with purpose and for the first time in *weeks*, she felt *right*. She felt like she was who she was *meant* to be.

As she went to go past him, he caught her arm, his fingers digging into her flesh, tight and merciless. It would leave a mark. He dipped his face low and sneered at her. "I think perhaps you've gotten it wrong. You're the clueless one. The man you killed—his brother works for me, too. Shall I send him to fetch your sister?"

Jerking away, she glared at him. The power flooded her—it felt like it was everywhere. *Everywhere.*

She didn't have to look to the blood to find it. It pulsed, breathed, sang in the air around her . . . hers for the taking. She'd felt weak for so long, but no longer. That power danced within her, shimmered in the air around her and flowed in the ground beneath her feet.

Where did it come from?

She didn't know. She didn't care. Her hand clenched. Power flexed. And she watched as Peter Sanders went white, gasping for air. He clawed his neck. Although she didn't touch him, she could somehow feel his hands. She could feel his neck under her fingers. She could feel his heart racing as he struggled to breathe.

"You will leave my sister alone." She pulled back on her power and listened as he sucked in a desperate breath of air. Then she started to choke him again. Without even touching him.

Manipulating the elements, she realized. She could do that—kill without even touching him. It wouldn't even weaken her.

The knowledge awoke the Leviathan within her, a great hulking beast, hungry for more power, for more blood.

No . . . a voice whispered in the back of her mind. *You mustn't.*

He deserves it! she thought. *He threatened Jazzy, used me. Why shouldn't I kill him?*

Oh, it's not the killing him that's the problem. You may well have to. But you cannot feed on the blood—don't go down that road again. You don't want that evil inside you and you don't need that power.

That was true . . . she *didn't* need the extra boost. She already had power. It sang inside her veins, erotic, pure and *hers*. Hers, not stolen.

"You will not touch the girl." She stared into Sanders's eyes. "Do we have an understanding?"

She jerked the Leviathan back under control, refusing to let it reach for that blood. Cutting off the flow of power, she let Sanders breathe.

"You stupid little cunt," he rasped. "You don't want to fuck with me."

She gave him a cool smile. "Again, you are clueless."

In the back of her mind, she suspected she might have to kill this man. But not yet. Jazzy had been right—they should have just left. They would. As soon as she made sure this goon didn't have people watching over her sister, as soon as she could make the plans, they were leaving.

I N the back of her mind, Jazzy could still think.

She couldn't move.

Couldn't talk.

Couldn't even turn her head to look around.

But she could still think.

All she could think, though, was, *Jazzy, you are in so much trouble.*

She still didn't understand why she'd taken the bike. She'd been prowling around, looking for a car to boost. Something old and plain, something that wouldn't attract attention.

The shining black-and-chrome Harley did nothing but attract attention.

She knew that.

Getting noticed had been at the bottom of her list of things to do. But she'd gotten noticed, and now she was in hot water.

As the man slowed his bike to a stop, she silently amended, *Scalding water.*

Though it was dark, she recognized the area. The pristine sand was dotted here and there with big, luxurious houses. This was where the money lived. Some were summer homes, while others belonged to the locals. The locals with money, of course.

This guy wasn't a local. She didn't know how she knew that, but she did.

He climbed off the bike first. It should have been awkward with her still perched behind him, but he made it look easy. He turned to face her, the watery moonlight illuminating his face. Fuck, his eyes—were they glowing?

"Get off the bike."

And just like that, she could move. She climbed off. Awesome. She could move. Now . . . could she run?

Fuck. No. The only damn thing she could do was fucking *stand* there, with every muscle in her body frozen, like a slab of ice.

Her mind was playing tricks on her. Or maybe the light. His eyes weren't glowing.

She needed to get away,

You don't have a chance.

Didn't matter—she wasn't going to just make it easy for him to do . . . *Oh, shit, I'm in so much trouble.*

For one brief second, she let herself think about Morgan. But Morgan couldn't help her—her sister was so screwed up in the head, had been, ever since she'd come home.

It was a miracle Morgan hadn't gotten herself killed.

There was no way she could count on her sister now. If she wanted to get out of this mess, she'd have to do it herself.

Run, her brain commanded.

But her body wouldn't respond.

Him. It had something to do with him.

He pointed toward the house. "Head up the stairs."

Once more, light flashed in his eyes. No, it was like the light flashed *behind* his eyes. And even though all she wanted to do was run, she realized her body was responding to his command. Again. She was walking up the stairs with him following close behind.

The door swung closed behind him and he flicked on a light. She flinched against it, lifting a hand to shield her eyes. Or rather, that was what she tried to do. But she couldn't move a muscle. Couldn't even blink voluntarily, she realized.

He came around to stand in front of her. "You can move." His eyes glowed, and she felt an odd little *push* on her brain. "But you will not scream. You will not try to run."

Like hell. She nodded—then stopped when she realized she could nod. "What are you doing? How can you do that?"

He shrugged. "Doesn't matter. You won't remember it in a few minutes anyway."

"Yeah? What are you going to do—hypnotize me?"

A faint smile curled his lips. "You got it on the first try. Smart girl."

Hypnotize . . .

"That is a bunch of bullshit." She sneered at him, even as some small voice of common sense screamed at her not to make him mad.

"Really? Don't you think it's kind of strange that you haven't wanted to run away?"

"Oh, I want to, believe me. I just . . ." *Can't.*

Swallowing, she looked away from him. She needed to get out of here. Why in hell had she boosted *that* bike?

"Relax. I'm just going to ask you a few questions. I won't hurt you." She felt that weird little push again, but it didn't seem so strong.

Jazzy snorted, careful to keep from looking at him. His voice was soothing, compelling. She *wanted* to look at him. Wanted to answer his questions. Wanted to relax, even to trust him.

But when she wasn't looking at him, it was easier to ignore.

Again, she felt something pushing against her mind.

"Look at me."

She kept her gaze focused on the window in the far wall. It faced out over the water and she could see the silvery glow of moonlight dancing on the surface. *Good. Just don't look at him. Good.*

Again, he ordered, "*Look at me.*"

The push on her brain was harder this time and she flinched.

Then, abruptly, it stopped. "Huh. You got a natural resistance."

From the corner of her eye, she slid him a quick glance. Then she focused on the window again. She heard him breathing—*Okay, really weird now. Is he smelling me?*

"You're a witch."

He said it so calmly, his voice so matter-of-fact. Shocked, Jazzy nearly looked him in the eyes, but quickly stopped herself. *"What?"*

He shrugged. "You smell like magic." His lashes lowered, shielding his eyes. "It would make my job a lot easier if you didn't have a natural resistance."

"What job?" She stared at him, forgetting that she didn't want to meet his eyes. "What do you mean I *smell* like magic?"

"You just do. As to the job, I'm looking for somebody. And I think you know who she is."

"Really." She gave him a sugary sweet smile. "Do you smell her, too?"

His nostrils flared. A strange look entered his eyes. Goose bumps broke out over her arms. The air around them felt tight, hot. Then he looked away and the moment was broken.

"Yes, as a matter of fact, I do."

It took all of her self-control not to gape at him. Mustering up as much bravado she could, she sauntered past him and flopped down on the couch situated just under that big picture window. "Well, I really don't know what to tell you. Whoever it is you're looking for? I don't know her—can't help you."

"Now, see, I haven't even told you who I'm looking for." A lopsided smile curled his lips and he shook his head. "How do you know you don't know who she is? I haven't even asked you about her yet."

S CARED *little rabbit*, Dominic thought. But he had a feeling she would bite when she was cornered.

He didn't want to frighten her, at least not any more than he had to. Settling into the chair across from the couch, he said, "She looks quite a bit like you. A few years older. And her magic is stronger."

Fear flashed through her eyes. The scent of that fear filled the air around them—sickly sweet. But she gave him another one of those cocky smiles, careful not to meet his eyes as she shrugged. "Magic . . . like, what . . . hocus-pocus crap? Man, you are nuts. That shit isn't real."

"Really. That's weird, because I smell it all over you." Drumming his fingers on his thigh, he asked, "Where is she?"

"I don't know who you're talking about."

"Liar." He leaned back in his chair and stared at her.

After thirty seconds, she started to squirm.

After two minutes, she came up off the couch and started to pace. "You can't keep me here."

Dominic lifted a brow. "You sound awful certain about that."

"This is called *kidnapping*. It is *illegal*."

"So is stealing a Harley," Dominic replied with a grin.

She gaped at him. "You're comparing taking a stupid bike to kidnapping a person?"

Dominic shrugged.

"You know what? You're right, I did steal your bike. Call the cops."

She made a good bluff. He studied her face, her eyes. She didn't look worried or afraid. But he could smell her fear. "I'm not going to call the cops. You don't belong in jail. You're a scared kid who made a dumb-ass mistake. You don't need to go to jail for that. But I do want you to help me. I need to find the woman. You know who she is. Tell me."

"I don't know who you're talking about," she whispered. But she wouldn't look at him.

The thick miasma of fear grew stronger, now tinged with the acrid, bitter sense of anger. "You do know who I'm talking about. I get the feeling she's in trouble. Am I right about that?"

Her eyes flicked his way and then darted off. "I don't know . . ." Abruptly, she sagged to the floor, drawing her knees to her chest. Folding her arms, she rested them on her upraised knees and buried her face. Her shoulders jerked with a suppressed sob.

Despair, now. Dominic came off the chair and hunkered down next to her. *Poor kid.* He didn't touch her. She stiffened, glancing at him from the corner of her eye. "I know you don't want to believe this, but I'm not going to hurt you. I don't hurt kids. I don't hurt anybody, unless I have to."

She sniffled. "If you're not going to hurt me, then why am I here?"

"I already told you that. I need to find her. You know who she is. Help me."

"Why should I?"

Ahhh, progress. At least she wasn't pretending ignorance anymore. That was the first step.

"Tell me so I can help her—before it's too late." Settling on the floor next to her, he said, "I get the feeling you care about her. You don't want her hurt. She's gotten mixed up in some bad things. Hasn't she?"

With an unsteady sigh, she nodded. "*Bad things* doesn't quite cover it. She's in a world of trouble, and I don't know how to help her. Why should I think you'd be able to? I don't know *you*. She doesn't know *you*. So why should you help us?"

"Because I have to." He held out a hand.

She gave him a suspicious look, staring at his hand as though it were covered with some unnamed, unidentified matter. Dominic cocked a brow. "You can read a lie."

Now, her eyes widened, and she scooted back a few feet on her butt. "How did you know that?"

"Because you're a witch. Witches can read lies. The same way I can smell them. The same way I can feel them."

"*Smell* a lie? What in the hell are you, a bloodhound?"

Dominic grinned at her. "Nope. What you see is what you get." *Mostly.* "You really do need to trust me. I get the feeling she's running out of time." *And so are you.*

If she didn't tell him what he needed to know, Dominic was going to get somebody down here that would make her. He really didn't want to do that.

Under that cocky bravado, she was just a kid. A scared kid with old eyes. Tired eyes. He'd say she was fifteen at the most, but she had done things in her life nobody should ever have to do. Lived through things nobody should ever have to live through.

It had made her cynical and very wary.

She'd had enough things forced on her. He didn't want to add to it.

She jammed her hands into the pockets of her worn jeans. "What's your name?"

"Dominic. You?"

"Jasmine. Everybody calls me Jazzy."

Once more, Dominic held out his hand. "It's a pleasure to meet you, Jazzy."

"Whatever." But she placed her hand in his.

"I won't hurt you—or her. But you have to help me find her."

Jazzy shook her head. "I have no reason to trust you. No reason at all." Then she tugged her hand away, tucking it back in her pocket. "So why do I feel like I'm supposed to?"

"Instinct. I can help."

She sighed, her thin shoulders rising and falling. Thin, too thin. She had the look of somebody rarely able to eat her fill. "Do you know her?"

"Sort of. But you know her better. You can help me help her."

Morose, Jazzy just stared at him. "I don't know her so well anymore. She's been gone a while. Maybe I never really knew her." She kicked at the plush carpet with the toe of her worn-out shoe. Shooting him a glance from under her bangs, she asked, "How come you're so sure you can help if you don't really know her?"

"I don't know . . . I just know I need to find her." He shook his head, hoping she wouldn't press. "It's too complicated to explain. We would need all night. Hell, we might need all of tonight, tomorrow night, plus the next five nights. And you'd probably want me to call a shrink. But we don't have that kind of time. *She* doesn't have that kind of time." He paused for a beat and then asked, "Does she?"

"Fuck, no." She flopped down on the couch and stared at him, her blue green eyes shadowed and worried. "Morgan's my sister. She thinks she's protecting me. But she's going to end up in a world of trouble . . . and probably drag me down with her, if I hang around. *Which* I am *not* going to do. I love her, but I'm not gonna stand around and watch her do this."

"Do what?" Dominic forced the question out past a tight throat. It was a good thing he didn't need to breathe—also that he didn't have much of a heartbeat anymore.

Morgan. She'd called her Morgan. For some reason, that name sent a fucking cold chill straight down his spine.

"Work for *him*—Peter Sanders. He owns these streets . . .

and once he decides he doesn't want her around anymore, he'll have one of his men kill her." Once more, Jazzy buried her face against her knees. "I just got my sister back. I don't want to lose her again."

N EED warred with duty.

Dominic couldn't leave Jazzy here alone. She'd take off. He could see it in her eyes. That would be bad news all around, for him, for Jazzy, and for . . . Nessa.

Hell. He didn't even know if she *was* Nessa. His gut said Nessa was *here*, and he could scent her all over this kid. But the kid kept calling her Morgan.

Morgan. Who in the hell was Morgan? The name had to mean something, otherwise it wouldn't have turned his blood to ice. Storming out to the deck, he pulled his cell phone out and made a call to Excelsior.

Kelsey's voice was bright and clear, despite the fact that it was two a.m. "Do you ever sleep?" Dominic demanded.

"Oh, sure. When people let me. But people have this annoying habit of calling at two in the morning," she said, her voice droll.

"Sorry. Question . . . does the name Morgan mean anything to you?"

Her silence said everything.

It stretched on for . . . ages. It was probably only a few seconds, but it seemed to take forever. Finally, her voice soft and worried, she asked, "Why?"

"Just answer the question."

"Yes. It means something. Bad news. Now answer my question. *Why?*"

"I don't know. Who in the hell is Morgan?"

There was a soft murmur—Dominic recognized Malachi's voice and he swore. "Damn it, one of you answer me."

Kelsey sighed. "Dom, it's complicated. This was one of things Malachi wanted to talk to you about before you left, but you weren't in the mood to wait, and frankly, it didn't seem to be anything you needed to know."

"Obviously, it would seem different. Who in the hell is Morgan?"

"She was a witch that Nessa fought a few years ago. One who nearly killed Nessa—hell, we thought she *did* kill her. She was a dream thief, and she used blood magic. She was bad, bad news, all the way around."

Blood magic. That bit, he pretty much understood. "What's a dream thief?"

"Rare talent. Kind of a psychic vampire. It's a witch who can slip into a person's dreams and suck their life force out of them while they dream. They can drain a person dry—even kill them." Kelsey's voice was heavy and tired. "Like I said, bad news."

"But Morgan is dead, right? Dead, buried?"

"Well . . ."

Just when Dominic thought things couldn't get any stranger. But things could always get stranger—always. Kelsey managed to break it down to the bare bones, explaining in under ten minutes, and even though she'd kept it simple and concise, his head was spinning when he hung up the phone.

So Morgan's *body* wasn't dead. Nessa's was.

Morgan's soul was gone, but Nessa's *wasn't*.

Son of a bitch, what in the hell was going on?

All the questions tumbled through his mind, but before they could take over, he shoved them all aside, because in the end, none of them really mattered. He had the answer he needed—he knew who Morgan was, or who she had been, at least.

Whether or not she was truly dead, he didn't know, but that didn't matter now, not to him.

No, what mattered to him was the fact that his woman was just miles away and in more trouble than she possibly knew. That was one thing he was sure of.

He came back inside and started to pace, turning things over in his head. From the corner of his eye, he watched Jazzy. She sat on the couch, pretending not to watch him watching her.

"Do you know where I can find her?" Dominic asked, coming to a stop. He turned to face her, and once more, he caught sight of the fear in her eyes. It was enough to turn his stomach. She was just a kid. The last thing Dominic had ever wanted to do was frighten a kid.

She shrugged, her blue green eyes meeting his for just a second before she looked away again. "No, not exactly. But I probably have a rough idea."

"A rough idea is fine," Dominic assured her. All he needed to do was get close enough to her, and he'd be able to track her down like a bloodhound.

Or a ravenous vampire.

"You . . . you're not going to try to go after her alone, are you?" She shook her head and said, "You can't do that. Sanders is a fucking psycho. I've heard that he kills people just because they looked at him wrong."

"Sounds like a paragon." Dominic smiled humorlessly.

Jazzy didn't look amused. "I'm serious. You seem to think I'm kidding around. But I'm not. He's bad news."

"I get that." Dominic wished he could reassure her. But he wasn't about to tell her some drug dealer and his lackeys just weren't much of a threat to him. She'd want to know why. He wasn't going to explain that part to her.

"There's a club." Jazzy sighed and tucked her hair back behind her ear. "It's closer to downtown, in an older building. His club is on the main floor. The second level for private areas." She curled her lip and added, "You can probably figure out what those private areas are for." She licked her lips and looked away. "That's where he keeps his girls."

Dominic didn't need to ask what the girls were for, either. He knew.

Jazzy rubbed her hands together, staring at the floor. "Now you need to understand, I've never been in any of his places. I don't like him. I keep my distance. But I do hear things. Last I heard, Sanders had a place on the third floor they use for business. He doesn't like to do any business in his home—it's always at the club. And I'm pretty sure that's where Morgan met up with him."

Morgan . . .

Dominic rubbed the back of his neck, staring off into the distance.

There was some seriously weird shit going on and if he had a hope of untangling it, he needed all the information he could get—starting with whatever this kid knew.

CHAPTER 14

Less than an hour later, Dominic was crouched in the alley outside the club. He had found it with no trouble. It had been harder for him to walk away from the kid than it had been to find this place—he hadn't wanted to leave her there, but he hadn't had much choice.

I'll take care of your sister, kid. Just trust me. Trust me and wait here, he'd told her.

She didn't trust him, but she was still young enough to hope, to *want* to trust him. He only prayed it was enough to keep her in the house while he dealt with all the other problems.

He could feel her now . . . *his* witch. His woman. Nessa . . . It didn't matter what name she was calling herself. He knew who she was. It was *her*. That pull was back. Deep inside, he felt it tugging on him, drawing him. It no longer felt like he was being pulled in five different directions at once.

He *knew* where he was going. *Her*. He was going to her. *He could feel her.*

Adrenaline crashed through him. His body responded as

it always did to the rush of adrenaline. His fangs throbbed in their sheaths. His senses were on red alert.

Inside the building, even over the throb and pulse of music, he could hear people talking. He could hear the beating of a hundred hearts . . . more. He could smell the drugs. He could smell the sex.

And . . . son of a bitch, he could smell Jazzy.

Swearing under his breath, he rose and began to pace back down the alley. She was here. He could hear her footsteps, the erratic beat of her heart.

Should've tied her up.

He should've known she would follow him.

Furiously, he thought, contemplating possible plans, discarding them almost immediately. He wasn't going into a fight with the kid at his heels. He couldn't risk it.

Even though *she* was so close . . . so close, he had even been able to sense the familiar lavender-vanilla scent of her skin.

It flooded his senses like a drug, a thousand times more potent than any of the illegal ones being passed around inside the club. More addictive than heroine, more seductive than ecstasy.

Close . . . so close. Just a few feet away.

After all this time, she was almost close enough to touch.

He ached. Ached to hunt her down, pull her close.

But he couldn't. Not right now.

He could feel the threat in the air—sweat, fear, drugs, money. A bad, nasty combination, the kind that often ended in death. He couldn't take Jazzy in there, and he couldn't go in and hope she had the sense to keep her distance.

If she had, she would still be back at the safe house instead of slinking closer and closer.

He wouldn't risk the kid but he couldn't go in there with his attention divided, which meant he had to deal with Jazzy. Why in the *hell* couldn't she have stayed at the beach house?

She was too strong-willed. He could have tried just laying a heavy dose of mind-control on her, but as it did with many of the gifted, vampire mojo crap would wear off if he wasn't there—he'd already seen that she had a natural resistance.

He'd hoped she'd listen to him, and wasn't that a fucking mistake? Should have figured something else out.

Closing his eyes, he tested the air.

Nothing.

His eyes flew open and then narrowed. Again, he checked the air.

Nothing.

He couldn't smell her—not now.

What in the hell . . . ?

One second, he had known almost exactly where she was, how far away she was, just by her scent. He had even heard her heartbeat, her unsteady breaths.

Now it was like she had disappeared.

Couldn't smell her, couldn't hear her.

With silent movements, he made his way to the mouth of the alley. He peered down the street, searching through the shadows for her. There . . . she was right there.

A bright, blond head of hair was visible down the street now.

He could *see* her—she was still more than a quarter of a mile away, and walking slow, keeping to the shadows. But it was Jazzy.

Hissing out a breath, he withdrew back into the alley, hiding in the shadows.

Everything felt blunted.

It occurred to him that it wasn't just Jazzy. He couldn't hear much of anything over the music coming from the club.

He couldn't smell anything beyond the trash in the alley and cigarette smoke.

He was scent-blind and his ears didn't work any better than they had when he was a mortal.

A spell . . . ? Jazzy hadn't felt that powerful, but could she have done some sort of spell?

No. That didn't seem right. Magic had a feel to it.

Witches had a feel. And even though he couldn't smell her, even though he couldn't hear her, he could still feel something coming off Jazzy . . . her magic.

Whatever this was, it didn't feel like her.

An engine roared, drawing near.

Looking away from Jazzy, he glanced automatically up the street. A Mustang convertible, raven-wing black, the top down.

Dominic narrowed his eyes as the car began to slow down.

His nose and ears might not be working, but his eyes were just fine. He recognized the man behind the wheel of the car. He also recognized the pretty blonde in the seat next to him. The kid in the backseat looked vaguely familiar, too.

As the car rumbled to a stop, Dominic retreated into the shadows of the alley once more.

A door opened, and Duke Lawson climbed out.

"Shit."

Although Dominic remained in the shadows, Duke's gaze landed on him unerringly and a wide grin split his face. The shapeshifter ambled toward him.

"I don't have time for this," Dominic growled.

"Yeah, hello to you, too. Long time, no see. What am I doing here? Oh, hey, I just happened to be in the neighborhood, along with my wife and her obnoxious brat of a brother. That brat of a brother kept telling me we needed to be somewhere . . . but he wouldn't say where. Then all of a sudden, I start feeling witch. Then I feel vampire. Then I feel blood. Now I know where I'm supposed to be, and why. Here. Right here, helping your sorry ass," Duke drawled.

Dominic stared at Duke. It was the longest speech he'd ever heard out of the shapeshifter. "What?"

The car door slammed again and he glanced up, watching over Duke's shoulder as Ana approached. The tall, lanky blond at her side looked vaguely familiar . . . her brother.

A memory flashed through his mind. A few years earlier, Dominic had spent a few days at Excelsior, after Rafe had told him he was showing Master tendencies. He had met Ana there, and her brother.

Brad, his brain finally supplied. *The boy's name is Brad*. He didn't look much like a boy now. He had one vivid memory of how this boy had sent a vampire hurtling through the air with just the power of his mind.

Although Dominic's instincts still felt off, standing this close, he couldn't *not* feel the power from these three. Especially the boy.

Power all but crackled off him.

Psychic.

He met Brad's eyes and then looked at Duke. "I don't need help . . . unless you feel like kidnapping a kid witch."

Duke rubbed his jaw. "The witch I felt earlier wasn't any kid. And there was a hell of a lot of blood."

"Wrong witch—there's a kid. I need her out of the way." He reached up and rubbed his nose. Still couldn't smell much of anything . . . he was barely even aware of his own scent. "I'll handle the other witch."

Running his tongue along the edge of his teeth, he looked from Duke's face to Ana's. She gave him a strained smile. Fear and nerves danced through her eyes.

Abruptly, he remembered something else. Something he had heard about Ana back at Excelsior.

"You." He stared at her, hard. "You are the reason I can hardly smell a damn thing, the reason I can't hear much of anything beyond that fucking music."

She gave a single, jerky nod. "I'm blocking. Have to, otherwise the witch will feel Duke, and maybe me and Brad. Definitely you."

Protectively, Duke placed his body in front of her. "I told her to. You got a problem, you settle it with me."

Dominic scowled at the shapeshifter. "Hell, if you three are here to help, who in the hell am I to complain about how you do it?" Then he headed back toward the mouth of the alley, peering around the corner.

Jazzy was getting closer. In another few minutes she'd be just outside the alley.

"There is a kid coming. The witch I want you to help with. You wanna help me, you get her out of the picture. Get her someplace safe." He sighed and rubbed the back of his neck. "Hell. Just take her to Excelsior. Dump her in Kelsey's lap. Kelsey will know what to do with her."

"What about the other witch?" Duke asked.

"She's mine."

M ORGAN shivered, the mysterious confidence from ear-lier gone—along with that unending well of power.

She still had the strength she'd gotten from the blood, but the rest of it? Gone, like it had never existed, and damned if she could figure out why. She stood there, confused and shivering, while her head pounded and her heart raced.

She tried to tell herself she was just tired, cold and hungry. She tried to tell herself she just needed some sleep. But deep inside, she knew that wasn't it. Something was *wrong*. If she was honest with herself, she might admit she was afraid. But screw that. *Tired, cold and hungry* sounded so much better than *afraid*.

And her head—her head was *killing* her, like it was trying to split apart from the inside out. Those annoying whispers kept coming and going, and she'd almost give her right kidney for some peace inside her skull.

Yeah, a headache, cold, tired, hungry—much better than afraid. She'd already shown Sanders she could deal with him and she damn well knew she *could*, right? She didn't need to be afraid of *him*. He was just a two-bit, mean-ass drug dealer.

All she needed to do was get through the night and make sure he hadn't set her up and planned anything to hurt Jazzy.

One night. Make it through one night and they were out of there.

But it was a night that seemed unending.

She had spent much of the past two hours in this exact same position. Arms folded over her chest, head lowered. Listening . . . and waiting.

She didn't even know what she was waiting for but there was something . . . something big. Something inevitable.

Her skin buzzed, adrenaline crashed through her veins and for reasons she couldn't understand, she was hyper-aware of everything. Despite the loud music pulsing in the club below, it seemed like she could pick up individual voices. The mingled scents of sex, sweat and smoke flooded her head, nauseating her.

Her ears caught every little sound.

Her eyes caught every little motion.

She felt jacked-up, but she couldn't figure out why. It was almost like the other night when that nameless sensation had pulled her from her sleep and sent her hunting. Almost.

Ready . . . be ready. In the back of her mind, she heard a voice murmuring to her. *Be ready . . .*

Be ready for what . . . she didn't know.

But she was ready for whatever in the hell it was. Standing in the shadows, she waited.

Her so-called boss sat at a table with several other men. There were two doors in the room and both were guarded by men with guns. Every once in a while, Sanders would flick a glance her way. His snakelike eyes were cold with dislike.

She stared at his profile and wondered where the courage from earlier had gone. She wanted him dead. Would do it as soon as she had a chance, but that cool, calm confidence of earlier was gone, like it had never existed.

It was just a matter of hours now. Once this night was over and done, she'd be back at home, she'd make sure Jazzy was safe and they'd get the hell out of town. Just like Jazzy had said.

Rubbing the back of her neck, she glanced around the room and started to pace. Sanders gave her a narrow look and she flipped him off as she made a slow circuit around the room.

So far, she hadn't done anything other than stand around and listen to them talk. The more they talked, the edgier she got. Every second that ticked by wound her tighter and tighter.

A warning whispered through her mind as she passed by the window.

Get ready. Get ready. Not much time . . .

Morgan closed her eyes. Her muscles were tight, but as she took a deep breath, they loosened, relaxed.

Somebody was watching her—no. Not *watching. Stalking.* She felt like she had a big, fat target painted on her back, even though none of them seemed to be paying her that much attention.

One of them was, though. One of them was watching her with way too much interest.

Danger. Danger there.

Heat formed in her hands, her magic concentrating in that one spot.

Opening her eyes, she looked at the men, from one to another, until her gaze landed on one in particular.

That one . . . threat.

He was a quiet one, sitting at Sanders's left hand. He continued to watch her, and the hair on the back of Morgan's neck stood on end. A smile curled his lips and the look of it made her blood run cold. His nostrils flared and she had the ridiculous suspicion that he was *smelling* her. It must've been her imagination, but a sickly sweet odor seemed to waft from her.

You're afraid . . . he knows it. He likes it. You have to get it under control.

Morgan swallowed, her mouth painfully dry. His smile widened, revealing perfectly straight white teeth. Blood roared in her ears and reality twisted inside out. An image superimposed itself over his features—he wasn't a man.

He was a monster.

His face deformed, an elongated jaw lined with wicked, sharp teeth. Fine hair covered his features. He looked like he was caught frozen between a bad Halloween mask and a wolf on steroids.

But it wasn't what she *saw* that told her he was evil.

It was what she sensed inside him.

Pure, undiluted evil. His heart was black with it.

Her heart knocked against her ribs, and the image faded.

She was left staring at a man. A perfectly normal man, with perfectly normal features, perfectly normal smile, perfectly normal eyes . . . that *glowed*.

Morgan hissed out a breath between her teeth and retreated a step. Her back bumped into the wall. She rested her hands against it, staring into those eerily glowing eyes.

In the back of her mind, a voice spoke.

Wolf.

Then it whispered, *Be ready.*

Amusement danced across his features. Amusement . . . and hunger.

Lock it down, she told herself. *Lock it down.*

It took all her strength to look away from him. All her control not to watch him, watch and wait for the attack. Paranoia and fear bubbled inside her but she battled it down, locked it up. Feigning nonchalance, she inspected her nails, picking at a hangnail.

He continued to study her but Morgan didn't look at him.

One of the other men at the table murmured to Sanders. He replied, his voice just as quiet. Then he glanced at her, a cold, sharp smile on his face.

She held his gaze for a moment, her brow cocked. Then she resumed her study of her fingernails.

"So are you going to tell us why I'm here?"

Although she didn't look up, Morgan knew who it was. The quiet man. The man who looked at her with a monster staring out of his eyes.

"Of course, Marty. In due time," Sanders answered with a vague wave of his hand.

From under her lashes, Morgan watched as Sanders leaned back in his chair and once more focused his gaze on her. The grin on his face widened. In the pit of her stomach, a cold, hard knot settled.

"I'd like you to meet my new . . . associate," Sanders said. "Gentlemen, this is Morgan. Lovely, isn't she?"

"Yes." It was Marty who spoke. The sound of his voice made her gut clench with fear. "Is she a new toy? I don't much care to take another man's leavings, but somehow I don't think you realize what you have here." He paused and then said, "Why don't you give her to me? Let me have her and we will call our debt even."

"To the contrary, Marty, I know exactly what I have here. Shall I demonstrate?"

Morgan narrowed her eyes. "I'm not a trick pony. I don't perform on command."

"Oh, you will do exactly that." Sanders narrowed his eyes. He said nothing, but the threat was there nonetheless.

She smiled.

Sanders pushed back from the chair. Over his shoulder, he said, "Gentlemen, if you'll excuse me just a moment, I need to speak with Morgan." He caught her arm, his fingers digging into her flesh. He squeezed so tightly, she knew there would be a bruise. But she didn't make a sound and she didn't try to pull away.

She let him drag her to the corner of the room and stood there silently as he glared at her. "You will do as you're told," he said, keeping his voice low. "Or I will have your sister retrieved. You will not like what my men do to her."

Staring past him, she watched Marty. He could hear them . . . she knew it as well as she knew the color of her eyes. He could hear every word they said. Tearing her gaze from him, she looked at Sanders. "I was under the impression you want my . . . help. It's wasted having me perform like some sort of circus freak."

"I don't give a damn what impression you were under. You will do as you're told. Otherwise . . ." His voice trailed off menacingly and he reached inside his jacket, pulling out his phone. He pushed a button and held the phone to his ear. "Send Eloy up."

The door opened and one of Sanders's goons came in. He glanced at Morgan and then at Sanders.

Morgan frowned as she studied him.

Afraid. He was afraid.

Sanders met him halfway across the floor.

Again, though they kept their voices low, Morgan heard them. So did Marty. But right now, she didn't care about the weird dude with the freakishly glowing eyes.

She wasn't there, senor. I looked and looked and waited and waited. Finally, I break into the house and it's a mess—like the girl decided to get out of there in a hurry.

Jazzy. Morgan had sent a man after Jazzy, but the kid hadn't been there.

Jazzy, where are you?

But she already knew. With a deep, certain knowledge, she knew Jazzy had taken off. Torn between pride and worry, she said a quick prayer that the girl was okay.

Of course, now that Jazzy wasn't in the picture, she didn't have to play nice, either.

Cold, gleeful anticipation settled inside her. Some of it must have shown on her face, because when Sanders turned to face her, he retreated half a step.

"Where is your sister?" Peter asked gently.

"At home in bed, I would imagine." She lied through her teeth and gave him a mockery of a smile. "That is certainly where I would rather be. It's getting late. Can't we just get this over with?"

"But you see, she isn't in bed." Sanders glanced at the newcomer. "This is Eloy. I asked him to go find your sister. I thought she might like to . . . join us. But she isn't home. Tell me, where could she have gone? After all, as you said, it is rather late."

Join us. You son of a bitch.

Rage slammed into her. Heat gathered in her hands, threatened to scorch her. *Burn.* She wanted to burn him, until he was nothing but ash. A cold sweat broke out over her, but all she did was smile and shrug. "Mama never really kept us on a tight leash. Who knows where she went? She'll be home sooner or later." Then she narrowed her eyes. In a quiet, cold voice, she added, "But, you really do need to know, she isn't welcome at any party of yours. I won't tolerate it."

"*You* won't tolerate it," he echoed. A snarl twisted his face and his hand shot out, closing over her upper arm. He jerked her close and dipped his head, murmured into her ear, "You still don't get it. You still don't seem to understand— I'm the one in charge. And if I decide I want your sister here, your sister will be here. Now where is she?"

Fear roused. And with it, the hunger. The monstrous, excessive hunger . . . the Leviathan. It stirred inside her, stretching, reaching.

Feast. It wanted her to feast.

Somebody chuckled. *Marty.* She knew it without even looking. "Peter, my friend, I told you. You don't know what you have here. Give her up before somebody gets hurt."

You can't have him, Morgan thought. *He's mine.*

His blood . . . Sanders's blood.

Morgan's hands twitched. She could all but feel his blood on her flesh.

No.

She shoved the hunger inside and braced herself. Not here. Not now. If at all possible, she was never going to do that again.

Some part of her babbled in fear, "*But you need it. If you want to fight him, fight all of them, and get away so you can protect Jazzy, you need it. Take it.*"

But she didn't need it.

"Idiots," she whispered. "The both of you."

The energy, that power she'd sensed from earlier, she could feel it again, wrapping around her, warming her. Tilting her head back, she smiled at Sanders. She lifted her hand.

His eyes darted off to the side, focused on her hand. Then she closed her fingers. Inside her mind's eye, she could see the element of air, responding to her command, closing around his throat, tightening. She could feel his skin. Feel his life.

Feel his blood.

No. Forget the blood.

Sanders's breath whooshed out of him in a high, tight

wheeze. His face went red. With his back to the others, nobody else could see him. Nobody else could see that he was choking, gasping for air. His eyes wheeled off to the side. Recognizing his intent, Morgan said, "Try to get help, and I snap your neck. I can do it. You know that. You will be dead. And frankly, anything they might do to me would be worth it, just to *see* you dead. So don't push your luck." She paused, peering into his eyes. "Am I clear?"

She eased her grip on his throat.

"Yes," he wheezed out, sucking in air through his damaged throat. "Bitch."

Releasing him completely, she folded her arms over her chest. "You screwed up thinking you could control me."

Keeping half of her attention focused on him, she reached out, trying to sense Jazzy. There was nothing.

Before she could panic, though, she realized it wasn't just Jazzy she couldn't feel. She couldn't sense much of anything. Not outside this room.

Everything felt . . . muffled. But that didn't make any sense. It was almost like the instincts she counted on didn't exist. That strange sense of hyperawareness was gone. She couldn't make out anything more than the beat and pulse of the music playing downstairs and that her head was no longer choked, clogged with the stink of others.

Her belly clenched into a tight, hard knot.

For the past few weeks, her normal state of being was *weak* and *tired*. When she was in a weakened state, she couldn't sense as much. All of her energy was focused on just getting through each day . . . and resisting the hunger for more power.

She didn't feel weak or tired now so she *should* have been able to feel more, a lot more. Without understanding how, Morgan knew that when she was strong, she should be able to feel her sister. She should sense the people down in the club, the people waiting outside this room. Ten minutes ago, maybe less, she *had* been able to sense those things.

And now . . . she couldn't.

She couldn't *sense* anything. And that was wrong.

Get ready . . . get ready . . .

Aware that Sanders still watched her, she gave him a cool smile. "Other than my sister joining us, did you have any other plans for tonight? I really am getting tired."

He backed away. But distance helped him find some of bravado, restored that cocky, condescending arrogance to his eyes. "Oh, there were other things. I'm disappointed. I had such plans for you and your sister. They can wait, though. They'll hold. For now."

"They'll hold forever." Morgan bared her teeth at him. "My sister is off-limits."

Behind him, Marty laughed. "She's a cocky little bitch, isn't she?"

Morgan shifted and looked at the other man. He met her gaze, staring at her boldly. His eyes ran over her, down to her feet and then slowly back to her face, lingering at her breasts. He smiled and stroked his tongue across his lips.

It revealed those white, gleaming teeth—teeth too perfect to be real. "So, Pete, if you're so certain you know what you're up against, why don't you show us? Give us a taste." He licked his lips as he said it. "I'd certainly like a taste . . . a good one."

Morgan curled her lip at him.

Sanders opened his mouth to say something. His lips moved.

But Morgan heard nothing.

Something rolled through the air. Silent thunder. Electricity snapped, raising the hair on her arms, along the back of her neck. Adrenaline, hot and potent, crashed through her system.

All of a sudden, she could feel.

Feel everything. Vaguely, she was aware of Jazzy. The girl wasn't close. She wasn't home, but she was safe. Safe . . . and pissed off. Morgan had no more time to linger on Jazzy's state of mind, though. There was too much going on inside her head.

She was also aware of other things.

Marty—full of a voracious, violent hunger. When he'd

said *taste*, she had the sickening sensation that he had been being rather literal.

Drugs—downstairs in the club. The air was thick with the stink of it.

Blood—it clung to every soul in this room, tainting them.

And more . . . there was so much more.

Some lingering presence, a powerful source of energy that she *should* recognize, but couldn't. She felt like she should know what it was, but she didn't.

Whatever it was, it wasn't here. No . . . not it. *He.* Whoever he was, he wasn't here. He was far away. Full of energy, full of life, full of purpose. But not a threat. In her gut, she knew that.

After making that call, her mind moved on, focusing on something else, with hardly any cognizant direction from her.

Another source of energy. Another presence.

Another man.

Powerful.

Male.

And *close* . . .

Tension spiked. Energy crackled through the room, mounted. It felt like a thunderstorm . . . no. Not a storm. Something *more*. A tornado. Powerful, devastating, destructive and close.

Too close.

Marty was on his feet, his eyes darting around. That weird, eerie glow was back, and he was snarling, growling. No human throat could make that sound. *Not human, not human.*

Something buzzed in her ear and she jerked her attention away from Marty, focusing on Sanders. He stood just a few feet, glaring at her. His mouth was moving. Vaguely, she realized he was talking.

Her ears tried to process what he was saying, without success.

Of course it didn't help that she couldn't seem to really focus on him.

Somebody was coming.

Him.

The man she'd sensed.

The power.

Him . . . her tornado.

Her eyes flicked all around the room, lingered on the window. Her breath caught in her chest.

It was like she had tunnel vision—all she could see was the window. And then, she couldn't see at all as the glass exploded inward. All around her, people jumped. The men at the doors swung their guns toward the windows. Somebody shouted. Everybody was surprised.

Except Morgan and Marty.

Marty was already on the move, pulling away from the window with fluid, inhuman grace. His eyes shot to Morgan. Energy crackled inside him.

Danger. Danger.

Her mind screeched out the warning. She flexed her hand, let the heat of fire flood her. She held it at bay, watching Marty from the corner of her eye. But then, she forgot all about him. It didn't matter that everything inside her screamed that he was dangerous—deadly.

Silence fell, and her breath caught in her throat as she realized a man had come through the window. Fast . . . so fast her eyes hadn't been able to track him. He stood there, head bowed, hands closed into fists.

Sanders swore and then barked out an order.

There was an odd popping sound—the guns. The guards had shot him . . . *No!*

She stared at the floor, bracing herself to see his bullet-riddled body.

But he wasn't there.

Holy shit, where is he?

She backed against the wall, swallowing the knot in her throat as she scanned the room. There was a crack, followed by a thud. That was all she heard—she saw *nothing*.

But two of the guards lay dead on the floor, their eyes staring sightlessly at nothing, their heads at an odd angle.

He broke their necks, she realized.

There was another sickening crack, and this time, she saw just the rush of movement—a blurred shadow, a shadow that moved faster than any human possibly could.

Now all four guards were dead, leaving only Sanders and his so-called associates. Sanders stood cowering in a corner, clutching a gun in his hand.

Darkness edged in on her vision and she sucked in a breath, rubbed at her eyes. She wasn't going to pass out . . . but then she realized, it wasn't *her*.

The room was darker. Almost bathed in twilight, even though the lights blazed brilliantly overhead.

A low growl rumbled through the room, and she edged away, creeping along the wall.

Something silver flashed, caught her eye. Morgan whipped her head around. *Marty*. He shot Sanders a dark look and growled, "I told you that you didn't know what you were messing with."

He swiped out a hand—fast, so fast. Morgan just barely saw the movement. Then all she saw was the spray of blood gushing from Sanders's throat.

She sucked in a breath. What in the hell had she just seen?

"Stay the fuck away from me," she warned, lifting a hand as Marty moved across the floor toward her.

"You want to get out of this alive, you're coming with me," Marty growled.

"I don't think so." That cool, collected arrogance settled back over her shoulders, a comforting cloak. She felt like a stranger in her own skin—yet oddly . . . *whole*. "Trust me, *you* don't know what you're messing with. You might think you do, but you're wrong."

He snarled. The bones in his face rippled. He turned his head, cracking his neck. When he looked back at her his eyes were glowing again and she'd swear his teeth were longer. "Stupid little witch, you really think you can handle me? Or *him*?"

She hurled fire at him. As he jerked back to avoid it, he nearly tripped over the body at his feet.

Morgan stared at the dead man, dazed. She hadn't even seen him go down. It was the third man who'd been at the table with Sanders.

Now only two men remained, Marty and the silent fourth man. That one was just a few feet away from the door, creeping closer and closer to it and swearing in Spanish. As their gazes locked, something ugly flashed through his eyes.

"*Puta.*" He spat it out, his voice harsh with terror. He reached inside his jacket and pulled out a gun, leveled it at her. "What are you doing?"

"She isn't doing it." It was a low, rough voice . . . the sound of it was oddly familiar, and it sent a shiver down her spine. "I am."

Marty swore. He shot her a narrow look and said, "We can't survive this if we fight each other. Help me deal with him and then you can do whatever the hell you want."

"Shut up, wolf. You're already a dead man." Abruptly, the shadows darkening the room were gone and she could see him.

The man . . .

She sucked in a startled breath as she caught sight of his face.

She knew that face.

She'd seen it in her dreams damn near every night. She'd forgotten so much of her life, ever since she'd woken up in front of that ramshackle little house, with Jazzy hovering over her. But she hadn't forgotten *him*.

He moved then, and once more his body was nothing but a blur. The man holding the gun cried out, jerked his arm up. A split second later, the gun was torn from his hand. Morgan dodged as it crashed into the wall next to her with so much force, the drywall split.

In the time it took for her to look from them to the gun and back, the fourth man was dead.

Now it was just her, trapped in a room with a living, breathing machine of death and Marty with his freakishly glowing eyes and teeth that would look more at home in the mouth of a tiger.

Or a wolf . . .

Marty looked at her as shadows descended on the room. Blind terror flooded his eyes and he demanded, "Don't just fucking stand there!"

But Morgan couldn't do anything else.

Once more, that comforting confidence was gone and she could barely breathe, could hardly think. The fear that lived inside her screeched, demanded she run.

Run, she whispered to herself. *He's going to kill everybody here. That's what his kind does . . . they kill.*

His kind . . .

"Not his kind," another voice whispered. *"Their kind kill . . . and our kind kill them."*

Pain swamped her, drowning out the voices in her head. Groaning, she grabbed her head. "Shut up. Shut up. *Shutupshutup*," she rasped, her voice rising with each word until she was screaming.

The pain in her head intensified, nearly doubling her over. *Run.*

But she couldn't move a muscle.

Not to save her life.

She looked around the room, searching for him. Marty was edging toward the open window. She could just barely make out his form, but the other man . . . she couldn't see him. Couldn't sense him.

And then he was *there*, standing between Marty and the window.

"Time to die," he said softly.

Marty growled. The muscles in his body tensed and she held her breath, certain he was going to leap for the other man.

But he did a backflip—son of a bitch, a fucking *backflip*—in her direction, landing just a few feet away.

The man's eyes flicked toward hers. She sucked in a breath and retreated until her back hit the wall. As the shadows once more faded from the room, she squeezed her eyes closed. Marty turned toward her and the man whispered, "Don't. Keep away from her . . . run now, and maybe you'll live another night."

Marty stilled, glancing from the man to Morgan. She couldn't hide her fear, not now. She watched as his nostrils flared. Smelling her. Then he smirked.

"You want her? Fine, vamp. She's yours." He shot Morgan a look and said, "Stupid bitch. You should have listened to me . . . you might have stood half a chance."

Then he was gone, disappearing out the open window with blinding, blurring speed.

She was alone with him now. She was surrounded by blood and death, staring into eyes of soft, velvety brown and listening to her heart race. Fear lay in the back of her mouth, a nasty, metallic film. She swallowed past the knot in her throat.

Was she next?

Yes, you stupid bitch. You're next. If you'd gone with the wolf, you might have lived through this. It was an angry whisper, full of hate, mockery and derision. *You should have run and now you're gonna die.*

"No," she whimpered.

Yes . . .

After all, she was in here with them . . . earlier, she'd killed a man. Last night, she'd killed a man. God only knows what she might have done for these bastards, if it meant keeping her sister safe.

Her skin prickled and she sucked in a breath.

The scent of him flooded her head. Male musk, soap, something else . . . something darkly seductive, something she could come to crave. She clenched her hands into fists, tight, so tight her nails bit into her flesh. Then she made herself open her eyes. She wouldn't see him, she thought.

Not until he was on her—ready to kill her.

But she did see him.

He stood right there.

Close enough to touch.

Close enough to kiss.

And then he *was* kissing her. Those hands that had so easily ended lives cradled her face, gently, reverently. His lips brushed against hers and her mouth opened on a gasp.

His tongue traced her lower lip, and then gently, slowly, oh so slowly, he deepened the kiss. His hands tangled in her hair and tugged her head to the side, arching her neck.

Morgan groaned and leaned against him, opening her mouth wider. Then she slid her tongue out, rubbed it against his. He caught it between his teeth and bit down gently, so gently.

Trembling, she reached up, clutching at his shirt, wiggling closer. She tangled her fingers in the worn, faded cotton stretching over his chest and pushed up onto her toes.

More . . . she needed more.

Something sharp sliced over her lip—a hot, quick flash of pain. The man's body shuddered, and then he tore himself away.

Caught off balance, she sagged and fell against the wall.

Her body ached. Her nipples stabbed into the silken material of her bra and between her legs, she was wet, painfully empty.

He stood on the other side of the room, staring at her. For one split second, it seemed like his eyes glowed . . . sunshine gleaming behind black glass. Then he lowered his lashes and when he looked at her again, his eyes were dark, velvety brown . . . beautiful, but completely normal.

His face.

That angelically beautiful face . . .

"Son of a bitch," she whispered.

Her dreams.

Morgan's breath caught in her throat and she tore her eyes away from him. It was either that or pounce on him. And while pouncing on him held an awful lot of appeal, her brain was still reeling from what had happened in this room.

He had just killed six men. Quick as a blink. With his bare hands.

Well, no. Marty had killed Sanders.

Lowering her eyes, she looked at each of the bodies and then back at the only man left standing. "You killed them. All of them."

His only response was a slow blink. Thick, curly lashes lowered, shielding his eyes for just a brief moment and then he was staring at her again.

"Am . . . Am I next?"

He cocked a brow and then he spoke. For a few seconds, she was too drunk on the sound of his voice to hear the words . . . slow, warm and heavy, with that lazy drawl of the South. It stroked over her senses like a velvet glove. If she were a cat, she might have purred and rubbed up against him, hoping he'd say something, *anything* else.

Then she blinked and understood *what* he had said.

"Some people deserve to die. I just gave them what they deserved," he said.

Some people deserve to die . . . and I'm probably one of them. Her breath caught in her throat. Her blood roared in her ears and her heart raced. Meeting his eyes, she demanded, "Am I next?"

He said nothing. He just stared at her, his dark velvet eyes staring at her as though he saw nothing else. Just her. Only her.

Jerking her chin up, she demanded, "Well, what are you waiting for?"

"You think I want to kill you," he said.

Deadly words. A deadly man. That voice. Damn it, that voice . . . rough, low and slow . . . that sexy velvet drawl. It had her remembering dreams where he had made love to her, whispering in her ear as he touched her.

You've lost your mind. You never saw him before now. He's never made love to you. In the back of her mind, a voice jeered, *"He's here to kill you . . . he might beat your sorry ass before he does it, but he's not going to make love to you."*

"Aren't you?" She flexed her hands and mentally checked her energy. She could fight, if she had to. But somehow, she knew she didn't stand a chance against him.

The thick black fringe of his lashes lowered, shielding his eyes. "I'm not here to kill you." He held out a hand. "Come on. We don't have that much time."

Morgan stared at his hand, shaken by how very much she wanted to put her hand in his. Shaken by how much she wanted to follow him, do whatever he asked.

He would keep me safe. With clear, blinding clarity, she knew it. So at odds with the angry, raging voice that even now whispered of her death . . . her death at his hands.

"He won't keep you safe . . . he'll kill you. Then he'll find Jazzy and kill her."

Mentally, she squared her shoulders. She wasn't going to have a fucking mental breakdown, and if she *was*, she'd rather do it because something really scary wanted her dead, *not* because the voices in her head wouldn't quit arguing.

As the voice started in on more of its nasty, slippery warnings, Morgan said silently, *Just shut the hell up already.*

If he wanted her dead, she didn't stand a chance anyway.

"How did you do that?" She glanced past him to the men on the floor. "Are you . . . How . . ." Her voice trailed off as she struggled to understand all the questions in her mind. "People can't move that fast. How did you do that?"

Although his expression didn't change, Morgan had the strangest feeling that she had startled him. His dark chocolate eyes narrowed on her face, his gaze heavy and intent.

"No time," he muttered, shaking his head. "We don't have time for this. Come on, we need to get out of here."

"I'm not going anywhere with you."

"Yes, you are. Relax. I'm not going to hurt you. I wouldn't."

She gaped at him. "You come in here like the Grim Reaper, kill everybody in just a couple of minutes. And I'm supposed to believe that you don't want to hurt me?"

A muscle jerked in his cheek. "If I wanted to hurt you, I wouldn't be standing here talking to you. If I wanted to hurt you, I wouldn't have kissed you the moment I had a chance." He cocked his head then, as though listening to something.

Although how he could hear much of anything outside this room other than the music, she didn't know.

"Time's up. We're going. Now."

It wasn't a request.

Narrowing her eyes, Morgan said, "I don't think so."

He stared at her. In the depths of his eyes, she saw . . . something. Her heart started to race. Warmth unfurled inside her. Without even realizing it, she started to lift her hand.

Out in the hallway, there was a crash. Voices raised. Then the door rattled on its hinges as somebody began to pound against it.

"Peter, open up, man. Everything okay in there?"

The man in front of her sighed. "I'm sorry."

"Sorry . . . ?" Morgan shook her head, confused. From the corner of her eye, she saw a blur. But it came too quick. Alarm barely had a chance to form in her mind before he hit her.

Darkness swirled up, pulling her under.

CHAPTER 15

SHE hadn't recognized him.

"Put it away, man," Dominic told himself.

No time for it. Not right now. These streets were too open, too unfamiliar . . . and that damn werewolf was out there somewhere.

Dominic should have killed him, but he couldn't risk it—if he had moved toward Nessa . . .

Somehow, Dominic knew she wouldn't have been able to handle it. Not in that moment.

With her slight weight draped over his shoulder, he ran through the streets. It was dark and late, most of the streets abandoned. Nobody followed him, but his handiwork had been discovered.

He was a quarter mile away when they had finally busted the door down.

Not for the first time, Dominic was grateful for a vampire's speed.

He was almost to his beach house when she started to stir. Putting on an extra burst of speed, he closed the distance. He was inside the house just as she woke up.

She didn't wake up happy. She began to kick and struggle against him as he closed the door behind him. "Fucking asshole. Put me down."

Dominic did just that, putting her on the couch. As he straightened, his eyes lingered on her face.

Damn it, your face . . .

This wasn't really happening, was it?

It was her. The woman he'd dreamed about for most of his life. Her pale, peaches-and-cream complexion, a pink Cupid's bow of a mouth, her heart-shaped face.

And those big blue eyes, so wide and confused and frightened . . . staring at him as though she didn't know what in the hell was going on.

That makes two of us, sweetheart.

There was no recognition in her gaze.

When he had seen her earlier, she had been standing off to the side. Although none of the mortals would recognize it, she had been terrified.

Dominic had recognized it . . . miles away. It had drawn him in, pulled him close. He'd felt her. Sensed her fear . . . even now, he could feel it, sense it, smell it.

It roused every protective instinct he had, and all he wanted to do was hold her close, promise her that nobody would ever hurt her again.

But it went deeper than that.

Looking at her, even from a distance, it had felt like home. It was like he had found some part of himself that he hadn't even realized was missing.

And she stared at him like he was a stranger.

Backing away, he stood in the middle of the room as she came off the couch. Her blue eyes blazed at him. "You hit me, you bastard."

"You didn't leave me with much choice." Dominic swallowed the bitter taste of guilt, knowing he had done the right thing. But even knowing that didn't make it any easier to swallow. "I needed to get you out of there and you made it clear you weren't going to budge. I didn't have time to fight with you, not if I wanted to keep you safe."

"You son of a bitch." She jerked her hands through her hair and started to pace. "You want me to believe you *hit* me to keep me *safe*."

"I don't expect you to believe anything you don't want to," he said, and he knew he lied.

Yes, he expected her to believe him.

He expected her to look at him and feel the same crazy shit *he* felt when he looked at her.

But she didn't . . .

Damn it, enough already. Just deal with it, you moron. Deal with it. You'll just have to figure things out as you go.

Yes. That was exactly what he had to do, and he knew he could. Because he had to—he'd *found* her, damn it, he could figure the rest of this out. He hadn't gotten this far, hadn't made it this far to quit now. They could figure this mess out, damn it, and they would.

Decision made, he looked at her. His heart broke a little as he picked up on the fear dancing inside her, spinning through her, drawing her tighter and tighter. She kept it hidden deep inside, not letting it show on her face, but she couldn't hide the signals her body was sending out.

Not from him.

"Okay," she said, taking a deep breath. "So you don't want to hurt me. Fine. You got me out of there. I'm safe. Can I go now?"

Dominic cocked a brow. "Go? Exactly where do you want to go?"

"How about home? It's late. I'm tired." Fear and worry hovered in the air around her, like a cloak. "Besides, I've got somebody waiting for me. I don't want her to worry when I don't show up."

"Jazzy isn't expecting you to come home."

She froze, her slender body rigid. She was strung so tight, it was like she'd shatter if she took even one deep breath. "Jazzy?" she parroted back at him.

"Don't worry . . . she's safe." But even as he said it, he laughed at himself. Ugly, acrid bitterness flooded him. How could he expect her not to be scared? She didn't know what was going on. She didn't know who he was—didn't know *what* he was.

Hell, he didn't think she entirely understood what *she* was.

How could she? She had thought he was going to kill her . . . *Stop it. Stop. One step at a time. One thing at time.*

"How do you know about Jazzy? And why wouldn't she be waiting for me?"

"I know Jazzy. She's the one who told me where to find you." He did know Jazzy—in the shallowest sense of the word. He'd met her. He knew her name. Not a lie, right?

Hell, he wasn't sure who he was dealing with, at least not entirely. She'd looked at him with utter fear, utter confusion— she didn't know what he was. Which meant she didn't know what she was . . . and if she didn't know what she was, she didn't know *who* she was.

Which meant he couldn't exactly trust her, especially considering he could smell the blood on her.

Blood.

She had blood on her hands. He had to make sense of that, somehow. Had to, but he didn't know where to start.

He knew where he wanted to start, though.

He needed her.

He ached . . . deep inside. Inside his heart, in a way he had never known. He knew, as surely as he knew his own name, that if he held her the pain would go away. No . . . not go away. It would *change*, change into that kind of ache that wouldn't go away entirely until he had that soft, sleek body under his, with her arms wrapped around him, clutching him tight.

Maybe a few dozen years of that would help.

If he could just make love to her, let the rest of the world fall away, then later, they could make sense of everything.

Of course, he somehow suspected she wouldn't be open to that idea.

He heard her moving behind him, drawing close. He turned and instinct had him stepping to the side at the same time. He was two feet away before she could try to brain him.

Caught off balance, she stumbled forward and the cast-iron poker she held struck the floor.

She scowled, spinning around to glare at him. "Damn it, how in the hell do you keep doing that?"

Okay. Might as well start with this, then. See if we can make sense of anything.

She looked completely, utterly confused, and it wasn't any sort of act. That would reek of lies and he scented no deceit on her.

Dominic ran his tongue along the inside of his teeth, then idly pressed the tip of his tongue to the sockets where his fangs rested. *Do I start there? Flash my fangs and see what happens?*

So . . . do you know you're a witch? Yes? No? Maybe? Here's another one to try on for size . . . I'm a vampire. And I'm the reincarnation of your long-lost lover. Whaddya say . . . wanna go to bed with me?

Somehow, he didn't see that conversation going over very well.

THERE was something seriously unnerving about the way he stared at her, Morgan decided.

It made her twitchy.

It made her edgy.

Be honest. Be honest with yourself even if you can't do it with anybody else. He doesn't make you twitchy or edgy.

He makes you hot.

She scowled and wished the voices in her head would start clamoring at her again. She'd had no thoughts but her own, and right now, she'd give almost anything to have those other voices whispering at her. Her id and her ego. Both of them were quiet and she was left alone to face the man in front of her.

With nothing to distract her.

Except him, of course.

And although it sounded incongruous, he could certainly

distract her. She should be trying to figure out what was going on, and she *was* . . . sort of. When she wasn't overcome with the urge to fling herself at him and sob on those wonderfully strong-looking shoulders. Or the skin-blistering lust that had her yearning to peel off his clothes and learn every muscle, every line of his body. With her eyes, her hands, her mouth.

Get it together, Morgan, she told herself.

"So are you going to answer me?" she asked, finally forcing a question past her tight throat.

He lifted a brow at her. "Answer what?"

"That . . . thing. Hell, I don't know what to call it. But you move fast. Too fast."

"Maybe I work out."

"Superman on steroids doesn't move *that* fast," she said sourly.

A grin curled his lips. When he smiled, he had a dimple in his cheek . . . and his eyes crinkled at the corners. It was that sort of smile that would lay women low . . . that boy-next-door kind of smile, with just a touch of wickedness.

"Superman wouldn't do steroids. It would mess with his mojo," he said.

She blinked at him, and then, to her surprise, she laughed. "Good point. And we can't have anything messing with the Man of Steel's mojo." Her smile faded and she shook her head. "But you didn't answer me."

"Because I'm not entirely sure how to do that just yet." He shrugged and rested his head on the back of the couch. "So, what's your name?"

Morgan narrowed her eyes. "I thought you knew my sister."

"I do."

"You know my sister, know her well enough that she told you where to find me, but she never mentioned my name," Morgan said slowly. *Not likely.*

He lifted his head just long enough to meet her eyes. "She was too busy sputtering about what a mistake you were making." He lay his head back down and murmured softly, "A bad mistake. The worst kind."

Yeah, she'd figured that much out. She'd known it going in but she hadn't seen another way out. *Actually, I just didn't look hard enough*, she admitted.

"Where is Jazzy?" Morgan asked, folding her arms over her chest.

"Someplace safe. I'm not sure where." He didn't sound too concerned with that fact, either.

"You don't know where she is."

"No."

Morgan ground her teeth together and tried, for about five seconds, not to lose it. Then she bit off, "I need to find her."

"Do you? Why?" he asked, his voice oddly flat. He came off the couch, his muscles uncoiling, that lean body unfolding. He hooked his thumbs in the front pockets of his jeans and watched her from unreadable dark eyes.

Morgan stared at him. "*Why?*" she echoed. "Damn it, she's my sister. *That* is why. She's *my* responsibility. I need to take care of her."

"You were doing a lousy job of it today."

She flinched as though he'd slapped her. It would have hurt less if he had. Tears burned her eyes but she blinked them back. Spinning on her heel, she folded her arms over her chest and stared at the wall. "This is none of your business, you know."

"I hauled your butt out of a mess of trouble. That kind of makes it my business, at least in some way," he said after a few seconds.

"Nobody asked you to haul my butt out of anything. I was handling it."

"You were scared to death."

Morgan glared at him over her shoulder. "I was *handling* it. It was my mess—it was my responsibility to clean it up."

"Yeah, it was your mess. And that's why I found your sister hightailing it out of town like she had demons chasing after her," he responded. He shook his head. "You honestly don't realize how much trouble you were in, do you?

Jazzy, that kid you claim is *your* responsibility, has a better head on her shoulders than you do. She knew something bad was going down and she had the common sense to get the hell out of Dodge. But you were lingering right in the middle of ground zero, admiring your manicure."

She flushed. "I wasn't *admiring* my manicure." She shot a glance at her nails—they were bedraggled, cracked and desperately in need of some TLC. The hangnail she'd been picking at was gone, revealing a small, tender red area. "I was . . ."

"Trying not to let that bastard see how scared you were?" he offered.

Somehow, she knew he wasn't talking about Sanders.

Tearing her eyes away from him, she started to pace the living room. It was a lovely space, the hardwood floors gleaming a mellow gold, the furniture white as snow, soft as a cloud. A huge window faced out over the ocean. It would be one hell of a view for an early bird with a desire to watch the sun rise.

She felt terribly out of place.

Swiping her hands down the front of her jeans, she glanced at him from the corner of her eye. "I was scared. I was in trouble, and I know that," she said quietly. "I do appreciate your help . . . ah . . . you know what? You never told me your name, either."

He was quiet for so long, she didn't think he'd answer.

She held her breath as the silence stretched out.

Then, his voice deeper, rougher, he murmured, "It's Dominic."

For some reason, for some bizarre reason that made absolutely *no* sense, his answer made her want to fall to the ground and sob.

Dominic.

What did you think he was going to say?

She swallowed and tried to smile. "Seeing as how you hauled my ass out of the fire earlier, I guess I ought to at least tell you my name. It's Morgan. Morgan Wakefield."

His mouth spasmed. Pain flashed through his eyes. It was fast, there and then gone. And if she hadn't been so aware of him, she would have missed it. His features smoothed out and he said, "Well, I can definitely tell you that it has been an experience meeting you."

"Yes." She licked her lips and glanced away from him. Okay, niceties done. She really did need to get out of there.

"Look, I appreciate your help, seriously. But I need to try and figure out where my sister went." She edged away, keeping him in her line of sight as she made for the door. "I get why she took off—she's a hell of a lot smarter than I am, I guess. But still, she's just a kid and I . . . *hey!*"

She'd almost reached the door. Almost.

Then he was there, one hand braced against it, the other braced at the wall just over her shoulder. Pinned between his lean body and the wall, she stared up at him. Her pulse raced. She could feel it, fluttering in her neck, and she could hear her blood roaring in her ears. She swallowed and his gaze dropped, lingering on her throat.

Hypnotized by the heated intensity of his eyes, she held still as he lifted a hand and brushed his finger across the hollow of her throat, rested it just above the mad beat of her pulse. "I'm sorry . . . Morgan," he murmured. His voice hesitated over her name. He tore his eyes away from her neck and met her gaze. With a slow shake of his head, he whispered, "I'm sorry, but I can't let you walk away."

She ducked under his arm, backing away from him. Her entire body shook, and the farther away she moved, the more she ached. She didn't want to move *away* from him. She wanted to grab him, lose herself in him. Her heart raced faster and faster and she felt out of breath. She hadn't done a damn thing, but she felt like she'd just got done doing ten miles at an all-out run.

"You can't keep me here," she said, her voice shaking.

You can . . . and why in the hell do I want you to?

Dominic sighed and rubbed a hand over his face. He stared at the floor, his shoulders slumped. He looked tired, exhausted to the bone and . . . sad. She could feel his grief. Feel his pain. It beat inside her heart, like it was her own pain, not just his.

"Look, Morgan. It's late. I know you're confused and scared."

"Scared," she muttered. She pressed her fingertips to her temples. Inside her head, it was quiet. Too quiet. Everything inside her seemed frozen . . . waiting.

Waiting for what?

She was staring at the floor and never heard him move, but as the shadows on the floor in front of her shifted, she jerked her gaze up. He stood there, less than a foot away. She licked her lips and watched as his eyes tracked the movement. She could remember his taste . . . she wanted more.

"I'm not going to hurt you," he said quietly. There was a plea in his eyes. Desperate and determined, as though he could will her to believe him. "I'm not. I've spent . . ."

His voice trailed off.

Morgan stared at him. "You've spent . . . what?"

A muscle pulsed in his jaw as he reached out, smoothing a strand of hair back from her face. He tucked it behind her ear and then slid his hand around her neck, cupping it in his hand. She sighed and leaned into his touch, even as she tried to remind herself she needed to get the hell away from this strange, disturbing man.

But she couldn't get away. And not just because he wouldn't let her.

He stroked her cheek with his free hand, feathering the roughened pads of his fingers over her face as though he wanted to memorize it. "I've spent too long waiting for you. Looking for you. Now that I've found you, there's no way in hell I'd let anybody or anything hurt you."

Time fell away.

She fell away.

Her breath lodged in her throat, and for the longest time, she wasn't aware of any sound but the beating of her heart, racing faster and faster. The world whirled around her . . . racing in time with her heart. And suddenly, she wasn't standing in a lovely little house on the beach with a dark, grim stranger with sad eyes that broke her heart.

No. She was . . . somewhere else. Maybe even some*one* else.

She was on the ground, and in her arms, there was a man. A man with sun-streaked golden brown hair . . . and sad eyes that broke her heart. His blood pumped out, hot and wet, staining the ground beneath them, turning the dusty earth into mud.

He watched her with those sad, grieving eyes as he reached up to touch her face. He was dying. In her arms, he was dying . . . this man she loved more than life itself.

My beautiful, foolish, wonderful girl. I love you so much. I will come back . . . I will find you again . . .

"No!"

She screamed, and the sound jerked her back to herself. Tearing away from Dominic, she backed up, shaking her head.

His voice echoed in her head.

So different . . .

I will find you again . . .

I've spent too long waiting for you. Looking for you . . .

All of sudden, those voices were in her head, again, clamoring. One of them was louder, stronger.

Calling out a name.

But Morgan couldn't make sense of it.

She took one more step away and then . . . darkness.

S HE might not know him *here* . . . but in her dreams, she knew him.

In her dreams, he was waiting for her. But she was too afraid to believe it.

Too afraid to come out of the shell she had crafted for herself, a shell spun of her magic. A spell . . . a spell that kept her pain at bay, a spell that split her from her memories.

She was on that wide, soft couch under the window, and he was there, with her, next to her, stroking her hair back from her face.

She reached up and with a trembling hand, cupped his cheek. "Is it you? Truly?"

He caught her hand and nuzzled it, pressing his mouth to her palm. "It's me. Dear God, darlin', I never meant to be gone from you this long."

"I can't believe this," she whispered, her voice thick with tears. They stung her eyes and she blinked them away, furious at those salty drops because they blurred her vision, kept her from staring at him.

He was so different.

But his soul felt the same.

And those eyes, those eyes . . . she would know them anywhere.

"Why?" she demanded, her voice cracking. "Why *now*? Don't you know how . . ."

How lonely I've been? How much it hurts . . . just living, every single day without you? Why now?

Now . . . Now. When she was so broken. So shattered inside. So unworthy of him. Of a second chance. Of happiness.

"I can't believe this," she said again, shaking her head. *I won't.*

"Why?" He stroked her hair back from her face, his hands gentle, so gentle and warm and strong.

"Because it's too late." The tears blinding her spilled over and she murmured, "It's too late for me. I've fallen."

"It's not too late . . . I've got you. I won't let you fall."

I've got you. I won't let you fall . . .

The words echoed inside, left her shaking, aching. *Too late . . . too late . . .*

I won't let you fall.

A harsh sob tore from her throat and she collapsed against his chest, crying.

This can't be real, she thought. *It's just my foolish loneliness, my empty heart, playing tricks on me. It isn't real . . . he isn't real. He can't be.*

He kissed her. As though he'd heard her internal arguing, he whispered, "I am real. Come back to me, my beautiful little witch. Please come back."

* * *

DOMINIC sat on the couch, cradling her in his arms. He stared at her face, stroking her tousled blond hair back.

She wasn't asleep. This was deeper than sleep. It was as though she'd gone some place deep, deep inside herself. But she couldn't escape the pain. And he couldn't escape her pain—it dug inside his heart, tearing, clawing.

She cried.

Tears slipped out from under her closed lids, and he wiped them away with his thumb, kissed them and rocked her, held her. "Come back to me. Come back to me, Nessa, my beautiful little witch. Please come back."

CHAPTER 16

MARTY Russo was thirty miles away before he dared to slow down.

So far, the vampire hadn't followed him. But he wouldn't bet on his luck holding forever.

So as he ran, he made plans.

It only took him thirty minutes to run those thirty miles. Though he ran over the ground in his wolf form, inside his mind, he was still human. Mostly. And he planned. Plotted.

What he needed was help.

Help to do something about the Hunter, in case the bastard came after him. He knew the stories. When a Hunter had your scent, they never let go. Once he'd taken care of that stupid witch, he might decide to come after Marty.

And Marty wasn't going to make it easy on him.

Hell, if he was lucky . . . maybe he could even kill the fucker.

The vampire was young—Marty could tell. Witches weren't the only ones able to sense that kind of thing with vamps. The Hunter was a strong bastard, too, especially for his years. But he was still young and that made him more vulnerable. Relatively speaking.

I can handle him.

He could. Especially if *she* helped him.

Under normal circumstances, they didn't like each other. They were two territorial predators, and she hadn't liked him encroaching so close on what she viewed as *her* land.

But she wasn't on *her* land now. She was in *his* territory and he'd allowed it. Allowed her to live.

She'd been weak then, but she wasn't now. She was stronger, and she was alive. Because of him. She owed him. Marty was going to collect. She would help him handle the vampire. Then, they'd call it even.

S UNRISE was pressing ever closer. Too close. Dominic flicked a glance out the window and then studied her delicate, heart-shaped face. Resting a hand on her chest, he let the steady beat of her heart reassure him.

She was breathing, strong and steady. He could feel the ebb and flow of her life, pulsing inside her.

She was still caught in whatever deep dreams held her, but it was nothing more than that.

Fear, nerves, they tangled inside him.

He couldn't fight the dawn but he couldn't risk her running away on him, either.

Here, inside this safe house, he didn't have to worry about her slipping away. Like so many of the Hunter safe houses scattered across the world, it was owned by some faceless philanthropist most of the world had never heard of. The documentation wasn't likely to be traced back to Excelsior or the Council, but they were the ones responsible for its upkeep . . . and its secrets.

All of the safe houses had secrets.

This house's secret was a hidden, interior room that was safe for a vamp to take a rest in during the day . . . and once he sealed the door, it wouldn't open again until he opened it.

Outside, the sky was beginning to lighten, the deep blue of the night giving way to softer hues. He didn't have that much time left. Blowing out a sigh, he lifted Nessa's still form in his arms and made his way to the safe room.

It was small. Considering the house's design, it had to be small. Although this house sat empty unless a Hunter was using it, they still guarded their secrets closely. They had no choice. The mortal world wasn't ready to accept them. Dominic didn't think they would ever be.

The room wasn't much bigger than a closet. It had a small cot tucked up against one wall. In the corner, there was a small refrigerator. There were no windows. He laid Nessa on the cot, pulled the blanket up over her.

Nessa.

Not Morgan. He couldn't think of her with that name. He just couldn't.

He left the room quickly and grabbed a pillow from the couch and then headed back into the safe room. As the door slid shut behind him, he punched a code into the small keypad, activating the locking mechanism.

Now, even if the power went out . . . or the electricity went haywire . . . the door wouldn't open. He could pry it open if he had to, but there was no way Nessa would get out of this room without his help.

In the back of his mind, an unknowing voice whispered, *She could always burn her way out.*

No. She wouldn't do that—too dangerous. She wouldn't risk hurting him. He was going to have to put faith in that.

She was as safe as she could be, for now.

He tossed the pillow on the floor and checked the locking mechanism on the refrigerator. The last thing he needed was her waking up thirsty and deciding to look for something to drink in there. It held nothing but bagged blood.

Sunrise . . . he could feel it. It hit his body like a tranquilizer, turning his muscles heavy, weighing his steps down, fatigue drawing him.

Sleep. Need to sleep.

Dragging his feet, he paused by the cot and stared down

at Nessa. Her face was averted, one thick blond lock of hair curling across her cheek. One hand rested on her chest, curled between her breasts. That was where he wanted to be. He wanted to stretch out and lay his head on her chest, listen to her heart beat as he slept the day away.

He traced one finger down the line of her jaw and then turned away.

Sleep . . .

Unable to resist another moment, he stretched out on the floor, turning on his side so he could look at her. Her face was the last thing he saw before sleep pulled him under.

In his dreams, he found her.

H ER name was Isis.
      That wasn't the name on her birth certificate, but the name *Marie* didn't suit her.

Isis did. She was a goddess among men, and a woman who should be worshipped . . . and feared.

The man before her now was certainly afraid, but that fear wasn't inspired by her. Still, that didn't keep her from drinking it in. It hit her system with a rush, a welcome one. She was still weak. Although her injuries were gone, she had yet to regain her full strength.

Damn that witch.

Damn her straight to hell.

Isis had failed to send her there.

No, she told herself. *It wasn't failure. Not my failure, at least. It's Morgan's. Useless little waste.*

If Morgan had had any strength to speak of, she never would have lost to that old crone in the first place. Then Isis wouldn't have had to deal with the mess her daughter had left behind.

It was Morgan's fault.

That damn witch showing up. The fight and now Isis's weakness—all Morgan's fault. Damn the girl.

That soothed the ragged edges of her anger and she was able to smile as she reclined on the ragged, broken-down couch. "Marty, you look like something the cat dragged in," she purred.

He curled his lip at her, sneering. "It's payback time, Isis. You owe me now."

"I owe you?" She arched a brow at him. "How exactly do you figure that I owe you?"

"You are in my territory. Had I chosen, I could have killed you. You were too weak then to fight me, and we both know it. I let you live, and now you owe me." His eyes glittered as he stared at her, his beast lurking just behind his gaze.

Angry . . . and afraid.

"Well, I'm not surprised you see it that way." She flicked a glance around the tiny hovel. It was even smaller than the house where her youngest daughter, Jasmine, lived. *Jasmine*. That treacherous little bitch.

It was nothing like *her* home. She had a lovely condo on the beach, a place she took her lovers, a place where she practiced her spells, a place where she indulged in her pleasures, however she saw fit.

For now, that place was off-limits to her. She couldn't go back to St. Augustine until she had figured out how to deal with the witch. If she stepped a foot back in that town without some sort of plan, Isis was dead.

It might well be Morgan's fault, but she'd still be dead and Isis was rather fond of life.

"How the hell else would I see it?" Marty asked. His lip curled and he watched her with disdain in his eyes. "I didn't take your life for coming into my territory. I let you live, and you know damn well I could have—and probably *should* have—killed you were you stood. But I didn't. More, I saw to it that you had a place to stay. You didn't spend those nights helpless and alone on the streets, now did you?"

Isis glanced around the small, cramped house. "I wouldn't exactly call this a place to live."

He gave a bark of laughter. "You ungrateful bitch. After

all the times you tried to kill me, did you really expect me to put you up at the Ritz?"

"Of course not. It's a bit too far away." She smiled and studied her nails. She plucked a file from the rickety table in front of the couch and smoothed the edge of one. "After all, this is where my home is. This is where my daughter is. I'm not about to run off. But you could have done much better than this mess."

"And I could've done worse. You could be dead," he reminded her.

Isis rolled her eyes. "So you said, repeatedly. It's becoming a bit boring." She tossed the file back on the table and looked up at Marty. "Exactly what is it you want me to do? What exactly should I do to make things level between us?" She smirked and murmured, "I'd rather not have any sort of debt to some worthless dog."

Marty growled. Deep and rough, it rumbled out of his throat, echoing in the small room. "I'm already pissed off, Isis. Don't make it worse."

"Oh, did the puppy have a bad day?" She cooed.

His hand shot out, grabbing her throat. In the span of two seconds, she went from sitting on the couch to being held upright over it, her body dangling from his hand. His grip on her throat was tight, too tight. He squeezed in warning, and murmured, "I'm not in the mood for this."

Isis reached up and closed a hand over his wrist. Her eyes glowed. Under her hand, the skin she touched went cold. The flesh turned white, and the white grew, spreading from his hand halfway up his forearm. He dropped her and stumbled back. "You stupid bitch, what in the hell are you doing?"

"Touch me again without my permission, and see what I do," she warned.

He gasped for air, weaving back and forth on his feet. Only moments ago, he had all but glowed with health. The energy of a shapeshifter had crackled inside him. Now he was gray, his skin ashen and his eyes sunken.

"What did you do to me?" he demanded, his voice a mere whisper.

"Nothing near as bad as I could've done," she said. He didn't need to know she was bluffing. She couldn't do much more to him yet, not until she returned to full strength. But Marty wasn't exactly a strong werewolf. It wouldn't take much to train him.

She sidled up to him and rested a hand on his chest, stroking him through the cotton of his shirt. "I could have killed you, you know," she murmured. She stroked a hand down, toyed with the button of his jeans. "I could have drained you dry, left you like an empty husk. You're not strong enough to stop me. You know it. I know it. So, Marty . . . don't piss me off."

After reaching up to pat his cheek, she returned to the couch. "Enough with the drama already. What is it you want from me?"

"There's a Hunter. In town." He spoke slowly, almost reluctantly. The color returned to his face, his altered body repairing the damage she had done with relative ease. She hadn't taken enough to damage him—just enough to scare him. Just enough to warn him.

With a shrug, she pushed her hair back from her face. "I already know about the Hunter."

"You know," he echoed. "You knew there was a Hunter nearby, and you didn't see fit to warn anybody?"

Isis waved a hand dismissively. "Why should I? You're not my responsibility. You are responsible for your own neck."

"I suppose it never occurred to you that the two of us are more equipped to deal with him together than on our own? You increase your chance of surviving by working with me, old witch," he snapped.

"I cannot face a Hunter right now. You're on your own with her. She almost . . ." Her voice trailed off. Scowling, she cocked her head and studied his face. "Did you say 'him'? This Hunter, he's a man?"

"Yeah." He frowned as he met her eyes. "I take it you thought it was a woman."

"I assumed it was the same witch I battled . . . the one who damn near killed me. She's a Hunter, as well."

Two of them. Isis rubbed her hands together. Her gut twisted, ran cold with fear. *No, not fear. I'm not afraid of a couple of Hunters,* she told herself. She didn't fear them. Closing her eyes, Isis focused. She needed to get control of the fear. She took a series of deep, slow breaths and then focused on Marty's face once more.

"Tell me about this male Hunter. Is he the only one you've seen? Have you seen the witch?"

"Son of a bitch," Marty swore. He shoved a hand through his hair and started to pace. She caught a glimpse of the glitter in his eyes and realized he was still very afraid . . . and it wasn't because of her. "Another witch. We don't need another witch around."

"Another . . . why do I get the feeling you're not talking about me?"

"Because I'm not," he snapped. Glaring at her, he said, "The Hunter I ran across is a vampire. Young, but not weak. He's got strength inside him. And he came here looking for a witch. Now you tell me you've run into a different Hunter—a Hunter who's a witch. That's two Hunters. Two different Hunters, and the witch beat you, so that tells me she's a strong one."

"She didn't beat me," Isis snarled. "It wasn't even my fight . . . I was cleaning up my daughter's mess. That stupid, useless waste."

Marty folded his arms over his chest. "I don't care what your excuses are. They don't matter to me. Bottom line . . . you fought and you didn't kill her. If you had won, you would have killed her, you would have drunk her power, and we wouldn't be having this discussion." He turned away and started to pace. "So now we have two Hunters to deal with. The witch and the vampire. With any luck, that idiot Morgan will keep the vampire occupied, for a while at least. Sunrise is coming soon and he will have to rest. That buys us until nightfall before we have to worry about him."

"Morgan . . ." Isis murmured. She shook her head and then asked, "Did you say Morgan?"

Marty waved a hand. "Yeah. She's the reason the Hunter is here. He was looking for her. I can't figure out what she's done to grab his interest, but she certainly got it. He was more interested in her than me, so she must've done something."

Morgan.

"Describe her to me," Isis murmured.

Marty rolled his eyes. "Trust me, Isis. That ditz Morgan is not going to be an issue. Hell, she might even be useful. She already has. She distracted the vampire."

"Damn it, you mangy wolf. Describe her to me." Isis shot up off the couch, glaring at him. Her power, always erratic when her emotions spiked, flared out of control and the light in the room flickered. And when Marty exhaled, his breath came out in a frosty puff of air.

He stared at her. "She's just a stupid little witch. Young, I don't know, in her twenties. Hard to gauge the age of the human, especially the witches. But she's not too powerful so I suspect she is as young as she looks."

"And what does she *look* like?" Isis closed her hands into fists, struggling to control her anger. Struggling to keep control . . . period. She couldn't spare the energy.

Plus, although Marty was annoying, he wasn't an idiot. That was why she hadn't killed him. If she had to have another predator living so close to her territory, she would rather it not be a fool. Fools did foolish things, and foolish things too often caught attention. Isis did not want attention drawn to her, or anywhere near her territory. That was how she avoided the Hunters. She kept under their radar.

Marty wasn't a fool, and that meant there was no way he could look at Agnes Milcher and not recognize her for what she was. One very powerful witch.

Which meant . . . *what*?

Morgan.

Isis narrowed her eyes. She sensed the barest remnant of Morgan's presence, but she'd dismissed it.

The second she laid eyes on the face that had belonged to her oldest child, she'd known she wasn't dealing with Morgan—no matter what the witch had pretended.

Hunters had a feel all their own, and Hunter witches— even more unique.

There had been *something* that felt like Morgan. An echo. A shadow. Hell, maybe Morgan had been haunting the bitch who killed her.

Or maybe . . .

A smile curled her lips. "So, she told you her name was Morgan?"

"Y ou have got to be kidding me."

Brad opened his mouth to respond, only to close it with a sigh as Duke's pale gray eyes narrowed and shifted to a point somewhere over Brad's shoulder. The car. The girl. The little witch.

"You so much as touch that door, kid, and you'll regret it," Duke said, his voice a rough growl.

Jasmine Wakefield muttered something under her breath. Brad couldn't quite catch it, but Duke did. Amusement flashed through the shifter's eyes, and he shook his head. "That girl is a brat," he said softly.

"Miracle she isn't worse." Brad shrugged. He hadn't ever met her older sister, at least not when Morgan had been the inhabitant of the body, but he'd heard some stories.

Bad news. That was what those stories said. She was nothing but bad news.

Jasmine might be trouble, but she wasn't bad news.

She definitely was trouble, though, and she was already proving to be a pain in the neck. Brad shoved his hands deep inside the pockets of the fleece hoodie he wore and waited until Duke's eyes shifted back to him. "There's no other way to handle this," Brad said.

"There's always another way. You think it's so fucking important for Ana to be there, then fine. I trust your instincts. But we'll all go."

Shaking his head, Brad replied, "We can't. *She* can't." He jerked his head toward the car. "That girl can't be anywhere around them right now."

"Why not?" Duke asked.

"She just can't. She's too vulnerable to them. None of us are equipped to protect a baby witch from other witches and you know it." Brad glared at Duke and demanded, "Do you trust me or not? You say you trust my instincts, and then you demand I do the exact opposite of what my instincts are telling me. We need to get that girl to Excelsior and we need to do it quick. You know she's too damn vulnerable out here."

"I am *not* vulnerable," Jasmine snarled, poking her head out of the car.

Brad shot her a look over his shoulders. A brat. With very good ears. But he didn't respond to her. He looked back at Duke and said, "You're the only one who can definitely get her back there. I could try, but if she managed to get away, I don't know that I could find her. *You* could— you could just track her. Plus, she'll have a harder time slipping away from you."

Ana had been standing quietly to the side through the exchange. As Brad glanced at her, she moved to stand by Duke, resting a hand on his shoulder. "Duke, it's not like I'm wading into some nest of vampires or something all on my own. Brad will be with me . . . plus, Dominic is there."

"Damn it, Ana." Duke's lips twisted in a snarl and he shook his head. "That might not be the best way to argue the kid's case."

Brad rolled his eyes. Part of him wanted to argue about the "kid" part, but he'd already realized that he was *always* going to be a kid to Duke—when the man had married Ana, he'd all but adopted Brad as his unofficial little brother. Not just a brother-in-law, either . . . a real brother.

"Dominic isn't interested in Ana," Brad said.

Duke's upper lip peeled back from his teeth. "Once upon a time, he was."

"Oh, for crying out loud." Ana crossed her arms over

her chest and glared at Duke. "Please tell me that's not why we're standing here arguing."

"It's not." Duke hooked a hand over her neck and drew her close.

Brad looked away as Duke pressed his brow to Ana's. They'd been married for a while now, but sometimes, it seemed like they were still on a honeymoon. The obvious love between the two of them still left him amazed. Even though Brad had seen this coming, he hadn't been fully prepared for it.

"It's because this isn't your job, Ana," Duke said quietly. He cupped her cheek, stroking his thumb over her lower lip. "You weren't trained for this."

She watched him, purple eyes dark with worry, fear. She no longer hid from him, which was a damn good thing, but he hated seeing that fear in her eyes.

"Duke, you know Brad wouldn't be hauling me along if he thought I was going to be in major danger. Especially not without you with me. For some reason, he thinks I can help with something . . . I have to try."

"No." He scowled. Sliding an arm around her waist, he pulled her close and muttered, "No. Damn it, Ana, we're supposed to be on vacation. Taking it easy."

She smoothed a hand down his arm and said, "If you wanted to take it easy, we should have just laid around the house back home instead of hitting the beaches."

"And I should have said no when the kid wanted to come along," Duke muttered. He lifted his head and glared at Brad.

Brad returned his stare, levelly, steadily.

The kid really wasn't a kid anymore, Duke knew. He also knew Brad was smart, sharp, savvy. He wasn't going to get his sister into some sort of danger. He adored his big sister—she'd spent her life protecting him. Now Brad was the stronger one, physically . . . and in other ways. He'd die before he let something happen to her.

But still . . .

"Duke."

He looked at her, watched as she gave him a strained smile. "Duke, I'm in good hands . . . and you know it."

Yeah. He did know. Plus, he also knew they couldn't leave the baby witch alone. She was problems just waiting to happen and they needed to get someplace controlled, contained . . . and hopefully somebody at Excelsior could undo the hint of darkness he sensed inside the girl.

If Brad was sensing something tugging at him, then Brad was the one best-equipped to handle it. Duke didn't feel a damn thing.

The kid's psychic skills were something of a wonder, and if he said there was a need for Ana, then there was a need for her. Her rather unique skills had come in handy a time or two, and Duke suspected he knew why she was needed.

Still, he didn't like it. At all.

Turning from Ana, he stared at Brad. Ignoring his wife, he crowded in on Brad, fisting a hand in the younger man's shirt. Brad didn't flinch or look away. His heartbeat spiked before he could control it, but that lasted only a few seconds. The kid's control was damn near perfect.

"You got any idea what I'd do if something happened to her?"

Brad snorted. "Assuming I didn't kill myself first, I figure you wouldn't leave enough to bury. You know I won't let anything happen to her, Duke."

A kid. He's just a kid.

But he wasn't. Brad hadn't ever been *just* a kid. And even though he was only nineteen, he had so much power inside him, so much control. He was one of the youngest called to serve the Council, and come fall, Brad was heading north to Alaska where Duke was going to mentor him for a while.

"Yeah, kid. I know."

Blowing out a breath, he turned and met Ana's gaze. She stared at him balefully and muttered, "I can't believe you're actually threatening my baby brother."

"The baby brother expects it," Duke said with a shrug.

"Not the point." She stood rigid as he moved to pull

her into his arms, but as he pressed a kiss to her neck, she sighed and slipped her arms around his waist. "Stop worrying so much, Duke. I'll be fine. Besides, if it was anything really bad, you'd feel it, too. I'll be fine."

He might have felt better about it if he hadn't seen the nerves in her eyes. The fear.

But Ana didn't let fear stop her . . . she never had.

He loved her too much to take that away.

*H*E *isn't real* . . .
　　Lost in a bank of fog, she held still, silent. Afraid to move, afraid to breathe . . . afraid to wake.

When she woke, she'd discover she was wrong.

That she was dreaming.

That once more, God had played a nasty, awful joke on her.

It seemed that was all her life was—a cosmic joke gone wrong.

Why now?

Something in the fog shifted and she looked up, found herself standing face-to-face with . . . herself.

"He isn't real," she said quietly.

"How do you know?"

"Because he can't be. It has been too long. It has been . . . ages."

"A lifetime." There was a sad sigh, and the fog thickened, tightened—it weighed down on them, heavy and oppressive.

"A lifetime."

Tears pricked her eyes, but they wouldn't fall. Here, lost in the land of dreams, lost in the magic of her own making, she couldn't cry. Not physically, at least.

But in her heart, she wept. She sobbed. Her soul screamed out at the cruelty of it, the injustice.

"Why now?" She swallowed and stared into her own eyes. "Why now? I finally said good-bye. I finally let go. I was finally ready to move on and now . . . this."

"Does this mean we think he is real?"

She shook her head. "I don't know. I just don't know."

Her other self smiled, a sad curl of her lips. "We want to believe. We want to think he is real. But if we're wrong . . ."

"If I'm wrong, it will destroy me. I'm so close already . . . so close to falling away."

"We've already fallen away. *You* have fallen away. You fell into darkness, into blackness . . . you linger too close to true evil. *Hunter.*"

She flinched. In her heart of hearts, she knew it was true.

But the pain . . . the loneliness . . .

She closed her eyes and sank to her knees, arms wrapped around herself for warmth. "I did not do this intentionally. I simply wanted to . . . forget."

"You willed it on yourself. On us. You cannot continue like this. *We* cannot continue. If we do . . ." Something dark, terrifying flashed in the eyes of her other self. "The blood . . . this body craves the power, even if we do not. If we give in, if we let ourselves get lost, there is little that can be done to save us. Little that will save those we love."

"I am in control." But even as she said it, she wondered. Rubbing the heel of her hand over her chest, she wondered at the fear in her gut, the coldness in her soul. The darkness that clawed in closer and closer . . . calling to her.

"You are . . . for now—while part of you still lingers. But if you stay like this for too long, you grow weak. If you are weakened, you are not in control. If that darkness taps into your power . . . lives will be lost. Blood will flow, a red river of death. There is none yet who are your equal in magic."

"I know," she bit off, narrowing her eyes. "I have control of it. Of *her*."

Her . . . that dark, angry soul haunting her.

"For *now*. But you cannot continue. You must return. *We* must return." Now her other self smiled, that frightening, dark anger fading away, replaced by warmth. "We are needed. We are Hunters. *You* are a Hunter. Needed . . . and loved."

"I am a Hunter," she whispered. "Needed . . . loved."
She turned away and shook her head. "I know this. But
I fear. I fear *him* . . . fear his memory, fear the tricks my
empty heart would play on me."

"And what if they aren't tricks?"

Her hands shook as she shoved her hair back from her
face. "In my heart, I want to believe." Then she sighed and
muttered, "No . . . let's be honest. It's just us, after all. Just
me. In my heart, I *do* believe, but I fear that belief is born
of desperation. If I return, and I am wrong . . ."

She turned back, faced herself. "If I am wrong, it will
destroy me. Destroy us. If I dare to hope, and those hopes
are dashed, I won't survive it."

"But if you do not return, and *soon*, it will be too late. You
will be lost . . . and if you are lost . . . she may well win."

"No." She shook her head and closed her eyes. "She
won't win. I won't lose. I don't lose."

A cynical smile curled her lips and she murmured,
"Even when I try to, I cannot do it."

Then she opened her eyes, to face herself, to decide.

But the dream shifted around her . . . and then she was
elsewhere.

In a little house on the beach, sitting on a bed with him
stretched out next to her. Neither of them wore a stitch and
as her eyes met his, something warm and hopeful flooded
her heart.

"A NOTHER dream," Dominic muttered.

"Hmmm. Dreams are not such a bad thing." Nessa
sat at his side, her legs folded, her eyes somber and sad.
"Dreams of you kept me sane all these years."

Guilt festered inside his heart, and he reached up,
touched her cheek. "I'm so sorry."

"Why?" She cocked her head, her golden hair spilling
over one shoulder. She was naked, and Dominic found
himself fascinated by the sight of her pink nipples peeking
through her hair.

Nessa chuckled and he glanced up, realized he'd been all but drooling. "You're such a male." She rolled her eyes and then, with a wide grin, primly smoothed her hair down, covering herself.

Dominic slid a hand up her thigh, over her side, until he could cup her breast. "Now I've got to be honest and admit, I don't know much more than what I've seen in my own dreams, but I'm pretty sure you enjoyed me being male."

"I did at that." She rested a hand on his chest, sighing. "I want to believe this is real, you know. I want to believe you are here, really here. But I'm too afraid."

"Is that why you're . . . not you?"

She pulled her hand from his chest and folded them in her lap. Lifting one shoulder in a shrug, she said, "I *am* me. I'm just . . . hiding."

Dominic rolled to his side, pushing up onto his elbow. Cupping her face, he said, "Then stop hiding. Come out . . . from wherever in the hell you are, stop whatever in the hell you're doing, and just come back to me."

Gold-tipped black lashes lowered over her eyes. "And if I do . . . and you aren't here, it will end me. I can't live through that, lover. It will kill me. Or worse."

"I *am* here." He caught her hand and drew it to his chest. Pressing it to his skin, he said, "I'm here. See? Touch me. Feel me."

"But these are just dreams . . . and I've had many a dream where I could touch you, feel you."

"Did they feel the same way this dream feels?" he asked. Then he shook his head. "I know they didn't. Something's different—something's been different in my dreams, and now I know why. I bet your dreams have changed, too."

Nessa's only answer was a sigh. She glided her hand over his chest, his arms, stroking down to his hips and thighs. Although his blood burned in his veins and he ached to touch and take, he held still.

She leaned over him, her eyes locked on her hands as she stroked him. She watched with rapt fascination, as though she wished to memorize everything about him.

"So different," she whispered. "Everything about you looks so different . . . but you feel the same."

"And how is that?"

She slanted a look at him. "Like the rest of me—the other half of my heart. I've felt broken, incomplete . . . ever since you left me. Five hundred years of that. And now I feel like I'm whole again. I'm me. It feels like there is life in me again."

She raked her nails up over his thigh.

That light touch left him shivering, and she smiled, doing it again. Involuntarily, his hips jerked when her hand drew near his cock. Her smile took on a devious slant and she started to stroke her fingertip in little circles high on his thigh.

As she lightly brushed against him, Dominic hissed out a breath. "You're asking for it," he muttered.

"Am I?" She bent over and pressed her lips to his thigh. "What exactly am I asking for?"

Then she touched her tongue to his skin.

Dominic groaned. Cool, slender fingers closed around his cock and he reached down, folded his hand around hers, squeezing. Gritting his teeth, he started to rock against her hand. She flicked her tongue against the sensitive flesh of his balls and he swore as fire tore through him.

"Witch," he muttered.

"Hmmm." Then she nudged his hand aside, using her hand to hold his cock steady. Watching him from under her lashes, she closed her mouth around the head of his shaft and began to suck.

She used her tongue, the edge of her teeth, her hands on him while Dominic tore at the sheets beneath him, rising to meet her touch.

She worked him close . . . so close. And then she stopped.

Dominic gaped at her as she straightened up and once more folded her hands in her lap. She grinned at him and said, "You taste different."

"You are a cruel, cruel woman." He caught her eyes and then moved, uncoiling from the bed and catching her slim body, tucked her beneath him. Pushing his knee between her thighs, he started to rock against her.

She was hot, slick . . . and wet. He shuddered as he rubbed his thigh against the damp curls between her thighs. He wanted to feel those curls brush against the head of his cock, wanted to push inside her and feel her clench around him. Catching her wrists, he drew them over her head, held them pinned there with one hand.

Heat flashed through her blue eyes as she tugged against his hold. "Going to hold me down, then?" she asked, her voice husky and soft.

He brushed his lips against hers. "Do you want me to let go?"

"Not on your life."

"Then I won't." He wedged his hips between her thighs and pushed against her. Steadying his cock, he pressed it to her entrance. Her gaze held his. In the blue depths of her eyes, he saw hunger, need . . . love. A love that he had been missing, every day of his life—of this *new* life. The only life he really remembered, but it hadn't even felt like a true life, not until he found out about her.

Like the rest of me—the other half of my heart . . . now I feel like I'm whole again.

Whole.

That was it, completely.

She made him whole.

In his dreams, at least.

As he sank inside her, one slow inch at a time, he stared at her face. Letting go of her wrists, he cupped her chin and angled her head. As he withdrew, and then sank deep, deep back inside her, he watched her face.

She arched underneath him, her knees coming up to grip his hips. She clenched around him, silky soft and sleek. "Please . . ." she whispered. Her lashes fluttered over her eyes and she blindly sought his mouth. Against his lips, she said it again, "Please . . . please . . ."

"Come back to me," he ordered, his voice rough and

harsh. Slanting his mouth over hers, he kissed her deep, shuddering at the taste of her, struggling against the deeper hunger that moved inside him. He needed more. He needed all of her. He needed to look into her eyes outside of these crazy dreams and see that she *knew* him. He needed to sink his teeth into her neck and let the taste of her flood him, fill him. He needed to lie down to rest and know that she was with him.

Everything . . . he needed everything.

And until she stopped hiding, he had no chance of having it.

He fisted a hand in her hair and jerked her head back. Against her mouth, he growled, "Come back to me, damn it. Come back . . ."

She cried out, her body twisting and rocking against his. Her nipples burned into his chest, tight, hard little points. She shivered and clenched around him and the silken muscles of her pussy gripped him, milked him.

Shoving back onto his knees, he tucked her against him. He hooked his elbows under her knees, holding her open . . . exposed. He stared down, watching as he withdrew, his cock ruddy, gleaming with the moisture from her sex. Then, he sank inside, slow . . . slow . . . slow. . . . She was shivering, quivering, shaking when he seated his length completely inside her.

Slowly. Then not so slow . . . then fast, faster, faster . . . driving into her with all his strength, and it still wasn't enough. Falling back over her body, he tangled his hands in her hair and arched her head back. "Come back to me," he pleaded against her lips. "Please . . . Please, come back."

"Shhh . . ." She stroked a soothing hand down his back. "Just love me . . . Just love me."

Broken, he whispered, "I already do. I always have. Even when I had no idea who you were, that you waited, I loved you then."

"Show me, then." She nipped at his lower lip, then cupped his face between her hands, staring at him. "Show me now . . . just love me. Give me now, and we'll sort out the rest later."

Not enough . . .

But he wasn't strong enough to pull away, wasn't strong enough to deny either of them. As she kissed him, he wrapped his arms tight around her, rocking inside until the pleasure burned too hot, too bright. As she begged and pleaded and whimpered beneath him, he made love to her and when she climaxed with a cry, he was with her.

I T could have been hours later. It could have been minutes. He lay with his head pillowed between her breasts while she combed a hand through his hair.

"I've wanted this," she murmured.

Glancing up at her, Dominic asked, "What?"

"This." A smile curled her lips and she shrugged. "Just this. To be with you, like this, again. Every day of my life, I wanted this."

"Then take it." He nuzzled her belly, breathing in the scent of her skin. She smelled of woman. She smelled of sex. She smelled of him. He nipped the soft skin. His fangs throbbed in their sheaths and he shuddered as the need to bite her, mark her, crashed through him. "Come . . ."

Her body stiffened.

Dominic tensed as he caught the edgy scent of fear. Even in dreams, he felt it, sensed it. Rolling off her, he crouched on the bed, waiting. "What?" he asked quietly. "What is it?"

He heard nothing but the racing of her heart, smelled nothing but her fear. Yet he knew something was wrong.

"No." Her eyes closed, her face crumpling.

Dominic swore and reached for her, drawing her against him protectively. "What is wrong, baby?"

"I don't want to wake," she whispered. She opened her soft blue eyes and stared at him, her gaze glittering with tears. "I don't want to leave here . . . leave you."

"You're not leaving me." Shaking his head, he brushed her tangled hair back from her face and said, "Wake up . . . and come to me. Stop hiding . . . stop . . ."

Even as he said it, she was fading.

In the span of one heartbeat, she was gone.

CHAPTER 17

M ORGAN came awake with a jerk.

For a split second, she didn't remember anything . . . save her sister and the fact that she'd screwed up royally.

Then she realized the ceiling overhead wasn't *her* ceiling and the bed beneath her wasn't really a bed. It was a cot, hard and narrow and unyielding.

Jackknifing into a sitting position, she stared at the dim room while her heart raced in her throat.

Filtered sconces on the wall provided the only light and it wasn't much, either. But she could see well enough, and as she came off the bed, she caught sight of one thing that made her heart stutter.

But whether it was fear, or something else, she didn't know.

It was *him*.

Blood rushed to her cheeks as memories from her dreams slammed into her.

She didn't remember much of those dreams, just his mouth on her, his hands all over her body . . . and she could remember doing the same to him. Touching him, stroking him, tasting him.

Shoving her hair back from her face, she looked around the narrow, boxlike room and tried to figure out how they'd gotten in there. She remembered arguing with him—Dominic—his name was Dominic. She needed to leave, find Jazzy. He hadn't wanted her to go.

Then . . . what?

Her head began to pound and she sank back down on the edge of the cot, cradling it between her hands.

I know you're afraid, he'd told her. Then he'd said he wouldn't hurt her.

Because . . . what . . .

The pounding in her head increased and her breath caught at the pain.

I've spent too long waiting for you . . .

Too long.

In her heart, she felt something clench.

Her breath froze. She started to rock unconsciously, trying to remember something more. Anything more. But there was just darkness. Followed by dreams. Crazy dreams. Hot and wicked dreams.

Pressing her hands to her flushed face, she swallowed. Her mouth was dry, painfully so, and her heart raced. Against the fabric of her bra, her nipples were hard, pressing into the material. It lightly abraded them, just one more little edge of arousal gathering inside.

"I need a damn drink," she muttered.

And a cold shower.

Preferably away from the very, very confusing man stretched out on the floor . . . right in front of the door.

The only door in the tiny little room.

Shoving off the cot, she made her way around the edge of the room, tried to decide if she could slip outside without him waking.

He hadn't moved an inch. A few feet away she froze, staring at his still body.

And she did mean *still*—hell, it didn't even look like he was breathing.

Squinting her eyes, she stared at his chest, waiting to see it rise. Fall.

Nothing.

"Oh, shit," she whispered, shaking her head. "Don't be dead."

Sidling closer, she knelt down, brushed her fingers against his wrist.

His skin was cool. Too cool.

No. No. No.

It was an endless refrain in her head and tears burned her eyes. Her heart screamed in denial.

Swallowing, she closed her hand around his wrist, her fingers seeking the spot on the inside. Pulse . . . needed to check for a pulse . . .

And then, in the blink of an eye, *her* pulse was racing.

Morgan yelped out in shock as he moved. One moment, he was as still as death, and the next . . . she was stretched out flat under him and the weight of his body crushed hers into the floor.

Shaken, she stared at him.

Time stretched out.

She was acutely aware of him, that lean, strong body, so unbelievably strong and fast. And cool. Too damn cool, but it did seem to warm against hers.

There was also the odd, unnerving little fact that he didn't seem to be breathing . . .

But even as she thought that, his nostrils flared and she heard him inhale.

His lashes drooped over his eyes and he lowered his head, nuzzling her neck. "You smell so good," he whispered, his voice rough and low, drowsy. His tongue touched her skin. "You taste good, too." He lifted his head, watching her with sleepy eyes.

"Do I?" she asked. She blushed feeling like a fool.

All he did was smile and lower his head back to her neck, taking a deep breath . . . like he was just breathing her in. "Yeah. Real damn good." He nuzzled her neck.

She cupped the back of his head and arched her neck, baring it for him.

His body stiffened.

Something hot and potent, a power so strong it was nearly tangible, rolled through the room.

Morgan gasped as heat and fear coiled inside her. Clutching at him, she burrowed against him. Closer. She needed to be closer.

And for about two seconds, she was. His hand tangled in her hair and she shuddered as she felt the press of his teeth against her neck.

Then, quicker than she could follow, he was gone.

She blinked and sat up, staring at him as he stood on the far side of the room. Not that he was terribly far away in the coffin of a room. The only way he could have gotten any more distance between them would be if he had started to climb the walls.

"What?" she asked, feeling more than a little bewildered. At him.

At herself. What in the hell was she doing?

He shook his head. "I need a few minutes."

"Ahhh . . . okay."

His gaze flicked past her, lingered on the door. He edged around the room, keeping a careful distance between them. "Would you excuse me? I need to open the door."

"Then open it already," she snapped defensively. Hell, he was acting like he'd woken up to find her pawing him. Against his will.

Which was just plain stupid, because she knew he wanted her.

She could *feel* the edge of his hunger, and it was going to drive her mad.

She gestured to the door, which stood a foot off to her side. "By all means, open the damn door."

Something dark flashed through his eyes, something that sent a shiver down her spine. "Back away from it."

"Excuse me?"

"Get the fuck away from the door, because if I get too

close to you right now, I'm going to spend the next thirty minutes fucking you."

Morgan's mouth went dry. Her knees threatened to buckle. A river of heat ran through her lower body, need cramping in her belly. "I . . . ah . . ."

She didn't think she wanted to move.

Dominic's eyes narrowed. Then, abruptly, he turned away. His shoulders rose and fell as he took one deep, slow breath, followed by another. "Morgan, I need a few minutes, okay? Just move away from the door, please—I'm going to unlock it and let you out. Just don't try to leave. I need a few minutes, then we'll . . . shit. We'll talk. Okay? I just need to . . . clear my head, you don't need to be that close to me. I'll just make things worse."

Swallowing the knot in her throat, she retreated, moving away from the door. Folding her arms around her middle, she stared at the wall and tried to understand what in the hell was happening. Inside her heart. Inside her head.

He'd been wrong.

Being close to him didn't make things worse.

Not being close to him did that.

T HE moment she slipped out of the room, he locked the door again and stormed over to the mini fridge. He deactivated the locks and grabbed a pack of bagged blood. He hated the stuff, but right now, he had no choice.

The hunger was tearing into him, and although he could control his actions, he doubted he could control his body's *re*actions. Namely the fangs, the eyes. Since his control was already shot around her, he had to manage the blood hunger better.

He used his fangs to pierce the bag and drained it. The taste of it, flat, nearly bitter, lay on the back of his tongue, and he tried not to think about how Nessa would taste. Tried not to wonder if he'd ever have a chance to find out.

It took less than two minutes, and he listened to her

through the walls the entire time. Even if he could stand the thought of not having her close, it wasn't safe—

As that thought drifted through his mind, he felt it.

He jerked his head, eyes narrowed as he stared off into the distance.

What was that . . .

It wasn't danger, or at least not anything he could recognize as danger. It was . . . odd.

Son of a bitch.

It took him less than thirty seconds to figure out just *what* he was feeling.

Or rather . . . what he wasn't.

He'd only sensed something like this once, but it hadn't been that long ago. It hadn't even been a few days.

Ana Morell . . . no. Lawson. Ana Lawson. Ana, with the very strange gift. It had to be her.

He hoped.

Shit.

Shit.

Shit.

He threw the empty blood bag on the bed and left the room, leaving the door unlocked.

He found Morgan in the living room, pale and shaken. She had a pinched look to her eyes, her soft mouth. With her arms crossed over her middle, she huddled against the wall, watching him as he drew near.

"I feel something really weird," she said softly.

He tucked a lock of hair behind her ear and murmured, "I know. I feel it, too."

"How?" She swallowed, then shook her head. "Doesn't matter. We need to leave. *Now. Right* now."

Dominic cocked a brow. "We don't need to leave. Relax. I think I know what's going on."

"What?" she demanded.

"Too complicated to explain, but don't worry, okay?" Dominic shrugged restlessly and cocked his head, straining to hear something outside the house.

But his ears weren't cooperating and it wasn't until the car turned onto their street that he even heard it.

"Don't worry," she muttered as she followed him through the house. "Don't worry, he tells me."

Dominic waited on the dark porch, peering out into the night. Sure enough, a Mustang convertible shortly turned into their driveway. As before, his ears and his senses might not be working as well as he'd like, but he could see just fine.

Fine enough to see that it was only Ana and the kid with her—her little brother. A little brother that stood damn near half a head taller than her, too, Dominic noticed as Brad climbed out of the car and came to stand by Ana, one hand resting protectively on her shoulder.

Duke wasn't there, and neither was Jazzy.

Brad mounted the steps, Ana following close behind. Brad's purple blue eyes moved from him to the woman standing just a few feet behind him, then back to Dominic's. "Guess you found who you were looking for."

"Yeah. Where are Duke and . . . his friend?"

Brad smiled. "Headed to Virginia. Figure that's a good place for the friend to be."

Yeah. Excelsior was about the best place imaginable for Jazzy, Dominic figured. "Okay. So . . . why are *you* here?" he asked, cocking a brow at Brad. The boy's only response was to tap his temple.

Dominic scowled. He didn't need Brad to explain in any more detail. The kid was a psychic. He felt a need to be here, so that's where he was going to be. It also explained *how* they were here—the safe houses weren't exactly advertised, but a kid like Brad wouldn't need a map.

According to the news Dominic had heard through the grapevine, Brad had been approached by the Council eight months earlier. The kid had spent much of the past few months completing the initial, intense training—rumor was it made boot camp look like something designed for sissies.

Brad had passed with flying colors, despite the fact that

he was still mortal—more or less—and physically weaker than many of the other Hunters.

Shifting his gaze to Ana, he said, "What about you?"

She shrugged and lifted her hands. "Ask him." She pointed to her brother.

Something rippled through the air, far off, at the very edge of Dominic's senses. Behind him, he heard Nessa's soft intake of breath. Shifting, he turned so he could see her, as well as keep an eye on Brad and Ana.

"It's okay . . . Morgan," he said, forcing the name out of his mouth.

It left a bad taste on his tongue, and he was surprised as hell she hadn't felt the lie. Calling her Morgan—it was nothing *but* a lie. To him. For him. He saw the surprise flicker across Ana's face as he spoke.

She'd recognized Nessa. He just hoped she didn't go asking questions right now, because there was no way he could explain anything just yet. Hell, maybe never. How could he explain what he didn't understand?

"She's doing this." His witch stood there, glaring at Ana with distrust in her eyes.

Ana swallowed. Dominic sensed the fear inside her, but she shoved it aside and angled her chin up. "Yes, I am."

"Quit it. It's not . . . It's not safe," she said, shaking her head.

"I have to." Then she cocked her head, peering at Nessa with narrowed eyes. Her eyes shifted to a point past Nessa's shoulder, as though she was looking at somebody. Something.

Her gaze was so intense that Dominic found himself doing the same thing, but he saw nothing . . . nothing but the night sky and the darkness of the ocean.

Brad rested a hand on his sister's shoulder, squeezed. She turned her head, staring at him.

Unspoken communication always left Dominic feeling tight, edgy. They said nothing, nothing aloud, anyway, but Dominic knew for damn sure they were talking.

Psychics. He shoved a hand through his hair and looked

away from them. His skin crawled and now he understood why psychics sometimes left other non-humans feeling more than a little on edge.

There was something downright spooky about that kid, about the unspoken conversation that passed between him and his sister.

"Dominic?"

He looked up and met Nessa's summery blue eyes. Giving her a smile, he said, "They're okay. They aren't here to hurt you."

She shook her head. "That's not it. There's . . . It's more than that. Something feels wrong." Her mouth twisted in a spasm and she reached up, rubbed the back of her neck. "I don't know. Man, my head is killing me."

"You're fighting it. Your head hurts because you're fighting too hard."

It was Ana's voice, quiet, soft, shaking just a little.

Nessa frowned and looked at the other woman. "Fighting what?" she demanded sourly.

Ana licked her lips and shrugged.

"Yourself." She glanced away, staring out at the ocean. "I . . . uh . . . well, I can see . . ."

"We're psychic." Brad moved, putting his body between Ana and Nessa. "We hear 'whispers,' both of us. And there's just a crazy amount of whispers coming from your head."

Dominic scowled. That wasn't entirely true . . . just the faintest bit of lie colored Brad's words. Catching Brad's gaze, he narrowed his eyes.

The young man returned his stare levelly.

Then, clear as day, Brad fucking *spoke* inside Dominic's head. *Not a good idea to go into any more detail than that right now.*

Dominic wanted to know why the hell not.

You'll just have to trust me. Then he looked away and met his sister's gaze.

Trust him. Dominic swore and pressed the heels of his hands to his eyes. "What in the hell is going on?" he muttered.

He lifted his head and slanted a look at Ana. "What do you call your gift?"

"Not much of a gift." She shrugged and tucked her hands into her pockets. "It's called 'blocking.' Not much more than me playing psychic chameleon. I don't have the instincts of a fighter and my instinct is to withdraw, hide away. When I sense something threatening, I 'block' and it makes it seem like I'm just a typical human, no psychic skill whatsoever. Makes it harder for non-mortals to sense me. But I can't limit my range, and when I'm blocking, *everything* around me is blocked as well. So nobody can really sense me, but they can't sense others, either."

"You're dangerous."

It was Nessa, her voice low and hard.

Ana's lashes lowered, shielding her eyes. "I'm aware it's not the ideal gift to have, but I didn't choose it. The best I can do is control it."

"Then why aren't you controlling it now?"

"Because something's coming . . . and I know that for a fact." Her eyes met Nessa's, held her gaze steadily. "Brad saw them. He knows how many, and he knows when. We won't *feel* them coming, but Brad already knows about them. And while we can't feel them, they can't feel us, either. They know about Dominic, and you. That's it."

A weak smile curled her lips and she shrugged. "Think of us as your ace in the hole . . . especially Brad. And trust me, he's one hell of an ace."

Morgan stared at the woman, wondering if somebody besides her realized how insane this sounded.

"Somehow I don't think a kid just barely old enough to shave and some chick who's afraid of her own shadow are exactly the people I want at my back if a fight is coming." Backing away, she glanced at Dominic and said, "I'm not hanging around for . . . whatever this is."

"You aren't leaving," he said, turning and meeting her

eyes. His voice was flat and level. He could have been discussing the weather for all the emotion he showed.

"You *can't* keep me here," she snapped.

"Yeah, so you've already told me. But know what? I damn well am."

She flexed her hand, tempted to reach up, smack that sexy, lean face. He watched her, pain in those dark eyes . . . longing. "Why, damn it? What in the hell do you want from me?"

A smile quirked his mouth. "If I tell you that, I'm really going to terrify you."

"I don't think I could get any more freaked out than I already am." She wrapped her arms around herself, rubbing at her arms. She was cold. Cold, tired and hungry. "Just spill it, Dominic. What in the hell do you want from me?"

"Everything." Then he turned away. He stared off into the night.

While she tried to get a grip on that, he took a step toward the waist-high railing on the elevated porch.

A car turned down the street.

Morgan tensed.

Dominic took a deep, slow breath. "Showtime," he said quietly.

CHAPTER 18

"YOU'RE sure they are here?" Isis demanded, glaring at Marty.

He curled his lip at her. "No, you stupid bitch, I'm not. I can't sense fuck, and something's messing with my nose, too, so I can't be sure I'm following the right scent. But this is the best I can do unless you can figure out what's screwing with my senses, my instincts."

Arrogant bastard. Isis wondered if she should just kill him when this was done.

If she did that, she left one of her borders open though and she really did hate that. But perhaps fate would smile upon her . . . and she'd be welcoming her dear daughter back into her arms. She laughed quietly. No, she and Morgan hadn't ever been on good terms, but the younger woman had the makings of a powerful witch and she'd gotten hooked on the blood magic early—there was no way she could fight those cravings, not while she lived.

If.

It was one big, fat *if.* She had sensed nothing but an echo of Morgan's presence when she'd fought the old witch that wore Morgan's body. But Agnes Milcher was strong. Damn strong. Isis suspected the old hag could have just suppressed any lingering traces of Morgan. If anybody could have done it, it was that old Hunter bitch.

She closed her eyes and extended her senses, trying to pick up . . . something.

Something. She didn't know what. "Can you smell anything? The witch? The vampire?" she asked.

Marty grunted. "I smell a woman. Think it's her, but can't be sure. Vamp is a little stronger, lingers in the air a little longer. But like I said, everything is faint."

Isis rubbed her temple, frustrated. She couldn't *feel* anything.

Not a vampire. Not a witch.

If a low-level witch was a buzz on her senses, then a powerful witch like Agnes would have been like an electric shock. But she couldn't feel a damn thing.

"There." Marty pointed ahead, at a house that stood apart from the others, a little closer to the water.

It was a small, elegant-looking cabin with a motorcycle parked in the front, along with a convertible.

"Why are we doing this again?" Marty demanded. "I'd rather just steer clear of the Hunter bastards. It's how I've stayed alive this long."

"Nobody lives forever." Isis smirked. "Do you know I had another daughter? Her name was Morgan. A few years ago, she got into a fight with a Hunter by the name of Agnes Milcher."

Marty's eyes popped wide. Something shifted in the depths of his gaze, the first shadow of his beast. The wolf stared at her from Marty's still normal-looking gaze, gnashing his teeth and snarling in fear.

"Agnes . . . shit, Isis, there is no way I'm going to square off with *that* old bitch."

Isis smiled. A few years ago, she would have said the same thing.

But then again, a few years ago, talk of the old woman seemed to . . . stop.

"They say she died," Isis murmured. "They say she died fighting my daughter. That's what the rumors were, but I've never been one to put much stock in rumors."

Especially not this kind—Morgan was a screwup, had always been a screwup. How could that idiot kid possibly have done enough damage to kill the strongest witch the Hunters had?

Marty stared at her, shaking his head. "What the shit are you talking about? What's going on?"

"Tell me, wolf . . . that idiot witch, did she look like this?" She brushed a hand over her face, felt the warmth of illusion settle over her features as she turned to look at Marty.

"Exactly."

A smile curled Isis's lips and she let the illusion fade. "The witch I fought a few weeks ago, she wore my daughter's face, her body. But her magic wasn't Morgan's. It was a Hunter's magic. She stank with it."

"The kid I saw earlier wasn't any Hunter. She smelled of violence. Bloody death."

"Yes . . . and she calls herself Morgan. It makes me wonder what happened the night Morgan and Agnes fought. Which of them truly died . . . and which one lived."

As the car glided to a stop, she peered up onto the porch. Her eyesight wasn't as refined as a wolf's—just slightly better than average. But the moon cast a watery, silvery light on the world, and she could see a dark haired man leaning against a railing.

Almost as if he waited for them.

"If you get me killed, Isis, I'm going to haunt your ass," Marty muttered darkly.

Isis ignored him.

"Showtime," she whispered.

As the car drew closer, Dominic squinted, tried to focus. He wanted his eyes to work *better* to make up for his ears and his nose working less, but it didn't work that way. Part of him wanted to tell Ana to let up, but he couldn't do that, not unless he wanted those coming to sense them as well.

"Morgan, I want you to take Ana, show her the inner room, the one where we slept." He wanted the two women out of the way. Ana was too vulnerable—she might be a highly trained psychic, but her skills were all defensive. She was better at hiding than defending herself.

And Nessa—hell, she still didn't know who she was. Probably didn't entirely understand *what* she was. Whatever was going on with her, it was too effective, because the power he suspected she *would* have had just wasn't there.

But of course, his witch couldn't cooperate.

"Why?" she demanded.

He turned his head, looking at her over his shoulder. "It's safer."

"Safer." She shook her head and said, "The hell it is."

He was lying about something, Morgan realized. She didn't know what. But he had been lying about something, and steadily . . . almost from the get-go. Until she knew what he was hiding, she wasn't going to do a damn thing he said.

Even then, she might not.

"No. Hell, no. I'm not letting you lock me away in that little coffin while you . . ." Her words trailed off as the car turned down the narrow, short drive, heading straight for the little beach house. "Besides, it's too late. They are already here."

"Damn it," Dominic muttered, raking a hand through his hair. "Morgan, get inside, *now*."

"No." She crossed her arms over her chest and leaned against the wall, staring straight ahead.

"Hiding won't do any good," the boy said.

Morgan glanced at him. He had young-old eyes, she noticed. Like he'd seen way, way too much, and it had weighed on him. A grim, heavy burden, one that shouldn't have been born by someone so young.

"They always find you when you hide," Morgan said quietly. She wrapped her arms around herself and rested against the wall. Tucking her chin against her chest, she held still . . . and waited.

I sis uncurled from the car, staring up at the porch.

    She could see him rather clearly now, despite the strange magic blocking her senses. He looked young—a very lovely man.

As she mounted the steps, he watched her, his dark eyes betraying no thoughts, no emotions.

Marty followed close at her back, stopping on the step behind her as she paused to study the vampire.

Isis couldn't help but appreciate the whole package. The body matched the face . . . lovely. Wide shoulders, a little too lean, a little too skinny, but still, nicely muscled and she knew he'd be deliciously strong. After all, he was a vampire.

Damned shame. He'd be fun to play with, but she knew better than to toy with Hunters.

His eyes flicked to her and then to Marty, still waiting at her back.

"Should have gutted you," the vampire said, his voice a low, rough drawl.

Marty growled.

The vampire ignored him, focusing on Isis. She surreptitiously studied the others standing just behind him. An unknown blond woman—she didn't smell of magic, and Isis's instincts told her she wasn't a witch. She certainly wasn't a vampire or shifter. So not likely a Hunter. She all but stank of fear. There was a boy at her side, a blond, a few years younger, probably not much older than Jazzy. A child, and not much of a threat there, either, she decided.

Then she shifted her gaze to the woman standing just behind the vampire. When she saw Morgan's familiar face, her eyes narrowed. "Treacherous little bitch," she hissed. "Damn it, where is my little girl?"

"Your little girl?" the vampire asked, cocking a brow.

His nostrils flared, and she watched as he drew in a deep, slow breath. *Odd.* He was scenting her. But he would have done that earlier, probably already pegged who she was—she smelled too much like her two daughters not to be a blood relative.

Vampires were like bloodhounds. He should have already figured out who she was. Unless whatever odd magic handicapping her had affected him as well.

"Yes." She let her voice wobble and then jutted her chin up. "My daughter. You've already sunk your claws into this one, but you can't have Jazzy."

A grin curled the vampire's mouth. "Well, that's an interesting tactic to try." He leaned a hip against the railing, hooking his thumbs in the pockets of his jeans. "I'm afraid the kid is out of your reach now."

"She's my *daughter*," Isis snarled. "I will find her."

A wicked light gleamed in the vampire's eyes. Smirking, he replied, "Well, if you try really hard, I'm sure you can figure out where we'd send a young witch who was more than a little confused about how to use her magic. But if you're smart—and I think you're a sharp one—you'll also know you don't stand a chance in hell of getting your hands on her."

"Bastard." She spat the word out. She didn't have to feign her hostility. No fucking way—they'd sent her daughter *there*?

No. She hadn't expected this. "You had no *right*."

The vampire shrugged. "Legally? You're right. We had no right. But then again, legally, you had no right to whale on her when you were pissed off. You had no right to let her go hungry and I can tell just by looking at her she's gone hungry in her life . . . a lot. There's probably a lot more, too, if we dig down below the surface." A cocky smile curled his lips and he drawled, "You and me, we both live in a world where the rules of mortals don't really apply quite the same."

He shoved off the steps, clearing them in one easy, agile

jump and landing in front of her. He gave her a taunting grin as he rocked back on the balls of his feet. "The kid is out of your reach now, witch. Deal with it."

Deal with it. Rage had her shaking, and all she wanted to do was knock that arrogant smirk off his face.

They'd sent her kid off to Excelsior. *Excelsior!*

It was the last thing she'd expected to hear. But then again, she hadn't known what she was expecting. She'd only come wanting to see Morgan with her own eyes, see who was living in that body.

Narrowing her eyes, she looked at Morgan and said, "Did you have some part in this, you old crone?"

The old crone would have just smiled. Or laughed.

But the young woman stared at her with a dumbfounded look. "Part of what?"

"Sending your baby sister off to that . . . that . . . *brainwashing jail.*" She'd be untouchable—there was no way in hell Isis could get her daughter away from the school. No way. She knew her youngest. Too well. She'd believe the lines the Hunters handed her—would believe that "greater purpose" bit, that she was to use her gift to serve, to protect.

But then again, Jazzy had always had that streak of weakness in her. The Hunters would exploit that—brainwash her. *Change* her.

Damn it, Isis hadn't seen this coming . . . Jazzy wasn't a strong witch, but she was a witch. She might not have blood on her hands, but she had done bad things, unpleasant things.

The Hunters shouldn't have wanted her . . . unless it involved seeing her dead.

Isis would rather see her youngest dead than in the hands of those brainwashing bastards.

The woman with her daughter's face shook her head. "I don't know what in the hell you're talking about. Do . . ." She snapped her mouth shut before she finished his name. Instead, she jabbed a finger toward the vamp and said, "He knows Jazzy, made sure she was someplace safe."

"Safe." Isis laughed. "Is that what he told you? Damn

it, Morgan, you've gotten even more stupid in the past few years. How is that possible?"

Morgan's eyes narrowed. "You . . . You're my mother."

"Fucking idiot, did you just now figure that out? What in the hell is wrong with you?"

T HE woman had a lot of hatred inside her, Morgan thought. A lot of hate. A lot of rage.

And evil. It clung to her, like a second skin. How could she have left Jazzy alone with *that*?

Giving her mother a sharp smile, she said, "Lucky me, I hit my head hard enough to forget every damn thing I ever knew about you. And now I'm wondering if there's a way to make sure that doesn't change—I'd rather not know."

"If you've forgotten me, then you've likely forgotten other stuff as well . . . like what kind of man this is," Isis said. She shifted her gaze to the vampire and murmured, "Do you have any idea who he is? What he does? What will happen to Jasmine?"

"Can't be anything worse than what you've done to the poor girl for her entire life. What you've done to her since I left. She told me all about it. She'd go days without eating, unless she could steal something on her own. You would disappear and she'd be alone in that house for days, weeks." Morgan shook her head. "Stop the caring mother routine—I don't remember you, but even I can tell you've never cared about another soul a day in your life."

"It has nothing to do with being a caring mother." Isis waved a hand. "It has to do with not wanting my *child* to end up like one of them."

"One of *who*?" Morgan demanded. She shouldered past Dominic, coming to a halt just a few feet away. "What in the hell are you talking about?"

Isis cocked her head, studying Morgan's face. Frustrated, she reached out with her magic, trying to read the girl, trying to get something off her. It wasn't easy. It was damn near impossible—all she picked up was the vaguest impression.

Isis hadn't ever realized just how fully she relied on her magic.

But . . . she didn't think Morgan lied.

She didn't know.

"You must have hit your head pretty damn hard," Isis murmured. "Sweetie, that's a Hunter . . . and he kills witches."

Morgan hissed out a breath. "That's bullshit."

"Is it?" Isis smiled. "Ask him."

The vampire curled his lip at her, but as Morgan turned to face him, the look faded, replaced by one that confused the hell out of Isis.

Tenderness.

Need.

For my daughter . . . ?

But as soon as he reached out and stroked a hand down Morgan's face, Isis had her answer. No. Not for Morgan. For Nessa—for the old crone who'd damned near killed Isis.

But this wasn't Nessa in front of her. It couldn't be, because the Hunter witch's power had been like a supernova and nothing could have completely eradicated that strength.

Even with her weakened gift, she could sense that much.

Granted, she didn't feel like *Morgan*, either.

That wasn't important, though. This wasn't Nessa—and *that* was what mattered more than anything else.

"W HAT is a Hunter?" Morgan asked, but she didn't know if she asked Dominic or Isis.

"Basically, they are just cops." Dominic's eyes stared into hers, the intensity of his gaze a weighty, palpable thing. It was like he was trying to tell her something. Convince her of something.

This isn't who you are . . .

That voice whispered in the back of her mind.

Swearing, Morgan reached up and shoved a hand through her hair, yanking lightly with the hope that small pain might clear her muddled head.

"*Basically.*" She shook her head. "It's more than that. I can feel it."

"It *is* more than that." He took a step closer, turning his back on Isis.

Oh, you shouldn't do that . . . Morgan shifted minutely so she could continue to keep an eye on the other witch. There was no denying they were related. The woman looked a few years older, but not by much. She could have passed for an older sister. But Morgan knew it was more—she'd come from that woman. And that woman reeked of evil.

Her belly churned, nausea roiling inside her. She'd come from that . . .

No. No, you did not.

"So tell me what else there is to it. Do you kill witches?" A hunter . . . a hunter of what? A witch hunter, maybe? Is that what Isis was talking about?

His eyes narrowed. "I have. But not unless I had to."

Morgan sputtered, a disbelieving laugh falling from her lips. This man killed witches—he'd admitted it. And he had Jazzy. *Shit.*

He wouldn't hurt the girl.

Snarling, she spun around and pressed her fisted hands to her temples. "Would you just shut *up*?" she spat out. That voice in her head, it was going to drive her nuts. If the pain didn't kill her. It felt like it was trying to split her head into a thousand tiny fragments.

"Exactly why would you *have* to kill a witch?" she asked, the words reluctant. They didn't want to be spoken. They felt *wrong*. "Does somebody order you to do it? Are you afraid of them . . . what?"

"Ordered? No. I don't kill on command." He moved up behind her. She sensed him, even though she didn't hear him. "I kill when I have to . . . to protect others. Like your sister. Like you . . . those men earlier, they would have hurt you, forced you to do things you couldn't ever undo, no matter how much you wanted to. I'm not a murderer . . . I don't indiscriminately kill witches or . . . well, anybody."

"He's lying," Isis whispered.

Morgan glanced up, watched as her mother sidled closer. Her platinum-streaked hair fell in a straight line to her waist and her blue eyes were a shade between the blue green of Jazzy's and Morgan's own summery blue. Completely lovely. Completely evil. Swallowing the knot in her throat, Morgan gritted out, "I don't remember you but I know enough about you. I know what my gut says . . . you're one of the best liars in the world. Why should I believe you?"

"Don't believe *me*." Isis shrugged. "Believe yourself. He doesn't speak the truth, or not the whole of it. You can feel that, the same as I can." She curled her lips and glanced around. "If you'd end this damned spell, you could sense even more of his lies."

"I didn't cast any spell." Her all-too-familiar headache settled at the base of her skull once more, pounding in time with her heart.

Out of the blue, she found herself staring at Ana.

You're fighting it. Your head hurts because you're fighting too hard.

That was what Ana had said.

Fighting too hard—fighting *herself*. The other woman waited on the porch still, standing silently by her brother. Her mouth was a thin, tight line. Fear clung to her, but she didn't flee. Didn't cower.

Courage . . . that woman had it in spades.

"Somebody cast this fucking spell," Isis snarled. "I feel almost powerless, and something is causing it. It's not *him*. So if it's not him, and you claim it's not you . . ."

Isis narrowed her eyes and understanding glinted in them.

As she turned to face Brad and Ana, the younger man moved, placed his body between Isis and his sister. With his hands tucked in his back pockets and a cocky grin on his face, he looked like some college kid.

Cute, confident . . . harmless.

Isis glanced at him and then to the woman behind him. Cocking her head, she said, "You're not a witch."

Ana said nothing.

"Whatever it is you're doing, stop it now or I—"

Brad laughed. "Damn, woman. You got balls. Making threats you can't possibly follow through on."

Marty slunk around behind them. How had he gotten up there? He'd just been down here only seconds ago. Now he was up there on the porch without making any noise. Quiet, so quiet . . . how could these people move with such utter silence? In the shadows, Morgan could hardly see him.

But as he lunged for Ana, the brother shifted and lifted a hand.

Morgan's jaw dropped as Marty's body froze in midair. His mouth was open, his eyes half wild. A snarl tore free from his lips. He shouted something, but Morgan had no idea what.

She was too busy staring at his mouth. His teeth. Long, wickedly curved. Utterly inhuman.

Shaking, she backed away. Her body brushed against Dominic's and she flinched. As his hands came up, she sidestepped away, keeping all of them in her sight. *What is going on?*

CHAPTER 19

Isis swore, staring at Marty's suspended body.

There was no magic.

She would have felt that.

There had been a faint, damn near unnoticeable crackle of energy, but it wasn't magic.

Psychic—

Her face contorting in a scowl, she looked at the young man. Him and the woman—she'd written them off entirely. They weren't witches, shifters or vamps, therefore they weren't worth her concern.

Wrong.

Utterly wrong.

She shot the vampire a dark look and then focused on Morgan's face.

Indecision swarmed inside. What did she do? She could run, and that might be the wisest decision. She'd live that way. Somehow, she knew the vampire wouldn't take the time to mess with her, not yet. Whatever he wanted from Morgan, it was his priority. She could live, plan and then try again . . . or just disappear, start all over.

No. You're not running. It's one damn vampire. A couple of psychics.

Morgan. This all had to do with Morgan. Everything came back to her. Morgan . . . Nessa . . . whoever she was, whatever she was.

Willing the woman to look at her, Isis said, "You know he isn't being honest. If he isn't being honest, then you're a fool to trust him. How can you trust him with your sister?"

Morgan's mouth twisted in a sneer. "Don't pretend to care about her. I don't remember you, but I *know* her. You never loved her. Hell, you *can't* love. So don't use her against me."

"Loving her and not wanting to see her mixed up with *his* kind are two different things." Isis shrugged. "One has nothing to do with the other. But you do love her. Can you really risk her?"

"Shut up," the vampire snapped, his voice cold and hard. He started toward Morgan, but she backed away from him, staring at him with indecision written all over her face.

He froze. His hands curled into fists, hanging useless at his sides.

There was pain in his eyes.

Isis breathed it in, tasted it. It was finer than wine . . . almost as good as the hit of power she got from fear. Almost as potent as death. Drinking it in, she closed her eyes . . . and that was one major mistake.

She sensed the movement, but not in time. A hand closed around her throat, and one heartbeat later, she was suspended in the air, her feet dangling a good foot and a half above the floor. The vampire's eyes glowed, glints of red dancing in his dark brown irises.

"Get it somewhere else, you parasite," he said.

She gurgled out a laugh, struggling to breathe past the hand that could crush the life from her. "Parasite . . . oh, now that's irony for you. *You* . . . calling me a parasite."

"I take no pleasure, reap no power from the misery of others." His fingers squeezed warningly and he brought her closer, holding her weight easily in one hand—untouched by it. "I feel it again, witch, you die."

Wheeling her eyes around, she gave Morgan a beseeching stare. "This is the freak you've chosen to trust?"

His hand tightened and black dots began to dance in front of her eyes. Terror bloomed in her mind and she struck out, calling for the one power in her arsenal that could really hurt him. The fire came, but it was sluggish, barely responding to her call.

She hurled it at him, but before it could so much as singe one hair on his head, it was doused.

She crashed to the floor, just in time to see Morgan coming for her.

A snarl peeled her lips back from her teeth and the sound coming from her throat barely sounded human.

Adrenaline spurred her movements. Acting on instinct, Isis reached down and drew the athame she liked to carry in her boot. Grabbing the hilt carved from bone, she jerked it up and lurched to her feet. Brandishing it in front of her, she snarled, "Come on, worthless bitch. You never did a damn thing to help me in your life . . . so I'll just settle for your death instead."

The knife Isis held didn't slow Morgan down—not for a microsecond.

She moved with a speed that Isis hadn't ever seen her daughter display. Speed . . . and skill. Her foot came up, swept out in an arc, knocking the blade out of Isis's hand. Isis hissed out a breath and backed away. The knife . . . she needed that damn knife.

There—

A fist came flying toward hers, clipping her on the temple. Pain exploded through her head and she went with it, letting it knock her to the ground. Nausea and agony roiled inside. Her head ached, pounded. Just a few inches away, though, she saw the glint of her knife.

Panting, she closed her hand around it, used her body to hide it as she rolled over and glared at Morgan.

Morgan pounced and Isis waited—waited—just before Morgan would have been on top of her, she whipped the knife out. Morgan jerked aside, just barely missing the blade.

Isis swore and then cried out, enraged. Hard, cold fingers closed around her wrist. With her face an implacable mask, Morgan battled Isis for control of the knife . . . and she was winning.

She fought with skill . . . confidence.

Isis had only fear on her side.

And her magic . . . she tried to call it to her hand, but she was still too drained. Just calling the fire had been too much for it.

"Worthless, *useless* bitch."

A DRENALINE dulled the pain.
Although Morgan's head ached, although those annoying, nagging whispers wouldn't shut the hell up, she wasn't blinded by the pain.

No, instead she was blinded by rage. Sheer, utter rage.

The bitch had pulled a blade on him. *Him* . . .

Without any conscious thought, she struggled with Isis, rolling on the ground, grappling for control of the blade. As the woman hissed out, "Worthless, *useless* bitch," Morgan gave her a taunting smile.

The pain swelled—like her brain was trying to split apart. In that voice that sounded so unlike her own, she taunted, "What is it the kids used to say? Oh, yes . . . it takes one to know one."

Isis shrieked, and in one last moment of desperation, she wrenched her knife hand free and swung out.

Morgan caught the wrist, closed her fingers around it, shifted with an ease born of long practice. *Natural.* It felt so natural to move like this, to fight like she'd done so her entire life.

Bone cracked. Isis still held the blade, but now Morgan was in control, her hand curled around Isis's hand, guiding the blade. Staring into the other woman's eyes, Morgan forced the blade into Isis's belly.

Isis screamed, and the warm wash of blood flowed over them.

The air was filled with the acrid, sour stink of a gut wound. Rising, she stared down at the other woman.

As her life ebbed away, that greedy, dark hunger rose inside, side by side with a cooler wash of energy. *You don't need the blood, do you now? Breathe now, girl. Come on . . . that's a girl . . . breathe . . .*

Groaning, she brought her fisted hands up, pressing them to her brow, mindless of the blood. *Shit*. The voices in her head—the whispers—that nasty black hunger. They were going to drive her insane—rip her apart.

As the adrenaline rush faded, the pain in her head returned, mounted. A hand came up, brushed her shoulder.

"Are you okay?"

Dominic . . .

Jerking away, she stared at him. Okay? No. She *wasn't* okay. Confused, scared. Terrified.

She forced the words out of her tight throat. "Where is my sister?"

"She's safe," he said, his voice gentle. "I swear to you, she's safe."

Truth . . . it felt like truth.

But Morgan couldn't . . . no . . . didn't *want* to trust that. This man . . . somehow . . . this man had the power to hurt her a great deal. Fear tore into her, vicious, jagged claws. She needed to get away—find Jazzy and get away—get very, very far away. Someplace where she could hide, where she wouldn't have to face whatever pain this stranger promised her.

"I want to go to my sister. Right *now*."

Dominic swallowed. "I can't take you right now." Then he turned, staring at the body sprawled at their feet.

"What do you want me to do with this one?" Brad asked quietly.

But Dominic barely heard him. His throat was tight. Too fucking tight for him to speak, and his head hurt, too much to think. His heart hurt, too, and damn it, it hadn't hurt like this in . . . forever.

No. Actually it was just a few centuries ago, he thought

to himself morbidly. Back when he lay dying, he'd hurt like this.

Just as now . . . he hurt . . . over her.

She still stood there, trembling, covered with the other witch's blood.

All he wanted to do was hold her.

And she'd pulled away. She didn't want his comfort or his concern or any damn thing from him.

"Dom?"

Lifting his head, he caught Ana's eyes and then glanced at Brad. Brad still held the werewolf in the air—effortlessly, it seemed. He hung there like some sort of life-sized piñata. Dominic smiled grimly at the image—he could find some blunt object and beat the bastard until his skin split.

Not trusting his rage, he looked at Brad. "You up to dealing with him?"

Ana went pale, but said something, turning her head to look at Brad. There was understanding in his young-old eyes and then he looked at the werewolf. "Yeah, I can handle him."

The wolf howled, snarled. "Damn it, I didn't do a damn *thing*."

"Yeah, you're all about hugs and kitties, aren't you?" Brad said, his lip curling. Then a mask fell over his face.

The air around them grew tight.

Dominic didn't bother to watch. He had a mess to clean up—soon, there would be two dead bodies—his ears caught the acceleration in the wolf's heartbeat, followed by a stuttering pause. Then the heart stopped. No, make that there *were* two bodies to deal with.

And Nessa . . .

Rubbing the heel of his hand over his heart, he tried to figure out just how he was to handle that. What was he supposed to do?

"Later," he muttered. He'd have to handle it later.

Looking at Ana, he said, "Can you stop now? It's safe, right?"

Ana looked at Brad. The young man stood there, hands

still tucked in his pockets. He had been looking at the wolf—still suspended in the air. When he looked away, the wolf's body fell, lifeless and limp, to the wooden planks of the porch. "We're clear."

The return of his senses was damn near deafening. Dom waited until his head stopped swimming before he moved. The bodies—he'd deal with the bodies first, get them tucked away before any nosy neighbors saw anything and then . . . and then . . .

Slowly, he turned, stared at Nessa.

She stood in the exact same spot, in the exact same position, a bloody knife in one small fist, her skin pale, splattered with blood.

And then—nothing.

Dominic didn't know what he was supposed to do now.

The woman before him was fractured, falling to bits and pieces, and so close to stumbling down a path that had no return.

He didn't know how to help her.

And until he could, his life might as well be over.

He had nothing without her.

He'd existed well enough *before* he'd learned who she was . . . who she was to *him*. But now?

Now . . . without her, nothing mattered.

CHAPTER 20

*J*AZZY.

Like a life preserver, Morgan focused on her sister.

She had to get Jazzy.

Breathing shallowly, she watched as Dominic spoke quietly to the young psychic.

Marty was dead. Morgan didn't understand how—or what. One moment he'd been hanging in midair and then the next, he was on the ground, his eyes all but bugging out, mottled bruises on his throat. Like he'd been choked, although nobody had touched him.

And Isis—her mother—she was dead, too.

So much death.

Jazzy . . . have to get to her . . .

The pain was an excruciating song inside her head and her hands were sweating, clammy. The knife in her hand felt slippery—too slippery. She almost dropped it twice and she couldn't do that.

She needed the knife. Needed it to find her sister—

Dominic. Had to get past him. But he wouldn't let her . . .

*Then you have to make him. Use the knife. Get away.
Get away from him.*

Like she stabbed a man every day of her life.

I can't. He hasn't hurt me . . . .

An insidious whisper insisted, *But he lies to you. You
can see that, feel that. How can you trust him?*

Trust him. Could she trust him? He *did* lie . . .

Pain tore through her head. Morgan gasped, stumbling
against the wall. Her head—it was spinning, flooded with
memories. No—not memories. Were they?

Screams and blood . . . Her head was full of them.
Screams and blood.

A gentle hand touched her face and Morgan jerked back,
swallowing the sob trying to break free. Shifting, she used
her body to hide the knife and with her free hand, she
smacked Dominic's wrist away. "Get away from me," she
said, her voice weak, ragged.

Can't breathe. She couldn't breathe.

He set his jaw and fell back.

She flinched as the force of his pain slammed into her.
Too much—she was feeling too much. Too much from him.

Away. Needed to get away. Find her sister.

From under her lashes, she watched as Dominic turned
aside.

Now.

She had to do it now. Had to get away from him and
find Jazzy. Then the pain would stop and the two of them
would be safe—

She shoved away from the wall, raised the knife. Clum-
sily, she lunged toward him. He heard her—she knew he
heard her, but he didn't turn. With a cry, she crossed the
final few feet between them and struck—

The pain sliced through her mind, and this time, it was
all-consuming. Brutal in its intensity.

She gasped, struggling to breathe past it, to think. Even
see—she couldn't see.

And then she could . . . but it wasn't her world she saw.
Wasn't her time.

She wasn't aware of Dominic as his lean body stiffened, as he staggered.

Wasn't aware of the blood that bloomed from the wound.

Wasn't aware of anything as time fell away.

"I do not fear your tests, William. Let Elias go. He has done nothing wrong."

William smirked. "If he has done nothing wrong, then by all means . . ." He glanced at one of the men and nodded. *"But first you must agree. You will be bound. You will submit to the tests. You will be cleansed."*

"Your men will untie him as I come to you. If you dare to be foolish, Sir William, you will know pain like nothing you have ever felt," she warned.

"Nessa!"

She lifted her head and stared across the distance separating them. They use ropes, Elias. You think I cannot get rid of a few paltry ropes? Run into the forest—to our cave. I will meet you there. And these simpletons can rot. We wasted months protecting them.

His dark brown eyes stared into hers with fury and desperation. Do not let him touch you, Nessa. I do not trust him—

She just shook her head. She would not risk Elias. She would not. She walked arrogantly toward William, holding her wrists out in front of her. He just smiled benevolently and gestured to one of his men.

"I shall deal with your husband," William said, his voice quiet and dignified. His eyes gleamed though, with something she did not like, not one bit. He would deal with her husband? Lower himself to free him? Instead of ordering his men . . . ?

Her ears pricked at those words. Her instincts screamed.

Rough rope bit into her wrists but she barely even noticed as she watched William walk over the uneven ground to where his men were cutting Elias free.

Elias shrugged away from them and started toward Nessa. She shook her head at him and she could see the argument in his eyes. Run, she said into his mind. Now.

She heard the argument in his head. Felt his refusal.

And then there was nothing but icy, sharp pain. She felt the brutal echo of it in her own heart.

They were soul mates—meant for each other even before birth. And it would have been better if that blade had killed her as well as Elias.

"*No!*" *she screamed out. She shoved at the sheriff's man, pushing away from him as though he were naught more than a child.*

"*Grab her—cover her eyes," one of the men bellowed.*

All around her people shouted—although some screamed in horror as they realized what one of William's men had done.

She barely even heard them. She was aware of nothing.

Nothing but the screams . . . and the blood.

It was Elias's blood, dripping from the dagger of a treacherous snake.

L OST in the fog of memories, she lifted her hands, pressed them to her eyes. A familiar scent flooded her head. Blood . . . metallic, strong. She lowered her hands, stared at the knife she held.

The bloodied knife.

Screams and smoke.

Anguish and anger.

Betrayal and blood.

Elias . . . his blood pumping out of him. His voice, weak and growing weaker, as he whispered, *I will come back . . . I will find you again.*

His eyes, so warm and dark, always so full of love . . . for her.

Those eyes—

Dazed, she lifted her head, seeking his face.

There. He stood there, sagging against the railing, half-turned toward her, staring at her with shocked, pained eyes.

Dark brown eyes.

So warm and dark, so full of love.

And pain.

"No."

Oh, dear God, what have I done?

The pain inside her head rose, swelling and swelling—a symphony of agony.

"No!"

She reached inside, grasped at something, without fully realizing what she was doing . . . or why.

A wall inside her head—a barrier. It shredded under the weight of her magic and as the weight of memories—five hundred years worth—slammed back into her head, Nessa staggered.

"Bloody hell!"

She stared at the knife in her hand . . . stared at the blood dripping from it. Deep, dark red . . .

"No."

She swallowed and looked up. Only seconds had passed—seconds for them. But it seemed a lifetime to her. Two lifetimes . . . more.

The man in front of her leaned against the railing, staring at her. Blood blossomed on the front of his shirt and she could see where the tip of the knife had gone completely through him.

The ugly red stain of his blood grew, spreading with every passing second.

"Dear Lord, what I have done?" she whispered.

Her ears might not be as sharp as some, but she heard rather well, and she could hear the erratic skip of his breathing, feel the pain. Hurling the knife down, she lunged for him as he staggered back.

His heart—

No. She'd stabbed high on the left side of his back, too close to the heart.

Too close—

Dominic gritted his teeth against the pain.

His fangs were out, throbbing and aching, desperate for blood, desperate for a fight. He'd been attacked, and all his body knew was that it wanted to attack back. Fight back. Sucking in a breath, he focused on that, the feel of air moving in, out of his lungs, as he reached for calm. For control.

He wasn't going to die.

As much as his instincts were screaming for a fight, he knew he wasn't going to die and he yanked his primitive urges under control, forced his body to respond. As his fangs slowly retreated, he made himself assess the damage.

It burned—too much. Silver in the knife. But not pure silver. It wasn't still inside him and it hadn't touched his heart, because if it had, he'd be on his knees. All in all, things could be worse.

With his weight braced against the railing, he stared at the ground. Could be worse . . . how?

She'd stabbed him—came at him from behind. The woman he loved. The woman he'd always loved. He'd been born just so he could find her again, have her again. And she'd stabbed him.

Sensing movement, he glanced up. Both Ana and Nessa. Moving toward him.

Ana pushed between him and Nessa, snarling as she shoved the other woman back.

He couldn't hear them, not a word. Not over the blood roaring in his ears.

She'd stabbed him . . .

B RAD caught his sister around the waist. Pressing a brotherly kiss to her temple, he said, "Back off, sis. It's cool."

"Cool? It's fucking cool? How in the hell can it be cool?" she spat out. "She just stabbed him. In the fucking back!"

"He'll be fine." Backing away, he pulled Ana with him.

Right now, the last place he wanted to be was between this witch and the vampire behind them.

He hadn't felt her power earlier, but now it slammed into him. Even Ana's gift wasn't strong enough to dull *that* kind of power. The light of this witch's power had been damn near extinguished just moments earlier, but now . . . hell, it was like trying to look into the sun. Too bright. Too painful.

"It's okay, Ana," he repeated again.

She struggled and drove her elbow back into his gut. Grunting, he let her go, still keeping between Ana and the witch. "Ana—I knew this was going to happen. And trust me. Okay? Just trust me."

N ESSA knew the other two were there.

But they were like gnats, in her way and annoying. And then they weren't.

All she could see was the man.

The man with eyes that had warmed when he looked at her. A man who smiled, like she was his reason for smiling.

And then she'd stabbed him—

Stop it. He lives. You can heal him . . .

Heat gathered in her hands. She wanted to look into those eyes, but for now, she didn't dare. Didn't dare.

"I . . ." She licked her lips as she drew close. "I'm sorry. I can't explain what came over me, but I . . . I can help."

He knew what she was. He'd been there, had seen. He knew. She wouldn't completely terrify him when she put her hands on him, healed him.

No, you did that when you stabbed him in the back.

Her hands shook, shivered so violently, they ached. "Let me help . . ."

He said something, but she didn't hear. Couldn't. Had to focus. On her hands. On the healing magic within them. She'd healed before. She could heal this man . . . and then maybe try to understand what was going on. Why everything inside him seemed to call to her.

Still not looking him in the eye, she placed one hand on his chest, the other at his back.

A gasp locked in her throat. Unable to stop it, she lifted her head and stared into his eyes.

Tears blinded her. Now, although she looked at him, she couldn't see. Couldn't see—

But she didn't need her eyes.

All she had needed to do was touch him. To *feel* him. Inside. In that cold, dark place that had been empty, ever since he had left her.

I will come back, he'd whispered. Had promised. And she had waited . . .

Inside her heart, something began to dance. To burn.

Through lips that trembled, she whispered his name. "Elias . . . ?"

A pained smile twisted his lips as he lifted a hand. He cupped her cheek in his hand. "Nessa . . . my Nessa."

His lashes drooped and then he sighed. It rattled out of his chest and he swayed on his feet. "My beautiful, silly little witch . . ."

CHAPTER 21

*S*HE *knows me.*

Dazed, wondering, Dominic stared at her face.

His chest burned and the flesh, reluctant to heal, was slowly knitting together. Silver-wrought wounds—such a pain in the ass.

Her hand covered his and she blinked, staring at him through a veil of tears. "What . . . how . . . ?" More words rose to her throat, but she couldn't speak. Couldn't think.

Didn't care to . . . he was *here*. That was all that mattered, all she could think about. Nessa launched herself at him. Her arms came around him, and Dominic grunted in pain as her hand touched the edges of his wound.

She froze and then low in her chest, she started to whimper. "No . . . No, this isn't happening—can't be happening. Dear Lord, what have I done?"

She tore away from him. "I can heal you—I swear, I can heal this. I've healed worse and I can heal this . . ."

She talked a mile a minute as she eased him to the porch floor, her hands gentle but strong. Because he wasn't feeling entirely his best, he let her.

Plus . . . she was touching him, her hands cool, soft and quick as she eased him facedown on the porch. "I'll heal this, Elias . . . for pity's sake, then we'll talk. How did this happen? How . . ."

He lost track of her ramblings as her fingers brushed against his skin. She sank her fingers into the rip of his shirt and tore it wide open. The noise seemed terribly loud, especially now that she'd gone abruptly silent.

"Oh." She touched him and he swore at the sheer heaven of it.

"You're . . . You're not bleeding," she whispered. Her voice trembled and then firmed as she said, "It's not bleeding. You're . . . healing."

Dominic rolled to his back and stared up at her.

They were alone, he realized abruptly. He didn't even know how that had happened. Distantly, he heard a familiar, powerful engine and he figured it was Ana and Brad, speeding away into the night.

With the bodies, too, because he couldn't see either the witch's or wolf's corpse.

Her blond hair tumbled in tousled waves over her shoulder and there was blood on her, in her hair, streaking her face.

She looked lovely—so lovely.

And her eyes—they were clear. Clear as the dawn. Clear as rain. Staring at him with recognition. Understanding began to glow there as she settled back on her heels.

Dominic sat up slowly, kept his hands to himself when all he wanted to do was grab. Grab, touch, take. Keep . . .

"Why are you healing?" she asked.

But she already knew the answer. He saw it in her eyes.

"You know why," he said, shrugging. Then he swore as he remembered the wound in his back, the slowly healing flesh. The movement pulled, tore at him and he gritted his teeth until the pain eased up.

"Vampire," she said quietly. She laced her hands together, squeezing so tight, her knuckles went white.

"Yes."

"When?"

"Ten years ago." Then he shoved to his feet, unable to stay there, so close, without touching her. The shirt hung in shreds from his shoulders and he used his right arm to tear it the rest of the way off before he looked back at Nessa.

Why wasn't she touching him?

Why wasn't he touching her?

"Does it matter?" he asked softly.

She eased closer, eyeing his mouth with something akin to curiosity. And something deeper.

His heart skipped a beat, and when she reached up, touched her fingertips to his mouth, he had to curl his hands into fists just to keep from touching her. "That you're a vampire? Does it matter to me? Not so much," she said, her voice absent and soft. She pressed her finger to his lower lip and Dominic turned his head away.

The feel of her, so close, the smell of her, flooding his head, it was too much. His fangs throbbed, sliding down from their sheaths.

"Look at me," she said, her voice soft, but insistent.

"It's better if I don't." He closed his eyes.

Her hand cupped his cheek, guiding his face back to hers. "Look at me," she whispered again. Then she leaned close, so close he felt the weight of her breasts against his chest, the soft curve of her belly. "Please look at me, Elias."

Elias—

Shit, they really did need to talk.

He opened his mouth to say something, anything. But then her lips brushed against his cheek and he shuddered. Unable to resist, he forced his lashes up and stared into her summery, soft blue eyes. Uncaring of the blood on her face, he tangled a hand in her hair and leaned close, pressing his brow to hers.

"You know me," he muttered, his voice raspy and low.

"I know you. I'd know you anywhere." She pressed a kiss to his lips.

Dominic chuckled against her lips, and the hope dancing inside him began to spin—ready to take flight. "You didn't know me earlier," he said.

"Irrelevant." She smiled against his lips. "I know you now . . . I'll always know you."

She kissed him and he groaned as she delicately slid her tongue into his mouth, avoiding his fangs with ease. Then she stroked the tip of one with her tongue, and he tensed as the taste of her blood suddenly filled their kiss. But when he would have jerked away, she fisted a hand in his hair and held him still.

Strong . . . so strong. So soft.

Groaning, he closed his mouth around her tongue and sucked away those few precious drops. Under his kiss, the cut faded away, melted away, but still the taste of her blood lingered. He wanted more—needed more.

Talk—yeah, they damned well did need to talk, but he needed this now. Needed it more than he'd ever needed anything.

Tearing his mouth away, he pressed his brow to hers and whispered, "I have to make love to you. Now."

With a smile curling her lips, she stroked a hand down his cheek. "Now sounds just fine to me."

He swept her into his arms and strode into the house.

There were things he needed to do—there was blood on the porch, on the ground that needed to be cleaned up before it dried, and he really should have been worried that somebody had seen them, or heard them.

But all he could think about was her.

Nessa . . . this woman he'd dreamed of his entire life . . . and now she was here. In his arms.

He wanted her so bad he hurt with it, shook with it—it was a vicious, throbbing pain, in his heart, in his gut, in his cock. Making love to her once wouldn't be enough. Twice, a hundred times, a thousand—

But instead of taking her straight to bed, he detoured to the bathroom. She was splattered with blood and sweat. Dominic couldn't have cared less but she probably wouldn't mind cleaning up. And he could still get his hands all over her, without pouncing on her like a savage lunatic.

He flicked on the light and settled her on the granite countertop next to the sink. Brushing her hair back, he caught her face in his hands and angled it up. Her lashes fluttered down and as he nuzzled her mouth, he whispered, "No . . . look at me. I need to see you. I need you to see me."

Her lashes lifted slowly and summery blue eyes met his. "I can't believe this is happening," she said, her voice thick.

"It's happening . . . it's real. I couldn't dream this. Not this." He caught her lower lip between his teeth, biting down gently.

She shuddered.

When he pushed his tongue into her mouth, she mewled deep in her throat and arched against him. Through her clothes, through his, he could feel the heat of her body against his cooler one, warming him. He was heating rapidly—too rapidly. It felt like he had fire in his veins instead of blood.

Nessa tore her mouth away, gasping for air. A soft sound— part giggle, part sigh—escaped her and she whispered, "You might not have to breathe anymore, but I do."

Her head was spinning, round and round like a child's toy. Sucking in deep draughts of air didn't help. Her head continued to spin and her heart raced . . . no. It danced. Within her chest, her heart danced. Lifting her eyes to his, she trailed her fingers across his cheek. She could feel the light growth of his beard scraping across her palm. His fangs bulged lightly behind his upper lip and his eyes, they glowed. Sunlight behind black glass . . . they glowed with warmth, love . . . all that emotion she thought she'd never have.

She laid her hands on his chest, stroking them down over the smooth lines of his body. His skin was perfect, a strange mix of pale gold and ivory—a naturally dusky skin color, but softer, somehow. Lack of sunlight would do that to a man, she knew. Back when he'd still lived as a mortal, he probably had skin of deep gold. His muscles were hard under her hands, and that incredible skin stretched over them without any flesh to spare. He'd been young when he was Changed.

Tears burned her eyes and she caught her lip in her teeth. The Change was brutal, painful. She knew—she'd seen it. More than a few died during the horrid process. She hated to think of him going through that . . . and she hadn't been with him.

Why?

"Doesn't matter," she muttered, shaking her head.

He cupped her neck, pressed a kiss to the soft patch of skin behind one ear. "What doesn't matter?"

Turning her head, she caught his mouth with hers and said, "Nothing. Not now. Now that you're here, nothing else matters." Pulling back, she fisted her hands in the hem of her T-shirt and stripped it anyway.

As his eyes locked on the swell of her breasts, she was hit with a wave of acute self-consciousness. She barely knew this body. Even though she'd spent the past few years living in it, she barely knew it. She rarely looked in the mirror, she never touched herself. Glancing down at the slight curve of her breasts, she couldn't help but wonder . . . this new body, would it please him?

"Fuck."

She looked up and her breath lodged in her throat at the look in his eyes. It was burning, so hot, so hungry. He caught her cotton-covered breasts in his hands, plumping them together. Then he dipped his head and pressed his face between them, groaning against her.

His arm, sinewy and strong, came around her waist and hauled her off the counter. Yelping in surprise, she wrapped her legs around his waist, gripping his hips with her thighs. She grabbed his shoulders. Against the sensitive flesh between her thighs, she could feel him.

Pulsating, hard and thick. Shuddering, she lowered her head and pressed her mouth to his neck. "Well, there's the answer to that question," she said quietly.

"What question?" He raked his teeth across the top of one breast, the sharp tips of his fangs lightly scoring her flesh. He reached behind her and a few seconds later, her bra fell to the floor.

Nessa groaned and fisted a hand in his hair as he lifted his head. Drawing him back to her, she said, "I was wondering if you would want me . . . this . . . this isn't exactly my body. I didn't know if it would please you."

He lightly bit her nipple. "It is your body, baby. How it came to be that way isn't the issue, but it's yours."

"Isn't it, though? She was but a child when we fought. I killed her, and now her body is mine."

Dominic sighed. Staring into her troubled eyes, he lay his hand on her cheek, gently stroked his thumb over her lower lip. "You fought a woman who already had a history of killing people. She was hooked on blood magic, and while I'm not an expert on witches, I've heard the deal with that—they get to craving it. They *need* it—need it the same way I need blood. But they only get their fix when they kill. And you know her history—she'd killed. A *lot*. As far as years go, she might have been a kid, but she wasn't innocent. You know that."

"Yes." She covered her hand with his, pressed down gently. "I know that. But perhaps . . ."

He pressed his thumb to her mouth. "No. No *perhaps*. No *maybe*. We focus on the now . . . on what is. Things turn out the way they do for a reason."

Dipping his head, he replaced his thumb with his mouth, tracing his tongue along the line of her lower lip, nipping her gently. "You're here. With me. That is what matters to me. That is *all* that matters to me."

Pulling back, he sank to his knees before her, staring up at her. As he reached for the button of her jeans, she sagged back against the counter, resting her weight on her hands. He stripped the jeans away, taking her panties as well. The low boots she wore came off with her jeans and the clothing, the boots went flying, landing against the wall with a muffled thud.

He leaned forward and pressed his mouth to her.

Nessa cried out, her fingers curling around the edge of the countertop, clutching it for balance.

Balance—hell, there *was* no balance, she realized as he used his tongue to part her flesh, licking at her like a cat. She might still be standing—mostly—but the room was spinning. The earth was spinning. Her head was spinning. Nothing was solid, nothing was still . . . except him, kneeling at her feet with his dark head between her thighs.

He teased her clit with his tongue, his teeth. Nessa cried out and whispered, "I'm going to fall."

Long-fingered elegant hands cupped her ass. Against her flesh, he whispered, "I've got you. I won't let you fall."

Her heart skipped a beat. *I won't let you fall.* He'd said that to her . . . before. But she couldn't remember when, couldn't think, couldn't breathe—

He used the tip of his fang to scrape over her clit and she screamed out, her back arched. The orgasm slammed into her, so hard, so fast, so sudden—she couldn't breathe, couldn't prepare. Her eyes went dark and she blindly flailed out a hand, smacking it against his shoulder. She caught a hold of him, gripped him, her nails scoring his flesh as the orgasm tore through her.

So strong . . . and over all too soon.

Sobbing for breath, she collapsed against him, sinking down across his thighs in a boneless puddle. He stroked her back, pressed soft little kisses to her shoulder and then eased her off his lap. When he went to pull away, she panicked and reached out, grabbing his wrist. "Don't . . . You can't stop touching me, not yet."

"Shhh . . . I'm just going to start the shower."

Slowly, she uncurled her fingers from his wrist, let him go. She watched him, every step, even though her lids felt heavy and she was so tired, she could sleep for a week. After he turned the shower on, he stripped out of his jeans. She held out her arms, but he paused by the shower, checked the water. Adjusted it.

Steam was starting to billow out as he knelt beside her and caught her in his arms. Wrapping her arms around his neck, she snuggled against him. "You can't stop touching me. Not yet. Maybe not ever."

"We might get some weird looks, but I'm good with that idea," he whispered against her brow. He climbed into the oversized shower stall, shutting the glass door behind him.

The water was warm, gliding over her flesh like silk.

"Can you stand up?"

Looking at him through her lashes, she asked, "Are you going to stop touching me?"

"No. I'm going to wash you."

"Ahhh . . . then yes, I can stand up."

But as his soap-slicked hands moved over her body, Nessa wasn't so sure. Could she stand? Her knees were weak, wobbling and with every glide of his hands, standing became more and more difficult.

There was a metal bar affixed to the wall and she gripped it with her hands, bracing herself. When he went back down to his knees, her stomach clenched. But all he did was soap her legs, strong fingers digging into her muscles, massaging them as he washed her.

He washed her everywhere, from her nape down to her feet. Her feet were treated to the same quick massage as her legs and she curled her toes as he finished. "You'd make a killing as a love slave," she teased him.

"Love slaves don't get paid." He kissed her naval and stood. A grin tugged at one side of his mouth and he asked, "But I'd be your willing slave . . . any day. Any night."

"Would you really?"

"Hmmm. Mistress, if it is okay with you, I'm going to stop touching you so I can wash up real quick."

Chuckling, she reached out and snagged the soap from his hand. "No, it's not okay for you to stop touching me. But I have a solution. I'll wash you."

His grin widened, hot and bright, flashing across his face. "Excellent solution." He held still as she soaped up her hands, but when she touched him, the muscles under his skin jumped.

It was a wonderful way to discover this new body, she

decided. He was lean, lanky—bordering on too thin, but those lovely, yummy muscles stretched over his frame. His thick hair was silky black and she couldn't resist pushing a hand through it, watching as the strands twined around her fingers.

Thick black brows slashed over his eyes. He had high, carved cheekbones and a mouth that was almost too soft, too pretty for a man. She pushed up onto her toes as she slicked her soapy hands over his chest, nibbling at his lower lip. He tasted divine—spicy, male, dark, erotic.

When she pushed her tongue into his mouth, she traced his fangs and smiled inwardly at his shudder.

Settling flat on her feet, she finished washing his torso and then knelt down in front of him to wash his thighs, his calves. When she stroked her fingers over his instep, he jerked and she laughed. "You're ticklish," she noted.

As he glared at her, she laid a hand on the inside of his calf, stroking up, up, up . . . until she could cup the sac of his balls in his hand. He groaned and sagged, wide shoulders pressing against the tiled wall at his back. "All clean," she whispered, leaning in closer. "Everywhere except here."

She licked the head of his cock and shot him a glance from under her lashes.

He fisted a hand in her damp hair and tugged. "Enough already. Come here."

"Hmmm . . . no." Then she licked him again before taking him in her mouth. She took him as deep as she could, until she felt him nudge against the back of her throat. Stroking her tongue against the underside as she pulled back, she took a deep breath and mentally focused. In her mind's eye, she sought out those muscles as she sank back down, coaxed them into relaxing. This time, when he brushed the back of her throat, she took him deep. Swallowed.

He shouted her name and his hips jerked, spasmed. She did it again, and again. He started to move, thrusting into her mouth, pushing deeper, deeper, and she loved it—loved feeling his frantic movements, loved sensing the deep, mind-bending hunger—

In one abrupt, hard motion he stopped and jerked her back, using his hold on her hair. Nessa shot him a dark look but when she went to take him back in her mouth, he bent down and caught her in his arms, spinning to press her back against the tiled wall.

"Too damn long, witch," he whispered. "Too damn long . . . when I come, it's going to be inside *you*."

She touched her tongue to her lip and then shot him a wicked grin. "If you come in my mouth, it *is* inside me."

"Here," he muttered, slanting his mouth over hers and cupping her in his hand. She shuddered as he pushed one finger inside her sex. "I'm coming *here*, inside this pretty little pussy."

Need cramped deep inside her and she cried out, arching against his hand.

"Then do it," she ordered. "Do it now."

Their gazes locked and he lifted her, hooked his elbows under her knees. She shivered as his gaze ran over her body, lingering on the exposed flesh between her thighs. "Put me inside you."

With a hand that shook, she reached down, closed her fingers around his cock. As she pressed the head to her entrance, they both caught their breath—held it. As he pushed inside her, she reached up with her free hand and hooked it over his neck, hauled him close.

As he sank slowly, oh so slowly, inside her, she sighed into his mouth.

At last—

He started to withdraw and she clenched down, trying to keep him inside her. Good—too damn good, she needed him inside, always—

He grunted as she tightened around him. Then he started to rock, slowly at first, but then surging against her, faster, faster. His muscled chest crushed against hers, her breasts pressed flat, her nipples tight and aching.

"I can't make this last," he gritted out.

Tipping her head back, she said, "Good . . . because the sooner we're done, the sooner we can do it again."

A wolfish grin curled his lips and he dipped his head, nipped at her mouth. "Good logic."

Inside her, she felt him swell, felt him throb. He shifted, angling his body so that each stroke had him rubbing against the tight, burning knot of her clitoris. Each stroke—

She shrieked, the sound dying away to a breathless gasp. She could feel it, the orgasm rising higher, higher— stretching her body tighter, tighter.

Blindly, she reached up and fisted one hand in his short, dark hair. Jerking his head to her neck, she bared it and said, "Bite me."

"No—"

She turned her face to his chest and opened her mouth, catching him just above one tight, flat nipple. Sinking her teeth in, quick and hard, she bit until she tasted blood and then she lifted her head, pressed her mouth to his, knowing even the taste of his own blood would set him to burning.

She needed that—needed to make him burn in every way possible—and she needed him to do the same to her.

He snarled against her lips and tore his mouth away. "Damn it, Nessa."

"Please." She arched her head to the side, once more baring her neck. "I need this . . . *we* need it."

He shuddered. His eyes flashed—one pulsing red glow— and then he released one of her legs and slid his hand up, tangling his fingers in her hair. He licked her first. His lower body continued to move, his hips rocking, his cock stroking deep inside her. Her lashes fluttered low as he scraped his teeth across her skin. Lightning sizzled through her veins as the tip of one fang broke her skin. He growled, licking up the scant drops of blood.

Pressing against his head, she said softly, "Do it . . ."

The words were still hovering in the air when he struck. As his fangs pierced her skin, she climaxed. Hard and fast, unending. Blood roared in her ears. Her heart raced. Deep inside, she felt him jerk and then he started to come, his cock throbbing inside her. She whimpered and convulsed around him, her inner muscles gripping him, milking him, draining him . . .

Just as he was draining her. His skin burned hotter and hotter and he growled against her neck.

Her blood . . . it was like nectar. Like ambrosia. The sweetest damn thing he'd ever tasted and he wanted to gorge on it. Wanted it—wanted it so bad. But instead, he lifted his head, stroked his tongue over the small wounds until they started to close.

She was still climaxing around him . . . still quivering, and as he covered her mouth with his, she sobbed out his name.

Elias.

Too drained to move, he collapsed against her, resting his head on the wall just behind her.

The water was starting to cool and he kept his body between hers and the spray. The cooler water didn't affect him and thanks to that unplanned feeding, he was plenty warm enough for both of them.

Elias.

They really had to talk.

Slowly, he withdrew, gritting his teeth as she whimpered and wiggled around, clutching him close. Laughing softly, he dropped a kiss to her brow and whispered, "I'm not going anywhere."

"Better not." Her lashes lifted just a fraction and then she sighed, closed her eyes. "I'll turn you into a toad."

"But then we couldn't do this again," he teased. He stroked a hand down her side and then groaned as she reached between them, closed her fingers around his length. "You're going to kill me."

She stiffened and Dominic lifted his head. The glimpse of pain in her eyes had him swearing and he could have kicked himself.

"Hush," he whispered as she started to cry. "Shhh . . . I'm fine. You're fine. We're here . . . we're together."

Silly little fool, Nessa thought, staring at him through the tears.

Tears burned her eyes, a harsh sob escaping her.

"Hey . . ."

The tears spilled free and try as she might, she couldn't stop crying. Desperate, she wiggled until she could wrap her arms around him, seeking out the wound on his back with her hands.

There—it was right there. She could no longer feel it on the surface, but inside, she could still sense it . . . healing. Healing *slowly*, but it was healing.

Another sob tore free. Then another, and another.

He moved and she cried out, clutching him tighter. He paused and then shifted, lifting her in his arms as he murmured to her under his breath.

Nothing he said made sense.

She couldn't think—couldn't breathe. Couldn't do anything but clutch him close and cry.

She was unaware as he turned off the water, as he climbed from the shower.

Unaware of anything, everything, but the fact that he was *here* . . . and she'd almost killed him.

"Silver—I can't believe I stabbed you with silver," she babbled, running her hand over the wound. From somewhere inside, she found the strength, the focus to call her magic and she covered the wound. Healing warmth spilled from her into him—he gritted his teeth and stiffened, and she felt the edge of his pain.

It had her swearing. "Sorry. Bloody hell, I'm so sorry—no reason to go and hurt you, but I did it. You died once because of me, and I almost killed you this time. Silver. I stabbed you with bleeding silver and I could have killed you and . . . and . . ."

He kissed her—hard and fast. Whatever else she was going to say died in her throat and she whimpered, once more wrapping her arms around his neck, holding him tight. So tight. She couldn't ever let go. If she did, she'd wake and realize this wasn't real. She'd wake . . . and he'd be gone.

"Don't leave me," she whispered against his mouth. "Please, you can't ever leave me again."

"Shhh . . ." he crooned. Lifting his head, he stroked her hair back from her face and cupped her chin. "I don't plan on going anywhere."

He kissed the tears away from her cheeks and shifted around, grabbing a blanket from the foot of the bed, pulling it over them. That was when she realized they were *in* a bed. She didn't remember even leaving the shower.

They lay there, wrapped in each other's arms. Occasionally, she'd find herself stroking the place on his back where she'd stabbed him. It was fully healed now, but she could still feel the echo of the injury inside. More, she'd see that mark on his gleaming, golden skin for the rest of her life. For always.

She had to swallow convulsively, bile churning up her throat, as she realized she'd stabbed him in the exact same place he'd been stabbed . . . before. Back in that other life.

"How did this happen?" she finally asked, once she could speak without tripping over her words, without choking on the tears that still clogged her throat. "How is it that you are here?"

"You're asking the wrong person." He shifted, shrugged. One long-fingered hand toyed with her hair, winding one strand around his finger. "I'm still trying to catch up."

Capturing her lip between her teeth, she sat up and studied his face. "You . . . You don't look anything like you used to. But then, again, I guess you wouldn't, would you? You're not exactly the same man, are you?"

"No. Not exactly." Lashes lowered over his eyes and his chest rose, fell on a sigh. Habitual gesture, she suspected. Although vampires didn't need to breathe, many still did, especially when they were nervous or worried. Reaching out, she laid a hand on his chest. His skin was still warm, from being pressed against hers, and from feeding.

She'd shared her warmth with him, her life. Of course, she'd done it *after* she'd tried to kill him.

He covered her hand with his, squeezed gently. Slowly, his lashes lifted, revealing the dark, melted chocolate of his eyes. "Some of me is the same . . . but some of me . . . well, it isn't."

As he sat up, she cocked her head. "You feel the same to me. If I had seen you walking down the street, I would have known you." Then she made a face. Closing a hand into a fist, she whispered, "But you had to find me when I was taking my merry little ride into the land of fuck-it-all."

"Hmmm." He linked their hands, lifted them so he could press a kiss to her knuckles. "And exactly how did you end up in the land of fuck-it-all?"

Nessa shrugged. A rueful grin curled her lips and she said, "Oh, that's been quite a journey. Five hundred empty years, and then I think I'm done, I'm finally done and I'll be able to go to you. Find you. And . . ." She trailed off, rubbing her brow.

He tucked her hair behind her ear. "I know what happened with Morgan."

"Then you're a step up on me," she sighed. "I still don't know what happened with Morgan. Or at least, I don't *understand* it."

He laid a hand on her cheek and she rubbed against it, so desperate for his touch.

"Anyway, for a while there, it was touch and go. I began drifting closer to the land of fuck-it-all, but mostly got straightened out. Ended up meeting this girl. A sweet, talented girl . . . she was like a daughter to me. One I never had a chance to have. And she died." Tears stung her eyes but she blinked them away. "Too much loss. All these years, there's just been too much loss."

Taking a deep breath, she continued, "I tangled with that witch you met earlier. Her name was Isis—mean as a snake, that one. I fought her and got careless. She caught me at just the right time and I went flying, scrambled my brain just a bit—not anything bad, but it was enough that she got away and I'd knew I'd have to track her. I was lying there, healing up and thinking . . . *I don't want to do this anymore. I don't want to fight. I don't want to live this life . . . I don't want to remember this life.*

She stopped and looked up at him, blood rushing up to stain her cheeks.

He blinked at her. "You thought it."

"Yes." She licked her lips and used her free hand to tuck her hair back behind her ear. "I thought it. And, I guess, some part of me really *wanted* it."

He shook his head and murmured, "Things like that don't happen just because you *think* it."

"They can if you've got the power to make it so . . . and the desire." Lowering her gaze to the sheets, she whispered, "I cursed myself, and I did a right fine job of it, too."

Cursed herself. Damned herself. Almost damned him, as well. Almost *killed* him. *Stop it—no more crying over that. Not now.*

She took a deep breath and looked back at him. He was staring at her, as though he didn't know what in the hell to think.

That makes two of us . . .

Forcing a smile, she glanced around the room. "So there is a real bedroom in this place, I see. Not just that tiny closet you had us in."

"Yeah." A grin crooked his lips and he shrugged. "I just like the inner room better. Don't have to worry about sunlight or anything in there."

"The inner room. This is one of the safe houses," she realized. Another realization slammed into her. Memories of the past hours became clear and as they did, pieces of the puzzle fell into place.

Hunter.

This was one of the safe houses—she'd stayed in enough of them to recognize one. The safe room, the mini fridge—likely a stash of blood, kept for the vampires.

Isis—bugger. That bitch had called him a Hunter.

Hunter. He was a Hunter—

His fingers skimmed down her cheek and she tensed, jerking her head up to look at him. He stilled, his hand lowering to his side.

The smile on her face felt brittle. "You're a Hunter."

"Yeah." He caught her hand, bringing it to his lips. He raked the heel of her hand with his teeth and then pressed a kiss to her palm. As he did it, he watched her face, a calm, measuring look in those dark brown eyes. "And I'm getting the feeling that bothers you."

"Bothers me." She closed her eyes and tried to figure out how to answer that . . . without lying. "Lover, everything about this bothers me. I can't understand it, not any of it. I keep thinking, *What is all this*? *What on earth is going on*?" She shrugged and shook her head. "And I have no answer. Part of me believes I am sleeping, just dreaming, and soon I'll wake up."

Her breathing hitched in her throat and she had to fight not to crawl back into his lap and wrap herself around him, clutch him tight, hold him close and never let go.

I will come back . . .

Taking a deep breath, she blinked away the tears and said softly, "And if that happens, I'm gone. I won't be able to handle it. I'm just not strong enough."

He cupped her face in his hand and said quietly, "You're a hell of lot stronger than you think."

"Maybe I used to be. Once." She turned her face into his hand, rubbing against him like a cat. His hand was callused, strong. She could imagine happily spending the rest of her life, however long that might be, feeling these hands on her every single day.

She'd waited so long for him . . .

He felt like Elias to her. He felt like her love.

But is that who he was *now*? Was this who he wanted to be?

Was she who he wanted?

She was so confused. And tired—blast it all, she was still so tired. But right now, she couldn't try to think anything through, she couldn't even try to rest. She wasn't capable of it.

Just enjoy it, she told herself. *Take what remains of the night and enjoy it . . . have a think through later.*

Giving in to the urge, she climbed into his lap and pressed her back against his chest. She drew his arms around her waist, settling against him with a sigh. "I'm going to make a guess, here. Your name isn't Elias, is it?" she asked, tongue in cheek.

"No." He kissed her temple and rested his chin on her shoulder. It felt so natural . . . so right. Like they had done this a thousand times before. And they had—not a thousand times, perhaps not even a hundred. Their time together had been so short. Too short. But he had held her like this. She'd rested in his arms, and felt so at peace . . . so safe. So loved.

"Then what is it? You're not going to make me guess, are you?"

She could feel him smile as he murmured, "No. It's Dominic. Dominic Ralston."

"Dominic." She glanced at him over her shoulder, eyeing the inky black hair, the smooth, pale gold of his body—golden, even though his skin hadn't seen the kiss of the sun in years. "Italian American?"

"Yeah. Via Memphis."

"Memphis." She grinned and pressed her lips to his jaw. "Memphis, Tennessee. That would explain that sexy drawl of yours."

"My drawl?" He cocked a brow.

"Yes. Very sexy . . . that Southern accent of yours, I have to say, I do like it, quite a bit."

He tugged on her hair. "I don't have an accent. You do. You sound like a prim and proper British schoolteacher and it makes me want to do whatever I can to ruffle your feathers."

"Ruffle my feathers?" She shifted around in his lap. "Trust me, lover. You have done much more than ruffle my feathers. You've shaken the very bedrock of my world." She skimmed a hand through his hair as she added, "And you damn well do have an accent—a very fine one, too. I swear, all it took was about two words from you and my knickers just about fell off."

Then she slid a hand down his chest and whispered, "And I'm no prim and proper schoolmarm, English or not. But if you'd like me to pretend . . ." She closed her fingers around his cock and started to stroke him. "I'd be pleased to oblige."

"Don't tease me." He shot her a lambent, heavy lidded glance. "You going to dress up in some cute little plaid skirt and swat my hand with a ruler if I'm not a good boy?"

A laugh gurgled out of her. "You pervert. And I'm certain it's the school*girls* who wear the cute little plaid skirts, not the teachers. I'd wear a skinny black skirt with some sexy little slit in the back. Perhaps pearls and a pair of spectacles."

"Hell, a pair of pearls and some spectacles would do it for me." He slid a hand down her back, resting it on her rump. In a low, rough voice, he muttered, "But you're doing it for me now, too, just fine."

She shifted around. As she took him inside, her breath caught in her chest. "Am I?"

CHAPTER 22

D AWN was close . . . too close.

Keeping her in his arms, he pressed a kiss to her naked shoulder and murmured, "I need to move to the inner room, Nessa."

She snuggled back against him. "No, you don't."

"Yeah, I do." He shot a look at the big picture window over the bed. It faced the east and already, he could see the sky lightening. It was probably going to be a beautiful sunrise—not that he remembered them too well. Sunsets, he could take, but dawn was a distant memory. Too bad, too, because he'd love to lay here with her and watch the night bleed away into day . . . holding her.

"No." She rolled over onto her belly and stared at the window. A glazed look entered her eyes, and they began to shimmer, swirl and glow. The air around him felt charged and the hair on the back of his neck stood on end.

Magic—shit.

It carried a punch, too, heavy and hot, like a summer thunderstorm—one with a promise of devastation.

Then she blinked, and it was done. Smiling at him, she

stroked a finger down his jaw and said, "You have the most powerful witch the Council's ever seen tucked naked into your bed, Dominic. You could take a walk along the beach at noon without fear, if you wanted."

"And if I could stay awake." He slanted a look at the window, a grin curling his lips. "I've been waking before sunset for a while now, watch the sun go down every now and then. Over the past few weeks, I'm waking earlier than ever. But . . . well, it's not the same as being able to lie in a bed during the day and not worry about waking with third-degree burns all over my body."

Dropping back down, he caught a strand of her hair and wrapped it around his finger. "This has been a very insane day, you know. I can't quite believe you're here."

"Nor can I." She snuggled against his chest and rested a hand just above his heart. She felt one faint beat and a few minutes later, another. *Here. With me*, she thought, amazed. *Alive.*

A vampire. Swallowing the knot in her throat, she whispered, "Tell me how this happened to you . . . how you came to be a vampire, how you came to be *here*."

"It's not a fun story." He kissed the top of her head. "It's one you've probably heard before though. I ended up in the hands of a feral—he bit me, left me to die. A Hunter saved me, brought me through the Change . . . kept me from killing myself those first few weeks."

"Why would you have killed yourself?" she asked, lifting her head and peering up at him. Her heart hurt. She could feel the echo of his pain, pain he was still working to make peace with.

He could try to make peace with it all he wanted, but she wasn't ready to even begin—she didn't even *know* and she was furious. She hurt, she raged . . . she wanted to kill. Kill whoever had harmed him, even though if he hadn't been bitten, she may have never found him.

The Change was brutal, and when it was forced on a person, even to save their life, it was so much worse.

He was quiet, and she pushed up onto her elbow, staring

at him. "Why?" she asked again. "Because you didn't want to be a vampire?"

"I didn't want to *live*," he said, his voice flat and hard. A dull, ruddy flush stained his cheeks and he looked away, shamed.

Fear curled inside her, a nasty, unwanted little worm that stretched and grew with every passing second.

This was a proud man . . . a confident one. And the Change hadn't caused it—she recognized the inborn strength inside him. He'd been strong from day one . . . in this life, in the last. Not many things would push a strong man to serious suicidal thoughts.

"The vampire who bit me—the feral . . ." Dominic sat up and turned his back, staring blindly ahead of him.

Slipping out of the bed, she came around and knelt in front of him, resting her hands on his thighs. Yes . . . she'd heard this story before. He didn't even have to speak the words. She already knew.

Her heart, it was breaking inside her chest.

And deep inside, the monstrous anger. Thirsting . . . craving . . .

Blood.

Pain.

It was alien—she'd craved vengeance before, many times, but never like this. Never so blindly. Never so . . . cruelly.

Shoving it down, she caught his face in her hands and guided his gaze back to hers. "What did he do to you?"

Dominic's hands closed around her wrists, squeezing tightly, near to the point of pain. But he didn't push her away . . . he held her closer. Tighter.

Desperately.

"Whatever cruelty you can think of, he probably did it, or some variation," he bit off. "That fuck taught me what it was like to be helpless, what it was to truly know fear, and to crave death, the way an addict wants another hit. When he was done, all I wanted to do was die."

"But you didn't." She pressed her lips to his chin.

"No." The hands on her wrists loosened and when she pulled away, he let her.

Looping her arms around his neck, she said quietly, "Because of the Hunter . . . this one who saved you."

"Yeah."

He wouldn't look at her. Wouldn't look her in the face, wouldn't meet her gaze.

Nessa rested her head against his shoulder. "Memphis . . . would it be Rafe?"

A brief pause, and then he said quietly, "Yes. You know him."

"Hmmm. Yes. There was a time when I knew nearly every Hunter in the world."

He looked at her from the corner of his eye and she took advantage of that, leaned in and kissed the corner of his mouth. When he turned his face to her, she deepened the kiss and then waited until some of the tension inside him, some of his rage and shame faded.

She kept her own feelings tamped down, locked up deep inside.

He had suffered so—the other half of her heart—and she'd done nothing. Hadn't even known.

"Nearly every Hunter," she repeated. Giving him a smile, she cupped her face in her hands. "That would be many, many Hunters . . . and now Rafe is my second favorite."

"Favorite?"

"Yes. You, of course, would have to be my absolute favorite." She pressed her breasts against him and gave him a coy smile. "While I was never prim and proper, I was a schoolteacher for many, many years." She paused, frowning. "Although by the time I was teaching, I wasn't any man's idea of sexual fantasy material."

His hands curled around her hips. "Somehow, I don't quite believe that."

"Hmmm, well you've no idea what I looked like five or six years ago." Then she frowned. "Was it five or six years ago? Bloody hell, I don't even know . . . I think it was longer, actually. Nevertheless, trust me, lover. I was no man's fantasy material."

He nuzzled her nape and whispered, "I know what

happened to you, and I have to admit, while I hate that I left you alone so damn long, I'm not sorry you're still here . . . however it happened."

"Such a smooth talker you are." Sighing, she curled her arms around his neck. "The two of us, we're quite a pair, aren't we? Here I am, well past five centuries, and you're . . ." Her voice trailed off and she scowled. "Do I even want to know how old you are?"

He laughed. More of the tension inside him had slipped away and the faded anger, the remnants of shame were no longer evident in his voice. "I was twenty-four . . . I think . . . when I was changed. Yeah, twenty-four."

"Twenty-four." She winced and asked, "And how long ago was that again?"

"Ten years. Give or take."

"So you're all of thirty-four. Give or take."

"Yeah." He tangled a hand in her hair and tugged her close. "But if it helps you feel like less of a cradle robber, I have memories that go back about as far as yours. Dreams. Crazy dreams. Up until a few weeks ago, I was convinced I was going insane."

"Dreams." She shot a look out the window. Sunrise . . . it was so close, and he was still awake and aware. He was a strong vampire—she had only to look at him to know that. In time, he'd be a Master, if he chose. But he was still young and his body would yield to the sun.

Time . . . it was slipping away.

Inwardly, she wanted to curl into a ball and hide.

Outwardly, she gave him a curious smile and hoped she could hide how terrified she was. "Tell me of these dreams."

His lashes drooped, and as though her thoughts had brought it on, when he looked back at her, the exhaustion was heavy in his eyes. "Dreams. They never made any sense, not until recently. Sometimes it was us . . . back then. I can remember the knife. You crying."

Her breath caught as he traced a finger down her cheek, following the line of her long-ago tears. "You cried, and

I wanted so badly to hold you, promise you everything would be okay. But I couldn't."

"It wasn't your fault," she said quietly.

"It wasn't yours, either." He caught her hand, kissed it, hard, desperately. "Don't think I can't feel how torn up you are inside. Don't think I don't know how much you've blamed yourself over these years."

"And why shouldn't I?" She snapped her mouth shut, wishing she could call the question back.

"You're not God, my pretty little witch," he said, a sad, bitter smile curling his mouth. "You were strong back then—I don't think I can say I *remember* much—what little is there, it's all hazed, foggy. But I know you were strong. Strong isn't the same as infallible. You aren't to blame."

She looked away. She didn't feel the same way—perhaps she couldn't. She'd blamed herself every day since it had happened. Blamed herself . . . blamed God. Even Elias—Dominic. She'd blamed him for leaving her. Leaving her, and not coming back as he'd promised.

But he was back . . .

He eased back on the bed, blowing out a breath. She lay stretched out atop him, holding him close. So close. But not close enough. She could feel the faint, irregular beat of his heart, and the scent of him flooded her head. Against her magical senses, he was a velvety, electric presence—she'd feel him in her sleep. In her every waking moment.

In every last dream she had.

"So you had dreams. But does that mean you remembered? Did you always remember me?"

"No." His lashes drooped low, lower. He took a deep breath and then opened them, smiling at her.

She felt the weariness. The deep, deep exhaustion.

"No . . . not always. But I always looked for you. Every damn place I went. Every woman I saw. Every voice I heard . . . I looked for you. I had no choice." His arms tightened around her and then he shifted around. "I had to find you . . . even when I didn't know what I was looking for."

Five seconds later, the sun pierced the sky.

Five seconds after that, he was asleep.

And she was left alone with her thoughts, wrapped in his arms . . . and worrying.

No choice.

He'd looked for her because he had no choice. He'd found her, because the same instincts that made him a Hunter would have pushed him to find her.

Had he *wanted* to find her?

Tears leaked from her eyes, and the confusion in her head spread, growing worse, and worse.

He had found her, because he'd been compelled to. Somehow fate had conspired to place him on a road that would lead him to her—after *five hundred fucking years.* And it had been one awful, horrid road.

He'd suffered. The weight of his pain, it bore down on her. Hurt her deep inside, a vicious, twisting pain that left her struggling to breathe past it.

Suffered, just so he would find her.

Because he had no choice . . .

"I could live with that," she whispered to herself. No matter what his reasons for being here, he *was* here, and although he barely knew her, didn't remember her, didn't *know* her . . . she could make him fall in love with her. She could—after all, wasn't that why he was here? Now?

After all this time?

"Why now?"

Squirming out of his arms, she sat on the edge of the bed and stared upward.

"Why *now*?" she demanded. "After what I did . . . after what I've become? How could you let me do that? How?"

Her voice rose until she was shouting. Through her tears, she stared up toward the God she no longer wanted to believe in. All this time, she'd waited all this time, only for her lover to return to her . . . and she was broken.

Fallen.

Lifting her hands, she stared at them. She could still feel the blood.

Still feel the song of its power.

In the back of her mind, as though she had just been waiting for the chance to slip out and torment, there was Morgan. And of course the leech had been waiting—the only time she could break free was when Nessa let her guard down.

Morgan's voice, angrier, more vicious than ever, mocked her. *"Yeah, why now? Why couldn't he have come back when you were a haggard, ugly old crone so covered with wrinkles, he'd never recognize you? Then he wouldn't have wanted you. But now you've got my hot self and he's all over your ass."*

"Oh, do shut *up*," Nessa snarled.

Surging off the bed, she stormed to the mirror and stared at herself. It was her reflection, but she didn't *see* herself. She saw Morgan . . . the ghost of the witch who'd owned this body, hovering around her, clinging to life . . . haunting her.

An abrupt, irrational wave of anger flooded her, swamped her. Morgan's body still remembered the rush from blood power. Craved it. If those cravings hadn't been riding her, would she have fallen so far?

"Oh, you can't blame me *for that,"* Morgan responded, laughing. *"You can try as much as you want, but it wasn't my hands that killed that man. I wasn't the one soaking up his power, his essence, feeding off his pain and his anger and his fear. It was* you."

Nessa slammed a hand against the mirror. It shattered. *"No."* She blew out a harsh breath and said quietly, "I might have killed him, but it wasn't my hands that reached for his blood—that isn't a power I even knew how to manipulate. That was yours, and you can't fool me into thinking otherwise."

"So fucking what? You were there and you felt the rush, same as me. You killed him and you got off on the power, just like I did. You'll crave it the same as I do."

"Actually," Nessa murmured, "no. I believe it will just be me craving the blood. I'll have to fight it on my own in the future."

Focusing on the anger, the rage, she wound her power around Morgan's essence, lingering so deep inside her mind.

Morgan, sensing Nessa's intention, shrieked and fought, tugging against Nessa's hold, struggling desperately.

"It's past time I do this, don't you think?"

"You can't—damn it, you old bitch, I'm part of you now. Take me out, you may damn well die."

"Then that's a risk I'll have to take . . . I won't live with *you* inside me."

She couldn't. She couldn't risk it . . . especially not now.

"I just fucking want my body back! My life." Then, oddly, there was a catch, a sob in her thoughts and Morgan whispered, *"I never really even had much of a chance. I only did what I had to."*

Calm spread over Nessa and softly, she whispered, "Yes. Perhaps you did what you had to . . . perhaps you had no choice."

Perhaps Morgan had just been a pawn—a pawn used in these odd circumstances that had led straight up to the moment Nessa had plunged that dagger into Dominic's back, so close to destroying the heart.

Blowing out a sigh, Nessa said, "Perhaps you had no choice. And now . . . I have no choice. You don't belong here, precious. Not anymore."

Nessa closed her eyes. The air in the room grew cold . . . tight. Brittle . . . as though it would shatter if she breathed too deeply, if she moved wrong, if she even thought wrong.

Trapped in the web of Nessa's power, Morgan's soul struggled, thrashed. Pushed for control, tried to edge back inside Nessa's mind.

But she hadn't the power, not now.

"I should have done this long ago," she said quietly.

Morgan screamed.

Nessa felt it echoing inside her head, reverberating like a gong. Hissing out a breath, she shoved the presence away. *Out.* Out of *her* mind. Her body.

It was almost anticlimactic—one moment Morgan was fighting, shrieking, struggling.

And then Nessa was alone—completely and utterly alone inside her head, left to stare in the mirror at her fractured reflection.

"My body." Hers—just as the awful, wrong choices she'd made were hers. Completely and utterly . . . hers. She hadn't asked for this body—hadn't done a damn thing to bring it about. Whether it was some weird twist of fate, some strange machination of the powers that be, she didn't know.

But she hadn't done this—it had been done *to* her. To both of them—to her, and to Morgan.

She looked back at her hands, remembering the blood. Remembering the choices she'd made. She'd taken lives during that foggy, surreal time when she'd forgotten herself. She could live with killing others—she'd done it hundreds of times, perhaps thousands. But always to protect another.

She could no longer say that, and she wasn't sure she could live with what she had done.

Her throat tight, she turned to look at Dominic. His long, lean body stretched out on the bed and he slumbered, peaceful and at ease.

Tears stung Nessa's eyes. She hadn't been at ease with herself in so long. Hadn't been at peace.

Now happiness lay just inches away.

But she no longer deserved it. She didn't deserve him.

Rising from the bed, she murmured once more, "Why now?"

But it didn't matter. She had made her choices . . . and even as she made them, she had questioned them—*known* they were wrong.

"But it didn't stop me."

She'd been making bad decisions for some time now. Even before the debacle with Isis, followed by her unintentional self-curse. So many wrong decisions.

"No more."

No more.

CHAPTER 23

He woke alone.

Dominic had been pretty damn sure that he wouldn't have to do that again. At least not today.

But he woke alone.

Sitting up, he stared out the window into the fading day and tried to understand.

She was gone. Not just in another room, but gone. And judging by the slowly fading scent, she'd been gone for a while—more than a few hours.

A note.

Maybe she'd left a note.

Hell, she *was* a Hunter—he knew what it was like to get that nagging, demanding call, one that jerked and pulled, demanded obedience. A Hunter had to follow that call.

So maybe that's what was going on.

But his instincts said otherwise.

His heart said otherwise. He might not want to believe it, might want to deny it, fight it, but in his heart, he knew.

For some reason he didn't understand, *couldn't* understand, she was gone.

Swearing, he scooped up clothes from the floor, uncaring that they were dirty, still stained with blood. He had to find her.

And fortunately, he knew how to do just that.

Off to the west, the sun lingered in the air, taunting him. It was a few hours before the sun was completely gone, and fate wasn't even being kind enough to give him an overcast day.

But Dominic didn't give a damn. He wasn't a brand-new vamp—it would take more than a little bit of sunlight to do him in, although this sure as hell wouldn't be pleasant. He didn't give a fuck. He wasn't spending any more time without her—not if he had a choice. And he damned well *wouldn't* do it, period, without understanding why.

As he stormed out of the cabin into the soft, pale golden rays of sunlight, he muttered, "I just found you. I am *not* losing you."

"W HAT is she doing here?"

Kelsey gathered her hair into a loose ponytail and shook her head. "I don't know."

Malachi scowled, staring across the campus at her. Roughly an hour ago, he'd sensed her just before she'd arrived—using the very handy skill some of the more talented witches had. Flying—much like his own ability to dematerialize—wasn't a common gift.

And for a witch like Nessa, it was as easy as breathing . . . part of the reason he was hesitant to go speak with her just yet.

"She feels like a storm," Kelsey said, her hand resting just above her heart as though it hurt. "Angry. Sad. Desperate."

"Then she still hasn't seen him." Malachi blew out a breath and rubbed his neck. "We can fix this, then. I'll track the lad down and . . ."

"No." Kelsey turned and came into his arms, wrapping hers around his waist and holding him tight. "She's seen him. She knows. I can feel it."

"But, if she's seen him, why is she here alone?"

"I don't know."

Malachi stroked a hand down her back, resting his chin on the crown of her head. "Then maybe we should find out?"

"No." Kelsey closed her eyes. "Not yet. Not until she's . . . well, a little less likely to fly apart."

"Don't suppose you want to tell me what in the hell you're doing here, do you?"

Sliding Kelsey a look from the corner of her eye, Nessa said in a flat, harsh voice, "I want to be alone. You're interfering."

"Too damned bad." Kelsey stormed into the cabin and gave it a dirty look. "You show back up at my school and think I won't want to know what in the hell is going on?"

"Your school?" Nessa smirked. "*Your* school . . . should I have begged permission first?"

"Don't give me that crap." Kelsey made a face. "Damn it, Agnes, you're one of my dearest friends—you've been mother, sister, teacher to me—damn near *everything*. Save for Mal, there is no one on earth I love as much as I love you."

Weary, Nessa reached up and rubbed her neck. "Yes, love. I do know that. I . . . I just need to be alone."

"*Why*? For God's sake, you've spent too much time *alone* and now that you don't *have* to be alone, you're *choosing* to be?"

"I don't deserve more than that." She swallowed the knot in her throat. With the shame clawing at her stomach, she met Kelsey's gaze.

"What in the hell does that mean?"

Tears glimmered in Kelsey's eyes and she stared at Nessa, all the love, all the passion, all the life she had inside shining in those eyes.

Such a true soul—so pure, so strong. She'd been willing to die, more than once, to save those she loved. And Nessa had spent the past few years tormenting those she loved, toying with death with no regard for them. So desperate to escape the life she'd been given, this second chance, so desperate . . .

"My dear friend, it means just that. I *don't* deserve him. I fell, Kelsey. And heavens . . . did I fall hard." Nessa shook her head. "I'm not even sure I deserve to be here."

"Bullshit."

Narrowing her eyes, Nessa looked at Kelsey. "Pardon me, but you weren't there, so you really don't know, do you?"

"I know what I *see*. If you didn't belong here, I'd see that clear enough, and I don't see it."

"I killed a man, stole everything he was through his blood," Nessa said, and she watched as Kelsey went pale.

The other witch stumbled back against a wall. "You . . . You *what*?"

"You heard me. Now, can you still look at me and tell me that I deserve to be here?"

"What . . . How?"

She looked away, so sick at heart, so full of shame. "A man attacked me—and I killed him. I could live with that. I've taken lives before, in defense of myself, in defense of others . . . in the name of justice. But while I've taken lives, I've never fed from one, until him. I fed from a life, Kelsey. The one thing we witches can never do, and I did it. I'll crave it now, for the rest of my life. I'll have to fight it, for the rest of my life."

"Blood magic."

Nessa nodded, rubbing one hand against the other. "Yes. I tasted it, and now I understand why so many of our kind fall prey to it. Morgan . . . she learned it from her mother, you know. She was too young to truly understand how wrong it was, and by the time she was old enough, she was addicted to it. Had to have it, and she cared nothing for those she killed while she was feeding it. She was a victim, too, at the bottom of it all, and I never even realized it."

Blowing out a breath, she said, "She had to die, Kelsey. I know that. She'd never have been able to stop, even if she wanted to. She would have killed again, and again. But she was a victim. Perhaps if we had been there for her—to

stop her mother—she might have turned out differently.
She might have had a chance."

Another thought hit her, another shame—Jazzy. That
child. Hazy, incomplete memories from *before* she'd remembered who and what she was ran through her head—Brad
and Ana arriving—Dominic had asked about Duke, vague
references about a friend. *Jazzy, please let it be Jazzy . . .*

Swearing, she covered her face with her hands. "Fuck
it all—there's a girl, too. Morgan had a sister—Jasmine.
Jazzy. I suspect she's with Duke—he's bringing her here
most likely. She needs to be here, needs to be trained. She's
not a danger. Yet. But she will be, if we don't see to her."

"One problem at a time, please," Kelsey muttered as
she turned away, her fingers linked behind her neck as she
lifted her face to the sky and stared upward. "Shit. The
girl, though . . . that's easy enough. Not like we haven't
handled that kind of problem before."

"True enough. Just . . . have a care with her. She's fragile."

"Perhaps *you* should be the one to deal with her," Kelsey
bit off.

"I think I've fucked things up quite enough already,"
Nessa murmured. "And until I get a grip on things, taking on the responsibility of a child is *not* what I should be
doing. I'm a danger to her now, Kelsey. Until I even know
if I can control this . . ."

"Oh, bite me," Kelsey snapped, shooting Nessa a narrow look before she resumed her contemplation of the ceiling. "You'd never harm a child."

Nessa only wished she could be that certain.

Silence stretched out between them, with Nessa watching the woman she loved as sister, daughter and friend,
while Kelsey continued to stare upward into nothingness.

"There are no answers written on the ceiling, Kelsey,"
Nessa murmured.

"Running away from Dom isn't an answer, either."
Dropping her hands, Kelsey looked back at Nessa. "This
isn't the right answer, Nessa, and I think you know. You

can't run from him—even if you think you somehow don't deserve him, *he* deserves better than this."

"Better than what? A broken witch who is now going to have to fight an addiction every day for the rest of her life? I *crave* pain now, dear. Don't you get it? I want to make people feel anger, feel fear, feel pain. Fuck me, I'm worse than broken—I'm *ruined*."

"Bull fucking shit," Kelsey snapped.

Nessa's eyes narrowed. She opened her mouth, but then closed it abruptly and shook her head. "No. No, I'm not doing this with you. Just go away, Kelsey. I've made up my mind. I've made my choice."

"And you didn't bother to consult *him* about it—not terribly kind of you, considering the hell he's been through."

"The hell he's been through," she said. Then she repeated, louder, her voice shaking, "The hell *he* has been through? Damn it, Kelsey, do you think this is *easy* for me? Do you have any idea how long I've waited? And now . . . here he is."

Her voice broke. "Here he is . . . and I've shamed myself—cursed myself. Not with the memory, though. Not with the losing of it. I cursed myself by using my magic *wrong*. I did something that goes against everything I am—everything I've ever stood for."

"So one mistake and you throw your life away? And his? Because damn it, that's exactly what you're doing."

"Oh, don't be so melodramatic," Nessa muttered. She pressed her fingers to her burning eyes, trying desperately not to cry. "He doesn't *know* me, dear. Doesn't know me at all. What few memories he has are from the girl I once was, and I'm no longer that girl. He's no longer the man he once was, either. We're two very, very different souls, and he deserves more than the woman I let myself become."

"If you've gone and turned into a fucking coward, then maybe you're right," Kelsey said. She crossed her arms over her chest and stared at Nessa. There was disappointment on her face, in her eyes.

Nessa could feel it beating against her shields and absently, she strengthened them. She didn't need to feel Kelsey's misery as well as her own. Her own was quite enough.

Something pricked at her senses and in the back of her mind, she looked, studied, examined.

Vampire. Close—drawing closer. Here at the school, it wasn't always as easy to sense one from another, not until they were very close. Like trying to isolate the light of a candle when the whole room blazed with a thousand lamps.

Nessa's heart skipped a beat.

Something inside her lightened. That damned hope . . . trying to crawl free even when she knew what she needed to do.

The familiar buzz of energy pressed closer and she opened her senses more—even as she recognized him, her heart sank to her feet.

"Are you really just going to walk away from this? Without even giving it a chance—without giving him a choice?"

"A choice is exactly what I *want* him to have. A life. A life free from the burdens I'd bring to it." Nessa closed her hands into fists, her nails digging into her skin. "A choice that doesn't involve a broken witch who's going to have to fight the call of blood power."

"That's a fucking *crock*. That is not giving him a choice."

"It's a hell of a lot better than the choice he was handed, before he was even born," Nessa snarled. "Dreaming of me—his whole damned life. Did he dream of me even as a child?"

The tears burned her eyes and she no longer had the self-control to hold them back. Staring at Kelsey's blurred face, she said, "I imagine you think it quite romantic, and maybe it seems that way. Maybe it even is that way for some. But every step he took in life was to lead him *here*—all the misery he suffered was to prepare him for *this* and where the hell was his choice in that?"

"So you think you're doing this to give him a *choice*? You're taking his choice away. He came back for *you*, damn it. He's spent his whole life looking for you, without even understanding why."

"That's my point exactly," Nessa whispered. "He spent his whole life looking for me, and nobody ever bothered to see if this was what he wanted."

The presence of the vampire drew closer, and Nessa turned away. "Kelsey, your dearest husband is searching for you and I'm not quite up to dealing with him, as well as you. Just leave me be."

Kelsey shook her head. "You can't leave it this way, damn it. You can't."

The door to Nessa's cabin opened, and she closed her eyes. "Yes . . . I can. Now take your man and go."

"Nessa—"

"It's not your choice," Nessa snapped.

"What about mine?"

A shiver raced down Nessa's spine. Her eyes flew to the doorway, and for the next ten seconds, all she could do was stare.

Oh, it was Malachi, all right.

But he wasn't alone. And she suspected that the ancient vampire had done nothing more than act as a Trojan horse. As far as vampire presences went, he was a thousand lamps and Dominic was a candle. Dominic wouldn't have pressed in on her Hunter senses, and she'd been shielding herself so strongly against everything, she couldn't have felt much else from him.

Swallowing, she turned away. "What do you want?" she asked as Kelsey and Malachi quietly slipped away.

"You."

"You don't know that," she muttered, shaking her head. She didn't want to look at him, but she couldn't stop herself. From the corner of her eye, she watched him as he came close.

He looked like hell. Tired, strained, worn thin . . . and there were telltale burns on his face. Nessa knew damn well what those marks had come from—he'd spent too much time in the sunlight, and he hadn't stopped to feed so he wasn't healing as well as he should have.

"Please tell me you didn't drive straight from St. Augustine," she said quietly.

"What in the hell did you expect? I searched through damn near half the country looking for you. Did you really think I'd let you walk away that easy?" He held something in his hand, and he hurled it on the floor before crossing to stand in front of her.

It was a motorcycle helmet.

She swallowed and tried not to shudder at the thought of him spending several hours in the sunlight. Even the fading evening sun would be too much for him. "You rode thirteen hours, wearing nothing but that sodding helmet? Have you even seen your face and how badly you're burned?"

"No. I made it in about ten and I don't really give a fuck about the burns. Why in the hell did you leave?"

"Because I had to." Her palms itched and she wanted to touch him, heal the burns on his face and then curl around him like a cat. The urge was strong, too strong, and she ended up tucking her hands in her pockets just to keep from reaching for him.

"Yeah, so I heard. You've got this really fucked-up idea that you're doing this for *me*," he snarled.

The fury in his voice was so thick, so hot. She could feel his anger blasting at her, beating against her shields and all she wanted to do was touch him, tell him she was sorry, try to figure a way to make this work. But, she just couldn't see the way.

"I am," she said, her voice shaking.

"Can you help me out and explain that?" he asked, his voice thick with sarcasm. "Because I'm just not seeing it. I spent my whole *life* looking for you and now that I've found you, you walk away, but you're doing it for *me*?"

Her throat ached and the sobs clawed, demanding release. She nodded and turned away, pressing her brow to the window. Sensing movement, she froze, holding still as he drew close.

"I'm not seeing it, baby. How is this for me?" he bit off.

"You never had a choice."

"Oh, the hell I didn't. I didn't *have* to come looking for you."

"Yes, you did." She turned around, crossed her arms over her chest. The pain inside her chest grew, expanded, hot and vicious, ready to tear her heart out, her soul. Ready to destroy her. "You have a Hunter's instincts . . . you wouldn't have ignored them. You can't."

Her mouth twisted in a bitter smile and she shook her head. "None of us can ignore that call, Dominic. None of us . . . not if we want to come through with any semblance of sanity."

"It wasn't the Hunter inside that pulled me." He braced his arms over her shoulders, hands flat against the wall. Then he dipped his head, nuzzling her nape.

The feel of him sent a shiver through her. He scraped his teeth down her neck and murmured, "It was the man. The man who was looking for the woman he loved."

"You don't know me." Her voice broke, and she turned her head aside, trying not to cry. "You don't know me . . . how can you love me?"

"I was born loving you."

He brought his hands to her face, cradling it gently. One thumb stroked over her lip and he watched, as though the sight mesmerized him. "I was born loving you," he said again. "And once I realized you were *real*, that maybe you were out there waiting for me, just as I waited for you, nothing would have stopped me from finding you."

Her breath hitched in her throat. That odd dancing sensation was trying to settle inside her heart again, but the darkness didn't want to let it in. "You love me because you've never had any chance to know anything else . . . and I don't deserve that love."

She twisted away, moving closer to the door. She needed to get away from him, before she shattered. Before she gave in. Before she begged.

"Why not?"

She lifted her hands and said, "I killed a man, Dominic. I killed a man, and instead of just letting him die, I fed from the power inside his blood. *Blood* magic, Dominic. Dark magic. It's inside me now, like a drug, and it will want more."

"So the fuck what?"

She blinked, shaking her head. "Don't you get it? I'm damaged now . . . I'll fight this for the rest of my life, and there's no guarantee I'll win."

"No, there's not. I don't know that much about it, but it sounds a lot like an addiction, and damn, that's got to be one serious kick to have you addicted after using it just once. Must be like a witch's heroin or something."

"Worse." She hugged herself, rubbing her palms up and down her arms. Cold to the bone. Cold . . . tired. So tired.

"So it's an addiction and your way of dealing with it is to . . . what? Are you going to hide yourself away now? Lock yourself up, apart from everybody else? Or is it just me you won't be around?"

Narrowing her eyes, she snapped, "There is no need to be flippant. Dominic, perhaps you don't understand how this affects witches, but *I* do. It's addictive and it's dangerous."

"Maybe I don't get it." He shrugged and leaned his shoulders back against the wall. The T-shirt he wore stretched across his muscles and she wanted to stroke her hands down them, learn every last one.

Mouth dry, she looked away, concentrating on the shelves along the back wall. Odd—they didn't seem to be the exact same shade as they'd been when she was last here. And she was certain the books weren't in the right order.

He moved closer, and she started to count the books. Count them, focus on them and not him and oh, he was just a breath away now. Closer. His hand fisted in her hair and he whispered, "I guess I don't get it, baby. Because all I can figure out is that you've got an addiction. But that doesn't mean it has to control you—doesn't mean it has to end your life."

"That's the whole *point*—it will want to control me and . . . well, it's just that . . ." Frustrated, she shot him a dark look and said, "You shouldn't have to carry this burden. It's mine. I made the mistake, I'll deal with it."

"So much for giving me a choice," he said, that heavy, bitter irony coloring his voice again. "You've got a problem, and instead of trusting me to do what I think is best for *me*, and to take part in making the decision of what is best for *us*, you're doing it, all on your own. I have no say in the matter. Is that how you give me a choice?"

She winced. "It's not that simple . . ."

"Yeah. It is." He cupped her chin and angled her face up.

Dark, furious eyes stared into hers and he snapped, "That's exactly what it is. You think I came after you because something *made* me . . . well, you're right . . . in a way. My heart made me. I listened to my heart, listened to everything inside me that demanded I find you. So that's what I did, because I knew, in *here*"—he slammed a fist against his chest—"I knew in *here* that the only way I'd ever be complete in my life was if I found the woman I'd loved in my last life. I didn't get to live it out with you then, and I should have. But now here's the chance to have that, and you won't let it happen? How in the hell is that giving me any choice at all?"

"You . . ." She licked her lips and shook her head. "I'm not that woman—the woman you knew then was nothing but a girl, a girl who still had hope, who still had dreams. I'm not *her* . . . and you said it yourself, you're not him, either. You don't know me well enough to know if you love me."

For one long moment, he was quiet. Then he let her go and moved away, no longer looking at her. "I'm going to ask you a question—you answer it, yes or no. *Just* yes or no. If you tell me no, and do it honestly, make me believe your answer, then fine, I'll get the hell out. But you have to make me believe it." Then he looked at her. "Do you love me?"

Pain tore through her. Did she love him?

She whispered, "Yes. You already know the answer to that, damn you."

"Look at me and say it."

She didn't.

He closed the distance between them, and when she would have backed away, he caught her around the waist, hauling her against him. "Do it."

She planted her hands against his shoulders and shoved. She was strong. Witches did tend to be a bit stronger physically than mortals and she was no exception.

But he was a vampire, and by sheer physical strength alone, she couldn't move him. Glaring at him, she said, "Yes, damn it, I love you."

"But how can you? You don't know me."

Her heart trembled . . . cracked. Shattered. "But I do know you." She laid a hand against his cheek. "I look at you and I see everything you are, I feel every pain you've felt and I feel your loneliness. Then I look at myself, and all I see is a woman who is too weak, one who broke and gave in to the nastiest sort of evil. *I* don't deserve you, damn it. Maybe I would have . . . once. But I broke. I gave in and now, any strength I might have had is gone, whatever decency was inside me, I killed. That's what this is all about."

He sighed and pressed his lips to her brow. The crushing grip he held her with gentled and he began to stroke his hands up and down her back, slow, soft caresses. "If you aren't strong, then nobody is," he said quietly. He kissed her eyes, the tip of her nose, each cheek. "If you aren't decent, then nobody is. You didn't *kill* anything but a bastard who wanted to hurt you."

She opened her mouth and he laid a finger across her lips, silencing her. "I don't want to hear it. Did you screw up? I've gotta say yes, but it's not like *you* were in complete control—you were off in the land of fuck-it-all, remember? And hell, after five hundred years, didn't you deserve some sort of peace?" He didn't wait for her to answer, just kissed her again, soft and slow, before lifting his head to look at her. "It was a mistake, a bad one . . . but how can *one* bad mistake undo everything you are? It can't . . . not unless you let it."

It was a mistake, a bad one . . . but how can one bad mistake undo everything you are? It can't . . . not unless you let it.

Pressing her lips together, she wrapped her arms around his neck and buried her face against him. A sob shook her and she couldn't hold it back. That simple—could it really be that simple?

But what . . . what if he decided he didn't want her later on? What if he realized he didn't really love her?

"And when in hell did I ever become a coward?" she muttered.

"A coward." He lifted his head, studying her face. "So now you're a coward, on top of being evil and weak?" Dominic laughed.

"I don't see the humor here, you know."

He grinned and said, "Baby, if you had any idea how ridiculous some of this sounds . . ."

"It's not ridiculous."

He dipped his head and nipped her lower lip. "Well, yeah, some of it is. Really. After all, aren't you the strongest witch the Hunters have ever had? Strong enough that you could make it so I could walk naked down the beach at noon and not get a burn?" He touched the red marks on his cheeks and grimaced. "And I've got to say, I'd like to arrange that if we could. Here you are, the legendary witch that all good little Hunters hear so much about. You lived through more mortal lifetimes than I could count and even when your body tried to die on you, your soul found another way to live on. Then, even though you're tired and lonely and just want to be done, you keep on going. That's strength. You faced a lifetime alone . . . and that's bravery. And here you are, trying to push me away, even though you'll be miserable after, because you don't want to . . . how did you put it? Burden me?"

He slipped his hands under the hem of her shirt, and her heart stuttered at the feel of them on her flesh, strong and gentle and . . . He swatted her rump and when she glared at him, he said, "You'd make yourself miserable to keep from burdening me. And although your logic is a little flawed, since you'd also make *me* miserable, that's not the choice somebody evil would make. Evil wants what it wants . . . it doesn't give a damn who suffers for it."

That simple . . .

Licking her lips, she shrugged and said, "Well, there might be a bit of humor in it." Then she sighed. Peering at his face, she lifted a hand and brushed it over his reddened face. She couldn't take seeing those marks on him. Not for another second. "You fool vampire, chasing me down even though the sun is trying to burn you to a crisp."

"You fool witch, running away from me."

As the healing magic raced across his injured skin, he closed his eyes. When she was done, he carried her to the nearby chair and sat down, keeping her on his lap. "I came here a few weeks ago, convinced I was losing my mind. When I walked by this cabin, I knew . . . I felt you, smelled you. And I almost went insane trying to figure out what was going on. All I could think of was you. You haunt me. In my sleep. In the night, when I'm supposed to be focused on the hunt, I think of you instead. Don't tell me that I don't love you, and don't tell me I have no choice. Maybe I don't have all that much choice, but I have what I *want* . . . you."

He cupped her cheek in his hand and rubbed his thumb over her lower lip. "If you're scared, I can understand that. Whatever this blood magic is going to do, or try to do, I'd probably be scared, too. But being *alone* isn't going to help you any, and walking away from me because of guilt won't help either. And for all your talk of choices, you're trying to take mine. You're deciding for both of us."

She swallowed.

The look in his eyes, it shook her to the core. The need, the love she had for him swamped her. The lonely ache of her heart screamed out for him—everything inside her screamed out for him.

Could she really walk away?

Yes. She could.

And she'd hate herself forever. For hurting herself—*and* for hurting him.

Blowing out a rough breath, she said, "Perhaps I am. I'm . . . oh, I'm such a mess. You do realize that, Dominic?"

"Figured that out." He kissed her neck.

She felt the lightest brush of his fangs and shivered. "A mess," she whispered again. Then she made herself look at him. "But it's more than just me. There's Jazzy, too. Right now, until I know I can control this, I shouldn't be near her. If I can control this, though . . . well . . . in an odd way, I'm the only family she has, even if I'm not exactly related to her. I've got a responsibility to that girl now. It's not just one messed-up witch you may be taking on, but two."

"I've got a thing for messed-up blondes; I ever tell you that?" His gaze caught hers, held it. "You'll get a hold on this . . . addiction, whatever. I know you will. And you'll find a way to make things works with Jazzy. I know that, too. Something else I know . . . you'd be more of a mess if you decided you really needed to walk. And so would I. You know what? I think after five centuries, the two of us really do deserve a break." He laid his hand over her heart and caught hers, brought it to his chest. "We deserve this . . . We deserve a chance to be happy."

He leaned in and kissed her gently. "I came back for you . . . only for you. You are my entire reason for existing, and I wouldn't have it any other way. I wouldn't have *you* any other way. I don't care if you think you're broken, flawed, evil as Satan himself. I know what I want . . . what I see when I look at you. I see the woman I want to spend the rest of my life with, and if it's any shorter than five centuries, I'm going to feel very short-changed."

Her heart skipped.

Tears blurred her eyes.

A giggle bubbled out of her. "Five centuries . . . you sure about that? It's rather a long time."

"With you, it will pass in a heartbeat . . . if you give us half a chance."

She blinked away the tears and stared at him, stared into those dark brown eyes. Everything else, it was so different . . . physically. But his eyes . . . they were the same. Warm and full of love and life and humor. Leaning in, she pressed her lips to his. "I suppose after five centuries we're entitled to that half a chance. And then some."

Turn the page for a preview of

DEPARTED
By Shiloh Walker

Coming soon from Berkley Sensation!

CHAPTER I

"Fucking crazy," one of the techs muttered, watching as Dez Lincoln stood in the middle of a desolate Iowa field with a smile on her face.

She was a beautiful woman—her black hair cut short, no more than an inch long, currently spiked up. Her skin was a light, smooth brown and her eyes were dark, so dark they almost appeared black, set under feathery, arched brows. Her body was all curves and long limbs, round hips, and a chest that was undeniably *female*. But there was no mistaking the strength—there was well-toned muscle to go along with those curves.

No doubt about it, she was gorgeous, and when she smiled, she could make the hearts of the men around her race.

But right now, her smile was fucking *freaky*.

Under her feet, they suspected, were dozens of bones. Unmarked graves.

The location of a serial killer's little playground. Or maybe his burial ground.

But she smiled. It was a peaceful, beautiful smile—a

Mona Lisa smile, and it didn't belong in the place of death and decay, the tech thought.

Fucking *freaky*. He muttered it under his breath again and went to turn away, only to realize he was the subject of intense scrutiny.

Special Agent in Charge Taylor Jones was staring at him, and he did not look pleased. If Desiree Lincoln was fucking freaky, then Jones was fucking scary, and that look never boded well.

Swallowing, he held that steely blue gaze and prepared himself for the fact that his head just might be rolling across the ground, figuratively speaking, in a second or two.

But all Jones did was stare at him—long enough to make sure the point was made.

*I*DIOT.

Taylor Jones didn't much like having any of his people being called crazy—they were unique, all of them. If they weren't unique, they wouldn't work for him. But unique didn't make them crazy—didn't make them freaks.

The tech flushed, and after another fifteen seconds Taylor looked away.

Still, he knew the tech's thoughts were echoed by a number of others. At least among the techs. Those on Taylor's team understood, on some level, how Dez's gift worked, and they were no longer surprised by her reactions, even in a place as disturbing as this. Others, though . . . they didn't like to see a woman smiling when she stood in the middle of what was likely an unmarked mass grave.

Perhaps, if he didn't know Desiree, he'd agree with them.

He knew her, though, and her gift had long since stopped unsettling him. Other things about Dez might unsettle him, but not her gift. He knew she didn't smile because she stood atop the possible grave sites of murder victims.

She smiled because one of them, at least, would find peace tonight.

To Dez, that meant a lot.

Taylor wished he could find some solace in that, but all he felt was a fiery hot rage, carefully hidden under a cold, professional veneer. Somewhere, buried under all of it, was exhaustion.

He couldn't let that cold professionalism crack and he couldn't give in to the rage. Later, sometime much, much later, he could give in to the exhaustion, though.

They already had the killer in custody. *Correct that*, he thought to himself. *The* alleged *killer*.

Alleged, *my ass*. Keaton Weiss was a brutal, sadistic bastard who had spent the past fifteen years preying on the Miss Lonelyhearts type, stalking them, seducing them . . . then kidnapping them, raping them and killing them. Bodies had never been recovered, although one victim had managed to get away, and that was how they had finally managed to catch Weiss.

And catching Weiss was what had led them here.

No . . . it was what had led Dez here.

All Taylor had to do was place her in the room where Weiss had committed untold atrocities on untold women and, one by one, the ghosts had started to whisper to her. Most of them, though, had been too weak, too faded or still too traumatized to connect with Dez.

She would work with them and hopefully, over time, she could help them move on.

But one of them had been able to establish a tenuous link with Dez, and that link had proven strong enough for her to lead them here. Here, they'd find the evidence they needed to put the bastard away.

Jones didn't have the gifts Dez had but he knew his people, and judging by the looks on the faces of some of them, they had hit the crime jackpot here. Some of them were all but chomping at the bit to get out there and start their own hunt, but they knew they needed to give Dez her space.

If they screwed this up for her, the ghost may never find the peace she needed.

Some of the ungifted techs didn't quite understand that. While Taylor was impatient in the extreme and itching to get out there, he knew if that ghost didn't find any sort of peace, she'd linger with Dez.

And that would torment her.

He couldn't do that.

Not to her.

He tried to force up some semblance of the cold, hard shield he'd perfected so long ago—he didn't have any sort of special interest in Dez Lincoln. He wouldn't wish the unrest of an agitated ghost on any of his people, that was all. He needed them all at their best, all the time.

But even as he told himself that little line, he knew it for what it was.

Nothing but shit.

He did need his people at their best.

All the time.

He wouldn't wish the unrest of an agitated ghost on any of his people. But he most certainly had a special interest in Dez Lincoln. And he had from the very beginning.

Not that it mattered, though.

She was a member of his unit and that made her off-limits.

And even if that wasn't an issue, Taylor Jones didn't do relationships.

Period.

WILL you find him? Stop him?

It was the third time Tawny Lawrence had asked Dez that question. The departed so easily forgot things, especially when they were agitated, and Tawny was most definitely agitated. Agitated, angry . . . and as they'd drawn closer to her unmarked grave, she'd gotten sadder as well, as though she'd felt the gloom and the darkness looming over her.

But Dez didn't mention the repetitive questions—she simply answered as she had the first and second time. "We have found him. He has been stopped. He won't do this to anybody else."

They were often confused—especially once they realized she could see them, hear them . . . talk to them. Some of them had spent years and years unable to speak to any-body, not even one another. A lot of the time, the souls of the departed were trapped in their own personal hells and until they could break free and move on, they weren't aware of anything or anybody.

Unless somebody like Dez could penetrate that shield.

Tawny's face, pretty and sweet, softened with a smile, and just like that, the darkness surrounding her began to lift. She didn't look like a ghost, didn't look like a murder victim.

In Dez's experiences, the departed were a reflection of how they remembered themselves in life . . . a washed-out mirror reflection. Tawny's pale face faded even more and she closed her eyes.

How long? Do you know?

Dez said gently, "You disappeared seven years ago."

Seven years . . . my God. She sighed and her image flick-ered. Then she focused on Dez's face. As her gaze focused, the air around Dez grew colder and the tension was thick enough to cut. *My son. I have a son. Do you know what happened to him?*

"Your ex-husband took him. Raised him—he misses you but it looks like his father did his best to make sure he had a good life. He's graduated from high school and he's in college. Going for a degree in criminal justice." A faint smile curled Dez's lips and she said, "I think because of what happened to you."

Something that might have been tears glimmered in Tawny's eyes. *He's a good boy. I'm glad . . . thanks for telling me.*

Dez wasn't surprised the woman had asked. She'd skimmed the file as they traveled up here, preparing for just this sort of thing. A lot of them had questions, and nothing made it harder for them to pass over than *not* knowing.

Unwilling to be the one responsible for holding some-body back, she did her best to make sure she could answer whatever questions came up. But she couldn't always answer every question, and often, those unanswered ques-tions were the hardest.

What happens to me now? Tawny stared at her, her gaze sobering.

"That's not so easy to answer, Tawny. What do you think happens?"

Tawny just smiled.

And as easy as that, she faded away.

Sometimes they asked so many questions. But the answers Dez had didn't always suit those who had passed over, and she hated like hell to cause any more grief to those whose lives had been ended all too soon, and almost always in an ugly, violent manner.

Once Tawny was gone, she turned and faced the rest of the team.

Her gaze locked on Taylor's.

He lifted a golden brow.

She nodded.

That was all he needed. Without a word from her, he turned away and the team sprang into action.

And just like that, Dez's job was done and she was relegated to the sidelines.

Good thing for her she'd brought a book.

She knew Taylor wouldn't be leaving here anytime soon.

CHAPTER 2

"Y ou're not supposed to be here," Taylor snapped, his voice flat and cold.

Dez ignored him, staring at the house with a rapt expression.

The voices . . . they called to her. *Their* call was impossible to ignore. The whispers were like a siren's song in her head. Responding to Taylor's blunt statement was pointless, especially since she couldn't even explain *why* she was here. She just knew she *had* to be here.

She hadn't been notified and that meant nobody thought her skills were required. If Taylor wanted her here, he would most definitely have called her.

After all, she lived just a little outside of Williamsburg. It wouldn't take her any time to get to the small, upscale subdivision where all hell was currently breaking loose. It made her gut hurt to think about the hell happening inside this posh, designer neighborhood. Some people thought bad shit didn't happen in places like this.

Dez knew better.

"There's a child in there," she said quietly.

"No there's not." It was Colby Mathis, one of Jones's newest bloodhounds, and under most circumstances she would have listened to him, agreed with him. She liked the guy, respected him, and she knew he knew how to do his job. He was the hard-core psychic and she was the one who talked to ghosts.

But he was wrong, this time.

Because there was a ghost standing at the door of the house, staring at Dez with desperate eyes, her mouth open in a silent scream.

"He's got a child in there, Taylor, and if you all move on him like you're planning, he's going to kill her," Dez said, her voice strained.

Colby swore. "We don't have time for this, Jones. The fuck's slipped away from us before—he's *not* doing it again."

Taylor looked from Colby to Dez and Dez stared into Taylor's eyes.

"Colby, give me one minute."

Taylor saw the frustration simmer in the other man's eyes, but the agent gave a terse nod and retreated, falling back a few steps as Taylor reached out and caught Dez's arm. He tried to ignore the soft, silken, warm skin of said arm, just as he'd tried to ignore the way his heart had skipped a beat when she had moved to stand beside him earlier.

He hadn't even seen her, and he'd known it was her.

Felt it, somewhere deep inside.

Guiding her away from the crush of bodies, he said, "You can explain what you're doing here later. But for now, tell me why you think there's a kid in there when all my intel is saying otherwise."

Dez flicked a look past his shoulder. "Something woke me up and I just knew I needed to be somewhere. *Here.* So I got up, got dressed and headed out. Ended up here—I didn't even know you had a team here, by the way."

For a period of about five heartbeats, all thought stopped. Taylor could think of nothing else but those words—*got dressed.* Meaning . . . what? Had she been sleeping in pajamas? Something slinky and silky? Something sensible, practical? Or had she been naked, that sleek, warm brown body bare?

Blood drained out of his head and he clenched his jaw, jerked his attention away from her and stared at the house until he could remember what he was doing, why he was here.

What he was about. He didn't have time to be thinking about Desiree Lincoln and her sleeping attire—or lack thereof—he had a job to do.

A mission. *The* mission. It was all that mattered. All that could matter.

But his body didn't want to listen to reason, and he had to dredge up dark, ugly memories to remind himself *what* he was about, *why* he did this. To remind himself of the mission—had to think about the mission.

All of it necessary to ground himself, something he had to do around her more and more.

He needed distance between them, a great deal of distance. But somehow, he didn't think she'd like it if he suggested she quit. And as his unit was rather unique, if she didn't quit, the only way he could get distance was if one of them requested a transfer.

Dez would never do it. She'd joined the FBI specifically to come work for him—she *needed* it.

Her dark brown eyes moved past him once again, lingering on the porch, and there was an expression in them that he had seen all too often. Haunted, angry and determined. That haunted look appeared in her eyes for one reason and one reason only.

She had a ghost riding her.

Shit. He might have intel on the outside, but it looked like Dez had intel on the *inside*, and if she did, he couldn't risk a child . . .

"What do you see?" he asked, his voice flat and cold.

H ER name was Richelle. In life, she had been a petite, pretty little angel, one who had probably driven her mom and dad insane, one they had probably loved dearly.

Her death would have left a hole in their hearts, and Dez wondered if they were the open sort . . . the kind of people she could sit down and talk to.

Could she tell them what she was? What she did? That she'd seen Richelle, spoken with her? Would it help them? Hurt them?

Could she tell them that Richelle had helped her save another child?

That's assuming you do *save her*, she thought grimly, as she followed Richelle's wavering form down the hallway. Taylor was at her back, shadowing her every move.

It was just the two of them, and it had taken every persuasive argument she had in her arsenal to get him to do this. If there was a child in the house, they needed to get her out. Dez had eyes—the ghost would help her, she knew it clear down to her bones, and she'd been right.

Richelle was doing just that. A petite, avenging angel. She was hauntingly lovely, and death had made her ethereal.

And angry.

Right now, her killer was ensconced in the front of the house, staring entranced out the front window and mumbling to himself.

Richelle insisted he had a girl with him, but Colby had spent the past twenty minutes saying otherwise. Hell, he was probably *still* out there trying to convince the rest of the team Dez was wrong.

Colby sensed people. *Living* people.

If there was somebody else in there besides their killer and Colby didn't feel them, then chances were the child was dead, and by letting in Dez, *alone*, with nobody but a ghost for a guide, they were likely giving the bastard a potential hostage.

Taylor, naturally, had agreed. So she wouldn't go alone. She could live with that—after all, she wasn't stupid.

Nor was she helpless. She held her gun in a loose, ready grip.

Hostage, my ass.

She might not be the typical agent and she may not be

the badass some of them were, but she'd made it through
the same training they had, and she still kept herself in
pretty decent shape. The day she couldn't handle herself
against a child-molesting, motherfucking pervert was the
day she'd put down her gun and take up knitting—just let
the ghosts drive her crazy, because she wouldn't be much
use to anybody, anyway.

She's in the closet. Richelle's ghostly voice, audible
only to her, drifted back to her. *Gave her something to
make her sleep.*

Dez hoped it was just drugs, but logically, she knew Colby
was likely to sense a child, even one knocked out by drugs.

Not many things would keep him from sensing the presence of a human.

Dez wanted to ask Richelle if she knew what the guy
had used, but logically, she knew it was a waste of time.
Richelle was only ten—a wicked smart ten and surpris-
ingly clear-minded, especially for one of the departed. But
still, the child was only ten.

And now, she'd never get to see eleven, or twelve . . .
never go to the prom, never get her first kiss.

Richelle stopped by the closet and Dez halted a few feet
away. She looked by Richelle to the front room and then
glanced over her shoulder to Taylor. He eased around her,
the bulky bulletproof vest he wore breaking the smooth,
perfect line of his suit.

He stopped just a breath away from Richelle and his eyes,
flat and hard, stared down the hallway, watching, waiting.

With him watching her back, she laid a hand on the
doorknob.

Slowly, oh, so slowly, she turned it.

O UT front, the rest of the team waited.
With Taylor in the house with Dez, Special Agent
Joss Crawford was in charge and, unlike Jones, he didn't
believe in keeping a polished veneer that never showed any
sign of emotion.

So when the message came up on his phone, he didn't bother suppressing the urge to swear. No, it ripped out of him in a long, ugly torrent, and then he looked over and pinned Colby with a stare. "You were wrong, Mathis. Lincoln found a child and she's alive."

TAYLOR suspected some manner of psychic ability was more common than people thought.

He didn't have any classifiable skill—wasn't telekinetic the way some of his people were and he couldn't talk to the departed, as Dez liked to call them. Nor could he hone in on the trail of a kidnapped child the way Taige Morgan, one of his sometimes "contract" employees, did.

He recognized the gifted, though. It was how he'd lured so many of them to his unit. He recognized them and that was his "gift," so to speak, that and knowing how to bring them inside, get them to work for him.

While he wasn't getting any of those vibes from this house, he wasn't in the least bit surprised when the bastard they'd been sitting on came roaring around the corner, like he'd been somehow alerted to their presence.

Instinct. It wasn't that far removed from some level of psychic skill, and this pervert's sick needs were about to land him in the worst sort of hell.

His name was Edward Mitchell. He liked to pick up pretty little girls just shy of puberty and rape them, dump their bodies in the James River. He wasn't going to go down easy.

They'd almost made it to the back door and Taylor even had a believable story concocted to explain why they'd been in the house to begin with—they did have a warrant, but they hadn't bothered to explain that when he'd picked the lock.

Dez had reason to believe there was a child in danger in this house and she was carrying that child in her arms now.

But as Taylor went to open the door for her, Edward came rushing down the hall, huffing and puffing, his pale, pasty skin gleaming with sweat and his eyes half wild.

"No!" he screeched.

And he raised a gun.

Taylor raised his own and fired, but the bastard managed to get a shot off. And as the sick fuck fell, lifeless, to the floor, Taylor turned. And the first thing he saw as he turned was the brilliant, dark wash of red staining the side of Dez's neck.

T HE night passed in a haze of bloody memories, the wail of sirens and the bright, blinding lights of the emergency department.

They tried to keep him out in the waiting room.

But either the blood they saw in *his* eyes, the badge or the gun he didn't bother to keep concealed convinced the medical staff that keeping him out was going to waste precious time.

Judging by the amount of blood Dez had lost, he didn't know how much time she had.

The child was already at the local children's hospital, alive . . . and that was all he knew. For the first time, he'd turned over the reins to another, allowing Crawford to take command while he stayed with Dez. God—Dez.

She couldn't die.

Not like this. Fuck, she couldn't die. Not Dez.

Although he knew her, too well.

She'd be okay going down knowing she'd helped save a child, and that's what she'd done. The girl was alive . . . because Dez had shown up when she had. Alive because of Dez and the ghost of another victim.

Another victim . . . somebody else Taylor hadn't been able to save. Another scar on his soul. It didn't matter that he hadn't known. It never mattered. All that mattered was that he hadn't gotten there in time, hadn't pieced it together in time . . . and another child, another little girl had been lost.

Dez . . . would she become another scar on his soul?

Her face flashed in front of him, her warm brown skin a sickly, ashen gray, her eyes wide with shock. The blood had soaked her clothing. Mitchell, damn the bastard. He was either a damn good shot or Dez just had lousy luck. Her vest would have protected her torso, but the bastard's bullet had hit her neck.

Stop it—he had to hold it together for now. At least long enough to make sure they took care of her. She was still alive. That meant she had a chance. But if he hadn't been right there . . .

"Don't think about that," he muttered, reaching up and pressing his fingers to his eyes. "Don't."

And he found he actually *could* push the image out of his mind, but only because it just wasn't acceptable. The thought of Desiree Lincoln's lifeless body was just more than he could handle. A hell of a lot more.

"Mr. Lincoln?"

Tired, so tired, it never occurred to Taylor the nursing staff might be looking for him. It wasn't until the voice came again, and from a lot closer, that he opened his eyes and met the tired gaze of a man dressed in pale green scrubs. "Mr. Lincoln?"

"No. Special Agent Jones. But if you're here about Desiree Lincoln, then yes, I'm here with her."

"Ahhh . . . I see. My apologies." The nurse smiled. "It's been one of those nights. There's a small lounge just down the hall. I'm going to take you there, if that's okay. Dr. Frantz will be in to speak with you shortly." He paused and then asked, "Does Ms. Lincoln have any family we should notify? There wasn't much information in her personal effects."

Taylor shook his head. Dez's mother was still alive, living in the lap of luxury in West Palm Beach. He knew that, because he'd researched everything about Dez when he'd discovered her. He knew all about how the girl had been abandoned—her mother had taken her to school one day and just never had come back for her.

Dez had gone through a series of foster homes after that. Nobody wanted the strange, pretty child who had talked to thin air.